"Ma'am..." Girty,  his shoulders and boun
nervously as he thought
I jest wanted to tell you   clear out of
Detroit." He looked around, his neck seemingly stiff.
"I can't say no more'n—" He stopped, his eyes becoming wide.

He was looking at a track across the Frenchman's cornfield, and Gwen followed his gaze. She had a sudden flash of terror. Indians were approaching single file, and at their head was Amaghwah. The camp children were racing toward him, obviously to tell that the white medicine woman was here.

Girty was on his feet. A scalping knife hung at his waist, but the Indians were armed with guns. He rasped, "You got to go, quick!" He beckoned for her to get away into the rushes near the river.

Gwen shook him off. She would not run.

"Git!" Girty snarled through his teeth. "You know what's coming! You ain't—"

"Let them come!"

Already the Shawnees—three of them—were running toward the camp, Amaghwah in the lead, his savage face painted red and white, tomahawk in one hand. He looked ready for a fight.

Girty whistled, "Lordy, mistress, but you're something..."

BETRAYAL

The Seventh Powerful Novel
in the Northwest Territory Series

AN UNSTOPPABLE ARMY OF REDCOATS
AND INDIANS DESTROYS ALL IN ITS PATH
AND THREATENS TO DRIVE THE REBELS
OFF THE FRONTIER... AND ONLY ONE MAN
STANDS IN ITS WAY

OWEN SUTHERLAND. He is as stubborn as a
Scotsman, as cunning as an Indian, and as brave and
resourceful as the proud folk of his beloved Northwest...

ELLA SUTHERLAND. Wife, mother, and leader
of her people, she knows she and Owen must go on,
even when the war claims their own flesh and blood...

JAMES MORELY. An ambitious young businessman, all he wants is to turn a profit, but the Revolution, a woman, and Owen Sutherland all ask
something more of him...

SUSANNAH SUTHERLAND. A romantic dream
makes life bearable on the war-torn frontier, but as
she grows to womanhood, she needs a man, not a
mere dream...

CAPTAIN DAVIES. He kills rebels for pleasure, yet the British trust him as the one white leader who can keep the Indians in line . . .

AMAGHWAH. This Shawnee renegade comes in handy to a redcoat officer who won't soil his own hands killing women and children . . .

GWEN BENTLY. An angel of mercy in the enemy's camp, she finds that even a rebel nurse is no longer welcome in loyalist Detroit, and must flee through the wilderness, with death stalking her every move . . .

SIMON GIRTY. A drunk, a traitor, and a sly opportunist, he's also the best scout the British have, and a man of most peculiar honor . . .

BRADFORD CULLEN. The aging merchant prince of the Northwest, he has brought the ruthless might of Cullen and Company down on all who oppose him, but at last his day of reckoning is due. . . .

NORTHWEST TERRITORY·BOOK 7

BETRAYAL

OLIVER PAYNE

Created by the producers of
Wagons West, The Australians, and
The Kent Family Chronicles.

Chairman of the Board: Lyle Kenyon Engel

BERKLEY BOOKS, NEW YORK

BETRAYAL

A Berkley Book/published by arrangement with
Book Creations, Inc.

PRINTING HISTORY
Berkley edition/February 1986

Produced by Book Creations, Inc.
Chairman of the Board: Lyle Kenyon Engel

ISBN: 0-425-08649-6

To the memory of the Ohio Valley
pioneers, strangers in an unknown land,
who united, made a stand against
the odds, and won

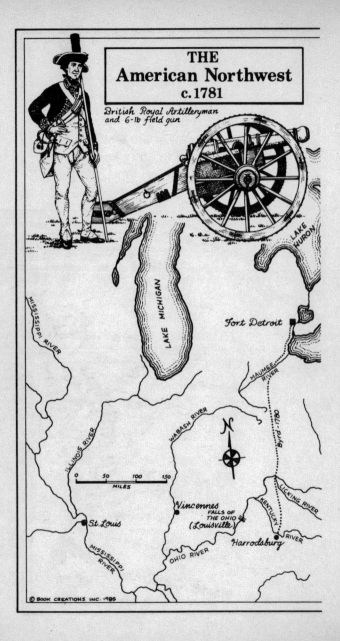

THE
American Northwest
c. 1781

British Royal Artilleryman
and 6-lb field gun

LAKE HURON

MISSISSIPPI RIVER

LAKE MICHIGAN

Fort Detroit

MAUMEE RIVER

ILLINOIS RIVER

WABASH RIVER

N

Byrd · 1780

0   50   100   150
MILES

LICKING RIVER

Vincennes

FALLS OF
THE OHIO
(Louisville)

KENTUCKY RIVER

St. Louis

MISSISSIPPI RIVER

OHIO RIVER

Harrodsburg

© BOOK CREATIONS INC. 1985

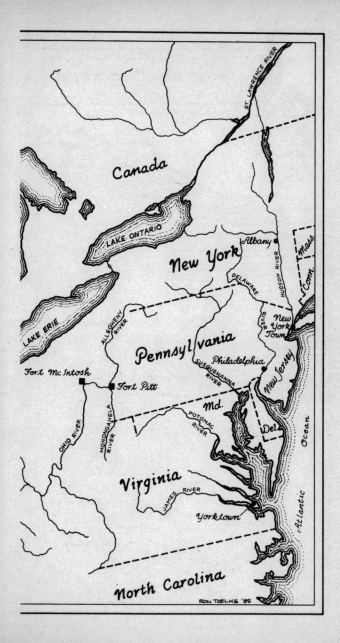

PART ONE

1779

chapter **1**

FORT DETROIT

It was almost evening of a sultry summer day in the settlement at Fort Detroit. Gwen Bently was struggling alone with the hospital laundry, boiling bed sheets in a great cauldron over a blazing fire in the yard.

With a long pole, she pushed and poked the bulky sheets, her arms aching, the reek of lye soap making her eyes tear. As if she had not worked hard enough today. More people had been dragged in, beaten and bruised, from the New York frontier, captives of the Seneca, who had starved and brutalized them all the way across the wilderness to Detroit, where the king's officers would pay for another triumph against the insolent rebel settlers.

Gwen had spent all day helping forlorn captives, tending wounded bodies and broken hearts. It was exhausting and depressing work, but she knew it well, having done it for nearly three years now. White or red, rebel, loyalist, or neutral in this war of revolution, there were plenty of patients for nurse Gwen Bently's hospital. Her labor was that much harder because her husband was not here to help. Only the Lord knew where Dr.

Jeremy Bently was at this moment, but Gwen prayed that it was somewhere safe from the horrors of the conflict that had made the country shudder during the past four years.

Gwen paused to wipe sweat from her brow, and to think, fondly, of her husband. Willing herself to see Jeremy's handsome, fair face, she tried to think of him without the scarlet British surgeon-major's uniform he had worn for King George the Third. She closed her eyes and smiled to think of her man, tall and handsome and easy to laugh. She could almost imagine his arms around her. . . .

Just then she heard the injured children crying from the hospital, though they had all been fed, their bandages had been changed, and they should be sleeping. One woke the other, and so it went, from slumber to pain and back again. Their mothers or other women would care for them now. Let them sleep. Please let them sleep soon.

Gwen opened her eyes and tried to work away the dismal sounds, singing softly to herself. She used the pole to haul a steaming sheet from the cauldron onto a line that stretched across the yard from a post at the far end to the square-timbered hospital that once had been a trading warehouse. Gwen was soaked in sweat, her hands blotched and raw, eyes running. Still, she was very pretty, and whenever a man passed by on the quiet street, he stole a long look at her if he could. In her middle twenties, she was slender but physically strong, and with long legs. Her frame was almost angular, but her movements were supple, and she carried herself gracefully and with confidence. Her blond hair was pinned up under a white mobcap, and she wore a linen apron over a light cotton dress that, in Indian style, reached only to her shapely calves.

Gwen did not mind that her work made her look like a scullery maid, for she had people to heal, and she labored harder than anyone else who helped in the hospital. Still, she would have taken more care of herself had Jeremy been here. She draped the sheet over the line, noticing that the crying had, mercifully, stopped. Then Jeremy was in her thoughts once more, as ever he had been these last months. He had not even seen his son, Richard Thomas Bently, born last autumn, not long after he had left for the Illinois country.

She again closed her eyes, not wanting to open them to see that familiar fenced yard, or another darkening sky at the end of another day without news from him. The settlement seemed so desolate on a Sunday night. Jeremy would have objected to her laundering on Sunday, but when else did she have the time?

In autumn she had seen him last, a splendid soldier of the king, an American loyalist off to quell a rebellion that he believed promised no better for the country than did the old colonial order. As a regimental surgeon, Jeremy had gone with British troops marching to attack the dangerous rebel colonel George Rogers Clark, who had wrested away the Illinois country and was threatening Detroit itself.

Then a letter had come, a letter from Jeremy that had jolted Gwen and caused her to rejoice. He had resigned from the British army! At last sickened by the murderous Indian frontier raids, he had rejected the army whose leaders condoned cruel assaults on hapless settlers, most of whom knew little about rebellion or loyalty and just wanted to be left alone.

But where was Jeremy now? All she knew was that he had gone off in search of his younger brother, who had been captured by loyalist Shawnees. The lad was a rebel, like the rest of Jeremy's family. Civil war and revolution went hand in hand, and Jeremy's own mother and stepfather were with the rebels; even he and Gwen were of different minds as far as the war was concerned. Yes, Gwen Bently staunchly favored the rebel cause, making her a stranger here at Detroit, the main loyalist stronghold in the northwest wilderness. She so loved Jeremy that she had stayed here with him despite the war, and at this hospital they healed the sick and wounded of both sides. They did not dwell on their differences, for their love was enough to bind them—more than enough, whatever came.

Wherever Jeremy was under this deepening sky, Gwen knew he was alive. He must be!

She looked down the quiet rue Saint Jacques, which was lined with log and timber cabins and trading houses. She could see all the way to the end of the street, and beyond to the wide, dark straits, shadowed by the setting sun. There was no longer a wooden wall to block her view, for the old, rotting palisades of the original fort had been torn down last year, and a new Redcoat post had been built a few hundred yards inland. Stronger than the old fort, the new citadel was better defense against the rebels. It had to be, for after Jeremy had resigned from the army, George Rogers Clark had captured the British lieutenant governor himself. Now loyalists at Detroit trembled whenever rumors flew that Clark was expected to appear suddenly at their doors.

Gwen's thoughts were momentarily distracted as she hung up the last sheet. Looking over it, she saw the elderly regimental surgeon, "Doc" Sennet, pacing back and forth behind the butcher's shop, thirty yards away. Tall and skinny, Sennet was bent over more than usual, and behaving strangely. Gwen paused to watch him rummaging about in a pile of bones—cattle and mule bones, for the most part. She knew he was nearsighted, but why was his nose almost stuck in the pile?

What was the poor dear up to? She liked Doc Sennet, a decrepit, harmless old fellow who was close to retiring from the army. He had been doing better lately at keeping away from the rum bottle. As it was with nearly all military surgeons, his only medical training had come through practical experience, born of emergency and refined by habit, and he possessed little formal knowledge of healing. Sennet was childlike in some ways, but worldly-wise in others, and was a good friend to Jeremy and Gwen, who had taught him something about modern medical techniques.

Gwen thought ruefully that Sennet must have gone back to the bottle, for he appeared drunk again. Now he was on his knees scrabbling at the bones, and to her surprise, he leaned forward and, with only his teeth, dragged a piece of bone from the pile. She briefly considered calling out, but that would have been embarrassing to him. He had best sleep it off.

As she went back to hanging the last of her laundry, she saw Sennet look around anxiously, as if afraid of being discovered in his silly behavior. The bone was still in his teeth, and he apparently did not notice her past the sheets. Next he put his hands behind him and walked deliberately backward, the piece of bone dangling awkwardly, for it was heavy and large. Gwen smiled and shook her head, about to turn away, but it was all too intriguing, and she had to watch. Sennet stopped after a few steps and let the bone fall from his mouth. Then he whirled, head held high, and strode off, not looking back. It came to Gwen that he was not drunk at all, but must be fooling with another of Mawak's superstitious Ottawa cures for some ailment. His behavior had all the markings of a magic remedy, complete with bones and walking backward.

Gwen thought poor old Sennet would never be able to go back to Maryland after the war, not like this. Not only would he be despised as an American who had served in a British uniform, but he would be the laughingstock of Baltimore because of his wilderness, Indian ways.

Gwen's musing was disturbed by the wail of an infant from inside the hospital building. She hurried away, glad it was the cry of her own baby and not the moan of a tormented little one who had come from the New York settlements. Gwen was heavy with milk, and ready for Richard to awaken. She went into the large, airy warehouse, which had been painted white inside and was spotless, smelling faintly of camphor and cleaning compound. The floors were scrubbed and sanded, and the neatly made beds, most of them occupied, stood in two long rows. As she passed she greeted people who were awake, glancing at a few who, at last, had fallen asleep. No one had died today, not yet. If only Jeremy could be here to help— could be here to see his son!

Evening was closing in, and she felt a little thrill of relief that she could feed Richard now, for it meant a quiet time. Tonight, she thought, she might even get some sleep herself, although she doubted it. Wounds hurt most at night, and so did broken hearts.

At the far end of the ward there was a smaller room, which she entered, and there she picked up the fussing Richard from his crib. Like Gwen and Jeremy, the baby was blond, with bright blue eyes. Gwen sat down in a rocker near a long table that was used for surgery. She tucked aside her bodice, folded her apron up to her lap, and gave the baby her breast. Weariness flooded away, and she closed her eyes, almost contented. These moments, with the child held close, were enough to see her through. She only hoped Jeremy would not be too long in coming, lest he miss the joy of the baby's infancy. She never let herself think he might not return at all.

After a little while, she heard someone come into the hospital, and by the sound of the creaking, gravelly voice, she knew it was Doc Sennet. She was glad for this, for if he was sober enough, he would look over the patients for her, then give her a fairly reliable report. Since he had begun to work with Jeremy here at the hospital, Doc Sennet had become much less enthusiastic about amputation, which formerly he had considered a solution for nearly every serious wound to a limb. He might even make a good healer one day, if only he would ease off on his rum ration—that and his attraction to Mawak's questionable cures, some of which made old wives' tales seem scientific. Ever since Doc Sennet had become good friends with the aged Ottawa medicine man, he had taken a fascinated interest in the most outlandish treatments. His latest notion was to make black hens walk over the bodies of people with chicken pox.

Gwen smiled to recall how Sennet had sneaked into her room when she was in labor with Richard, and had slipped an Indian tomahawk under her bed, a tomahawk specially feathered and decorated by Mawak. It was supposed to ease the pain, Gwen knew, but even Mawak could not explain just why or how. The white women caring for Gwen had given poor Sennet a browbeating for such foolishness, yet none of them had removed the charm—and Gwen's labor had been gratefully short.

She had just finished nursing Richard when there came a knock at the door, and Sennet entered quietly, smiling in that twisty way he had, his face gnarled and leathery. He was a career soldier—the oldest, in fact, in the Eighth Regiment—and one of the few native Americans among the Redcoats stationed at Fort Detroit. Nowadays the generals trusted only British-born men or German mercenaries to fight American rebels, but out here, hundreds of miles away from the nearest rebel settlement, veterans like Sennet could be safely depended upon.

As usual, his army wig needed powder, and his old scarlet tunic was a faded pink, but he was obviously sober. Right away Gwen saw that something was troubling him, for his watery eyes were even more watery than usual, and his jaw seemed swollen. At first she thought he had been punched, but when she asked, he said it was a terrible toothache.

"Not to worry," he said, rubbing his jaw as Gwen got up to put the sleeping baby back in his crib. "I'm taking care of it. Old Mawak gave me a recipe that'll do the trick, and no mistake about it!"

She came over to take a look. As she did so, into the room padded her rawboned, powerful dog, named Cape, who sniffed at Sennet and lay down by the crib. The big, sandy-brown Cape was a southern African lion dog, and a formidable protector for Gwen.

Gwen suggested a dose of *elixir paregoricum;* this was an opium-based medicine that combined licorice, camphor, and alcohol to help the patient sleep through the worst of everything. Sennet shook his head at her offer, but paced restlessly, showing that he suffered.

"What are you doing for it, pray tell?" Gwen asked, following him back and forth. "Perhaps you should have the tooth pulled."

Sennet waved that off. "I scarce have a tooth left already! No, no . . . I've used a remedy that's said to work every time . . . though it might take some patience, some waiting."

He looked at her sideways, as if he thought she would not approve or believe in it; but *he* did believe, or wanted to, and would not have his faith shaken, or even questioned.

Gwen nodded. "Mawak's idea?" She had considerable respect for Indian remedies, but there were those that made sense and those that did not, and one had to be choosy.

Sennet replied that this remedy made sense "—and make no mistake about it!" He paced some more. "Why, I think it already's working . . . bless me if it ain't!"

He stopped, eyes alight, and stared straight ahead, while Cape looked up at him, as if wondering what Sennet was about now.

"Pain going away?" Gwen asked, seeing wonder and inexpressible gladness come over Sennet. He clasped his hands together, and loudly declared Mawak to be a prince, a genius, a healer *par excellence*.

"Who would have guessed it possible!" he cried, while Gwen, not wanting to disturb the patients, kindly shushed him.

"I'm cured!" he burbled.

Gwen laughed lightly, saying she was happy for him. "Nothing worse than a toothache that will not go away," she said, then asked just how it was cured.

Sennet chuckled and waved at the shelves of potions, tinctures, pills, and powders that lined the walls of the room. He shook his head and spun the other way, his arm outstretched to take in all the wares around him.

"Let me have old Mawak practice for one day in an English

medical school, and I'll turn those whippersnappers round about
with all their theories of electricity and—" Carefully he said,
"—and exan-the-matologia!" He clapped his hands together
and straightened his disheveled wig. Gwen smiled to herself,
knowing how hard he had studied to say that right.

"What's the cure?" she asked again, cheerfully, going about
the business of cutting up old sheets for bandages. The strutting
Sennet felt at his jaw and chuckled some more.

"I wouldn't normally give it away," he said, "'cept seeing
as you're quite medical yourself . . ." He thought a long moment
before saying, "And seeing as you just now witnessed the cure
with your own eyes! I'll tell you if you promise not to play
me for a fool. Promise?"

Gwen giggled once and tried to concentrate on her bandages,
but promised all the same.

Sennet squinted his rubbery face, saw Gwen was attempting
to be serious, and said, with much gravity, "Very well." He
tried to straighten his wig, but it stayed askew. Then he folded
his arms, cocked his chin, and said, in an emotionless tone,
"Picked up the jawbone of a calf with my teeth, walked backward exactly nine steps, dropped it, never touching it with my
hands . . ." He eyed Gwen, who was for the moment more
amazed than tickled. "Mustn't touch it with the hand, mind
you!"

"Of course." She was beginning to smile, but he became
more serious.

"It worked! You saw it work! Did it by the book—by Mawak's book, leastways! And didn't a soul see me do it, no!
Make no mistake, you got to do it by the book for it to work
perfect. Not a soul may see you, or the charm fails every time."

He grinned and chortled, rubbing his jaw as if it had never
felt better.

"But I saw you," Gwen said innocently, cutting another strip
of sheet and smiling to herself. Then, abruptly, she realized
she had said the wrong thing. She looked up quickly, and sure
enough, poor Sennet was pale, his mouth dropping open, pain
creeping back into his eyes.

"You saw?" he whispered. "You didn't! Ahhh . . ."

The pain had definitely come back. Worse than ever. He
grasped his jaw, tongue and gums working. Gwen felt awful.

Why did these charms always have to have some fool require-
ment like that!

"Oh, Mr. Sennet!" she said plaintively, and laid aside the
sheet and scissors. "Maybe I was wrong . . . maybe I—"

He shook his head, unable to speak for the awful, throbbing
pain. Gwen began to recommend another, more usual, remedy
for the toothache, but he simply lowered his head and went to
the door, eyes watering again. Poor thing!

"There's another jawbone out there," he said thickly. "Just
. . . please don't—ah—"

"Oh, no! Never!" She held up her hands. "I won't! I
won't . . . look!" As he went out, she said, "Come back if it
doesn't—"

But he was gone, hurrying off. Gwen bit her lip, trying not
to laugh, feeling sorry and tickled all at once. The baby fussed,
and she went to him, leaning down to the crib, fondling big
Cape's floppy ear as she spoke to Richard. She gave him a
turtle-shell rattle, a gift from Lela, an Indian woman who helped
at the hospital. Like Gwen, Lela lived across the straits from
Detroit, and Gwen would visit her tomorrow.

There came a shouting outside, and the sound of men running. Harsh, angry voices joined with cries in Shawnee.
Wounded were coming in. Gwen's brief quiet time was finished. She opened the door to the ward. Already, men were
stamping hurriedly into the far entrance of the hospital, heedless
of the patients, who were startled awake, children crying again.
Through the dim room came two swarthy figures, and someone
was lashed between them, carried on a makeshift blanket litter.
Gwen took a deep breath, prepared herself for the worst, and
called them to her.

Suddenly, into the light came the fierce and ugly face of the
Shawnee Amaghwah, a brutal old warrior whose war paint was
smeared and whose leggins were crusted with dirt and blood.
He was helping to carry the wounded man, whom she could
not see. At the other end of the litter was the scout Simon
Girty, a dark, stocky fellow, grizzled and beady-eyed.

These two were among the hardest cases in the northwest,
the worst enemies of rebels, and both knew Gwen favored the
rebel cause. Her heart beating fast, she stiffened and backed
away from the doorway as they pushed roughly in. She mo-

tioned for them to lay the man on the examination table, and
her stomach turned at the sight of the filth, blood, and pus that
fouled the blanket.

She could not see who was being rolled onto the table, for
the blanket and the two men were in her way. She heard
Amaghwah growl, "Best keep him alive! We carry ten sleeps,
no stop!" Amaghwah turned and pointed a dirty finger at her
face. "You fix him!"

"I'll do my best," she snapped, not wavering. "Now leave
and send word for Dr. Sennet and Mistress Annie Ross to—"

Gwen saw who it was and caught her breath, her hands
shaking. She put them behind her apron as she moved closer
to the man lying so stiffly on the table. It was a face she had
hoped never to see again.

Lying there, eyes shut, mouth open and dry, Captain Mark
Davies looked so like a corpse that Gwen might have thought
him already gone had his bearers not insisted he was alive.
Crumpled awkwardly, no trace of a British uniform on him
because he had been fighting as a partisan with the Indians,
Davies looked a wretched, dismal creature. Yet his delicate
features could have been almost handsome, had they not been
so twisted over the years by unrelenting hatred.

To Gwen's dismay, the life of this awful man, her husband's
worst enemy, was in her hands.

From behind, Amaghwah grasped her arm and wrenched
her around. His ugly face came very close to hers, and she
could smell the stink of him as he snarled, "Your man do this!
Yes! Your dog of a man cut my captain—"

Suddenly Simon Girty yanked him away, hurling him against
the wall, and at the same moment Cape sprang at the Indian,
snapping and biting until Gwen called her off. With a glancing
kick toward Cape, Amaghwah fled from the room, cursing,
pushing through a group of curious patients who had come
from their beds to see what was happening.

Simon Girty edged forward now, removing his dirty, flat
hat out of respect. Without meeting her eyes, he said, "I'm
sorry for that, ma'am—" Cape growled at him, but Gwen told
her to lie down.

As Gwen turned back to the wounded officer, Girty went
on, "But 'tis true enough, lady—Dr. Bently done for him."
He seemed to want to spit tobacco juice, but thought better of

it, then bowed a bit and backed out of the room. "Best ponder twicet about staying here at Detroit after word of this gits out, lady. Your man's a turncoat now, a traitor. Best think of that afore it's too late."

Girty's shifty gaze found Gwen, and she stared hard at him, comprehending with a shock that Jeremy had actually gone over to the rebels.

Girty was right. She must soon leave Detroit.

The baby began to cry as Gwen hurriedly prepared for the operation. Davies lay still, as pale as death.

Gwen started by washing out the nastiest wound, a dangerous sword thrust that had torn the man's side open, and now was infected and foul. Davies's rescuers had lugged him back, but they had nearly killed him in the process, failing to clean the wound or to change the makeshift bandages that covered it.

Gwen was no stranger to hideous injury, and she shut out the thought that Jeremy himself had laid open this flesh. But what had happened to him in the fight? She swabbed and wiped and scraped away pus and loose scab. What had happened to Jeremy? He must have lived, or Amaghwah would have boasted about his death. That realization made her light-headed with emotion. The baby was crying louder now.

Gwen lit tallow lamps against the gathering darkness and sang softly to Richard as she worked, a lullaby about butterflies and meadows and pretty little horses, dapples and grays . . . pintos and bays . . . and Richard found his thumb.

Davies was in a bad way, having lost too much blood, yet his heart was still beating steadily, as if he simply refused to die. Richard cooed, and Cape put down her head. Someone out in the hospital called that a pot of tea was on, and did Gwen want any? She would have something soon, she called back, but thought that first she needed help, for the heavy body, the tattered, filthy clothing, and the need for clamps and needles and sutures were more than she could handle.

Just then, in came her cousin Annie Ross, a young woman of Gwen's age who lived not far from the hospital. Her dark eyes flared with dislike when she saw Davies on the table, but she said nothing, tucking her long auburn hair under her mob-cap, readying to help with the treatment. Though once she had been queasy at the sight of blood, Annie now was one of Gwen's most dependable aides. Without a word, Gwen glanced up at her cousin, who was lovely of face, trim, and shapely, and she felt a rush of gratitude. Annie took up a sponge and began to help clean Davies's wounds, her delicate features shining in the lamplight, looking grimly determined for all their refinement and polite breeding.

Davies groaned as the suture needle went in and out. It was the first sound he had made, and a sign that he was not too far gone. He might even recover, if their work was done well and no serious complications set in.

Annie was handling a clamp as Gwen sewed, and she spoke after releasing a sound of amazement: "How strange that you should have to save this . . . this bad man!" She looked at Gwen, who was intent on the work and did not reply. "But I suppose you can do nothing else but try, even though you'd be better off with him dead. When it's done he'll still be your enemy."

Gwen pursed her lips and glanced at Annie, who sometimes could be very blunt, despite her normally ladylike disposition. Annie had once been in love with Jeremy, and for a time had felt bitter toward Gwen for winning him instead. Now it seemed she was over it, and Gwen was grateful for her cousin's support. Gwen had always thought Annie the real beauty of the family, and it was not right that she should not yet have found a husband among these handsome officers and bold merchant traders who came from every part of the British empire. Did Annie still hold a flame for Jeremy? Gwen hoped not, and looked again at her cousin, who gazed back and asked whether Gwen was all right.

Then Gwen saw tears in Annie's eyes, and that caused her to stop sewing, but Annie urged her on, saying not to mind. Over in the crib, Richard was restless, making little cranky noises, as if he needed to be burped. Annie wiped her hands on her apron and went to pick up the baby. She walked back and forth with him, sniffing all the while.

Softly, Gwen said, "Don't cry, cousin."

Annie sighed and caught her breath, then turned to Gwen with a determined expression, although the tears now ran down.

"You know you must go away!" Annie declared, while nervously patting Richard, who still would not burp. "That beastly Indian Amaghwah, and others like him . . ."

Gwen finished her sewing, and only then said, "I'll heal their beloved partisan fighter . . . their king's officer in bloody buckskins! If the war department knew he was fighting out of uniform, they'd cashier him *and* his commander. It's a sin the way Lernoult let this devil loose among the poor settlers—"

Annie gasped in surprise. Gwen looked up. There, in the open door, was Captain Richard Lernoult himself. Clearly he had heard Gwen's accusation, and he had a black look about him. His tricorne was held stiffly under one arm, brass and braid glittering in the lamplight. His white wig was perfectly powdered, and his features were square and strong.

Before saying anything, Lernoult stepped in to look at Davies. Gwen rapidly began to bind Davies's torso. The bleeding was stopped, the wounds were clean, but there were other things to be attended to, including bathing him and getting him to a bed.

Lernoult indicated the officer with a curt nod. "Will he live?"

"Perhaps." Gwen did not look up from her work.

"I hope you have done your best."

Gwen stopped and stared at Lernoult, but he did not look back. Annie stepped over, and unlike her usual demure self, stuck out her chin and said sharply, "Gwen always does her best, even for sick snakes that slithered into our farmyard when we were children back in Tarrytown, New York!" Not waiting for a reply from the puffing, annoyed Lernoult, Annie whirled about, and just then the baby gave a loud and aromatic burp into the startled officer's face.

Gwen gasped.

The man scratched his ear, pulled his nose, and glanced over at the baby, whose wide, innocent blue eyes were staring as he bobbed up and down on Annie's shoulder. Lernoult looked at Gwen, back at the child, and then chuckled, slowly shaking his head.

"Dratted unmilitary around here . . ." He grinned, relaxing, and said with a nod, "Forgive me, Mistress Bently. But you must understand my position now that your husband has . . . joined the rebels." He thought a moment, and both Gwen and Annie softened. Lernoult was a good man, and fair. Richard burped loudly again, and Annie gave him over to his mother.

Lernoult sighed, paced a bit, and said he knew all that had happened, and "deeply regretted" that Jeremy had fought Captain Davies. Though he did not say it, his words implied that Jeremy was a traitor.

Afraid for her husband, Gwen protested: "But we don't know the whole story. Besides, he wrote to me that he had resigned formally, and his resignation was accepted by Governor Hamilton. . . ."

Lernoult had raised a hand and was looking blankly at the floor. "Your husband is with the rebels now, according to Simon Girty; there's no way around that, madam. None, though I rue it heartily."

"At least," Annie hissed, "he's not pretending to be a civilian while really being a king's officer! He resigned, and never pretended to be what he was not! He was not dishonorable." Before Lernoult could protest, she added, "What has our king's army come to, Captain? What disgrace when Captain Davies dons a woodsman's outfit to fight like a spy, like an Indian marauder?"

Lernoult was pale and angry, but had no good reply. Officers were not officially allowed to serve in civilian clothes—none but this Captain Mark Davies, who had received special permission from Henry Hamilton himself. Indeed, the war department would be furious if they knew about it, for Hamilton clearly had overstepped his authority. Gwen knew the British were desperate to win the frontier war in the northwest, even if it meant letting king's officers dress as frontiersmen and lead Indians against the settlements. Normally only loyalist volunteers were given command of war parties, but things were changing, it seemed.

As if in answer to Gwen's thoughts, Lernoult pinched his lower lip and spoke with an embarrassed harrumph: "It will not happen under my command, ladies; no officer will ever be permitted—" He caught himself, as if disturbed that he should find himself obliged to explain military matters to civilians—and women, at that. To Gwen, he said, "Mistress Bently, we are grateful for all you have done in the past for our troops and for the king's loyal subjects, but I must tell you to my regret that our men will no longer be permitted to be treated in your hospital."

Gwen was confused. What difference did it make who healed them? Who else could?

Lernoult backed off a little and nodded to a pair of soldiers waiting with a stretcher at the door of the room. They moved in to fetch Davies.

Lernoult said to Gwen, "Security reasons, don't you see?" She did not see. He tightened his lips. "Men talk . . . especially wounded men who are delirious."

British soldiers would not be placed under the care of a rebel sympathizer whose husband had fought alongside rebels. That was that.

As Davies was lifted, he screamed hoarsely with pain, coming suddenly conscious. Still holding Richard, Gwen moved to Davies's side as the startled soldiers inadvertently let him fall back onto the table.

His eyes were glazed, but he obviously recognized Gwen, and made an animal sound as a horribly ugly expression came over him. His lips frothed with spittle, his muscles contorted. Davies looked insane. Cape growled.

"You!" he rasped, quivering as he struggled to speak through his agony. "You'll pay for . . . for what he did! You'll pay!" He pointed a shaking finger at her.

Gwen gaped at him as if seeing a monster, an abomination of hell, and Davies looked the part, fierce and vengeful and evil.

"You!" he shrieked, and the troubled Lernoult ordered him carried away, saying Lieutenant Sennet would finish the treatment.

"You'll pay! I'll be avenged! I swear it!"

Outside in the ward room, the patients stared as Davies was borne past. A child began crying. Several sick regular soldiers were told by Lernoult to come up to the fort in the morning and find a bed in a new infirmary being prepared there. From out in the darkness, Davies's shrieks could still be heard. Then Lernoult, too, was gone, without even a good-bye. Gwen was numb.

Annie took the baby back. The child looked about, bewildered. Gwen sat down heavily, her forehead in her hands, but she would not lose control. Her breath came in short gasps. She must not lose control, but she knew she had to leave Detroit soon. They thought her a spy! They would watch her.

"Mistress Bently—" Doc Sennet came sheepishly to the door, wringing his thin hands as he looked from her to Annie and back. "Cap'n Lernoult asked me to tell . . . to ask you please not to leave the fort without getting a pass from him."

"For how long must I get passes from him?" Gwen demanded, now seeing that the British meant to keep her here, a virtual prisoner.

Sennet shook his head sadly. "Don't know, ma'am. But please, please don't defy the man." He chewed his lip—his tooth still hurting, it seemed—and said, "Lernoult's decent enough, but don't force him to clip your wings, because he will if he has to, and no mistake."

With that, Sennet departed, saying he would come to visit her, no matter what the other soldiers did. He went away muttering to himself, "Don't care what your man done, spy or no. . . . It ain't nothing you should have to suffer for, and no mistake."

Gwen wanted to scream that neither she nor Jeremy were spies. Instead, she banged her fists against her legs and bowed her head, furious and sad and confused. What was the use? She would not stay here, and they would never be able to keep her, not as long as she could walk. But where could she go, and what would she do with Richard?

chapter **2**

KIDNAPPED

Before dawn, Gwen awoke, sitting up suddenly. She saw that Annie was gone from the cot she had slept in, refusing to go home for the night. No doubt she was already hard at work with the patients. Beside Gwen lay the baby; she had taken him from his crib hours ago, for an early feeding. Gwen wished she could get Richard used to sleeping through the night, as he should be doing by now. But her own life was too busy and muddled, and often she was kept awake by patients. Thus, the baby frequently awoke and had to be fed to settle him down. It was tiring. If Jeremy had been there, he could have helped her through this wearying time.

She put her feet on the floor, hearing people stir in the main hospital room; yes, they were being tended by dear Annie. Gwen was so very tired. Jarringly, the memory of last night, of the insane Mark Davies, of Lernoult, and of the disgusting Amaghwah swept over her. She closed her eyes, waiting for her mind to clear. It came to her again that somehow she must get away from Detroit, like the Sutherlands, and perhaps forever. But how?

She could not travel alone toward rebel country, through a land filled with Indians, lawless whites, and wild beasts. Or could she? If she was in danger here, would there be any other choice?

Gwen's mind was filled with these troubling thoughts as she rose to wash and dress. The baby was deep asleep, and that was good. She laid him in the crib and stood a moment to gaze down at him. Jeremy would take such pride! Then it came to her that to flee rashly with the infant would risk his life. She had to stay, until some safer solution was at hand. Perhaps Lela or Mawak could help her.

She finished washing and dressing and went out to the hospital, where Annie was treating a widowed settler who had been badly beaten by her Seneca captors. Gwen opened the door to let Cape go outside, and then she joined Annie to comfort the woman, who was weeping, nearly hysterical. In the four days since being brought in by the Senecas, she had not spoken a word. During the journey, the woman's baby had been killed by the Indians.

Gwen felt a sudden grip of fear, and she stood up straight, looking back at the dim room where Richard lay alone. She rushed into the room and stared down into the crib, her heart pounding. He was there, thumb in mouth, sucking contentedly. Gwen was trembling. The baby stirred, almost waking, and Gwen cooed him back to sleep. Then Annie came in and took her by the shoulders, offering a cup of tea and some mush.

Half closing the door, they went out into the ward again and sat down at a table near the iron stove that had been lit against the morning chill. The hysterical woman now was in the arms of a friend, who tried to comfort her. The room was busy with folk preparing breakfast, women and children in one section, men in the other, with a canvas sailcloth separating them.

Gwen was utterly exhausted, having slept poorly, on top of everything else. Annie did not bother her with small talk. Everything was foggy; her mind felt slow, dull. There appeared to be nothing she could do for herself, nothing except wait for whatever was to come. But there was much that had to be done for the ill and the wounded.

Then a sergeant of the Eighth Regiment, one of the soldiers Lernoult had ordered to come back to the fort, approached, touching his forelock, holding his black tricorne in big, strong hands. He was a hulk of a man, with heavy eyebrows and thick features, plain but for his alert blue eyes. He was in full uniform, wearing a scarlet coat with blue facings, and his waistcoat and breeches were a crisp white.

"Good morning, Sergeant Bailey," Gwen said with a wan smile. "Have you and your two friends recovered from your . . . intestinal problems?"

Sergeant Edward Bailey grinned, his face puffy from a recent shaving, and he bowed slightly to both women, saying in a thick North-of-England accent, "Thanks to thee, Mistress Bently, me and the lads've thrown off what ailed us these past few days." He sought for words, the hat working round and round as his eyes searched the rafters of the hospital.

Gwen could see why he was a sergeant, being a fine example to his men, clean and erect, and utterly unbreakable. He was typical of what was best in British troops—honest and direct, with inexhaustible strength. Unlike many frontier Redcoats, however, Sergeant Bailey was a stranger out in this wilderness; though superbly trained for battle-order drills and fighting in rank, he still had much to learn of frontier ways.

He said after a moment, "In all of my years soldierin', mistress, I ain't seen the likes of that there stomach illness, by gum! Why, I sweated hot when I was icy cold, and the corporal and private there turned a pure pea-green and raved that their hair and fingernails was a-falling out!"

He shook his head, muttering in dismay that even in the India service he had never experienced such an illness. As he hitched at the crimson sergeant's sash around his waist, he said he had been sure they were all about to die.

Then he straightened up and looked very much the line soldier, professional and tough, but there was a certain disappointment in his eyes as he spoke softly: "Mistress, the lads'n me . . . we want to thank thee from the bottom of our hearts, that thy work has been given so freely, and that thee asks . . . asks no payment—"

Gwen held up a hand and smiled at him, wanting to ease his embarrassment. Normally, soldiers who went on sick call had their pay stopped for the time they were off duty, and on top of that, they were required to pay their military doctor fourpence a day, even though they earned only eightpence a day in all. She seldom asked any payment from soldiers, most of whom were poorer than the poorest settler, and only officers were charged for hospital services.

Before Gwen could reply, Bailey said hastily, "Mistress, please don't think all us soldiers holds something against thee! I mean, please don't think we'll forget all thee've done on our behalf!"

They both were at a loss for words. Finally Annie spoke up. "Just remember, Sergeant, the next time you and your lads get sick from drinking trader's high wine, Dr. Sennet might not be able to explain it away to your commander the way Mistress Bently has!"

They all had a chuckle at that. Out here in the northwest, unscrupulous traders made their own explosive alcoholic concoction from corn whiskey, oil of turpentine, water, cayenne pepper, a plug of tobacco for color, and whatever else was potent and handy. Indians drank it, knowing little better, but whites stayed away from "high wine," which was illegal to sell. Bailey and his friends had been green enough in wilderness trade to acquire a jug of this poison, and had drunk so much that it had almost done them in.

He said, "I thought it was the cat-o'-nine-tails that initiated a soldier to army life, but here on the frontier it's trade whiskey does the job!" He looked a bit queasy just at the thought of it, and again thanked Gwen for all she had done.

Bailey returned to the men's sleeping section, where the other soldiers were packed and ready to go back to the fort. Gwen observed three soldiers sitting one behind the other on a bench, braiding one another's queues before putting on their regulation wigs. She said quietly that she would miss helping the regulars, for they were mostly good souls for all their harsh life. She and Annie returned to their breakfasts, and Gwen became thoughtful once again.

In the back of her mind, she heard a thud, as of a door being closed somewhere. Idly, she looked around to see who was coming in, but the front door to the hospital had not been opened, nor was anyone closing a window. The sound must have come from her own room. Her mind became sharp, senses keen. She felt that chilling shock again and stood up. Was someone in the room with Richard? She shuddered. She had to settle down, get hold of herself. He had to sleep. She sat again, but her fingers thrummed on the table. The buzz of voices from the hospital only irritated her the more, for she was listening to hear whether Richard was awake. The hysterical woman was whimpering softly now, embracing her friend, who was patting her on the back.

Gwen tried to eat some mush but could not. She just had to look in at Richard. She moved swiftly, now that she had made up her mind to go. Something did not feel quite right. She pushed the door all the way open and went to the crib. In horror, she cried out. The baby was gone!

With a terrible scream Gwen rushed out the back door, into the gray morning light. Nothing was clear, and only a few candles and lamps gleamed here and there at nearby windows. There was no sign of anyone! Nothing. She cast back and forth, looking up and down the street. Soon Annie was with her, just as frantic, calling Richard's name.

No one was around! Gwen was cold all over.

Suddenly she heard a vicious snarling, and someone was cursing in anger and pain. The commotion came from behind the hospital. The two women dashed there, toward the deeper shadows. They were desperate, almost mad with frenzy. It was Cape, fighting someone in the alley. A shadowy figure, tall and awkward, was writhing, the dog at his chest, driving him backward.

Gwen rushed in and threw herself at the man, clutching at greased flesh and stinking buckskins. It was Amaghwah, who was nearly knocked off his feet by her assault, but he regained his balance and struck wickedly at her with a fist. Under his arm he had the baby, wrapped completely in the crib blanket. Gwen screamed in fury, punching and kicking, Cape at her side, the dog's teeth now in Amaghwah's ankle. The Indian was strong, though, and determined to get away with the baby. He fought and kicked, but he must have either dropped his knife or had no chance to get it, for he used only his free, bare hand. He was a match for the woman and the dog until Annie rushed him, scratching and biting and yanking at his greased scalplock until his head bent down so that Gwen could kick him in the face.

Amaghwah still would not give up, but finally Cape brought her great bulk to bear and piled the Indian down, crashing into his chest and snapping for the throat. The presence of the baby held Cape back, however, for the Indian pressed the bundle at the dog, who knew enough not to bite it. Amaghwah was trapped. Now it would be hard even to get away before help came for Gwen. With a brutal effort, he hurled the baby at Gwen. She stumbled and caught it with a cry, then struggled to unwrap the blankets, afraid for what she might find.

Amaghwah fought to his feet, staggering Cape with a terrific kick to the head. He knocked Annie down with a blow from the back of his hand, and it was then that Gwen saw the Indian's scalping knife flash in the dimness. She cried out as the Shawnee moved at Cape, who was about to spring. The knife came up. Gwen tore the blanket from the baby and threw it at Amaghwah, causing his aim with the knife to go awry just as Cape struck him, knocking him off balance. Then there was a shout from the head of the alley. The three Redcoats from the hospital were there, Sergeant Bailey in the lead, and they barreled into the alley, lanterns in hand.

As if by magic, Amaghwah was gone. He had sprung away onto a shed roof, then darted across to the other side of the building and into the dimness, leaving Cape bewildered and barking. Richard was all right. He kicked and fussed, crying furiously, to Gwen's inexpressible relief.

She bundled him in the blanket and hurried back to the hospital, leaving Annie to show the angry soldiers where Amaghwah had gone. Gwen clutched the baby close, Cape bounding at her side—and then she saw another Indian, standing at the hospital's back door, watching her. This one was portly, ponderous, and disheveled, and Gwen was glad to recognize old Mawak, the Ottawa medicine man who had been a friend to the Sutherlands for many years. He stared sadly at Gwen, as if he realized what had happened.

Gwen was badly shaken, but she could tell Mawak wanted to say something important. They left the commotion that swirled around them and went into the small room, closing the door. Gwen took a seat, shutting her eyes, holding Richard close.

Mawak was musty and needed a wash; his three or four layers of trade shirts had long ago lost their garish colors. Despite his almost clownish appearance and his love of alcohol, Mawak was wiser than most who lived at the straits, and Gwen had great respect for him. Indeed, at times he understood things with a clarity that seemed almost supernatural. No one could figure out how men such as he knew what they knew, but their "medicine" was almost always powerful.

Gwen, still trembling, hugged the baby in her arms, while Mawak remained standing, as if contemplating what had to be said. Only after the sounds of confusion outside the hospital settled down did he seat himself on the floor, cross-legged. He refused with a shake of the head when Gwen offered him food and drink, as was proper according to Indian custom. Already, Richard was quiet, asleep in his mother's arms.

When Mawak spoke at last, his voice was gravelly, his words slow and weighty. He spoke in Ottawa, which Gwen understood well by now.

"I have known for days about Dr. Bently's change of side," he said, black eyes shining, intense as he stared at the floor. "Many villages have heard about it, and have passed the word, although the white soldiers knew nothing until Girty brought the wounded Captain Davies back from Shawnee lands." Gwen asked why Mawak had not told her this earlier.

He answered: "I feared you would act foolishly, attempt to flee immediately, and that would make them follow and arrest you for a spy."

Gwen flinched at the thought of such a foul accusation. Mawak said he had hoped that Captain Davies would die, for that would have ended much of the danger for her. With Davies alive, however, she would be always in peril, if not from Amaghwah, then from someone else.

"You must take care in all you do, Mistress Bently, but know that none of my people will help this low dog Amaghwah, who is an outcast of the Shawnees!" His expression hardened. "We will kill him if we find him. . . ." He shook his head. "But the Redcoats will likely keep him as a scout on the eastern frontier. They will not be able to prove that he has done this thing today." Mawak snorted. "They are desperate, the Redcoats, and they need Indians like him on their side for this war."

Mawak explained that many a village had recently refused to send men to fight alongside the British soldiers. The army was paying costly bribes, giving presents and supplies of unprecedented value to keep the Indians loyal; but ever since Clark had shattered the security of loyalists in the northwest, the Indians around Detroit were not sure the Redcoats could lead them, defend them, or even supply them for very much longer.

"It goes badly for the sons of the great white father across the sea, and his red children are afraid to obey him much longer." He became thoughtful a while, before saying, "The soldiers must prove beyond doubt to the Indians that they are stronger than the *Bostonnais*."

Mawak used this old term for enemy—"Bostonians"—a name given British colonials by the French, who had led Indians in the century-long war with the eastern colonies. Boston was the main staging area for the greatest campaigns against the French lands, and many of the troops who fought the Indians came from New England, near Boston. Now the British were opening old wounds by calling all rebels Bostonians, to keep the Indians eager to fight them.

But even that strategy was losing its potency, Gwen knew.

"The villages will not easily join the British—not the older warriors, anyway, the ones with good sense. But there are enough young ones . . . some bad ones, too, ones who have a taste for blood and pillage and do not know they will leave their own bones on the trail. It is these who will go with the British when the time comes."

Gwen laid Richard in his crib and sat down again, listening to Mawak say that a major campaign would take place next spring, and the British had sent out the red tomahawk of war, calling on all the tribes to muster their young men.

Mawak said, "I have seen visions, and they are dark, stormy, and terribly bloody, as never before seen in this country!" Gwen anxiously listened, but Mawak did not relate any more. Stiffly, he rose and repeated that Gwen must take care, adding that if he could find Amaghwah, he would personally slay him. Gwen shuddered, and thanked the Ottawa for his offer of protection.

Before departing, he said, "Men like Davies will lead the Indian astray, lead them through my stormy vision. Davies will take revenge against rebels where he can, and the British are desperate, so they will let him fight the *Bostonnais* his own way."

Gwen and Mawak stared at each other a moment, until the Indian said, "My dreams have foretold that it might be better, when you have the choice, to let Davies die."

Then he was gone, leaving Gwen with a grim puzzle and profound uneasiness. Anyway, Davies was not in her hands now, and she thanked the Lord she did not have to take that awful responsibility.

chapter **3**

FALLS OF THE OHIO

In dappled sunlight slanting through the forest, the young buck moved slowly, a brown shadow, feeding on leaves, now and again raising his head to scent the wind.

Sighted along the barrel of Owen Sutherland's rifle, the buck was an easy shot. Its meat would be appreciated back at the settlement, for deer were scarce in the Kentucky country now that so many settlers had come down the Ohio. Sutherland let the buck move a bit more, waited for the shoulder to come around square into his sight.

Concealed in thick undergrowth, his long legs stiff from crouching, Sutherland had been waiting half an hour for the buck to drift into range. The play of sunlight on his deerskin jacket and leggins made him indistinguishable from his surroundings, and the buck had no apprehension. Any moment now . . .

But Sutherland did not squeeze the trigger. He sensed that he must not, that he must wait, must watch. Though he was only a couple of miles from the well-guarded settlement, he sensed Indian danger. Even the deer had now lifted his head.

Standing stock still, the buck sensed something. But it was not
Owen Sutherland.

Sutherland heard more than saw the first arrow. It hissed
from bushes close at hand. The buck leaped forward when hit,
letting out a bleat of shock. Another and another arrow flew,
until five in all struck the animal, even before it could leap
again. It went down with a crash, kicking, unable to get up
and run. In the next instant, Sutherland saw Shawnees bound
from cover, five of them. With a start he realized they were
boys, all so young that there was scarcely a feather among
them. They romped to the deer, as gleeful as if they were safe
in their own hills, not in country patrolled by mortal enemies.
None was older than twelve; they had not even earned the
Shawnee crest, the ridge of greased hair a warrior preened
down his back.

For all that they were foolish boys, they were brave, and
Sutherland smiled ruefully, settling back to watch them gut the
deer and struggle to sling it on a pole that one of their number
had slashed noisily from some saplings nearby. They were
indeed bold, these impetuous young Shawnees, to have come
across the Ohio River to Kentucky country, because this was
now white man's territory. There would be no mercy if the
boys were caught by tough woodsmen or rebel rangers on a
patrol.

For countless generations of Indians, Kentucky had been a
battlefield and hunting ground—"dark and bloody ground," its
name meant. But now, with the coming of the whites and their
war, these woods were more dangerous than ever for the red
man, and by venturing over here without even a rusty musket
with which to protect themselves, these boys were taking their
lives into their hands.

Had it been another frontiersman watching them—another
as wily and tough as Owen Sutherland—these Shawnees would
have been dead meat. As it was, they were such novices that
their excitement and hunger got the better of them, and they
took greedy, happy bites of the liver, passing it around. Blood
ran down their chins, like the war paint they one day would
earn the right to wear. If they lived that long.

But Owen Sutherland had no will to kill them, as he could
easily have done. These boys were hunters who had strayed

too close to danger; they were not scouts or a war party. He admired their courage at having come across—probably against their families' orders. No doubt they needed that buck more badly than his own people did. Well, he would let them have it, and with it the honor they would earn. He only wanted them to get away quickly, back to Indian country, before some rangers stumbled on them and wiped them out.

He was glad when at last they got the deer trussed. Triumphant, laughing more loudly than was prudent, they hurried along the trail toward the Ohio River. From here, the raging of the rapids could be heard, and it would not be long before the Shawnee boys were in their canoe and skimming across the water to safety.

Sutherland stepped from the thicket, into brighter sunshine, and followed them. He meant to make sure—for their own good—that they departed immediately. Rifle at the ready, he padded silently along the trail. He was ruddy, clean-shaven, and hatless, his dark hair clubbed at the nape of his neck. At his side hung a weighty sword—an unusual weapon for a scout in the woods. Sutherland was big and muscular, but he moved gracefully, hard to see against the shadows of the trees, and he wanted it that way. Lurking everywhere these days were Shawnee scouts—fighting men, not just boys off on a daring lark—watching the new settlements taking shape in Kentucky, and attacking and killing whenever they could.

Shortly, Sutherland was looking down at the boys, who were dragging a canoe from cover. He was concealed once more, and watched them lunging and stumbling with the heavy deer, trying to load it into their craft. He could not help but smile to see them so plucky and intent on their work, so serious, and yet so vulnerable. They were years away from learning how to hunt in a no-man's-land. He thought to give them a lesson.

Making sure there were no other Shawnees about, Sutherland waited until the boys began to push the canoe into deeper water, the deer now in the middle of the boat. Then he cupped his hands and yelled a terrifying war cry he had learned as a young fighting man from the Highlands of his native Scotland. The boys yelped in fright, and in a clatter of paddles and bows scrambled aboard, almost upsetting the craft as they frantically strove to get away.

Sutherland chuckled, waited until they had hauled a fat

laggard among them into the stern of the canoe, then cupped his hands once more.

In Shawnee he bellowed, "Come back here again, and by the manitous I'll truss you all like that deer and have your hearts for breakfast! Get! Save yourselves, thieves! And never come back! On pain of death!"

He followed with the terrible battle cry that ended in a hearty laugh, for he had never before seen a canoe paddled so quickly yet so awkwardly. The boys were so disorganized that at first they could make little headway, flailing their paddles at the water until the canoe nearly circled back to shore.

Finally, however, they got hold of themselves and fled out into the broad Ohio. Sutherland was satisfied, and set off for home. The settlement was not far downriver, where the rapids foamed into swirling, treacherous eddies known as the Falls of the Ohio.

He walked along the river trail, and after a while came to the edge of the settlement, where cattle and horses peacefully cropped what little grass grew in the clearings that had been freshly slashed out along the riverbank. The place was bathed in bright sunlight, and was alive with men building, women and children cultivating gardens, and people coming and going on the rutted street that passed between primitive cabins and disappeared into the gate of the stockade beyond.

Near the gate, Sutherland saw his daughter, Susannah, strolling in the sunshine with James Morely, a tall young man she adored, although he was in his twenties and she was not yet of marriageable age. Susannah looked fresh and pretty in a yellow dress, and Sutherland paused at the edge of the woods to observe her a moment and admire her. Almost a woman, Susannah had a mind of her own, and no father could have been prouder than Owen Sutherland. Yet he was concerned for her, uneasy that she was so infatuated with the Morely lad. A year ago, Sutherland would have been pleased to see her with James, who had the makings of a good man. Lately, however, there had been problems. . . .

Sutherland put aside this troubling line of thought, decided he did not want to go to the settlement just yet, and turned away. He began walking up a wooded hillside toward the crest of a ridge he favored as a good place to think. At the last moment, he saw that Susannah had noticed him, and they waved to each other before he pushed on into the trees, out of her sight.

Soon he was standing in sunlight on a rocky outcrop, the wind in his face, fresh and cool. Below was the settlement, and beyond it the foaming Ohio. He gazed across the river, toward the Shawnee hills, as if he could see over them, far beyond, to the distant grasslands that rolled northward into broad, flat country. Many weeks' travel in that direction was another river, wider than the Ohio, and to it his thoughts drifted.

Across the river, near the outpost called Fort Detroit, was a fine house, clapboard sided, white in the morning sunshine, and he could imagine it standing there, waiting. Waiting for him and Ella to come home. The house was named Valenya, and he had been away from it for four hard years of war. Revolution, some called it, and gloried in the name; but to most Americans it was a bloody civil war, harsh and brutal and seemingly unending. Many folk, like the Sutherlands, had been forced from their homes because the other side was in power locally and had driven them out. Detroit was held by loyalists; the Sutherlands were rebels, and that was why his family was here at the Falls, in a squalid little fortified settlement of folk attempting to make a fresh start in a new country.

Between loyalist Detroit and this rocky outcrop in rebel Kentucky were hundreds of miles of forest, and thousands of Indians, nearly all of whom had declared for the king. They were sworn enemies to rebels like Owen Sutherland.

With a long, weary sigh, he sat down on the rock, rifle across his knees, the claymore that he once had worn as an officer of the famous Black Watch Highland regiment resting in its scabbard at his side. The sword, the token of a gentleman, contrasted with his buckskins and linen shirt, the dress of a frontiersman. Sutherland closed his eyes and smelled the fragrance of river and forest—the forest of "Indian country."

Indian country. Until the war began, he had never really thought of the northwest wilderness in that way, for it had become his own, his homeland, even more than was his native Scotland. He knew the Indian heart and had once had an Indian wife; that was why he had so admired those Shawnee boys at their hunting. Looking at the rest of the world from the straits of Detroit, living happily as a friend of the Indians, being regarded as the leading trader in all the vast northwest, Sutherland had seen the country above the Ohio River in a far different light. It had been a land rich with profit, peopled by friends and hearty companions—Indian and French.

The sun was warm and soothing, the breeze fresh, and Sutherland imagined he was sitting at the doorway of Valenya, watching the river, or seeing wheat ripple in the wind. He wished he were thinking about the fur trade, not about war. . . .

There was movement nearby. He grew alert. Someone was coming quietly through the bushes. His right hand moved casually to his leg. Were there more Shawnees than he had seen? Was one of them after a prisoner to drag back across the river?

Abruptly, the bushes behind him parted and a figure sprang through. Sutherland whipped around. His Scottish dirk flashed from his leggin. The attacker was leaping right into the blade. But it was Susannah. He gasped, catching her lithe body a fraction from the dirk tip, and held her off. She stared, wide-eyed, and Sutherland trembled, as few things ever could make him tremble.

"Lassie!" he hissed, sudden anger coming over him as he steadied her on her feet. "You should know better than to slip up. . . . What in the name of . . ."

Slim and blond, her blue eyes blinking as she stared at the dirk still held at her breast, Susannah could not find the words at first, and, recovering, tried to laugh it off. Fast becoming as beautiful as her mother, she was wearing a clean linen apron over her dress. Her head was uncovered and her brushed long hair hung free, like her mother's. Standing erect before Sutherland, she looked tall, much older than her fourteen years.

"May I join you, Pa?" Her voice shook a little, and she cleared her throat as they sat down side by side on the rocks.

For days he had hoped she would come to him, to talk, and to forgive, and to start over again after the trouble that had passed between them of late.

Hands in her lap, eyes distant, Susannah was the picture of innocence to her father. No man loved his daughter more, but he wondered anxiously what she felt for him just now.

He said softly, "I'm glad you're here, lass. . . ." His voice had a gentle Scots burr that would not be lost, though he had been in America twenty-five of his fifty-odd years. "But next time, announce yourself before you leap at my back."

He looked intently at her, searching for some hint of what

it was she had come to say. After a moment, with Susannah's eyes filling up—though she clearly was trying to be strong and to keep back tears—Sutherland reached over to touch her hand. She gripped his, but still could not speak what was in her heart.

That was all right, for Sutherland was content that at least she had come to him, to let the anger between them drain away in silence. For all his trials during a life in the wilderness, there had been few more painful than seeing hatred in his daughter's eyes. His heart wrenched at the memory of it, though it had been weeks ago. Since then, they had scarcely spoken, for he, too, could be awkwardly stubborn, especially when hurt by the resentment of his only daughter.

"Pa . . ." she began, and a tear rolled down her cheek. "I'm sorry . . . I did not mean to hurt you, and I know you were only trying to do what is best for me. . . ."

He could tell she had practiced this, and he knew how hard it was for her to forgive him, and to ask that he forgive her.

"Pa," she breathed, sniffing, and wiping her eyes clumsily, "you have to talk to James. You have to tell him you . . . you don't hold anything against him . . . that you understand what he meant to do, and that you want to work with him just as you always have."

Sutherland knew this was what she would say, what she had to say. His daughter was hopelessly in love with the ambitious young trader James Morely, though she was not old enough to marry. Now she was looking at her father, and he wanted to find the right words, to tell her he did not want to hold anything against James. All his grown life, James had been a member of the Frontier Company, and his father had been Sutherland's partner in establishing the company back in 1764. Sutherland was nominal leader of the company, and no one more than he wanted James a part of it, but he was not sure that was possible anymore, after all that had happened.

"Pa?" Susannah could not bear the quiet. Sutherland did not blame her for her impatience.

"Lassie, if the lad wants to remain in the Frontier Company with the rest of us, he's welcome—you know that, and so does he. But if he chooses to ally with Bradford Cullen, he can't do business with me as well."

Seeing her lower her head, he again reached to touch her trembling hands. He sought the right thing to say, but it was easier to council with Indians at war, or to face down an enemy. . . .

He got up and stared at the river, feeling Susannah watching him, as if to fathom his thoughts. He tried to keep away the dark fury that came over him as he considered how James Morely, in rash confidence, had nearly led Susannah and others into a fatal ambush—an ambush set up by Bradford Cullen, of that Sutherland had no doubt. The most corrupt and most powerful merchant prince on the frontier, old Cullen was always looking for a way to destroy the Frontier Company, and with it Owen Sutherland, his enemy.

Sutherland was sure Cullen had tricked the less-worldly James into taking a convoy of flatboats down the Ohio from Pitt a few weeks ago, boats laden with goods and munitions for the rebel leader George Rogers Clark, who was headquartered here at the Falls. Promising that a fortune was to be made, wooing the young man with flattery and lies, Cullen had even offered financing, and finally persuaded James to ally with him in an expedition that was never meant to reach its destination. Only Owen Sutherland's arrival in time to defeat the Shawnee ambush had saved the convoy—and saved his family and friends, who would have been wiped out, to Bradford Cullen's satisfaction.

Yes, Sutherland had openly blamed James Morely for the near-disaster. And that had broken Susannah's heart, and set her against her father for the past weeks.

He sighed. A brilliant, promising young trader like James had to be forgiven for rashness now and then. It would be better, however, if James would admit that Cullen had set up the ambush. He did not, and that angered Sutherland all the more.

He did not say these thoughts to Susannah, for it only would have made things worse, and would have sent her crying back down to the settlement. Instead, he turned to her and said simply, "I'll hold nothing against the lad, Susannah, for we all make mistakes—"

"Pa—" She began to protest at his tone of voice, but then she held herself back, fingertips touching her lips, as if in prayer.

"But never forget, Susannah," Sutherland said, staring hard at her, "Cullen means to ruin the Frontier Company, to dominate the northwest trade completely. He always has and always will bend good men like James to his will—men whose vanity is too easily flattered—"

"Pa!" she pleaded. "Don't start that, please, not again!"

He raised a hand. "Aye, lassie, I'll say no more about that in your presence."

"Or in James's! Please!" She reached for his hands and squeezed them tightly. "Please, please go to him, before he goes back up to Fort Pitt! Won't you, Pa? Talk to him. For me? At least don't let him go away hating you!"

Sutherland softened again. "No, I don't want James Morely hating me."

James's father, Garth, had been one of Sutherland's best friends, before being killed by white renegades years back. The widow was with her second husband, down in the settlement. Down there, too, was James's brother, who was married to Sutherland's foster daughter. No, there was no good in leaving James full of bile at the mention of the name Owen Sutherland.

"I'll go to him, Susannah." He gave a little dry laugh. "Lord knows he won't come to me."

A voice spoke from the woods nearby. "But he will, sir." James stepped from the trees, hat in hand, face drawn and pale from the ache of a broken collarbone and other wounds suffered in the fight with the loyalist Indians. Sutherland glanced from James to Susannah, who was on her feet, and he saw that she, too, was startled by the young man's unexpected appearance. She had not set this up.

Admiration was in her eyes as she gazed at James, who was tall, well dressed in a good light-brown shirt and breeches, with matching silk stockings. The bandages that swathed him from shoulder to waist bulked up under his shirt, lending weight to his slender build. His eyes were brown and intense, his face darkly handsome, his chin and mouth firm. Sutherland knew he was in considerable pain from his wounds, but he had come all the way up the hill to talk.

Susannah moved to James and touched his arm. He smiled at her as she said she would see him later. Excited, she glanced anxiously at her father before hurrying down the slope, along an open trail to the village. Sutherland got up to watch her go; she was in sight nearly all the way.

James watched her also, as she skipped down the trail like

a nimble deer, her blond hair flying behind. Sutherland took note of the softness in the lad's eyes, and then James glanced back, intensity coming upon him again. Sutherland waited.

James broke the silence, saying, "It's for Susannah's sake that I've come to you, Owen."

Sutherland nodded, and they sat on the rocks. The sun was hot, the air clear and breezy. Though he did not voice it, Sutherland hoped James would not have to pay too great a price for being duped by Bradford Cullen. Whatever that price might be—and there surely would be one—Sutherland was determined that Susannah would not also suffer for it.

Sutherland said, "I'm grateful you've come to talk to me, lad, and I'll do my part to keep us from breaking forever."

He regarded James closely, and for a moment saw an image of the bright and charming young fellow he once had known, the cheerful boy who had always been so honest and able in the trade. Then there was another image before Sutherland, that of a good man going wrong, turning toward the lure of fortune, of power, turning away from the idealism that had forged and tempered the Frontier Company over the past ten or more years.

Sutherland shook off that impression and said, taking a deep breath, "Whatever you want to charge for your own part of the cargo you've hauled down here is your decision, son. But as for the Frontier Company, our goods will be sold to Colonel Clark at whatever he can afford to pay—whether it be in Virginia paper money or Congress Continental dollars."

He looked to James for a reply. James was stony. Both those forms of payment were almost worthless, for no one knew when Congress or Virginia could ever redeem them for hard money—if the rebels won the war.

James said, "I came to talk of Susannah, not of business."

Jolted, Sutherland straightened up. He was prepared to discuss business differences, not to speak seriously about what was to be for his daughter.

After a moment, Sutherland said, "Talk." His voice was unexpectedly hoarse.

James licked his lips and looked at the ground. "I know she's very young—"

"True enough."

"But she's nearly a woman—"

"Nearly."

"And I've no intent to rush her into anything—"

"Her mother and I would be obliged if you did not."

". . . and yet, it's time, I think, for us to speak man to man about . . . Susannah's future."

Sutherland looked closely at James, who stared back resolutely. The lad was solid enough, but not nearly so wise or experienced as he would like to think. There was a heavy silence.

James pressed on, forcing out the words: "I love Susannah . . . as I think is apparent, Owen."

Sutherland wondered whether James really knew what he was saying. Did he truly love the child with all his heart, as Sutherland and Ella loved her? Would he protect and care for her as a father demanded?

After another awkward pause, James said, "In three years she'll be old enough to marry, and at that time, Owen, I wish to ask for her hand . . . with your blessing, and with your respect, I sincerely hope."

Sutherland knew well that James felt a lack of respect from him. Yet Sutherland knew James was brave, even in blood combat, and could be every bit the man Susannah required for a husband. If only Bradford Cullen did not corrupt him with promises of power and wealth.

Sutherland tried to smile, but what appeared on his weathered face was a wan, almost ironic expression.

"James, laddie, when the time comes, and Susannah's old enough, I'll not stand in her way . . . if she loves you."

James became suddenly eager. "That she does!"

"Today she does. But she's yet a girl, and I'll only heed her in this when she's more of a woman."

There was silence, save for the wind picking up and the steady rush of the river. James shifted in his seat, obviously in pain from his many wounds; but he did not complain.

Staring hard, he said, "Then you'll not stand between us?"

Slowly shaking his head, Sutherland said, "Not if you're a free man in three years."

James asked sharply for an explanation.

"Not if you're your own man—I mean separate from Bradford Cullen."

James sighed, head stiffly raised, lower lip tight against his teeth. "Can't you ever forget Cullen? Owen, my dealings are for me to decide, no one else. Commerce is commerce! Business is business. Do you ask those Indians you trade with whether they've been good this past season, whether they've kept off the warpath, haven't killed a wife during a drunken stupor, or haven't murdered some other trapper to steal his pelts? Can you read the truth in a beaver skin? Some good, some bad? Are all your trade goods always clean, Owen, or did they perhaps come from a pirate hoard, stripped from a dead Spaniard gutted by a Carolina buccaneer sailing under the Jolly Roger?" He slapped his leg. "You can't be sure!"

Getting to his feet, despite the hurt of his body, James was obviously trying to control himself.

Sutherland, too, stood. "I'm speaking plainly, young man, and I need not explain myself further."

James scarcely restrained anger. "You attempt to put conditions on me that I will not allow any man to ask! I've made mistakes, and I'll make more, but I can look out for myself! Bradford Cullen has no power over me, and never will! I outwitted him again and again in the Albany trade, and made a pretty penny for the Frontier Company, to boot! But you know I've had no great love for your Revolution, and I have no respect for anyone who throws away the chance—" He looked away, forcing himself to speak calmly, but with emphasis. "I have no will to throw away what I have fairly earned, simply because I earned it by making a transaction with Bradford Cullen."

"Choose your way, laddie, but I'll not speak of it now."

James reached out his right hand for Sutherland to take it. Before Sutherland did so, James said, "I'll always respect you, sir. You know that."

Sutherland took the young man's hand in both of his.

"And I have always respected you, James."

As if startled to hear this, James rose to his full height, recovering dignity. He said, "When Susannah is old enough, I will ask for her hand; God grant that you will be proud to give her to me."

Sutherland felt that catch at his own heart. "So do I pray, James. For Susannah's sake."

• • •

Owen and James went back to the newly built settlement that sprawled raw and muddy in the summer heat beside the river.

As they descended the trail, they were watched by Ella Bently Sutherland, who stood at the side door of the flatboat that had brought her and the rest of the family downriver from Fort Pitt a couple of weeks ago. Ella was still a beauty at forty-five, with bright hazel eyes and long hair, golden in the sunlight, hanging free over her shoulders. She wore drab linen and cotton, but her plain clothes lent her loveliness all the more radiance.

The flatboat, her home for the past weeks, was tied up to the riverbank, behind a sandbar. Here and there around her its pine planking bore the scars of battle; it was pitted with bullet holes, and gashed where tomahawks and axes had struck—but at least the bloodstains had been scoured away. The large deck-house, behind Ella, was similar to some of the plank cabins on shore, with a stick-and-daub chimney, a few shuttered windows—now open to the river breeze—and a door at the side. Indeed, many a cabin here at the Falls was a dismantled flatboat that not long ago had floated down from Fort Pitt, loaded with people escaping the fighting in the East. They were mostly families, from Virginia, the Carolinas, Pennsylvania, Maryland, and New Jersey, and they believed they were putting the civil war—the Revolution—far behind them. They were sick of fighting other whites, but were willing enough to fight Indians if they must, and expected they would have to do so for many years to come, no matter who won the eastern war between king and Congress.

Sutherland and James approached, passing through ragged clusters of children who played with hoops and balls as they ran back and forth around three-sided lean-tos, canvas tents, and earthen mounds thrown up for rifle pits. Ella watched the two of them and thought they looked good together, complementing each other, though they were such very different men. She hoped the hostility between them would be overcome before long.

The two men parted, and Sutherland shouldered his rifle and came toward Ella at the flatboat. She waved, and so did he as he began to trot through the settlement. Ella would be glad to get away from here, the middle of nowhere, a ramshackle clutter of dwellings that reeked of river mud, overused latrines, and rotting garbage. As he ran, Sutherland was joined by his big white husky Heera, no longer young, but still spry and formidable.

Ella took her man's hand as he came up the gangway and laid his rifle aside. For a moment, she watched James move off, toward Susannah, who was sitting alone on the grassy bank of the river, reading a book that presumably was Shakespeare. The girl and James both loved reading the sonnets, and lately had taken an interest in the plays. Beyond Susannah, on the shore, was the palisade of Clark's new fort, close to long rapids that made this part of the river difficult to pass without portaging or very careful piloting.

A few months ago, Clark's brave men had joined with anti-British French from the Illinois and marched hundreds of miles to conquer the Crown's lieutenant governor, taking him prisoner in the hope that the Indian raids spawned by the British would be curtailed. It was yet to be seen whether Clark's triumphs had turned the tide of frontier war.

As she greeted her husband, Ella thought Owen looked tired. She took his sword belt and told him to come in for dinner, adding that her son Jeremy was inside, waiting to talk.

She took her husband by the arm. "Will James ask for Susannah's hand?" She was certain of the answer, and when it came, she was glad to hear it. "Three years will go by quickly, Owen, but when it's past, I hope the young ones will have a peaceful country." A cheering thought came to her. "Perhaps they'll want to live near Valenya! We might all be together, at last!"

Sutherland smiled at that and squeezed her against him when they were partway through the door of the deckhouse. He said he had been thinking the same thing.

Ella said, almost desperately, "This killing can't go on forever! The king and Parliament must know they can't win, even if they kill half of us!" She wanted Owen to agree with her, but his reply was slow in coming as he took off his buckskin jacket and hung it on a peg just inside the flap of their own partition in the dim main room. The deckhouse was fragrant with a cake baking in a brick oven at the far side of the room. Besides the Sutherlands, two other families lived here; Jeremy was staying with friends in a rented shack.

At last, Sutherland said, "We need one big victory, one win to rattle the bones of Parliament and the Tories! Clark and Virginia are talking about sending two thousand mounted men against Detroit next year, and that would pull all the tribes off the frontiers."

Ella had heard all this before, and she followed her husband into the common room, where Jeremy sat at a table, the sun from an open window falling on his blond hair, throwing his big, powerful frame into sharp forms of shadow and light. Yes, Ella had heard all this wishful talk before, but the war dragged on, even though the French had come in on the rebel side with money, supplies, ships, and guns. Yet there had been no decisive victory since the rebel triumph at Saratoga, two years past.

Ella poured tea for her husband and son. On the table was the map Jeremy had drawn of the country between this lonely post and Fort Detroit. She paused to look it over, and thought how enormous the distance seemed. Hundreds of miles of forest, swarming with Indian war parties and hunting parties. It troubled her to think of the danger, and yet nothing would keep her husband and son from going. Nor would she want them not to go. Up at Detroit was her grandson, Jeremy's new child, and the baby and mother were in danger.

Jeremy voiced another fear, as he tried to sit comfortably— his wounds were serious, and the knife-thrust in his side was not healing well—"When we take Gwen away, the house . . . Valenya, might be lost to us."

Ella looked at the floor, the teapot weightless in her hand. She wished Jeremy had not brought that up. Owen said there were friends at Detroit who surely would care for the house, as it had been cared for when they had first been forced to leave, under pressure from loyalists who wanted rebel blood. For the past couple of years, Jeremy and Gwen had lived at Valenya when not at their hospital in the fort. With Gwen gone, however, there might be no stopping men who would take pleasure in seeing a rebel's home burned to the ground.

Especially Captain Mark Davies, Jeremy said.

Ella moved to the wood stove and put down the teapot. Word had come in from Indian friends that the Redcoat Mark Davies had survived the recent fight when his Indian followers were beaten after attacking the Sutherland flatboat convoy.

Davies was a maniac, a bitter enemy of all rebels, and a man with a vendetta against Owen and Jeremy.

Jeremy said, "Davies must have reached Detroit by now, and surely he'll lie, claiming I was a rebel spy all the time I was in the army—"

He hesitated, grimly staring at the map. Ella knew the heaviness of his heart. No man of honor wanted friends to believe he had been a spy against them. Jeremy spoke no more of it. He and Sutherland began planning their journey, intending to travel with only Tamano, the Chippewa warrior who had been Sutherland's friend for many years. Tamano was out on a scout just then; it was he who had learned of Davies's survival.

Ella worked with a fork over the stove, preparing a cornmeal dish to be followed by the raisin cake baking in the oven. She could hear the men talking about leaving in a few weeks, after Jeremy had healed well enough to travel. It would be a journey that might last through the winter.

Ella felt weakness coming over her as she thought of losing her man again for so long a time. She closed her eyes, the hand with the fork falling to her side. Then Owen was there, turning her to face him. He was trying to smile, and doing well at it, in spite of Ella's sudden paleness.

"We'll be out of there before they even know we're in the country!" He took the fork from her and gave the food a stir, sniffing at the aroma. "I'll miss your cooking, lass."

Ella smiled. She knew now she would not cry, not until they were gone. How she wished they could get over the war and return to a normal, peaceful life—back to Valenya, where they belonged!

Musing, Jeremy said, "There's lots of friends who're watching over Gwen and Richard. Even old Mawak comes over from his village to make medicine for their safety." With forced cheerfulness, he added, "Richard'll be almost a year old by the time we get him out of Detroit. I haven't seen him myself yet!" He became thoughtful. "Do you think he'll know me?"

Ella laughed and took the fork from her husband, shooing him away as she opened the oven to test the cake. "You had best get on the trail, then, before the baby thinks old Mawak is the father and takes to drinking firewater and cracking lice with his teeth!"

Ella thought how much she would like to go up there and

see the baby and Gwen, whom she had never met. She would love to have them at Valenya, to spoil the baby a little, and to work in the orchard with Gwen.

She looked around her, pausing before taking out the cake. This little flatboat was all they had in the world right now. It would be hard to winter here at the Falls. The flatboat would have to be hauled out of the water, but there was no time for Owen to pull it apart and build a decent cabin with it.

There was little hard cash at hand, either. The Frontier Company's money was invested in goods George Rogers Clark was parceling up and shipping to his small garrisons up and down the Ohio and Illinois rivers. As to when payment for those goods would come from Clark's Virginia or the Continental Congress, no one could guess. For now, Ella Bently Sutherland, who once had been like nobility in the northwest, was little more than another poor settler among thousands of poor settlers struggling to survive on the edge of Indian country, waiting for better times to come.

She looked at Owen, who was standing over Jeremy, but staring at her. Could he know her thoughts? She did not want him to worry. When he said softly that there was still a pouch full of Spanish pieces of eight that would see her through the winter, she forced herself to shrug, trying to ignore his uncanny intuition.

When Jeremy got up to wash his hands, Owen came and drew Ella close to him. How strong and fine he was! It would be all right, she knew, rich or poor. . . .

She said, "Promise you'll come back to me, my love!"

He kissed her softly and smiled.

"Don't ever worry," he said, but she wished, this time, he had plainly promised to return. He did not, however, and she did not dare ask why.

chapter **4**

FAREWELLS

"Have I betrayed him, Pa? Have I?"

Susannah Sutherland pleaded for an answer as her father stood there, full of love for the young woman—or growing girl, for she was both at once, and yet neither completely.

Sutherland and Susannah were standing at the edge of the settlement, near the river, and brilliant sunshine bathed the clearing. It was late afternoon, and hot for September, not a breeze stirring. Nearby, in the shade of a big willow, a dozen ragged, barefoot children sat watching, but they were not close enough to hear the conversation. These were children of the Kentucky people, and Susannah was teaching them their lessons and, at the moment, proper manners. They sat fidgeting on split-log benches, and in every lap was a board with a sheet of paper containing writing that had been laboriously copied by Susannah from the text *The School of Manners*, subtitled *Rules for Children's Behaviour*.

Susannah had almost forgotten her class since her father arrived and announced he was about to depart for Detroit. Plans had been changed, he told her, and they had to go right away.

Word had come of a big Shawnee war party moving near the trail he meant to take, compelling him to get through before the Indians crossed their intended route, cutting them off, and forcing them to make a much longer journey through more densely inhabited Indian country.

Now even Sutherland's plans were put from his mind as he considered what Susannah—in a rush of emotion and confusion—had just told him.

She asked again, "I broke my promise to James by telling you about his . . . his falling sickness. Oh, Pa, was I wrong?"

Sutherland put an arm over his daughter's shoulder, and they walked off a little ways toward the edge of the river. The children were beginning to act up, and a girl was yelling as she was teased, but the two of them ignored the commotion.

Susannah had explained that James had suffered for years from fainting spells that he had kept secret from everyone but her. The only way she had learned about them was that she had been with him once, a couple of years ago, when he was on sentry duty and had fainted. Unfortunately, it had been just before a band of Shawnees had attacked the settlement where the Sutherlands and others were living. As a result of James's lapse, there had been no alarm, and Ella Sutherland had been nearly killed, and Benjamin captured and carried off.

Unwilling to admit he suffered from what he considered a mortal weakness, James had begged Susannah not to tell anyone of his fainting, not even in order to defend him against the accusation of dereliction of duty. Now, however, with her love for James overflowing, Susannah had blurted out everything.

As her father stared at the river, she declared, "Don't hold that incident against James! Pa, don't blame him for cowardice, for shirking his duty!"

Sutherland turned to face her, his thoughts whirling. He realized now why James was often so defensive. The lad was forever trying to prove himself. For a moment Sutherland wondered whether James really loved Susannah, or if she was simply a symbol to him, a way of proving that Owen Sutherland would accept him as a son-in-law. Sutherland did not want to think of that, however.

Susannah was standing before him, lovely and innocent, her hair in pigtails; it was the way he wanted to remember her when he ventured once again into enemy territory. Sutherland had a strange premonition that something terrible was in store for him. He could not explain it, but the feeling was stronger than any other premonition he had ever had. He did not want to talk about James Morely now, but he had no choice.

He smiled and put his finger under Susannah's chin, lifting her head slightly so that he could imagine the beautiful young woman she would one day become.

He said, "You have not betrayed him, lassie, because you are speaking the truth for his own good." He smiled and kissed her forehead, and she took his hands, as if finally realizing the moment of parting was almost upon them. Sutherland saw her eyes soften and was glad for that.

He spoke gently: "James has the makings of a good man, Susannah, but there's no need for you to worry or to rush into things yet, don't you see?"

She nodded, her eyes closing. The hint of tears appeared there. Sutherland felt unexpected relief as his daughter came into his arms. In the distance there was the chatter of unruly children who were not minding their manners at all. Neither father nor daughter paid them any heed.

Sutherland and Susannah stood there a bit longer, and he saw Ella appear, her hands folded before her as she watched them and waited. With the canoe, in a cove below the rapids, Jeremy, too, was ready, and so was Tamano. The time had come. The party would head downriver for a few days before crossing over at night and concealing their canoe. Then they would take a little-used hunting trail northward into the hilly forests.

Sutherland noticed children racing about, kicking an inflated sheep's bladder, and he said, "I think your class is dismissed."

Susannah smiled, wiped her eyes, and walked with her father to where Ella stood. Arm in arm, the three of them strolled toward Jeremy and Tamano, who were pushing the loaded canoe into the water near the Sutherland flatboat. The Chippewa was tall and athletic, though his hair was graying; he was about the same age as Sutherland. His quiet manner and reputation for great courage instilled confidence in those who knew a good man when they saw one. James was also there, self-conscious, but fine-looking, and he shook Sutherland's hand.

In response to James's sincere wish of godspeed, Sutherland

said, "I'll come to you at Pitt when I can, and we'll talk more about the company, and our future."

James nodded and glanced uneasily at Susannah, who was leaning at her father's side.

To Sutherland, James said, "I truly hope that all will be well, sir."

"And I."

Just then, a tall boy of fifteen appeared, walking through the group of friends who were there to say good-bye. Looking downcast and a bit sullen, the boy was lanky, but very strongly muscled, bearing a marked resemblance to Ella, although he was dark like Owen. Benjamin Sutherland wanted to go with his father on this expedition to Detroit, but he was needed here, with his mother and sister. He well knew it, and had not tried to argue. Benjamin's duty here would be every bit as dangerous as the attempt to get to Detroit. He simply was not happy with parting with his father again, and missing the adventure with him and Jeremy. As he moved toward his father, Benjamin was distracted by a large blue-jay that landed on his shoulder and opened its mouth to squawk, but made no sound. This was Punch, the boy's trained pet—a jay that had, through an injury, lost its voice.

Benjamin shook hands with his father, who clapped him on the shoulder. "Use your head," Sutherland said, smiling but serious. "Take no chances." Then, impulsively, Sutherland unbuckled his heavy claymore and gave it to the lad. Ella caught her breath in surprise. Benjamin was too stunned to accept the sword, and everyone else fell silent. Everyone but Sutherland, who laughed and said cheerfully there was no use for a sword in the woods.

"All these years I carried it for sentimental reasons—I could have better used a good Indian ax!" He looked around, seeing friends and family watching him closely, all of them wondering why he was doing this. He wanted them to smile bravely, as ever, and not take this gesture as an ill omen. He tossed his head and pushed the claymore into Benjamin's hands. "Keep it, son, and when I return, I'll show you how to wield it properly."

Benjamin embraced his father fiercely.

Then Sutherland turned to Ella. They had said their farewells already, in private. She took his hands, and they held each

other without a word. Quickly Sutherland cut the good-byes
short and waded into the water toward the waiting canoe. On
shore, handkerchiefs came out to wave, and to dry eyes. At
least twenty people were gathered now to bid them off, on
what was said to the rest of the settlement to be only a prolonged
scouting trip. Secrecy saved lives. Sutherland took up his paddle at the stern of the canoe, Tamano kneeling in the prow,
and Jeremy sitting in the center with the rifles and supplies.
They were traveling light, intending to live off the land.

Sutherland looked back as the shore drew away and the
choppy rush of the Ohio caught the canoe and drove it out into
the middle of the current. Quickly, the people on shore dwin-
dled, until soon they were very small, their white handkerchiefs
still fluttering. Never before had a farewell seemed quite like
this to Sutherland; he did not know just what it was he felt.

Then Tamano was loudly singing an Ottawa paddling song,
and Jeremy took up the words. The past seemed suddenly far
away, though it was actually no more than half a mile away
on the southern shore. The present was here, in this canoe,
three strong men heading into danger. At first, Sutherland did
not sing, but listened to the excitement in Tamano's hoarse
guttural voice, and in Jeremy's refined British-American voice.
They were both going for their wives and families. It would
be a welcome change in their lives. Those two were heading
straight toward their future, to make it their immediate present.
Sutherland was leaving his present behind, and the future was
only a vague impression, fraught with trouble, hardship, and
loneliness.

He struck deeply with his paddle and caught the vigor of
the Ottawa song—a song of travel, of sunrise, of wind, and
of the freedom of the northern rivers. It was as if they really
were going off on a carefree hunting trip, or going to trade
with distant villages, as so often they had when he was younger.

Just then, Tamano called out in Chippewa, which both whites
understood: "I have a nice trade tomahawk in my pack for you,
Donoway—" He used Sutherland's name as an adopted Ottawa.
"Needs nice decorations, but you can have it if you'll take care
not to chip it too much on the skull of Mark Davies!"

There were more good-byes to be said back at the Falls of the
Ohio, for James Morely was leaving that same day, sailing

northeast, against the river's current, back to Fort Pitt, where his business had made its new headquarters.

Just before the moment came for James's whaleboat to cast off, Ella Sutherland left Susannah and him alone on the deck of the flatboat. It was a busy time around the wharf, with a dozen hardbitten Virginia riflemen whose enlistments were up saying farewell to friends as they prepared to set off for home. They intended to reach their cabins before winter set in, and James's whaleboat would travel with their two canoes part of the way.

Susannah was worried about Indians lying in wait, but James was casual about it—not falsely brave, but confident that so many fighting men would be able to hold their own. Still, it would be dangerous, with Indian snipers all along the shore, and campsites frequently a target of ambush.

James said, "There're so many folks traveling downriver now that we'll likely always find people to camp with." He smiled and became thoughtful. "This country's filling up quickly, Susannah, and one day there'll be a mighty market right here!"

To Susannah, it seemed James was almost passionate about the growing commerce; it was as if he viewed the settlements as markets rather than as people's homes, and settlers braving Indians as buyers rather than as simply men and women. She did not want to think too much of what all that might mean, and as James looked at her, his large brown eyes caused her to flutter inside.

He said, "People like us have a future that will know no bounds, Susannah! In three years . . ." He meditated a moment, and Susannah thrilled, thinking he would say that in three years he would ask to wed her. ". . . in three years there'll be a hundred settlements up and down this river, and twenty thousand people, all of them hungry, eager for black powder, tools, cloth, and molasses, and—"

"In three years," Susannah said breathlessly, "I'll be almost eighteen, James!"

He put his head back and chuckled quietly before looking again at Susannah, his happiness and ambitions making the hurt of his wounds unimportant. He became sober and gentled his enthusiasm.

"Ah, yes, Susannah." He glanced about and saw they were alone where they stood on the flatboat. He took her small hands, and she thought his were very strong, for all that they were not muscled like a tough woodsman's, or gnarled with hard work and frontier living. James was a civilized man, but he knew the wilderness well, having been brought up at Fort Detroit, friend of French and Indian. As Susannah stood there with him, hoping he would kiss her, she saw all the good that was in him, all the wisdom and strength and raw genius that one day would set him apart from everyone else, even her father.

Suddenly, a question sprang into her mind, one she felt she had no right to ask, but which had nagged her for months. She could no longer hold it within.

"James..." She swallowed, blushing. "James, do you... do you have strong feeling for..."

He listened intently as she struggled to go on.

"...for Jeanette Defries?"

There, she had asked it—the most intimate question about her dear friend back in Albany, the daughter of a partner in the Frontier Company. James had been close to the Defries family not so long ago, and Susannah feared that he had been infatuated with Jeanette, who was undeniably beautiful, and older, too. She had not had the pluck to ask about it, until now.

James smiled and moved a little closer to her.

"Jeanette is wonderful—"

Susannah's heart sank.

"But I'm not in love with her, if that's what you mean."

Susannah's heart leaped in her joy and relief. Again she wanted him to kiss her, but loved him all the more that he did not, for she was too young. He said it was time to go, but he would come back down next spring "with a load of store-bought goods and all the credit the Sutherlands could ever want until they get back on their feet again."

"Ah, James," Susannah whispered, "would that we lived in another time and place...like Verona, where lovers like Romeo and Juliet need not be...be of age!"

He smiled at that and squeezed her hands. Voices called out that the flotilla was about to get under way.

James said, "You will be in my thoughts, and every day that passes will bring us closer together."

In her mind, Susannah heard the word "Forever!" Though it was not said, she was certain James felt it. He must! Her

young heart pounded with emotion and love—love she was
sure no older woman could ever experience more intensely.

She watched him, tall and handsome, embracing his portly
mother, Lettie Grey, and his big, broad-shouldered stepfather,
the former Redcoat Jeb Grey. As James bid good-bye to his
brother, Tom, and Tom's wife, Sally, Susannah observed his
every graceful movement, and how he kissed little Timothy,
his nephew, and said he should have brothers or sisters to play
with soon. Susannah nearly began to weep, but she held it in,
though she knew her mother, nearby, was well aware of her
unhappiness.

He came to Susannah last, kissing her hand, and speaking
softly words from their favorite Shakespeare—*Romeo and
Juliet*. It was the part where Romeo is about to pass Juliet's
garden wall:

> "Can I go forward when my heart is here?
> Turn back, dull earth, and find thy center out."

Susannah went limp momentarily, though in truth she really
was not quite sure just what those beautiful words meant. In
that moment, however, they were romantic beyond description.

Then James was gone, and Susannah stood waving, as the
white canvas of the whaleboat billowed against the far green
shore of the Ohio. Ella put an arm about her daughter and drew
her close.

Soon, Benjamin was beside them, saying he had to go on
a scout that afternoon, to where Indians had attacked an isolated
cabin. He would take the husky, Heera, he said, and would be
in company with half a dozen other men and boys whose turn
it was to serve as militia this month.

The day's routine returned quickly to the lonely settlement
of the Falls, where Susannah would hang on until better times.
Although the frontier these days made a woman like her mother
feel young, because she had to be strong and fearless and make
the most of every minute, it made Susannah feel older than
anyone could possibly think her to be. She plodded away to
her afternoon class of rowdies, determined to shake them up
and make them appreciate having their loved ones close at
hand. This afternoon she would teach these wild children from
the uncouth Virginia frontier what it meant to have correct

manners. . . . Then another thought came to her, a better one, one that was inspired! She dashed off, pigtails flying, toward the flatboat to fetch her Shakespeare book. She would read them *Romeo and Juliet*!

Surely, more than anything, such beauty would make them think twice about their lives, would make them realize that there was more to the world than their little wilderness cabins and tumbledown hovels, that there was an entire culture awaiting them if only they applied themselves, minded their manners, and showed respect to their teacher, who was a symbol of that cultured life.

If not, they would get a hickory switch across their bottoms, and they could think about that instead. Susannah was only fourteen, but she was a dedicated teacher.

The whaleboat that carried James was hardly out of sight of the Falls of the Ohio when he saw three great flatboats and two wallowing rafts coming downriver, their long keel oars each manned by two fellows, who tried to steer a course in the middle of the current.

James hallooed them as they passed, and the Virginia riflemen in the canoes fired raggedly into the air, copying the northern French and Indian custom of saluting with a simultaneous "fire of joy," as it was called. James thought of how different this southern border of the northwest territory was from the Detroit region and the lakes. Up north there were few people, mostly Indians, along with sophisticated merchants and wilderness-wise white and half-breed traders. In the north, much money was to be made in the peltry trade, it was true, but furs were increasingly monopolized these days by the powerful new association of free traders called the Northwest Company.

Here on the Ohio, a whole new trade was developing, the likes of which had not been seen in America since the first colonists stepped off the boats and were supplied exclusively by clever, rich merchants from back home. It might be the same here for decades. Here, in the Ohio Valley, was the beginning of a whole new people, a mixture of backwoods folk and eastern artisans, wilderness fighters and wealthy refugees from the Revolution. James's pulse quickened to think of all they would need—virtually everything, from sawn lumber to beans and glass—and of how he was in a perfect position to supply them from Fort Pitt. It was a whole new start to the world, a new age in America, and it lay squarely at his feet.

He struck up a conversation with a Philadelphia gentleman who had come downriver on some legal business—something to do with land patents and surveys—and was on his way home. He was an attorney named Noah Maxwell, and was well dressed, a peacock in silks and nankeen next to the frontier hawks in their calico and leather. Maxwell, too, had a great vision of the future of the Ohio Valley, and he saw the development extending deep into the northwest and Canada.

While James took a turn at the oar, Maxwell leaned back in his seat—he had paid well to be a passenger, not a rower—and smoked one of those newly fashionable tobaccos called cigars. The twist was long and thin, imported from Spain, and it made the lawyer look the part of a rake. Maxwell, like many modern young men, including James, wore no wig. He wore trousers similar to the leggins of frontiersmen, spurning the stockings and knee breeches that were common with older men and the more conservative. A thin man, tall and lanky, Maxwell was slightly stooped, and his eyes seemed to take in everything. His bicorne slouched on his head, and he held the cigar between his teeth as he spoke about the prosperous future of the northwest.

"Every blessed independent state wants it, or will claim it and use that claim to bargain for other things they want from the Continental Congress." His voice was smooth, refined, almost soft. "We'll take this country from King George and his ministers, and then we'll go to war against ourselves in a bloodier battle than ever we've seen!"

James knew well what Maxwell meant, and even as they talked, a fight broke out on a passing flatboat. From here they could see that one man was a woodsman from Virginia, wearing the usual white woolen hat, and the other was evidently a Pennsylvania farmer. As the flatboat drifted past, a general battle erupted on board, with men taking sides and being hurled into the water or beaten to a pulp. It was brutal, a typical example of the hatreds between men from the Pennsylvania and Virginia backcountry.

One of the men traveling in the canoes shouted, "Have at 'em, Virginia!" Before any of the other Virginia riflemen could join in the shout, however, their officer stood up and bellowed for them all to hold their tongues. James knew the man; he had fought at Saratoga, shoulder to shoulder with Pennsylvania rebels.

Maxwell laughed, sniggering that it was well the officer had cooled his Virginians, for in the other end of the whaleboat a few brawny Pennsylvanians were hot already, and would have gladly stirred things up if they thought they were being insulted. It would be a long trip back to Pitt if these two groups broke their temporary truce. And truce it was, because for fifteen years both Virginia and Pennsylvania had claimed Fort Pitt and the surroundings, just as South Carolina claimed all of Kentucky, and New York wanted part of the northwest, and even little Connecticut said her charter gave her the rights to vast acreage above the Ohio.

James said, "Need a strong hand out here when the time comes to rule it."

Maxwell eyed him a moment, then said, "Will it be you or Bradford Cullen?"

James did not take that lightly, or think it was funny, though Maxwell grinned, showing strong teeth, stained yellow. Cullen was the real power, and had the money and influence James wanted. Cullen had already offered James partnership in the northwest trade if the flatboat convoy to Clark were brought safely through from Pitt. Well, that had been done, and although Clark's bills had been paid with a promissory note—a draft on Virginia that Clark himself had written—there would eventually be a tremendous profit that even Bradford Cullen could be proud of. Moreover, the remarkable accomplishment of supplying George Rogers Clark, hero of America, darling of Congress, and spokesman for the settlers of the Ohio Valley, had brought James's reputation to a new height. He was known as a man who could make things happen, and when he said he could do something, no one would take him lightly.

James put aside the memory of the river ambush, and how Owen Sutherland had narrowly come to his rescue in a bitter fight against Davies's Indians. That had no relevance now. Still, his wounds yet ached, and he rubbed his shoulder as he recalled how Sutherland had berated him in front of everyone for allying himself with Cullen. Sutherland had even believed Cullen was the one behind the Indian ambush. James could not accept that idea.

James thought of the future, Sutherland of the past. Perhaps Bradford Cullen was the power today, but he was more than eighty years old, for all his toughness and iron will. Tomorrow, it would be James Morely in power. Even Owen Sutherland's star had passed its zenith, and was soon to set. It was strange to imagine that James would be selling the Sutherlands ordinary household goods, and they had to have credit to buy.

He shook his head as he thought of this. What a pity that the Frontier Company was failing after all these years, and just because Sutherland and the other misguided rebel members of the company were so blindly idealistic that they had spent their last penny to support the cause of the Revolution. James no longer wanted any part of the company his own father had helped establish. He was on his own now. Sutherland and the others had been foolish to give away all they had to rebels whose money was bad and whose credit was shaky at best. What would the company get back, even if the new states defeated Britain? Worthless continentals? What would a rebel victory mean?

Maxwell said it, as if he had read James's mind: "There'll be more blood out here soon enough, and not just between Indian and white, bless me!" He puffed on his cigar, held it in his teeth, and said, "Need a strong hand, indeed! And a young one!" He spat over the side, and said casually, "Owen Sutherland's not the man, though. And Bradford Cullen's too old and too hated by everyone he's squeezed and manipulated. His empire will crumble when he goes under . . . unless, that is, the young men at his elbow are the sort who can master that empire as well as he did, or better."

James knew that was true, but he said nothing, cocking his hat over his eyes and momentarily resting his arms on the oar and listening to Maxwell and the river.

Maxwell sighed, "Would that I could have a crack at lording over Cullen's wealth and empire! Might even be willing to marry that homely daughter of his . . . what's her name?"

"Linda." James observed him from under the corner of his hat. "You would take her?"

"That's right—Linda." He chuckled and winked at James. "You know her well, I'll warrant, and I'll warrant she's fluttered her cow eyes at you, like she has at every other likely bedmate who passes her long nose!"

James began rowing again and said that Linda was not after a bedmate; but he knew Noah Maxwell was partly right: homely Linda had flirted quite seriously with him. She was her father's darling and, in Cullen's eyes, came even before his empire. The man with the stomach to marry Linda Cullen would have the empire, too. Cullen had even intimated as much to James, and that could only mean that the old scoundrel would be glad to accept James as his successor. What a prospect! James could not help but smile to himself, for this was yet another proof of his ability. If the mighty Bradford Cullen would have him as an heir, as the successor who would assume control of the greatest trading company in all America, then James must have proved himself worthy beyond doubt. As he rowed, he imagined himself as the merchant prince of the future in America.

Yet it was strange, he thought, that Owen Sutherland did not seem to feel the same about him as Cullen obviously did. Perhaps that difference in judgment was an example of why they were such archenemies, Cullen and Sutherland, and why Sutherland clearly was losing the struggle.

chapter 5

AMAGHWAH AND GIRTY

Gwen Bently was at Valenya, that beautiful but empty house across the river from Fort Detroit. With Gwen and the baby were Annie Ross and her father, the merchant Cole Ross. Annie and Cole were out near the river, talking to a Frenchman who had been passing in his pony cart, while Gwen was standing in the common room, idly gazing out the window at the river, so wide and blue this quiet afternoon.

This was not Gwen's house, but she loved it after having lived here for three years as Jeremy's wife. It was here that Richard was born last autumn, and attending her had been Lela, Tamano's pretty, plump Ottawa squaw. Lela was the sister of Owen Sutherland's first wife, who had been killed during Pontiac's rebellion. Lela lived nearby, and kept watch over the house.

Gwen moved closer to the window and looked to the left, at the great, dark standing stones that loomed near the shoreline. She could just see the grave marker of Sutherland's first wife, in the center of the stones. The standing stones were sacred to the Indians, and that Owen Sutherland had been allowed by

the Ottawas to live here was testimony to how much they
revered him. Valenya must have been part of Sutherland, Gwen
thought. And now it was part of her, she part of it.

Standing in the sun-filled common room, with the grand-
father clock ticking peacefully away in the hall, Gwen wondered what Ella Sutherland must be like. She could almost
imagine her mother-in-law here. Ella had designed this house,
had furnished it, had breathed life into it, but had enjoyed it
for only a few years before being forced to flee, when loyalists
of the worst sort had threatened her as the wife of a rebel
fighting in the East.

Now Gwen was in a similar situation. Her own husband
was believed to have been a spy, an accusation passed in rumor
by liars who hated Jeremy—no doubt henchmen of the wounded
Davies.

As she looked across the straits, she saw canoes moving
back and forth, and a sailboat that seemed to be making for
the Valenya wharf. She wished Jeremy would be on board, as
often he used to be; she wished he would leap ashore and stride
toward the house, and she would be in his arms even before
he reached the front door.

Gwen sighed shakily. That was not to be. Cole and Annie
waved good-bye to the Frenchman, whose cart rattled off at
the usual breakneck speed of *habitant* drivers, and Gwen's
visions were interrupted. She turned to the room, sensing she
would soon have to say good-bye to this place.

The large, long common room had a wonderful kitchen,
with a brick oven and a fieldstone hearth, and even a stone
sink that drained outside into a puddle that served the ducks
and geese. Off to Gwen's left was the spinet that Ella Bently
had owned ever since she first came out here in 1763. In the
center of the common room was a magnificent trestle table that
Gwen had just finished oiling, and it shone in the sunlight.
The room spoke of wealth and good taste. Where were the
Sutherlands now? What was their life like? The floor was over-
laid with bright rag rugs, and, in Ella's fashion, a few small
Persian rugs lay on tables and sideboards.

Gwen sighed and moved to look at Richard, who was fast
asleep on the floor. At hand, still lying on the settee, was a
well-thumbed copy of *Robinson Crusoe* that Jeremy had been
reading before he departed with Hamilton's ill-fated Illinois

campaign. This was Jeremy's favorite book, read at least once a year. Gwen picked it up, realizing how seldom she had been here at Valenya in the tedious months since his departure. Day after day at the hospital. Patient after patient. It had been endless and sorrowful, yet often inspiring, because she had helped so many who otherwise would have died without her experienced hand. Old Doc Sennet likely would have lost half of those who were seriously wounded, and his surgical saws would have done in a good deal more. She wondered how the old fellow was doing, for it had been several weeks since Captain Lernoult had ordered the ill or injured regular troops to stay out of her hospital. Sennet must be busy with them at the fort's infirmary. Gwen had heard from Sennet that Davies was slowly recovering, although he was not yet on his feet, as she thought he should have been by now.

But that was not her affair. Plenty of civilians were still coming to the hospital, and a few times, under cover of darkness, soldiers had slipped in for Gwen's treatments. Even Sennet had come once to consult her when he could not diagnose a man's fever.

Gwen heard her uncle Cole and Annie step onto the wooden porch. It was time for them all to have the picnic they planned, and to fetch Lela and her two children for the fun. It was a delightful day, and Gwen needed the distraction.

She crossed the hallway and glanced into the back room, where she and Jeremy had set up their very first clinic three years ago. The room was still stocked with bottles, glasses, and jars on its many shelves, and there was an examination table, seldom used since the hospital had opened across the river more than two years past. Also on this side of the hallway was their bedroom, and upstairs were two other sleeping chambers. The house, Virginia style, had a door at the front center, and another at the back center, so that when both were opened there was a powerful, refreshing breeze that kept the place airy and feeling clean. It was very windy outside this afternoon, and so she played a trick on Cole and Annie by opening the back door just as they opened the front. The blast of air disheveled Cole's new wig and blew Annie's hat back out the door.

As they fussed, Gwen went laughing into the common room

to fetch Richard, leaving the others to chatter in mock annoyance at her impudence.

Then there came a shout from down near the wharf, and they saw that the sailboat Gwen had earlier thought was heading here had indeed tied up. Doc Sennet was creakily piling out while a young soldier held the boat fast against the wharf. Gwen went to meet Sennet, who came gawkily up the gravel walkway, waving and calling for her to hurry. He whipped off his hat, almost taking the grimy wig with it.

"Captain Lernoult wants—*begs* that you see him, Mistress Bently!" He puffed and wheezed, bent over, his face red from strain, and perhaps from embarrassment, for when Gwen asked what was wrong, he said, "It's Cap'n Davies, ma'am." He glanced uneasily at Annie and Cole, who listened closely. "Ah . . . well, it seems the fellow's taken a turn for the worse, and he's . . . well, it might be that . . . ah, mistress, don't you see, I can't do nothing for him, and Lernoult wants that you come and save him."

Gwen was angry, grim. She thought of the fight with murderous Amaghwah, Davies's confederate, and knew that a beast like him surely would try to hurt her or the baby again, if he had the chance. Perhaps Davies would condone, even prompt it. Gwen wanted no part of Davies, and was shaken to remember Mawak's prophetic warning that she might have the choice to save him or let him die.

"After all he's done!" She caught her breath, her hands trembling with anger. Then she thought of how it was Jeremy's blade that had nearly killed Davies, right or wrong. She thought of all the fighting men, white and red, rebel and loyalist, whose lives had been in her hands. And she thought of what Jeremy would want her to do. What was her duty? Was it not her duty to save lives?

Sennet's head was bowed, and he apologized, saying, "I understand, mistress, and it ain't right that you be asked to do this, and no mistake. But it seemed to me that if you was just to give me the least bit of advice . . . you know, just lean over my shoulder—" He grimaced and knitted his fingers over the hat, held in front of him. "It's just that I think he don't have to die, if only I could do better than I've done!"

When Gwen touched his thin shoulder, he looked up, watery

eyes searching. She said, "I see you still have your toothache."

He smiled wistfully and glanced at the others, saying, "Aw, it ain't so bad, though. I mean when a man's got a lot to do as I have nowadays, he don't have time to think about such things as toothaches." He shook his head. "I never knew so many soldiers had so many pains and complaints afore, and not a one of 'em credits me for my skills! Every last one wants you, ma'am, and they curse Lernoult as bad as they curse me, and no mistake! I think Lernoult will ask you to tend the troops again—if you be willing."

That did it. Gwen said, "I'll come immediately."

Had Sennet been more spry, his heels would have clicked together as he leaped for happiness. "All right, ma'am! Infirmary's all ready in the fort!" Annie was about to get the baby but Gwen said she would go over alone and see them all later, when she could.

"Richard's weaned now, so he'll be all right, Annie."

She was pale and felt blank as she went down toward the boat with Sennet. She could not get Mawak's warning out of her mind. Davies would lead the Indians if he lived. She tried to change her thoughts, but did not know what to expect over at Fort Detroit, or what it would take to save Davies, if it could be done at all. Still, there was a certain feeling of satisfaction and accomplishment as Sennet piped on about how he had seen to it that the infirmary had been washed and swept, and was cleaned every day. He had taken to their ideas of sanitation. Gwen and Jeremy would be proud of him, he burbled, saying, "And I ain't cut off more'n a little finger these past three weeks! And that one was just to keep in practice."

He winked at her, and she shoved her hand behind the old man's elbow. He almost strutted as they went. After all, Sennet wanted only the very best medical care for his fellow soldiers, nearly all of them being his friends, except for Davies. Never mind whether Davies lived or died. Mistress Bently was coming back for the sake of the men, and Doc Sennet was delighted.

Gwen saved Captain Mark Davies.

She worked three days straight over his infected, weakened body. She bled him, medicated him, cut him open, and sewed him up. She bathed him in cold water when he was hot, and bundled him warmly when he was chilled near to death. She stayed with him all that time, hardly sleeping, yet still finding the time to advise Sennet, and to tend to a long line of grateful young Redcoats. It seemed that every man of the hundred-strong garrison had an ailment, and when they met with Gwen, they spoke kindly to her. She began to realize that none of them believed Jeremy had been a spy. Nor did most of the people of the fort and settlement believe it. That made Gwen happier than she had been since her husband left.

Captain Lernoult apologized like a gentleman and said she needed no pass to come and go, but he warned her that there were those who had no love for rebel sympathizers, and so she should be discreet, mindful of voicing her opinions, and careful of being alone in the wrong places. She appreciated his warnings and arranged to tend to the soldiers regularly or whenever otherwise necessary. By now she was like a sister to them, although a few were surely lovesick whenever they saw her.

The first day Davies was able to eat again, Gwen looked in on him, the baby in her arms. She saw he would be fine and, without speaking to him, turned to leave.

"Wait..." he said, his voice hoarse, eyes glassy. He was pallid, but there was an inner strength and force that fairly burned and flared from him. "I know you are the one who kept me from dying—"

"No need to say anything—"

"There is, by damn!" He was sitting up, clearly in great pain, but he had declined opium, for he wanted control of his senses, as he had told Sennet. He had things to think about, plans to make. "I owe you my, my thanks—" He winced from the hurt. "Upon my honor, I thank you. I thank you most sincerely. I am...at your service." He was determined to be correct.

Gwen moved resolutely forward, the baby held at her side.

"Then, Captain, I will ask one thing of your service."

He nodded.

"Keep your Shawnee friends away from me. Keep them away from me and my baby. Promise me that, if you're honorable!"

Slowly, he sighed, and said, "I heard of what happened—" The pain in Davies's eyes seemed to be more than physical. "I never ordered anyone to...to harm your babe."

Gwen was fierce in her indignation. "You can order them

to keep away!" She turned to leave, but then swung around again. "If you were honorable, you would promise me that!"

Davies scowled, the corners of his mouth turning down involuntarily. "I would never order the killing of a white child!" He stared blankly at the bedsheets. He was weakened, his morale shattered by all he had endured.

She tried again. "Promise to keep Amaghwah away."

Davies suddenly contorted. "I cannot! He is not mine to command! Look at me! I'm a broken man! Can't you see that? You healed me, but I'm beaten within! I'm finished! All I can do is live! I'm not the man I was!" His face darkened, and he fell to the side, burying himself in the pillow, whimpering that he was ruined, his military career ended.

Gwen moved forward, actually feeling some sympathy for the wretch. "You will live; you can regain your full strength if you rebuild yourself."

He cocked his head and looked out of one eye. "Is that possible? Is it true?" He tried to sit up, but was so dizzy that he lay back, murmuring. "Is it true, then?"

"It is true." She felt dull, empty. "In three months, or maybe five, if you have the will, you'll be . . ." She did not want to say back in battle.

Unexpectedly, he glared out of that one eye. "Back on the warpath?"

To Gwen's dismay, he cackled and buried his face again, his legs moving slowly back and forth in excitement. Gwen shuddered and backed up, but before she could go, Davies looked at her once more through that one, piercing eye, so blue and cold.

"On the warpath! Maybe only half a man, but on the warpath!" He laughed, spittle running down his chin. "I'll give you your promise, Mistress Bently. My Shawnees will not *kill* your brat. That is my word . . . my word of honor!" He laughed again, that shrill, lost laugh of a man whose mind is hopelessly twisted, and whose heart has been corrupted by hatred.

Before Gwen pulled herself away, Davies became suddenly calm, as if overtaken by another compulsion that soothed his madness, and he sat up in such a way that Gwen wondered how he could bear the agony of his wounds.

Now he looked the part of Captain Mark Davies, British officer, gentleman, and coolly correct soldier of the king. He bowed his head, saying politely, "Good day, mistress."

Gwen knew he was utterly insane, but brilliantly insane, and well aware of his power, and the power of his rank as an officer. As Gwen ran out into the sunlight, she heard him cackle in that same high-pitched laugh that had haunted her whenever she had thought of him and of how he wanted to destroy Jeremy. She would not take this meekly. She would fight back, and strike first if she must.

As soon as she reached the hospital, Gwen hurried into her room and closed the door, feeling breathless and afraid, angry and determined at the same time. She laid Richard in his crib, then rested for a while on her cot. She steadied herself, exhaustion coming over her, and before long dozed off. Half asleep, she listened to the comfortable, familiar sounds of the hospital and the street outside.

Soon, Annie came in, pale and trembling. She closed the door behind her, then stood staring at Gwen. Sitting up, Gwen asked what was the matter.

"Simon Girty asked me to bring a message to you, cousin." Annie moved to the crib and then turned to look at Gwen, her eyes filling with tears. "He says you must leave Detroit... immediately. It's life or death!"

Gwen felt that sharply, although she had known it was coming. She closed her eyes, whispering, "Oh, dear God..." Then she sighed and shook her head as she stood up to take Annie in her arms. Annie was even more shaken by this than Gwen, who comforted her.

Gwen asked why Girty had not brought the message himself. Annie said he was apparently too ill at ease to say such a thing in Gwen's presence, especially after he had been involved in the fighting against Jeremy and the Sutherlands. Strange how Girty, a killer when he hated, was a boyish bumpkin with white women like Gwen or Annie.

"Why is he warning me?"

Annie shrugged. "I don't really know. Who can understand these woodsmen and their uncouth ways? Suddenly they're polite as gentlemen of the first rank, and next they're like wild animals."

Gwen knew there was more to Girty than just the woods rover who had been raised by Indians after his family was massacred. Also, she was sure there was some bond between him and Owen Sutherland, both of whom had fought in colonial campaigns against the Indians over the years. They had come through the worst of dangers together, and Girty had also been with Jeremy in a few tight spots. The man had his own warped code of honor, even though he had ties to the worst of rogues, like Amaghwah and Davies. He likely would not break those ties as long as he profited from them, and as long as they served his lust for fighting the rebels, whom he resented for having treated him badly.

Gwen had an idea, though it was a risky one. She pushed Annie back a moment and said, "Where is Girty?" Annie said he was camped outside the settlement, with some Indians of the "Poordevil" tribe.

Despite everything, Gwen could not keep back a smile. "Poordevil tribe?"

"That's what Girty told me they were named," Annie said between sobs.

Gwen giggled, her unrest and anxiety mingled with the sudden urge to laugh, but Annie was startled. "Annie, that's just a backwoods name for any Indians who are poorer than the poorest, not a name for some tribe!"

Annie paused to think about that, a tear still running down, but then she could not help but grin, and soon they were both laughing about laughing at such a frightening time. The laughing became funnier than the joke, and for the rest of that morning they could not stop giggling about nothing every time they looked at each other. After all, how was life to be borne if they could not laugh in spite of it all?

By afternoon, however, Gwen had decided to find out exactly who was threatening her, so she could do something about it.

She did much thinking as she worked at the hospital that afternoon. No matter what happened, she would eventually have to leave Detroit. She had to leave to be with Jeremy again, but she must go on her own terms, and in a way that would be safe for Richard. That meant waiting, planning. She had to protect herself until then, and the only way she knew was to make a point very strongly with those who were menacing her.

She did not know how much Simon Girty was involved in

this, but if anyone could tell her what was going on, and in which quarter the danger lay, he could. She borrowed a horse late that afternoon and set off for the little encampment of "poordevil" Indians, ten minutes' ride from the fort. She went alone, lest anyone claim it was too dangerous and try to stop her. Even Cape was left behind, for he might attack and botch her plans.

The hut where Girty was said to be holed up was on the weed-grown field of a drunken half-breed *habitant*, a worthless man who let poor Indians camp on his land in return for an occasional share in their hunting or for a pelt now and again. The camp's cooking fire was on a sandy bank near the river, and around it were three ragged lean-tos that a good wind would have leveled. There was also a Plains-type teepee that had seen better days. Its sides had once been painted with colorful images of the buffalo hunt, but the paint had faded, the hides had tattered and rotted, and the door flap hung limply, in sad need of repair.

Gwen rode into this smelly, littered camp and dismounted as though she were Captain Lernoult himself. She tied the reins to a tree as a toothless, ageless squaw greeted her insolently. A gaggle of filthy children collected to stare at her as if they had never seen a civilized white woman before, even though the fort was close by. The stench of urine and rotting meat drifted with the campfire smoke, and a flyblown, peltless beaver carcass lay near a lean-to. Gwen ignored it all and asked the Indian woman where Simon Girty could be found.

The woman's eyes slitted and she gazed at the old teepee. At that moment there came loud laughter from inside the teepee, and an empty rum bottle flew out, followed by a half-naked Indian girl, who cursed and spat and kicked at the teepee as if she would knock it down.

The laughter became anger, and out of the door barged Girty himself, to give the woman a stinging smack on the rump that sent her sprawling, much to his delight. Then they both saw Gwen standing there, dressed in an expensive riding habit, her head high, a clean and radiant beauty amid the squalor.

Girty swayed, collecting himself, as if he were wondering whether the drink had fuddled his eyes, or was the wife of Dr. Bently actually standing before him?

"I must have a word with you, Mr. Girty." Gwen's heart was pounding, but less with fear than with raw determination to get to the bottom of things.

Girty tugged at his pants, wiped his scraggly black beard with slender hands that he then dried on his shirt. He was a small creature, but powerfully framed, a bit bowlegged, and hunched over like an aging Indian. His stringy hair hung down, and from under it his eyes gleamed as sharp as a bird of prey's, even through the liquor.

With a mumbled greeting, he gestured for Gwen to come into the teepee. She shook her head, saying she preferred to sit by the river. She wanted her back to the water, guarded from that side, so she could see everything else.

Girty grunted, his face red from liquor and self-consciousness. By now, the young Indian woman had moved away to another lean-to, where she sat combing her hair, gazing with jealous curiosity at Gwen.

When Girty and Gwen were settled near the river—she on a stool he brought, and he crosslegged on the ground—she asked him bluntly: "Who wants to kill me, Mr. Girty?"

He was troubled, his eyes darting, unable or unwilling to look into her own. Unwavering, she repeated the question.

Girty cleared his throat and said hoarsely, "Ma'am, it ain't right that you should be here—"

"If you have any honor, Mr. Girty, you'll tell me the truth! Won't you at least give me a fair chance to defend my baby?"

Girty squirmed and looked at the river, then back at Gwen. He was growing sober, and his gaze almost met hers. "Ma'am, you shouldn't oughta be out here on your own. It ain't safe."

"I trust you, Mr. Girty." She said this simply, and knew he was touched by her words.

He raised a grimy hand. "And so you kin! And so you kin do jest that, ma'am! I sent the warning by the other mistress, and you kin trust this hoss, that's a fact!" He glanced about uneasily, saying, "But I ain't no Shawnee chief! I ain't got the say-so over them what . . . what don't mean right by you."

"Who does have the say-so?"

It was as if she had struck him, for he winced and looked at her with eyes half-closed.

She demanded, "Captain Davies?"

He sucked in his jowls, biting his lower lip. For a fearless frontiersman, Simon Girty was rattled. Gwen knew his kind well enough by now. Man to man, they were brutally direct, hard, and fearless. When a woman of substance confronted them, however, their upbringing and inborn disposition to show the utmost respect and deference came to the fore. Simon Girty, she knew, was not a man to want any part of an attack on her.

"Ma'am..." He shrugged his shoulders and bounced his knees up and down as he thought what to say. "Ma'am...I jest wanted to tell you that you best clear out of Detroit." He looked around, his neck seemingly stiff, his legs uncomfortable. "I can't say no more'n—" He stopped, his eyes becoming wide.

He was looking at a track across the Frenchman's cornfield, and Gwen followed his gaze. She had a sudden flash of terror. Indians were approaching single file, apparently coming back from the hunt, and at their head was Amaghwah. The camp children were racing toward him, obviously to tell that the white medicine woman was in camp.

Girty was on his feet, standing like a defiant warrior, no longer a backcountry drunk. A scalping knife hung at his waist, but the Indians were armed with guns.

He rasped, "You got to go, quick!" He beckoned for her to get away into the rushes near the river. "I'll bring back your mount."

Gwen shook him off. She would not run.

"Git!" Girty snarled through his teeth. "You know what's coming! You ain't—"

"Let them come!"

Already the Shawnees—three of them—were running toward the camp, Amaghwah in the lead, his savage face painted red and white, tomahawk in one hand. His ridge of hair had been stiffened and preened, two new eagle feathers adorning the scalplock. He looked ready for a fight.

Girty whistled. "Lordy, mistress, but you're something!"

He caught his breath and told Gwen to move a bit to one side while he moved to the other, to give Amaghwah "more to think twicet about."

Gwen was amazed that she was no longer afraid, now that the danger faced her. She knew what was about to happen, but

was ready to meet it squarely. For an instant she thought about
Richard, and about Jeremy and how much she loved them both.
Then she tensed.

Amaghwah was hurrying forward, a terrible grin on his face.
The old squaw stepped into his path, fearfully shouting for him
not to do anything, and he pushed her aside. The other two
Indians, both quite young, apparently were not so sure about
what was happening. They slowed. Murdering so important a
white woman at a place where news would spread quickly
would mean they would be hunted down as outcasts.

Gwen knew Amaghwah was another matter. Mark Davies
was his ally, and even if it meant he must flee into Indian
territory, he would have rewards from the captain that would
make him a very rich Shawnee. Furthermore, he hated Jeremy
Bently, and was surely still furious for having been bested when
he had tried to kidnap the baby.

Amaghwah came straight at her. Girty called his name in
warning, and the Indian slowed, surprised that Girty had his
scalping knife out.

The Shawnee stopped five yards away, the grin leaving his
ugly face. Gwen could see there was a longing in him that
cried out for satisfaction. He tossed his rifle to a companion,
his eyes on Gwen.

Girty warned him off again, but Amaghwah spoke harshly
to his friends, who overcame their uneasiness and moved
toward the scout. Girty eyed the younger Shawnees and
Amaghwah, who was about to go for Gwen.

"No!" Girty yelled, and went to block Amaghwah. The
Shawnee shifted away, and beckoned for his men to grab Girty.
They approached, and Girty pointed the knife at them. They
hesitated.

Gwen stood unmoving.

"I know you understand English, Shawnee dog!" Her words
rang out, and Amaghwah darkened at this insolence.

Girty wailed and shook his head, wishing she would shut
up and just get away. It was too late now, though.

Gwen said, "You would make war on us, and so I have
come to warn you that it will mean your death."

The other Indians were startled, but Amaghwah just grinned
like a hungry wolf. He laughed at Girty and then stared men-
acingly at Gwen.

"Will you rub this Injun out?" he said with a hiss and a laugh, then took a step forward.

Girty moved with his knife, but the two other Indians were stronger and quicker, and they cut him off, wrestling him, cursing, to the ground as Amaghwah watched with approval. Girty screamed for Gwen to run, and Amaghwah turned to face her again, his eyes glittering. He toyed with the tomahawk at his belt. Looking at Gwen's long, fair hair, he murmured, "Fine! Fine scalp!"

He went at her.

Out from behind her riding cloak came a pair of dueling pistols, the very best kind, certain not to misfire, and they were aimed at Amaghwah's shocked face. He staggered to see death just inches away. From under his captors, Girty hooted softly with admiration.

"You've chosen the wrong woman," Gwen said, her heart beating with excitement, breath coming short and quick, but without the slightest fear. Both hands were raised, the pistols cocked. For a moment she thought to end it right there and simply kill him on the spot.

Amaghwah scowled, fear plain in his face. He half turned, as if to speak to the others.

"Watch it!" Girty yelled, and sure enough, Amaghwah let the tomahawk fly, quick as lightning.

But Gwen was ready for it. As if she were an experienced fighter, she moved her head slightly to let it whisk past. Amaghwah was as good as dead. Frozen in place, he leaned forward, eyes on the pistols.

Gwen knew she must not show weakness. If she did not fire, he would come back. He would try again. Now she had to—

Amaghwah dropped to all fours and scrambled forward. Gwen leaped aside and fired once, the bullet striking Amaghwah in the left shoulder, driving him hard to the ground, and he shrieked with agony and terror. Gwen saved the second bullet, watching Amaghwah writhe and crawl away. She could have killed him easily. His two companions were confused, not ready to attack. Girty suddenly kicked one between the legs and gave the other an elbow in the face. They went down, and the scout grabbed for their tomahawks.

"God-rotting fools!" he yelled. "You had it all right living

out here! Now you'll have to clear out for good! I'm done with
you all! God-rotting varmints!"

He cursed and threatened with the axes, and they moved
away, dragging the wounded Amaghwah into a lean-to, where
he lay helpless, near to fainting. Gwen knew, however, that it
was not a death wound, if the squaws took decent care of it.

Girty stood before her, his wrinkled, bearded face beaming,
and he shook his head, chuckling. "Mighty fine brace of pistols,
ma'am." Then he whispered, "You gonna finish him?"

Gwen suddenly shook, sweat breaking out and pouring down
her face, soaking her clothes. Was she going to finish off
Amaghwah? She shuddered violently, and looked at the unfired
pistol in her hand. She closed her eyes, smelling the closeness
of Simon Girty, who could easily have killed her, if he was
one who wanted to curry the favor of mad Captain Davies.
She opened her eyes as he whispered:

"I think it's best for you if you go and finish him off now.
I'll see them two bucks won't interfere, and nobody'll be the
sorrier about the basta— I mean . . . I mean it's a sign to them
that you're brave enough to kill, but if you don't . . ."

Gwen had control now, but powerful emotion had drawn
tears. She wiped them away and said firmly, "Let Amaghwah
think what he wants of my courage, but I'll warrant he'll remember this day."

She turned and walked away, pistols dangling loosely. She
mounted up and urged her horse back to the fort, knowing that
word of what she had done would spread quickly enough, and
for certain it would make any other agents of Mark Davies
think twice.

Behind her, Simon Girty laughed to himself as he bundled up
his gear. He had best find some friendlier accommodations,
where he did not have to worry about somebody slitting his
throat at night. It was a pity to leave here, for that little Indian
wench had been a good time, for all that she had a nasty temper.

He was glad enough to have a reason to split with
Amaghwah, although Davies had ordered them to stay together
and await his recovery. Girty despised the aging Shawnee, and
Davies could not rightly now object to his leaving the man for
good. After what had happened, the army or the fort's con-
stables would come hunting Amaghwah to arrest him for at-

tacking a white woman. The Shawnee had best put some distance between himself and the authorities. It might be that Gwen Bently would not file any formal complaint, but Simon Girty would head into the fort that very afternoon and tell all that had happened, making sure Lernoult heard. It was an easy way to be rid of Amaghwah without having to kill him.

It was bad enough to have to put up with the arrogant Davies, that English bastard! But then Davies was powerful, influential, and knew how to make war on the damned rebels. In time, Davies would be an important man in British territory, and could do a lot for old comrades like Girty. Davies had a future, if he did not keep tangling unsuccessfully with the Sutherlands and Bentlys. Amaghwah was finished, though, for even Mark Davies could not justify to the army keeping that dog in its pay as a scout.

Girty chuckled, thinking of how slickly Gwen had done her work. He laughed aloud at the Shawnees as he went to the teepee to fetch his gear and his last bottle. The two young braves scowled at him, but the fight was out of them. Amaghwah was grunting in pain, a miserable sight, lying in the shadow of the lean-to.

"Best keep away from that straight-shooting lady, old hoss!" Girty repeated it in Shawnee and cackled.

Amaghwah glared at him, sweat and dirt streaking his face, his chest heaving quickly for air. His clothes were bloody, and there was a nasty wound on his left shoulder. Girty walked away, looked back once, and knew that Amaghwah was certainly not finished. Amaghwah was a man who took revenge once he swore it, and Gwen Bently was not free of him yet.

Girty clucked and muttered, "She shoulda done for him. I told her so!"

chapter **6**

LACOSTE'S BILLIARDS

Seldom had Owen Sutherland traveled more slowly through enemy territory than he did on this journey with Jeremy and Tamano toward Detroit.

For five weeks they had posed as traders from Saint Louis, a Spanish-held town populated with French and half-breeds. Sutherland had let his beard grow, as had Jeremy, and they looked as scruffy as any shiftless wandering traders drifting from one Indian village to another, trying to make a small profit. The Indians paid little attention to them, for it was near the end of the good hunting season, and enough game had to be brought in before winter. The weather had turned chilly, and as usual, every able-bodied Indian not far away on the warpath was after game. Those Sutherland met were scarcely interested in traders who did not have firewater to exchange.

Sutherland's party had bought horses from a village of Miamis on the Illinois River, and then had headed for the Wabash, following little-used trails that were so overgrown that the travelers had to lead the animals much of the time. All three of them were acquainted with many an Indian in this country, so they steered clear of villages, making cold camps at night, cooking and resting in the late afternoon, when their smoke would not be seen. After eating, they moved on a few more miles before dark, to sleep concealed, off the trail.

It was a hard march, and Jeremy's wounds were still hurting him. The trail was always fraught with the danger of chance discovery by Indians or French *habitants* who would recognize them. They knew the country well, however, and so were successful in covering many scores of miles without a serious mishap. Things would become more dangerous near populous Detroit, they knew. At least there would be friends there, and Tamano's own family, to shelter them. By now they were weary to the marrow, and of late had eaten poorly, because Indian hunting parties had scattered all the game. They were near the source of the Wabash when, at the end of a long day, they decided to look in on a half-breed trader, a distant relation of Tamano's wife, who had a tavern. Pierre Lacoste was a grumpy, surly fellow, but he bore no love for the British, and had done plenty of business with Sutherland over the years. He was said to have offered supplies to Clark whenever the Virginian led an army this far north.

They approached Lacoste's cottage carefully, stopping in a thicket of trees that were changing from pale green to yellow. They observed the cottage, with its steep, cedar-shingled roof, and a rickety barn nearby. The place seemed abandoned, not even a chicken scratching in the yard. Lacoste was gone at a time when he should have been busy getting ready for winter. It came to Sutherland then that, ever since Clark's success in the Illinois, the British had tightened their security in this region, often ordering suspected rebel sympathizers away from their homes. This, no doubt, had happened here.

After watching the deserted place for half an hour, Jeremy slipped up on the house to make sure there was no one at home. After he signaled all was clear, Owen and Tamano picketed the horses, concealed, in the trees and went to the house. It had been broken open and plundered. They would have savored some of Lacoste's homemade spruce beer just then, or some Detroit wine. But there was nothing to be had, and the inside of the house was a mess—furniture broken, glass crunching underfoot, and an empty beer keg cracked open behind the bar. Indians probably had looted the place of everything valuable, but there was firewood near the hearth, and it would be fine to get warm and sleep under a roof.

Jeremy came out of the back room and joined Sutherland and Tamano, who were in the tavern room, opening and closing closet doors, searching for some change to their monotonous diet of pemmican and hardtack.

Despite his wounds, Jeremy said cheerfully, "At least there's some diversion for our souls, Pa." He nodded toward the room he had just left, where a long billiard table, balls, and sticks were ready at hand.

Sutherland laughed, saying, "Almost as good as eating!" He rubbed his hands together and entered the room, looking eagerly at the green-covered table. "Haven't played a decent game since I left Detroit." He glanced at Jeremy. "You still remember how?"

Jeremy went to the table, picked up a cue stick—it was the old-fashioned style, with a sort of shovel at the end for pushing the ball—and deftly caromed the white ball off the red, and sank it in a side net pocket. Sutherland laughed, and Tamano settled down in a chair near the window to watch the trail that opened on the farmyard. It was dusk, and no travelers in their right minds would be on the trail at this late hour, but Tamano was vigilant just the same. They would light a fire after full dark, and with closed shutters it would not be seen.

Sutherland picked up a cue stick, and the game began. The failing light of dusk was just enough to make playing possible; the click of balls and their thud against the cushion was a homey sound to Sutherland. He and Jeremy forgot their hunger and satisfied another appetite, for both were experts at billiards and had been avid competitors in the old days.

The game was as skillful and pleasurable as ever, and the two of them laughed and joked as if the tavern were full, beer mugs at hand, and a few pelts or shillings wagered on the result. All that was wagered, however, was who would wash their dishes for the rest of the journey. Sutherland was apparently about to lose when Tamano hissed, and they sprang to the window. There, at the end of the clearing, were three mounted Redcoats, a patrol no doubt heading for a nearby Miami village. They were making for the house, apparently to bed down for the night, and there was no way Sutherland's group could get out in time.

The soldiers approached casually, tired from their journey. They, too, spoke about the billiard table inside, and were betting who would play best after they had some dinner. They dismounted, and a private tiredly led the horses toward the barn, to leave them for the night. The sergeant was Edward Bailey, the friend of Gwen's, and the other two men had been in the hospital with him after the bout of drinking trade liquor. Bailey and the corporal came unsuspectingly into the house, throwing open the door, as if there was no war on, no threat of danger, and this was simply another everyday stop at a cozy wayside tavern for dinner and a straw bed.

"Damn my eyes, but it's getting cold, Harry!" said the ruddy-faced Bailey, who rubbed his thick hands and drew his white blanket coat close about him as the wind gusted behind. He closed the door and sat down before the empty stone fireplace. "Be quick about getting a blaze up, and warm yer sergeant's old bones like a good lad!"

Harry Scruggs was the corporal, half the age of the sergeant and, like his companions, of the King's Eighth Foot. Being inexperienced wilderness fighters, these men from the garrisons at Montreal and New York were easy prey as they listlessly concerned themselves with warmth and food instead of being cautious. The sergeant untied a bundle of food while Harry fumbled with a tinderbox at the pile of kindling in the hearth.

In came the private, letting in a blast of autumn wind that blew out the tinder Harry had just started. That caused some complaints and arguing for a while, until the blaze finally roared up the chimney and threw heat into the room. Outside, stars were coming out, the last glow of the sun hanging on the tops of trees.

"Whatever happened to the old frog-eater who lived here?" Corporal Scruggs asked the sergeant, who was vigorously blowing his red nose. "Is it true he died upstairs in his bed— shot himself, like, when the army told him he had to leave?"

Sergeant Bailey glanced at the ladder that led to the trapdoor of the sleeping loft, then shrugged. Alf Higgins, the private— a skinny, pockmarked fellow with close-cropped hair—piped up as he hung his wig on the back of a broken, three-legged chair. "That's what I heard. Sorry devil was like to cry hisself to death in bed when he heard he was supposed to leave. Imagine he was afraid he'd never get back home after we run him out."

"Bah!" the sergeant grumbled. "Truth was he knew we'd confiscate the bloody lot of all he had, 'cause he was a collaborator with the damned rebels. Poor sod, just the same." He shook his head and brought out a flask of liquor, drinking and passing it around. He glanced at the ladder again. "Died up there, eh?" He was uneasy. "I mind when I came here last year—we got a good feed, and he had a couple of clean squaws who were willing."

The corporal wiped his mouth with the back of a hand and grinned. "I mind that. I was here, too. Same time last year as now. . . . What's the day, today?"

The private answered that it was October 31. Then they paused a moment and looked at one another until the corporal said softly what they all were thinking: "It's All Hallow's Eve. Haunting time."

There was silence, except for the crackle of the fire and the sound of wind rattling the shutters. All Hallow's Eve meant witchcraft and ghosts to superstitious Englishmen—and these were among the most superstitious, although the sergeant bluffed, breaking the silence with a scoff and a swig of whiskey.

"Who gives a damn about what eve it is?"

The private said with a forced grin, "Hell of a night to spend in a house where a frog-eater just deaded himself, ain't it?"

The sergeant grumbled, and the corporal moved a little closer to the fire. The sergeant said someone had to go fetch water. There was no response. Slapping his knee, he said loudly to the private, "Get water, then! Hop to it, Alfie! The well's out behind. Necessary house is there, too, so you can do your business at the same time and won't have to go out later on with your spooks and All Hallow's Eve haunters. Go on!"

Alfie was reluctant to move until the corporal said he might as well use the necessary house at the same time and would keep the other company. When a shutter slammed, they both jumped, one grasping the other's sleeve.

They laughed nervously, and the sergeant cleared his throat, saying to the corporal, "Well, Harry, you don't just need to go out as yet, do you?" He thought for a moment, then said, "Fire wants building up, and Alfie'll be back directly. Besides, I'll be using the necessary house later myself, and we can go along together if you're still afraid."

He cleared his throat and warmed his hands, stealing a sideways glance at the others. Harry said he might just as well go now, but, "If you want some company later, Sergeant Bailey, I'll accompany you round back."

Sergeant Bailey scowled and waved a meaty hand at that, saying "Aw, go on, then! I'll stay alone! I ain't afeared of ghosties, like you two pups! Go on, afore you drop your loads on the floor! I don't want no nervous skitters stinking up this place if I'm to sleep here tonight." He laughed to himself, returning his attention to the fire.

Before the men went out, the private said, "Maybe we could keep moving tonight, Sarge. I mean the village ain't so far, and this place gives me the creeps."

The shutter banged again, and there was a strange sound in the loft, as if someone was moving up there. They listened, eyes wide. Then the sound stopped, and the sergeant seemed to be considering whether he might as well accompany his men outside, rather than sit here alone. But he let them go without saying anything more, and sat rocking in a creaky chair, the firelight playing on his lined face.

When a shutter groaned and the noise above began again— it sounded just like feet shuffling—he stopped rocking, to listen. Then it was quiet, except for the many unexplained sounds of an empty house, and the moaning of the wind.

He picked up a long stick and prodded the fire, muttering, "All Hallow's Eve, by gad! Hell of a time to wind up here—"

He sat up. His ears might have grown longer, the way he was listening. Billiard balls were clicking in the other room. Or were they? He sat still. The sound had stopped. Had it been there at all? He was on the edge of his chair, as if about to get up and check the billiard room. The stick was firmly in his fist. Silence. After a moment, he started rocking again, floor and chair creaking in unison.

Click. It was the sound of a cue striking a ball—then a ball thudding around the cushions. The sergeant got to his feet. He was no coward, and had been through plenty of battles. Ghosts were something else, however. He called out the names of his companions. Were they trying to play him for a fool?

"Harry? Alfie? You there?"

No reply, save for the clack of a carom, and the sound of a ball being sunk in a pocket.

"Damn my eyes!" he hissed, and went to the front door, opening it to call for the men. He did not call too loudly, lest they think him afraid. The wind answered, no one else. "Damn my eyes!" he muttered, coming back to stare at the darkened doorway of the billiard room. Click. Thud, thud.

"Harry? Alfie?"

Click, thud, thud, thud, thud, thud. That last ball was hit hard. The sergeant poked the stick into the fire and got a blaze going for a torch. He plucked up his courage and went slowly into the billiard room, his light flaring over the green tabletop. No one was there, but a ball was in the pocket, and a cue stick lay on the table. The splash of torchlight flickered on the rough plastered walls, and he raised the stick to penetrate the blackness, trying to see into corners that were difficult to illuminate without going right into them.

He should have known there would be no sight of anyone. He felt cold, and his skin crawled. He turned back into the welcome light of the tavern room and sat down heavily, sighing and muttering about All Hallow's Eve, and wondering aloud where the others were off to.

"I want some tea!" he said to no one in particular, scratching his itches and looking about, the flaming stick still in his hand. Then he reached swiftly down into his pack and pulled out his Bible, whispering, "They say if the Good Book's opened in a haunted room . . . and a candle's lit, too, it's protection against 'em."

He carefully laid the book out near the fire and drew the stub of a candle from his pack. He lit the candle with the torch and set it carefully beside the Bible.

"There, done!" He seemed to feel better at that.

Click. Thud. Slowly. Thud.

He stiffened, eyes narrowing.

Upstairs came that shuffling, back and forth.

"Harry?"

What was that sound? Was someone in the house moaning in pain, or in fear, or were they laughing? Or was it just the wind?

"Alfie!"

There came a horrible shriek of terror and a loud crash from outside, and the sergeant leaped from his chair, dropping the fiery brand so that it struck his feet and made him jump. Quickly he kicked the torch into the fire, accidentally knocking over the candle. The door flew open, and with a shout he sprang around as it crashed against the wall. In rushed Harry and Alfie—both with their breeches down, and they were pale with fright.

"Sarge!"

"What—"

"Spooks!" Alfie wailed, tripping over his breeches, bumping into Harry, who was shaking, too frightened to pull up his pants.

Alfie cried, "Haunts! They knocked over the damned outhouse, and us with it! Spooks! Goblins, demons they were! Saw 'em with my own eyes! Hairy and with fangs! Near got me, they did!"

Harry was furiously nodding, quivering almost out of control.

Click.

"What was that?" Alfie gasped.

The sergeant tried to maintain composure. "They're playing billiards."

"Oh, blimey," whispered Alfie. "Harry, pull up yer drawers, quick!"

When the ghost began to laugh in a sound of yowling derision, the soldiers had endured enough. In a twinkling, Alfie yanked up Harry's pants, the sergeant threw their gear into a pile that he picked up all at once, and they dashed out the door, vanishing into the darkness.

The screech rose from the house and followed them across the yard, rushed them toward their nervous horses, and sent them galloping off into the night. They fled back down the trail the way they had come, as far from that spook house as they could get without losing their way.

Into the tavern room came Tamano, the firelight playing on his handsome, weathered face. At the open outside door, he cupped his hands to his mouth, leaned back, hurled another blood-chilling whoop into the darkness, and ended with laughter that doubled him up, sounding very unghostly.

"Close the door, Tamano!" Sutherland called from the billiard room, where the clicking had begun again. "We'll finish our game and then sit down with you at that cozy fire."

Tamano patted his stomach and fetched a bag of pemmican to be roasted over the flames. Now and again he chuckled to think about those soldiers, all of whom he knew fairly well from Detroit. As soon as they had come in sight, Jeremy had said they were good men, decent, and no one wanted to hurt them. Tamano laughed, shaking his head as he unpacked the food.

There came a shuffling upstairs again, and at first he hardly noticed it, but Sutherland stepped from the billiard room, cue in hand, gazing up at the beamed ceiling. Tamano looked around as he heard the sound, too. Was someone up there? Jeremy played the balls, then called for Sutherland to take his turn. The shuffling continued. Sutherland suggested Tamano go up the ladder and see what was about. Tamano declined and kept slicing meat, now and again glancing up at the creaking floorboards.

Sutherland and Jeremy exchanged looks until Jeremy shook off his uneasiness and scrambled up the ladder, throwing open the trapdoor and calling for a torch so he could inspect the loft. The noises stopped. Jeremy thrust the torch into the darkness.

"Empty!" he declared, coming down and letting the trapdoor slam overhead. He tossed the torch into the fire and said it was Sutherland's turn to play.

The sound came again.

"Just the wind, Pa."

Sutherland turned to go into the billiard room. The shuffling was followed by the distinct sound of laughter, soft and distant. It came from the loft. Sutherland, Jeremy, and Tamano swallowed simultaneously, a sound heard clearly in the quiet room.

Jeremy cleared his throat. "You want to play any more tonight, Pa?"

The shuffling went on.

Sutherland also cleared his throat, and with a casual shrug shook his head and said, "It's enough for another couple of years, eh?"

The shuffling continued. The eerie voice—or was it the wind?—drifted down.

Tamano cleared his throat. In Chippewa, he said, "Pemmican's cooked enough. Eat it quick, and let's get on the trail to make a cold camp. Safer."

"Right," Jeremy replied, listening to the laughing wind. "Let's just go. I can eat on horseback."

Sutherland fetched his things from the other room, where they had been concealed in a small closet built for people to hide in during an Indian attack. The shuffling moved right across the ceiling. Sutherland looked briefly up at the loft floor and said, "Anyway, I'm not used to having a roof overhead these days."

Jeremy gathered his gear, saying, "Just would make us soft."

They hastily saw to it that the fire was broken down, and a metal grate placed in front of it as a screen, then they got out of there. It was a relief to be back in the cool, windy night. Winter was coming on fast, and it might have been good to get a night's sleep indoors, but on All Hallow's Eve none of them wanted to be in a strange house with an unhappy past.

They found the horses, and as they began to ride off, Sutherland looked back to see the glow from the dying fire light the cottage windows. It would be warm in there tonight, for the first time in a long while. Old Lacoste would like that, and Sutherland did not begrudge him this small pleasure, even though the half-breed had always been a surly rascal. When he was alive, Lacoste was forever enjoying a prank that caused someone discomfort. He had not changed at all.

Owen had been gone more than five weeks, and Ella missed him so, as ever she did when he went off like this. She well knew something was not right with him, and he had given Benjamin his claymore. . . . She tried not to think about that, or what it might mean.

There was so much else to think about, with winter closing in, and little enough to eat. Game was scarce, and the hunters had to rove farther and farther afield to bring home deer or turkeys. It was dangerous to go too far, for Indian hunters had the same problems, and would hunt the same land. New settlers were still taking up dwelling places even this late in the season, and all they could depend upon for food was what little they had rafted down the Ohio and what they could hunt in the woods around the Falls and the other settlements to the southeast, on the Licking and South Licking rivers.

When a man was not hunting, he was often sent on a scout, or better termed a patrol, for few of the settlers at the Falls were scouts, or what were commonly known as Indian spies, or woods rangers. Only a handful were skilled enough to prowl the forests alone, searching for Indian sign, noting the presence of war parties, and sometimes surprising and killing unsuspecting Indian hunters. Small, brutal engagements were the foundation of the Indian war, and no quarter was asked or given.

Though he was only fifteen, Benjamin was one of the best rangers in Kentucky and was delegated to watch the western trails, which might be used by a stray party of Chickasaws or Creeks coming up to Kentucky for hunting and whatever pillaging they could easily accomplish. But a man could not spy out Indians and hunt at the same time, could not dash off and warn isolated settlers to abandon their cabins until danger was past and still bring home meat. Ella's people needed game.

Tom Morely, James's brother, was a fair hunter, and went out when Benjamin was too frequently called up by George Rogers Clark to go on a scout. But Tom and other hunters were unable to range very far without the protection of several experienced wilderness fighters to guard them and scout the woods where they were hunting and dressing meat. There simply were not enough real woodsmen at hand.

In their flatboat home, Ella, Susannah, Benjamin, and Tom and Sally Morely with their young son were warm and well protected, but they had to be careful with their food, and there were no luxuries to speak of—even a bar of rough, homemade lye soap was a luxury if it could be had from a recent migrant with some to trade. This was far from the prosperous life Ella had known at Valenya, when the Frontier Company had thrived, and goods from half the civilized world came to Detroit in exchange for peltry. Because Detroit was easily accessible by water, merchandise often reached there even faster than it could be shipped to some of the eastern cities. At the Falls, she was living in the most remote American settlement of all.

One warm autumn afternoon, Ella sat on the deck with Heera at her feet, while she spun wool on an old but serviceable wheel. The regular thump of her foot pressing down on the treadle and the whir of the spindle were homey, comforting sounds, and perhaps it was good that she should have to learn to appreciate what little she did have. Of course, back at Detroit she could have bought the finest French-spun yarn and spent her time weaving instead of spinning. Often she had bought the best Dutch cloth to make clothes, or paid a skilled *habitant* seamstress to fashion garments according to the latest pattern from London or Paris.

Ella smiled to herself to recall their past. It gave her a good feeling to think of how one day they would go back to Valenya, and it would all be better than ever. She could not let herself think otherwise, just as she could not let herself think of Owen giving the claymore to Benjamin. There were many things she did not think too much about, for she had to be strong, had to be an example to the others, even to her son, who was a boy but was living the life of a grown man.

At the moment, Benjamin was sitting on the prow of the flatboat, staring at nothing, his long legs dangling over the water. He was tough and brave, and Ella loved him so. She slowed her spinning to watch him while he did not know his mother had her eyes on him. The blue jay, Punch, was hopping about nearby, pecking at the boards; Benjamin was ignoring him, simply gazing across the water toward Indian country. Ella noticed that the claymore lay across his knees. Surely he was thinking about his father again.

The lad had not been the same since a recent patrol to a cabin that had been attacked and destroyed, the family murdered. Though he had seen much of death and killing in his fifteen years, the horrors of this latest carnage had shaken him badly. Ella paused in her work, letting her hands drop to her lap as she regarded him. He was growing so big and so fine. How she wished he did not have to experience this misery at all.

Just then, Susannah drifted out the side door of the deckhouse and paused near Benjamin. She was reading Shakespeare, hardly aware of her brother's presence. She leaned against the deckhouse, head cocked to one side, lips working while she whispered the words of some romantic scene. *Romeo and Juliet,* no doubt.

Ella returned to her spinning, and in rhythm with the wheel, her thoughts drifted as she savored the warm sun that appeared from behind a cloud. The autumn world was orange and flaming red, the sky blue above the Ohio River. It was peaceful, almost serene, if one did not think too hard. Ella closed her eyes. The sun felt good.

She heard her children's voices, Benjamin laughing, Susannah mildly annoyed and scolding. Susannah was saying, "Hear this, you dolt! Hear what one's life should be like! Maybe you'll never understand, but hear this if your ears aren't stopped up with mud from your slithering and snaking through the slimy woods all day!"

Benjamin snickered and agreed to listen. Susannah began in a halting but firm voice: "...*Romeo:*

> "If I profane with my unworthiest hand
> This holy shrine, the gentle sin is this;
> My lips, two blushing pilgrims, ready stand
> To smooth that rough touch with a tender kiss."

There was a pause, and Ella heard Susannah sigh, long and passionately. Then Benjamin muttered something incoherent before adding:

"Why must poets be so hard to understand like that? Now, Pa is a poet who makes good sense, with common words, and he writes about things we all understand, about the wild, the people, politics."

Another pause, until Susannah spoke.

"He once wrote poems of love, for Mother."

Ella's heart skipped as she heard that, and she smiled, biting her lower lip. The sun was wonderful, soothing. If only Owen were here now.

Benjamin was saying gruffly he never cared much for those poems, but he especially liked the biting, humorous essays his father wrote under the pseudonym Quill, a fictional Indian sage who criticized misguided policies of both Britain and America when it came to ruling the northwest.

Susannah insisted they talk about Shakespeare, for his was the sort of poetry young folk could understand far better than "the old, past history" about which her father wrote.

Ella's eyes opened, and she looked down to see Benjamin staring at Susannah's book as the girl pointed out several passages in *Romeo and Juliet*. The youngsters were sitting on deck while Punch hopped from one shoulder to the other, as if he, too, wanted to see, and he wound up on Susannah's finger as she said:

"Our parents simply cannot understand what it means to be young these days, to be full of life and hope! All they've ever known is war and hatred—"

Benjamin said, "And so have you, child!"

"Don't say child to me, dolt! You'll be as thickheaded and slow-witted as these Virginia backwoodsmen if you keep traipsing the woods with them!"

"You are a child! You're only fourteen!"

"Juliet was only fourteen, and that was old enough to love Romeo, and know very well the meaning of love! To love Romeo and take him to her breast, and . . . and die for the tragic, beautiful love of him!"

Benjamin snorted and shook his head. "Maybe she was better off dead, if she didn't know any better." He grinned.

Susannah slammed the book shut and gave him a shove. "You're no more than a clodhopping—"

He mumbled an apology. "But is there nothing lively, funny, in any of this? I need amusement. . . ." His voice dropped. "Lord knows I've seen enough of dead people."

There was another silence. Ella's heart was wrenched. She studied them, sitting there, shoulder to shoulder. It was apparent that Susannah, too, had been touched by what Benjamin had just said. Then the girl gave him an elbow and declared that he should listen. She proceeded to recite the play's opening, in which Capulets and Montagues comically insult one another as a brawl breaks out. Benjamin enjoyed that, and before long, Susannah was off again with her reading, and now he was interested in the entire play.

Ella began once more to spin, the treadle rising and falling, the sun warming her with its last strength before the onset of cold weather. Ella had been brought up with Shakespeare in her home, a grand English country house. She came from gentry, had fallen in love quite young with a dashing New Englander, and had sailed with him to his America. Those had been happy, simpler times, with Jeremy being born. Then her husband had died as the result of wounds suffered during the French and Indian war. That was twenty long years ago, and now she was happy again. She would be happier when her

Owen came back. She thought of him just as Juliet, on the balcony, spoke to Romeo, Susannah reading it beautifully:

> "My bounty is as boundless as the sea,
> My love as deep; the more I give to thee,
> The more I have, for both are infinite."

chapter **7**

THUNDER GUNS

Matters grew worse for Gwen Bently at Detroit. Even though Amaghwah had not been seen since the shooting, and no other attempts had been made to injure her or the baby, it was clear her continued presence here was barely tolerated. True, the settlement's loyalists no longer maintained that Jeremy had been a spy; instead, in many small and irritating ways, they often took their anger and their hatred of all rebels out on her.

Loyalist women who despised Jeremy's abandonment of their cause shunned Gwen completely, and there were so many of them that her life became steadily more lonely. Close friends and family did what they could to comfort her, but the unguarded hostility that met her during everyday chores and on simple shopping trips through town became almost too much to bear.

Grudgingly, even some of her worst detractors were obliged to come to her for medical treatment, and being with them in the hospital, she felt their resentment all the more. Try as she might to overcome it, there was no way to change the minds of folk whose cause was badly losing, and who might at any time find George Rogers Clark's fierce Virginians hammering at the door.

The only noteworthy improvement in her days was brought about by the unexpected arrival of an orphan boy named Jake Smith. His parents had been killed in a raid in Pennsylvania, and he was living with a foster family in the settlement. Jake, who was nine years old, arrived one morning to ask for work, and Gwen could not resist his big eyes and doleful but brave appearance. His clothes were poor and uncared for, he needed square meals and regular washing, and clearly he could use some tender care. Gwen, with her big heart, took him in as an errand boy and as a helper who could do many of the simple tasks and cleaning around the hospital. She paid him a penny a day and gave him meals and clothes. Soon he came to be called Little Jake.

Jake was bright, keenly observant, but very quiet. He seldom spoke, and Gwen wondered whether he really appreciated her efforts at civilizing and currying him. He did not outwardly object to being forced to wash twice a day, nor did he show much enthusiasm for the new clothes she gave him—better clothes than he had seen in his whole life, no doubt. Sometimes Gwen wondered why he had come to her, and what he really wanted. Yet it was understandable that he was so reserved, almost cold, because he had suffered much, and had seen too many terrible things.

He was always there to help when needed, however, never shirking, and he worked hard all day long. He declined to sleep in the hospital, though, and always seemed anxious to depart by evening, as if he had something important to do. When Gwen asked about this, he mumbled incoherently and avoided an answer. She did not ask again. Soon she became attached to the child, finding him a great help.

Of all the people at the hospital able to bring the boy out of his shell, Tamano's pretty wife, Lela, was best at it. She often came across the river to help Gwen and Annie, and was Gwen's dearest friend, next to her cousin. From the very first time Lela met Little Jake, she found a way to make him laugh, saying his curly hair reminded her of a buffalo, and calling him bull calf. But she won his heart by teaching him how to play the popular Indian gambling game called Hand. Normally,

Hand was played with two lines of participants, kneeling in front of one another as they passed a small object—usually a bullet or a dried pea—back and forth behind their backs. Once the passing stopped, the other line had to guess who had it. Lela showed Little Jake how to play alone, opening and closing one or the other hand in full view of the opponent, shifting the object until it was impossible to follow which hand held the pea or bullet.

At Hand, Lela was deft and elusive and was a good teacher. So was her ten-year-old son, David, who, like his twin sister, Catherine, was tall for his age and good-looking. David also became friendly with Little Jake, although the Indian boy was more mature and far different in character, being cheerful all the time, even though his father was gone and no one knew when he would come back. The boy adored his father and believed he would return safely, no matter what the danger. Gwen was grateful for all that Lela and her children did for Little Jake, although he remained unusually withdrawn.

Lela was a great support for Gwen, too, and sometimes, when Gwen looked at the Indian woman, she imagined what Owen Sutherland's first wife, Mayla, would have been like, had she lived. Lela often told Gwen about the past, about Pontiac's bloody war, the defeat of the Indians, and about Owen Sutherland's many adventures in company with Tamano. Gwen thought it ironic that Sutherland, one of the greatest heroes of the northwest, should be forbidden to come back here upon pain of death as a rebel. Had it not been for him and for his Ottawa wife—Mayla had given warning of an impending surprise attack by which Pontiac easily would have destroyed the garrison—this country might now be in Indian hands, if not back in French control.

The Indians had been allied with the French for a hundred years of warfare against the British colonies, and had chosen the wrong side. When the French lost, surrendering Canada and the northwest, the British had taken control of the defeated Indians, of the fur trade with them, and of key strategic positions on their rivers. It seemed, Gwen thought, that most Indians had again chosen the wrong side in a white man's war, for the British and loyalists were bound to lose. The fighting in the East was going hard against the king's troops, and the warfare along the frontier was tipping against the desperate

Indians and loyalists trying to stem the rising tide of white migration down the Ohio River.

The cold autumn days passed swiftly, with everyone preparing for winter, storing food, chinking cabins, hunting far afield for meat to pound with buffalo grease and berries into pemmican that would keep for months. Gwen wished she could remain at Valenya and never cross the river for the coming season. There she would be away from almost everyone except Lela, and Annie and her Uncle Cole could stay with her. At Valenya, it would be so peaceful and cozy.... But there was too much doctoring work to be done at the settlement, and Gwen would not avoid it. She longed for Jeremy, but Richard consoled her, growing fast as he did, and being such a delightful baby—and not such a baby anymore, for he was more than a year old. A year old, and his father never having seen him!

One dreary morning all Detroit came out to greet the arrival of a whaleboat convoy filled with Redcoat reinforcements. These men were replacing the troops lost during Hamilton's defeat, and they included several companies of experienced soldiers from Montreal, whose presence would strengthen Detroit considerably. They were led by a portly, red-faced captain named Henry Byrd, a man without enough wilderness experience, it was rumored. Still, for defense, he and his men would make Clark more cautious in the future.

Also with this force were two brass field cannon, unusual weapons for the northwest. Heavy guns were often mounted on boats and in forts, but field guns were hardly known, for it was almost impossible to take them on campaigns, since they were so unwieldy and the wilderness trails so rough. Gwen wondered what the British planned to do with them.

A few days after the reinforcements had arrived, on a gloomy Sunday afternoon when the first signs of snow were in the air, Mark Davies himself came into the hospital. He was cheerful, and fairly spry, considering how badly he had been wounded. Dressed immaculately in scarlet, white, and gold, he stood before Gwen in the examination room and said he had some exciting news to tell.

Gwen had been preparing packets of Glauber's salts, the contents of the bottle in a little mound on the counter before her, a pile of cut papers nearby for enclosing appropriate doses.

Though startled to see Davies, she did not show it, and glared at him without replying to his offer of news.

He smiled almost stupidly, closed the door behind him, and rocked on his heels. Gwen was uneasy and glanced about for something with which to defend herself if need be; but Davies was not there for violence. He meant simply to torment her.

"By springtime, the frontier settlements from Kentucky to Fort Pitt will be no more." Davies's voice was languid, sweet, matching his foolish grin.

Gwen gave a start and looked up, but then went back to her work, so as not to show that her heart was thundering. What was he getting at? Those settlements were doing very well defending themselves against loyalist partisans and Indians. They were growing stronger, if anything.

Davies cocked his bewigged head. "You don't believe me?"

"Go away, before I call my dog to rip the pants out of that pretty uniform of yours!" She worked harder and faster. "I mean it, Davies! Get out."

He smiled and nodded slowly. "Very well. I had no intention to tell you very much—just enough to give you something to ponder over this winter."

He began to open the door, then said casually, "Those new troops and the field cannon are to be sent against the settlements as soon as the weather breaks—with a thousand Indians behind them."

Davies hesitated, and showed his satisfaction at seeing Gwen so astonished.

He chuckled and said, "Pity you didn't know all this a month ago . . . when there would have been time and good weather for you to run off and warn your rebel compatriots about what's coming down on their scurvy heads!" His face and voice changed from mild sweetness to bitter anger as he said this; then, just as abruptly, the scowl left his face, and he added: "Have you any friends or family at Ruddle's Station, or Martin's, or any of those squalid pigsties in Kentucky?" He laughed humorlessly. "Wouldn't you like to scurry off and warn them? But you should have got there before winter, so they'd have time to prepare, to stock powder and strengthen their forts. When the springtime comes to rebel country, so will we! It will be a feat of arms, an achievement worthy of glory as we manhandle those guns through the wild!" He grinned and whispered, "Long live the king! Death to the rebels!"

Davies went out the door, greeting Little Jake—who had just appeared—and affectionately rubbing the child's curly head as he went.

Gwen was left alone, save for the boy, who gazed without emotion at her. It was as if Jake wanted to know what she would do, and he stared at her so hard that Gwen had to tell him to be about his work. When he left, Gwen stood at the window, which was rattling with icy snow. She felt utterly helpless. She knew about an impending disaster, but winter was indeed coming down, and for her to try to get away with her baby in her arms was courting death.

Outside ice was forming on puddles. It was cold, and getting colder. Richard awoke and stood up in his crib, but his mother paid him no mind. Her hands were in fists, and she was crying.

For the next few days, Gwen went about her business with hardly a word for anyone. Even the silent Little Jake was talkative by comparison. She felt a kinship with the lonely boy, whose quiet seriousness was the result of the same kind of devastation that might soon befall the people of the settlements, and which she often lay awake imagining.

Jake seemed to be always watching her these days. One morning he amazed her with his skill as he practiced stitching a buckskin hide, the way Gwen had shown him once when he had asked how she closed up a wound. Then he startled her by saying plainly:

"My pa would've lived if I could've done this for him."

Sitting nearby, Gwen paused in her cleaning of surgical instruments and observed the boy, who kept working, as if there had been no feeling at all behind his words. She knew well enough that his feelings were closed off, buried, but not forgotten.

After a long, quiet moment, she replied, saying, "One day maybe you'll be able to use what you learn to save someone . . . and your pa would be proud of that."

He stopped stitching, the needle trembling a little in his fine, strong fingers. Then he glanced at Gwen, but avoided her eyes, and said, "I'd like to learn how to do that, ma'am."

She smiled and, trying to lighten the mood, began to say

that he surely would, but grim Little Jake went on bluntly, "Lots of my folk would've lived, and I wouldn't have to stay here with them mean old varmints that took me in! I could've saved folk as cared for me, folk what didn't have to die if'n I was a doctor, like you, ma'am." He shook his head and continued to sew. "Someday I'll be there when people need help, and I'll stitch 'em up, and they won't have to die like Ma and Pa and Grandma and my little sister—"

"Jake!" Gwen was sharper than she meant to be, and he looked up at her, that cold, blank expression of his making her feel all the worse. "Jake," she said softly, "I'm sure you'll be a good doctor if that's what you want, but one day there won't be any more wars out here, and all you'll have to do is help folk with the usual aches and sicknesses." She tried to smile, yet could not help but see the fire behind those eyes of his, eyes that would not show the hurt. She saw the burning cabins, the bloodstained fields, the prisoners, and the heartless killers.

Gwen rose quickly and took the instruments from her apron, laying them on a towel. She tried to shake away what had come over her, yet she could not. She could not stop thinking of how it all was going to happen again, worse than ever, when Mark Davies took Indians on the warpath this spring. It must be stopped! But how? Who could do it?

Gwen sent Little Jake off on some chores, and in the privacy of the back room, she let herself weep. She was wiping her tears and fussing near the mantelpiece when Doc Sennet came through the half-open door and saw that she had been crying. Overcoming his embarrassment, he tried to cheer her up. He said she should take better care of herself, and that she might be falling ill from the hard labor at the hospital. As was to be expected, his recommendations were obscure remedies that Gwen recognized as being in part effective herbal cures. The combination of genuine cures with bizarre rituals such as walking on one's knees or facing an old hickory tree made her laugh a bit, and that was enough to ease her heavy heart.

"Dear Mr. Sennet," she said gently, "thanks for your kindness, but what ails me is not to be solved by medicines or remedies."

"Sure?" he asked. "You might have a mild case of rheumatism and not know what's troubling you." From his pocket he drew out a buckeye chestnut dangling from a string, and said, "This here's the cure for the rheumatis', mistress—just carry one in your pocket. I ain't never seen one better."

Gwen thanked him and began folding clean sheets for the hospital beds. "But I had thought you were learning modern medicine, Dr. Sennet."

"What? Oh, well, so I am, mistress! So I am, and gladly!"

"What about all these superstitions, then?"

"Superstitions?"

"The buckeye."

"Superstitious, me? No, I ain't superstitious about that, mistress. I jest don't want to get the rheumatis', is all."

Gwen looked at him as he muttered to himself, shoving the buckeye back into his pocket. She began to giggle again, and masked it by inquiring about the condition of Sennet's bad tooth.

"Has Mawak another charm for that? You seem to be over it."

"Aw, mistress," Sennet began, looking a bit embarrassed, "I was a fool to try them Injun shenanigans at all! Course they didn't work, though old Mawak told me up and down they'd do the trick if I believed hard enough in 'em!" He guffawed, slapping his leg and shaking his head, but before he could go on, the door opened, and in came the regal Ottawa medicine man himself.

Mawak had heard him, and said, "That's why Great Spirit make you a white man, sawbones! You no believe manitous, no believe what good for you! By damn, sawbones, you never get better with Injun medicine if you don't believe! That's why you be white man, and got sore teeth!"

Mawak folded his arms, giving Sennet a moment to bluster and ready a reply. Sennet flexed his shoulders, squinted through one eye, and said with disdain, "What do you redskins know about teeth that white men don't? Nothing! Nothing at all! You hardly got a fang in your mouth! That's why yours don't ache!"

Gwen loved it, and stood there folding her sheets and grinning, as Sennet declared his toothache was long gone, and no thanks to any Indian cure.

Mawak grunted, turning his head slightly. Sennet leaned his pointed chin forward and said he had been cured of the toothache by good old white man's common sense. In an aside to Gwen, he said his cure had been a well-known, time-tested practice rather than some modern scientific method, as she would have recommended.

Together, Gwen and Mawak asked, "What cure?"

Sennet shrugged his shoulders a few more times, his face working, and he squinted again at Mawak. "More'n one method, of course . . ." He squirmed a bit before saying, "One well-known cure is to use toothpicks from a lightning-struck tree."

Gwen looked at Mawak, who began to chuckle and shake his head, belly heaving. Sennet became more agitated, declaring that he had used toothpicks of that sort every day for a week, and it had helped stop the pain.

"That and taking certain . . . commonsense precautions, as I said! You know, making sure I don't do things the wrong way . . . you know, being plain sensible about . . . certain things."

Mawak's eyes narrowed, and Gwen asked, "Like what?"

Sennet became quite prim and raised his chin, saying, "Surely you know a man always has to put his left shoe on first in the morning if he wants to prevent the toothache—"

Gwen and Mawak were laughing, and that made Sennet all the more indignant as he declared that the remedy had worked. He was better, was he not? Certainly no Indian superstition had helped him. Mawak seemed to feel pity for Sennet, and again slowly shook his head, muttering "Left foot first!" as he broke into laughter once more. Gwen covered her mouth and went to put away the sheets.

Just then there came the loud clap of a cannon, and then another, followed by a distant cheer mingled with Indian screeches. Sennet said the new artillery was being tested on the common ground, and Captain Lernoult had invited the Indians to watch, "To give them that's wavering in our cause something to think about."

Gwen picked up the baby, and the four of them went outside, where many folk from the settlement were making their way along the frozen street, through a thin glaze of snow. Beyond, in the fields just west of town, hundreds of civilians, soldiers, and Indians were gathered. Although she had never witnessed such an event, Gwen knew the army regularly gave Indians a demonstration of military firepower, which was an effective way of intimidating them. Nothing was more intimidating to Indians than "thunder guns."

When Gwen, Mawak, and Sennet arrived at the edge of the

crowd, they saw a group of soldiers hauling the two brass field cannon across the bumpy ground. The soldiers, perfectly trained, moved swiftly, carrying out orders barked by a sergeant, as if they were on the battlefield. In close coordination, they maneuvered the guns into firing position. Gwen saw that heavy timbers had been set up a hundred yards off—apparently leftover portions of the original old fort palisade, which had been removed from around the settlement. The target looked just like a fort's gate, and above it, as if standing on ramparts, were several dummies made to resemble frontiersmen. The message was clear to the Indians, as well as to the civilians crowding the near side of the field, where the entire garrison was paraded in stiff red ranks.

At the shout of sharp commands, the cannon crew loaded and aimed. Nearby was Captain Lernoult, and beside him was Captain Henry Byrd, hands behind his back, his belly prominent as he proudly watched his gunners perform. Gwen realized it would be Byrd who would lead the invasion in the spring. He seemed too amiable, too sure of himself, or perhaps too sure of the power of his military rank. By now she had learned that he was at the defeat of St. Leger at Oriskany in 1777 and had been unable to stop the army's Indian allies from retreating en masse, which had compelled the regulars to fall back from the brink of victory. It was said he loathed Indian fighting habits and demanded harsh discipline, which they resented. Was Byrd the man to control these Indians?

The cannoneers were ready. As the match was touched to the hole, there came a fizz and the first gun leaped, its bang causing Gwen's ears to ring and Richard to howl in fright. The gate shuddered and gave, hanging on its leather hinges. Many Indians were capering about, and when, in the next moment, the second gun fired, they howled with redoubled excitement as the gate splintered, collapsing inward, and the dummies were hurled to the ground.

Mawak said to Gwen, "Big trouble come—look!"

Before anyone could stop them, a hundred young Indians, many just boys, went storming at the shattered gate, playing at attack. One of the nearby Redcoats jokingly ran out of the gate and threw up his hands in mock surrender, but the aroused Indians, some of them obviously drunk, rushed forward and, to every white man's surprise, roughly bore him down, whoop-

ing and pretending to scalp him while he angrily fought with
his fists and feet. A few other soldiers ran to help, but the
Indians were so agitated that they seemed to have lost their
senses, and a general brawl broke out at the gate. The fighting
was not stopped even when a guard detachment from Lernoult's
paraded troops darted forward on command, bayonets presented. They ran in military style, with their knees lifted high,
trotting in unison, like puppets at regulation drill. The excited
Indians broke and swarmed away when the soldiers pushed into
their midst, but something had caught hold of their savage
spirit, and they gathered again, yelping and screeching, preparing to charge the handful of troops who were blocking the
way to the make-believe fort.

Gwen could see that Captain Lernoult was upset, and Captain Byrd looked furious, but completely at a loss. His puffy
cheeks were flushed, his eyes wide as he stared at the mob of
Indians. A real fight was about to begin, and no one seemed
able to stop it.

Then there came a blast on a hunting horn of the style used
by English fox-chasers. Everyone looked off to Gwen's right,
where a tall Redcoat officer was striding across the field. To
Gwen's surprise, it was Mark Davies, appearing quite fit and
capable, though she knew he must still be in pain from his
wounds. He was calling to the Indians in their guttural tongue,
speaking slowly, his right hand raised.

They hesitated, pushed back and forth in a seething mass,
and looked to their leaders, especially to the Shawnee chiefs
who had been at the forefront of the fighting against rebel
settlers and knew Davies. Clearly this was a white officer they
respected: a man both ruthless and cunning, who was not
squeamish about massacre, and who despised the American
rebels and all they stood for.

The Indians stopped their frantic shouting and waving of
clubs and knives as Davies approached with utter calm. He
called out in several languages for the chiefs to control their
young men and to show respect for the soldiers of their great
white father across the sea, for they were his sons, just as the
Indians were his children, and therefore all of them were brothers. . . .

In a little while it was settled, and Lernoult awkwardly took
over from Davies, addressing the chiefs and saying firmly that

the king would frown upon those who shed the blood of any of his children. He offered gifts of white bread and beer, then called the demonstration to an early halt. Mawak moved off to enjoy some beer along with the high-spirited mob of Indians, leaving Gwen to think that Captain Byrd might as well not have been there at all.

It was a premonition of things to come, Gwen knew, as she turned away from the spectacle. The amazed Sennet stayed, watching the cannon being hauled away, and hardly noticed she was gone. The frontier war was taking a whole new, wicked twist. Even if the British were to lose the main eastern fighting, they seemed determined to clear the frontiers of rebel settlers, to push back the people swarming into Indian borderlands. The Crown intended to hold the northwest for the king and the loyalists, even if it meant widespread carnage for civilians. Gwen cared nothing for the politics involved, but it tormented her to think of the wanton killing and torture that would come of Byrd's campaign.

She heard someone call and, as she turned, saw Mark Davies standing there, looking alert and much stronger. He was chuckling, grinning broadly, but said nothing. Gwen wrenched herself away, trying to ignore his mocking laughter. The war was changing, but what could anyone do about it? Yet the settlements had to be warned. No one could help her do it, however, for virtually all the Indians here were loyal to the king, or at least would not risk being a spy for the rebels. Even an uncommitted Frenchman dare not venture far southward into rebel-held country, for the arm of the British government was long, and Lernoult's informants would surely know if anyone went off that way. Discovery would mean punishment for the family or business left behind, and the messenger would never get back home again.

No one would bring the warning to the eastern settlements— no one could but Gwen, and that was a risk that involved Richard as well. She did not know what to do, until she realized how many children like Richard and Little Jake would suffer if no one gave the warning.

For Gwen, there was no other choice but to go herself.

Little Jake came into Gwen's hospital room late that afternoon and saw her preparing a pack, with clothes, equipment, food, and medicine. She was startled to see him standing there, in the light of a candle that was lit against the gray of early twilight. He might have been watching her for some time. She asked what he wanted.

The boy said nothing, but his large eyes took everything in. Gwen said hastily that tomorrow she was going over to Valenya for a few days, but that he should mention nothing about it to anyone else. Annie knew already, she said, and would take care of the hospital for a while.

Little Jake still said nothing, but stood a moment longer, looked closely at the traveling pack, and then went out, not even saying good-bye.

Gwen sighed and wiped her sweating brow. She was nervous, her stomach queasy. She had packed enough, and her canoe had been repaired and was ready. Annie thought she was going to Valenya for a needed rest and believed that Gwen wanted to be alone for a while. Had Annie or any of Gwen's friends known what she was really up to, they would have forcibly stopped her, and would have watched her every move until the winter became so severe that not even someone as desperate as she would risk going out.

Gwen hardly slept that night, and before dawn she was ready to go. In the dimness, she glanced around the hospital, Cape standing nearby observing her, tongue hanging out as if she anticipated a walk. The patients were sleeping. Gwen would miss them and this place, and she felt a pang of guilt that she could not stay to help them all recover. She would miss Annie, too, and the rest. She released a long, shaky sigh, and with effort kept her composure, but she could not still her pounding heart. There was nothing else for it.

She must hurry, or it would be too late. It was the hour before full dawn. She would slip through the settlement, down to the river, and put Richard in her small canoe. They would set off, following the shoreline of the straits until, in two days, they reached the broad channel where the waters emptied into Lake Erie. From there it would be especially perilous, cutting across the width of Erie, trying to reach the Apostle Islands to rest during darkness. Then she would cross to the mainland near Sandusky, where there was a village of kindly Moravian, Christianized, Indians. She knew those people well, having gone to tend them several times with Jeremy. If she was lucky, and they did not ask too many questions, someone would surely guide her southeastward, or put her on the trail to a rebel settlement.

The God-fearing Moravians had remained neutral in this war, but they helped all travelers who came to them, red or white. That caused them problems, because loyalist Indians abused them for not going to battle against the rebels, and rebels accused them of harboring and spying for Indian raiders. Still, they were Gwen's only hope of getting away.

There were many risks, including bad weather and possible injury, but once she was safely in rebel territory, Gwen could get a message to Jeremy somehow. At the same time, she could begin to spread the alarm to rebel settlements in the Ohio Valley, western Pennsylvania, and Kentucky.

Gwen shouldered her gear and sent Cape on ahead. With Richard sleeping, slung over her back Indian style, she went quietly through the ward room, hesitated at the front door, and looked around. The darkened hospital was warm, secure, the sounds of snoring peaceful. Outside, the wind rose and clattered shutters, bringing with it a drizzling mist, cold and uncomfortable. Perhaps she was a fool! For an instant, she wavered.

It came to her that there were many other folk just like these out on the frontier, and their lives were in her hands—just as the life of her baby was in her hands. She thought of her many friends among the tribes of Indian country, people who owed their lives to her, and who would help if she could only get to them. They would see her through, as long as she could escape from Detroit, escape from Davies and Amaghwah. Those two were the real danger, not the Indians of the wilderness.

Gwen stepped outside, quietly closing the door behind her.

At that very moment, the first pale rays of a cold, mist-shrouded sun were lighting the back of the house at Valenya across the river. Crouching in a thicket near the water were Owen Sutherland and Jeremy Bently. Tamano had slipped off to his own lodge, to find out all he could from Lela, and to alert her that the moment to leave had come.

Jeremy was disappointed to see that Gwen was not at the house, which was obviously unoccupied. "I should've known she'd be at the fort hospital, working double hard because I'm not there to help." He glanced at Sutherland, whose own expression was a mixture of excitement and nostalgia as he looked at Valenya, the house he had built and had intended to be his permanent home.

Sutherland shook himself clear of emotion and became suddenly grim. "Once we get Gwen away from here, Valenya likely won't last." He turned to his stepson and saw that Jeremy was also troubled by the thought that the house might be destroyed.

Jeremy said, "Perhaps it was all a dream, anyway, to think you and ma could ever come back here again." He looked at the house. "If the British can, they'll hold on to the whole northwest after the war's done."

Sutherland nodded and lay on his side, gazing across the dark straits at the distant lights of cottages and Indian lodges twinkling faintly in the deepening mist. "Congress will have to bargain for a lot of things, and the British will want to hold Canada and this country." After a moment, he said, "Unless we take it by force, before a treaty's signed."

Quiet came between them, and a cold, wet north wind whipped down the straits, shaking treetops and howling between the standing stones a hundred yards off to the right. Sutherland listened, the sound so familiar to him. The sound of home.

Jeremy stirred and said, "I'm going to the house and take a look around." He saw that Sutherland was staring at the great stones, longing in his eyes. "Why don't you go down there, Pa? I'll meet you in the common room, when you're ready."

They separated, and Sutherland slipped through the drizzle, moving like a shadow in deeper shadows, toward the standing stones, to the gravesite of his first wife, who had died with his child in her womb.

The stones lamented as Sutherland knelt at the gravesite. It might be for the very last time.

Gwen had chosen the perfect time to go. It was a dreary Sunday morning, and no one would be working at the landing, or even awake yet. Unseen, she slid her small canoe from its rack and got it partly into the water. Cape eagerly splashed into the shallows and clambered in as Gwen held the boat steady from dry land.

She shivered, perhaps from the cold, then fetched her baby,

who was asleep in a thick blanket. Laying him in the center
of the canoe, on a leather sling suspended from one gunwale
to the other, she thanked heaven he was sleeping. As Gwen
tied a thong about the baby, securing the other end to a thwart,
Cape nuzzled the child, almost waking him, and Gwen scolded
the dog in a harsh whisper. Cape lay down in the bow as Gwen
loaded the food and gear. She pushed the birch boat all the
way into the water, clumsily struggling to climb in without
getting her feet wet. She succeeded, but the canoe rocked
sharply, so that Richard stirred and began to awaken.

Gwen shushed him, singing softly. For once, she wished
Richard were younger, easier to handle. She dreaded the thought
of his beginning to cry, sitting up, and attracting attention.

"Sleep, my little darling."

She sang the song he loved, of horses and meadows and
butterflies. She slowly pushed the water with the paddle, and
the boat turned its nose out into the gray, misty river. Gwen
sang, and Richard cooed. She could smell that he needed changing. What a time for it! He always howled when his diapers
were dirty. Please, not now.

Gwen suddenly felt as if she were being watched and turned
to look at the shore. It was quiet, though; a light or two could
be seen back in the settlement, but the mist lay soft and peaceful
on the ground, concealing the walls of the fort beyond. No one
was around.

Richard coughed and became fussy. Gwen sang to him, and
said she would change him soon, after they had gone a safe
distance. She spoke soothing nonsense to him, but he would
not be stilled and began to whimper.

"Please, dear little one! Please be still!"

Then Gwen heard a noise ashore, and she looked sharply
around. There, beside the canoe rack, was a tiny figure, as
gray as the mist, and looking right at her. It was Little Jake!
Gwen could not imagine what he was doing there, but she
played the part and waved cheerfully to him, hoping he would
not shout back. Jake was quiet, not waving. He stood there,
sullen and forlorn, as if he knew she was running away. He
could not know, could he? Gwen waved, blew him a kiss, and
smiled. He did not respond.

Then, to Gwen's horror, Mark Davies appeared behind the
boy, patting him on the shoulder, staring hard at Gwen. His

scarlet tunic was like fire in the mist, his white breeches and smallclothes seeming to be those of a phantom. Why was he there? What did he know? And with Little Jake?

Looking away, feeling cold and almost faint, Gwen rapidly steered the canoe across the river, glad for the gathering mist that was shutting her out from shore. Surely all Davies could think was that she was going to Valenya! He would not see her turn downstream, and could not possibly know any more than Jake did about her plans. He simply could not! She looked back quickly, and saw Jake wrench away from Davies, kick and twist, and run, with the man trying to hold him, but too pained by his wounds to follow.

Suddenly Richard was crying. He was uncomfortable and hungry, and soon would be cold. Gwen had to find a place to stop and build a fire so she could change and feed him, warming him up for another few hours' travel. She had to put miles between herself and Fort Detroit. She had to go fast, and the melancholy that earlier had troubled her was gone. Now she was simply afraid, alone, and determined to survive.

chapter 8

ISLAND IN THE MIST

Owen Sutherland stood in the large common room of Valenya, his rifle butt on the floor as he leaned on the muzzle. His mind was almost empty, like this house. He simply wanted to stand a moment, to be there, forgetful of past or future. Yet, for all that he did not want to think, he could not avoid feeling that the straits at Detroit were no longer his home. Much as he wanted it to be, after all the years of building, after all he had done here, this was not his home.

There was no way to deny that hollow feeling. Perhaps, in time, he would return to Valenya—return as a conqueror over those loyalists and Indians who stayed. For now, however, he did not belong here. It hurt to think that. He had been away too long, and too much had happened. If he and Ella ever came back here, it would be like starting over again, except for this house. If it were still here when he came back, there would be no better place to begin.

Sutherland wondered what was keeping Tamano. His family was to depart, also—the Chippewa was fetching them from

Lela's lodge a short distance away, in the cove beyond the standing stones. Jeremy was on his way to the lodge to help, and then Lela would cross the river to get Gwen.

Suddenly there was shouting down at the river, and Sutherland hurried out the back door, closed the padlock, and swung around the house to see what was happening. It was Lela, and running ahead of her was a small white boy, dashing toward the house.

Lela was shouting Sutherland's name, and she looked frantic. Clearly there was no enemy around, lurking in the fields or fencerows or behind the new hay barn, so Sutherland stepped out to meet the boy, who flew at him, crying that Gwen was in danger.

With one arm, Sutherland caught the lad and lifted him, seeing his dirty face was scratched and tear-streaked, and his clothes were torn as if someone had beaten him.

He panted, "You got to save Mistress Bently, sir! You got to keep 'em away from her! Go quick! Please! Please!" He raved, almost hysterical, and Lela rushed up to tell Owen that Gwen had fled downriver, and Mark Davies had sent Indians after her.

"Little Jake told us everything!" Lela cried, in a mixture of Ottawa and English. "My man's getting our canoe ready, and Jeremy's getting your gear and food! There's no time! No time! Come quick, Donoway!"

Sutherland was already moving. Little Jake was crying now, as though a dam had broken, releasing all his misery. Sutherland tossed the boy onto his shoulder and started off along the shoreline toward Lela's lodge. Out on the water, Jeremy came into sight in their canoe, stroking swiftly, his face set in determination.

They all reached Lela's lodge together, where Tamano was hurrying his two children and whatever they could carry into one canoe. Sutherland and Jeremy took Jake in the other, pushing off quickly. By now the boy had explained through sobs that Mark Davies had paid him to spy on Gwen. Jake wept, saying he had known it was wrong, but had not known just how wrong until now.

Jake was bent over, crying, in the center of the canoe, as Sutherland and Jeremy darted it out into the open water. Soon, the two canoes were cutting through the mist that still hung over the straits, Tamano's craft close behind. He was in the stern, Lela and Catherine paddling hard in the middle, and David in the bow. The mist would help prevent them from being seen by passersby, and they would use their knowledge of these waters to steer right for a cluster of islands downstream from the fort. Gwen would surely be there by now, for she had a lead of two hours. She would not go fast in the driving mist.

Jake said Amaghwah had met with Davies, and then the Indian had taken a canoe in pursuit of Gwen about an hour ago. Sutherland knew that Amaghwah would make right for the narrows near Grand Isle, where she had to pass eventually. There the Shawnee would intercept her.

Jeremy had not spoken much, but Sutherland realized what was in his stepson's mind. Their only chance to save Gwen lay in her moving erratically, perhaps delaying somewhere to get her bearings, or to feed the child. At any rate, the chances were that Amaghwah would pass her in the fog.

They drove on and on, paddling deeply, powerfully. Through this murk, few other men in the northwest could have found their way more precisely than these. If only they had enough time! There was not a moment to be lost, and they must not be delayed.

Gwen was terribly afraid, and at times felt as though her whole body trembled uncontrollably. It was difficult building a fire on the little island she had landed upon, but she got it going and hoped it would be unseen, the smoke concealed by mist. Because of her fear, it was even difficult to change the baby, for her hands shook badly. She was more worried for Richard than for herself—more afraid he would take ill from exposure than she was of being discovered by the British. Her anxiety was intensified by the raw cold, the oppressive, gray atmosphere, and the incessant rushing, rushing of the foaming waters around the island.

Gwen thought about where she would stop that night. She wished she could stay here, sleep beside the fire, right through until morning. It seemed like a dream, a nightmare, but it was real; she had fled, and now she must not be caught. She had to push on, to get far away from the fort. Davies could give the alarm to Lernoult and declare that Gwen was proving herself to be a spy running away to the rebels. If he did that, she surely would be captured, for there would be dozens of search parties, and they would have to find her. Ironically, her chances might be better if Davies decided to murder her. Then he might not report to Lernoult, but instead send Amaghwah after her and Richard. Davies was still too weak and in too much pain from his wounds to undertake the chase himself.

Gwen hastily kicked out the campfire, then laid Richard in the center of the canoe, which was half in the water. Cape got in next and lay down heavily near the baby. Gwen had lost track of time, but she knew her way well enough, and had only to keep toward the river's right bank past Grand Isle, through the quieter passage between island and mainland. Soon her canoe was into the current again, and she was feeling weary but excited. It was good that Richard was asleep, suspended in the harness, snug and warm. He would stay that way for some time, and she could travel far. If only she could keep to quieter water, then there would be no danger from the straits. Becoming disoriented, however, might result in being caught in tricky currents, or dashed against rocks.

She paddled on into the mist, listening to the steady sound of water rushing past rocky outcrops. She steered carefully along shorelines with which she was fairly familiar, or should have been—but in the shadowy dimness, the rocks and forest took on a different, perplexing character. Headlands appeared suddenly out of the drizzle, as if they moved on their own, and sunken trees wallowed stubbornly in her path, threatening to punch a hole in the birch boat. She was forced again and again to change directions, more than once causing her to lose her way.

Yet she pressed on, unwilling to wait for the mist to rise, for though it endangered her, it also concealed her against searchers. The canoe shot between rocks, sped along by the current faster than she wanted at times, but on she went, feeling alone in an overpowering and dismal environment. It was as if she were surrounded by silent watchers, and did not know whether they were friends or enemies.

Then she recognized the point of Grand Isle, and saw the huge twisty pines that marked a favorite picnic spot. She was relieved, having struck just where she wanted to be. Now, if she kept to the right side of the island, she would be through the narrows in a few hours and then could camp for the night. Relaxation came to her for the first time. At least she knew where she was, and tomorrow before dawn she would set off again with renewed strength. Then she was startled, as Cape let out a deep growl of warning.

Something was moving on her right. A boat was in the water—an Indian canoe. She strained her eyes to see it, felt fear, then quickly swung her canoe's prow left, toward shore. She looked hurriedly back over her shoulder. A lone Indian was silhouetted in the boat. She paddled hard. She looked again. He was heading right at her. His scalplock was preened straight and high, in Shawnee fashion. Gwen's heart leaped in terror. In the distance she heard him laugh. It was Amaghwah!

Gwen rushed toward an inlet that she knew was somewhere ahead in the fog. She put large boulders between herself and Amaghwah, so that, for now, he could not see her. She would get ashore, and there she and Cape could fight him. That was a chance, a slim one, but she would not surrender. She would fight to the last.

Not far away, Sutherland's two canoes sped through the mist, the passengers silent. Little Jake was wrapped in a blanket, sullen and angry with himself. By now Sutherland had learned all about the ambitious British plans to attack the settlements with field cannon that spring.

His thoughts were busy with this danger until he noticed Jake was holding a small pouch in his hands, one used for carrying coins. The boy weighed it once or twice, contemplating. Then he lifted it as if meaning to drop it overboard. Sutherland asked what he was doing.

Jake's mouth twitched, his eyes soft and sad. "This is . . . this is the dirty money I earned from Davies!" He was about to let it plop into the water, but Sutherland used his paddle to knock the pouch back into the canoe, causing Jake to turn, confused and questioning.

Sutherland knew how much that small amount of money meant to the child, and he was moved that the boy had decided to throw it away.

He said, "Keep it."

Jake shook his head and stared at the surface of the water whisking past the canoe. "I don't want it."

"Keep it," Sutherland said firmly. "What you've done is done. You'll need that coin someday, and Mistress Bently would want you to keep it."

Jake was uneasy as he looked at Sutherland, and then at the pouch lying in the bottom of the canoe. He did not pick it up.

Jeremy called, "Grand Isle up ahead!" There in the dimness were the same twisted pine trees Gwen had just passed.

"Push on!" Jeremy said, and they paddled deeper and harder, pulling away from Tamano's boat, which was dropping steadily behind, even though there were four paddlers in it.

Suddenly there came a loud and cheerful "Ahoy!" from somewhere nearby. Sutherland looked to the left to see a military whaleboat, sail lowered, with three bedraggled Redcoats rowing, and a fat officer standing in the bow, waving and calling, "Ahoy, the canoe! Heave to, will you, gentlemen! We're lost!"

The officer broke into fluent Parisian French that no *habitant* of the northwest ever would have understood. He said they had been visiting Indian villages downriver, and the mist had confused their sense of direction. Jeremy grunted to Sutherland that he thought the three soldiers might be the same men from the tavern on the Wabash. They would recognize Jeremy, who had been their doctor last year, so he paddled hard to get away.

But the officer was determined.

"Ahoy, gentlemen!" Again in French, the man demanded, "Be good enough to assist us! Stop!" In English: "Damned frog-eating rascals!"

The whaleboat was laboring across the river, obviously having been trying to beat its way back upstream. There were many treacherous currents here, and a sudden gusting crosswind might catch them unawares, sending them to the bottom if they did not take care. Among snags and rocks, these men were in serious trouble if the fog did not clear to show them safely to land.

Sutherland called back in French that they were sorry but could not stop. At that, the officer blustered angrily and ordered the sail hoisted. The whaleboat turned downstream and, with the current and breeze behind it, picked up enough speed to close on the canoe, coming within a hundred feet. Tamano's craft was not in sight; obviously he had heard the officer's loud cries and was keeping cautiously back.

Jeremy glanced over his shoulder at the soldiers and declared quietly to Sutherland that he would shoot them if they tried to interfere. Sutherland made no reply, but was prepared to do the same.

"Hold! Stop! In the name of the king!" The officer was speaking English now, and yanking out a pistol. In French he cried, "Rest on your paddles, or I'll be compelled to fire!" He was less than forty feet away now, but just then the soldier at the stern yanked the tiller to one side to avoid a rock, and the whaleboat heeled over awkwardly, like some giant lame bird. The current rushed hard from behind, making the boat ungainly, almost swamping it as the tillerman fumbled at the stern.

Sutherland called back in French that they would gladly meet in camp on the mainland, but the officer screamed in anger that he wanted to come alongside and ask a few questions about direction, for he had no time to go into camp, and was already overdue back at Fort Detroit. Would they obey, or must he arrest them?

Momentarily, Jeremy and Sutherland let their paddles dangle in the water, slowing the canoe as the whaleboat came closer.

"Well, then," said the officer, putting his pistol away, and blustering his relief that he would not be compelled to shoot them. "That's more like it—"

He stopped short and caught his breath, for Sutherland had grasped the side of the whaleboat and had presented his own pistol, while Jeremy was pointing two more pistols as he knelt in the canoe.

"What is the meaning of this outrage?" The officer, sputtering and bewildered, was none other than Captain Henry Byrd, paunchy and rosy-cheeked; the last thing he had expected was for a couple of vagabond *habitants* to menace a boatload of regulars. "Who are you?"

Sutherland nodded to the three soldiers, all of whom were dismayed, heads hanging, and he saw they were indeed the three who had almost run into his party at the tavern on the Wabash.

He said, "Your troops recognize us, sir, and they also know we're in deadly earnest when we tell you to make for the mainland immediately, or we'll be obliged to shoot you."

Sutherland spoke to Sergeant Bailey, who politely greeted

him and Jeremy, much to the dismay of Byrd. The officer sat down heavily.

"The notorious rebels?" the captain gasped, as much in astonishment as in frustration that he had been taken prisoner by men whose capture would have guaranteed his career, would have made him the most famous British soldier in America after General Cornwallis himself.

Held together, both boats were being swept downstream by wind and current. The disconsolate Sergeant Bailey, at the tiller of the whaleboat, had for the moment forgotten to steer. Corporal Higgins and Private Scruggs should have lowered the sail, but they, too, were in shock at having been taken prisoner.

Sutherland felt the canoe swing hard around, but he dared not lower his weapons to get the paddle. He shouted to the soldiers to master their craft, and they jumped to it, but it was too late, and the whaleboat lurched, the wind filling the sail and quickly tipping the boat over. Sutherland's grip was torn from where he had held the canoe and whaleboat side by side. Jeremy sat down, and Sutherland laid his own pistol aside to grab his paddle. The canoe was safe, but the whaleboat was capsized completely in the foaming water. Oars clattered and flailed. Men screamed in terror as they tried to stay with the overturned boat, which slowly spun out into the narrower, swifter channel, off to the right. It was only a matter of time before they would be swept against the rocks and drown. Their screams for help rang out through the mist that slowly gathered over them.

Sutherland cursed, adding, "Confound the damned British army!"

He and Jeremy exchanged the briefest of glances, then paddled rapidly toward the helpless soldiers. Sergeant Bailey was holding Scruggs from going down a second time, and the other two were fighting to keep a grip on the boat. Jeremy muttered a prayer for Gwen as he paddled, and with Sutherland steering from the stern, they came alongside the whaleboat and stopped it from spinning away. Then Tamano's canoe appeared, cutting in at the other side of the whaleboat, and as Lela and David held rifles on the soldiers, the Chippewa helped Sutherland begin to guide the boat toward a quiet, shallow inlet ahead to the left.

Byrd clung to the mast, his soaked wig falling over one eye, and he spat out water as he said, "I am in your . . . your debt, Mr. Sutherland!" He groaned as he slipped, losing hold again, and he went under. Sutherland reached down to yank him up, keeping him afloat. Slowly, the whaleboat was brought in to shore. As soon as they got these men to safety, they would be off. Gwen had to be somewhere nearby. Lord grant that she was not in danger, that they were not too late.

Had the weather been clear, they would have seen Amaghwah paddling swiftly, about three hundred yards ahead of them, making for a cove not far from the one to which they were ferrying the soldiers.

Amaghwah was confident he could finish off Gwen after he shot the big dog with her. Now, just a little distance off, he spotted her canoe floating, apparently abandoned, close to shore. She must have jumped out and rushed into the woods. So much the better. He would track her down, and when the dog came at him, he would kill it quickly. Licking his thin lips, he stopped paddling and reached down into his bundle to see that his tomahawk, scalping knife, and a small pistol were there. A fine rifle also lay at hand, but Captain Davies had suggested using the pistol for close-in work, especially to kill the dog.

Amaghwah would take care, knowing how cunning this white woman was, and that she would be armed. He stayed low in the canoe, eyeing the shoreline and the trees in case she was concealed there, a firearm at the ready. It would be no easy shot for her from there, and if she fired now, she would not have another chance. He could drive ashore before she could reload, and the dog would be no problem at all.

There, on land, he saw Cape, big and lumbering, springing out of the trees to bound back and forth, barking at Amaghwah. The Shawnee slowed, now nearly alongside the abandoned canoe, which still had everything stowed in it, covered with a blanket. He picked up his rifle to shoot the dog. His canoe drifted in slowly, and Cape presented an easy target, tail high, the large head inviting Amaghwah's bullet. The Indian brought the rifle to his shoulder and cocked the hammer. Cape was standing still now, and one slow squeeze of the trigger . . .

It was then that his canoe gently bumped against Gwen's, and something whacked down his rifle, which fired, unaimed.

Gwen was in her canoe, having thrown off the blanket that covered her and the baby, and she again swung the paddle at Amaghwah, throwing it, striking him in the face. He reeled, and before he could recover, Gwen held the two dueling pistols that had nearly killed him earlier. They were coming up to bear on his chest. She meant to finish him this time. For just an instant, Amaghwah was so startled that he was unable to move.

A pistol fired, but it flashed in the pan and did not send its bullet. That was all Amaghwah needed. As the second pistol fired, he tumbled aside, his canoe going over with him, and he splashed into the water.

Cape was barking wildly ashore. Richard was kicking and howling, trying to get out of his sling. Gwen sat there, eyes wide, her two useless pistols pointed at the bottom of the Shawnee's canoe. Had she hit him? Yes! She saw blood in the water.

Quickly, she recovered and reached for the second paddle, meaning to move a little distance away and reload. She dug in with the paddle blade, and the canoe shot away. She was shaking harder than ever, trying to get to shore to pick up Cape and then to get away before anyone could follow. If Amaghwah was not dead, then it would take a long time for him to right his canoe.

Abruptly the prow of her craft leaped into the air, as if it were alive, rising so high that she was thrown back against the stern. There came a terrible scream of fury, and behind her she glimpsed Amaghwah trying to climb in, both his legs curled up over the gunwales of the canoe, his hands on the high, curving stern of the boat. Gwen dropped her paddle as she struggled frantically, trying to get her balance. Amaghwah nearly was aboard. The canoe jerked violently to the side and flopped down again just as Gwen found the paddle and swung at Amaghwah's clinging legs and hands, but she missed each time, as he tugged the canoe first this way, then that, and she was wrenched off balance from side to side.

Richard had fallen from his sling bed and was wailing as he pitched to and fro in the center of the boat. If the canoe capsized, he would drown. Gwen desperately tried to get to him and fight off Amaghwah at the same time, but she could not get her balance. Howling, Amaghwah mocked her helplessness, and she screamed in anger as her paddle struck at his hands. She could not land a solid blow, for he was quick, and the canoe rocked and tilted, taking on water as its stern dipped lower. Amaghwah lurched mightily, and Gwen nearly fell overboard.

"Richard!" she screamed, and Amaghwah yelled back, laughing.

Gwen groped for the baby as he bounced around like a doll. She got a hand on him, but now Amaghwah was coming over the end of the boat. Gwen turned and slashed with the paddle, driving him back down. He began to yank the boat back and forth again. There was no escape.

At last Gwen sprang for the baby, and found herself on the bottom boards, the child in her grasp. She clutched him close, water splashing over her, Amaghwah's horrible cries ringing out. The boat swung from side to side, suddenly rose up high on its stern again, and Gwen was sure this time it would turn over. It smacked down hard, wobbling sickeningly, and then steadied. She fought to sit up, expecting to see Amaghwah aboard, but he was not there, and his shouting had stopped. Quickly she laid the baby down and snatched up the extra paddle, prepared for his head to appear at the gunwale. Nothing. Richard wailed, but there was no other sound. After a moment, Gwen looked over the side. The water was calm, except in one place, where there were bubbles and blood.

In the next moment, Gwen gasped to see Cape surface, and behind the dog rolled Amaghwah, face down. Cape swam slowly toward the canoe, and Gwen saw with overwhelming relief that Amaghwah was dead. Cape was hurt, though, and much of the blood was hers.

Weak with shock, Gwen paddled the few strokes to shore, then clambered out and waded through the water, Richard in her arms, the dog limping beside her. Cape had been stabbed repeatedly and needed attention. Gwen had rolls of bandages, and quickly she stanched the severest cuts. She was relieved to see Cape would be all right.

They were all wet and cold and shivering, but before Gwen could make a fire, there came another haloo from out on the water. Through the mist appeared a pair of canoes, and to her inexpressible joy she saw her husband in the bow of one.

"Jeremy!" she cried, and, picking up the baby, rushed into the water to meet him as he leaped out of the boat and embraced her. "Jeremy! Oh, my Jeremy!"

Lifting Gwen and his son in his arms, without speaking, Jeremy carried them ashore.

In the canoe, Owen Sutherland rested his paddle over his knees. He looked over at Tamano and Lela, and they all smiled, Lela's eyes wet with tears as she watched Jeremy hold his son for the first time. Young David and Catherine were more spontaneous and cried out cheerful greetings to Gwen, who waved with one arm, while her other was tightly around her man's neck.

It was not until they were camped safely, far downstream, that Sutherland learned from Gwen exactly who the officer was he had rescued from drowning and left marooned back on Grand Island. Captain Byrd had introduced himself correctly, despite his bedraggled, drenched condition. He had been polite—all military manners and proper decorum—even though Sutherland had further dampened his spirits by breaking the oars and slashing the sails of the whaleboat as a precaution against pursuit.

If Sutherland had known, back there, that Byrd would be the one to lead the assault against the settlements, he probably would have taken the man prisoner and hauled him back to Kentucky and Colonel Clark. Well, it was too late to return for him now, and the fugitives had to hurry on, before Byrd got back to Detroit and organized the chase.

It was a long way home, Sutherland thought as he sat before the campfire, smoking a short-stemmed clay pipe. In a lean-to just out of the firelight, Jeremy and Gwen lay, their baby beside them. Off to the other side of the little camp, Tamano was with his wife, with the Indian children and Jake fast asleep, wrapped in blankets beside the fire.

Sutherland was glad for all of them. Plans had been to make for Kentucky right away, so he would be with Ella and the children again, before winter came. The wind lifted and rushed through the trees, blowing cold and crisp from the north. The mist was gone, the air chill and dry, good for traveling far and fast by canoe. They would cross Erie swiftly and, if they were

fortunate, be on the trail toward the Falls of the Ohio within
a week. Back with Ella by Christmas—that would have been
fine.

But it would not be possible. Sutherland had to part with
his companions. He could not go back with them, for he had
to warn the settlers farther to the east of what was coming.
Jeremy and Tamano could pass the word through Kentucky,
but he must go to the settlements along the upper Ohio, as far
as Fort Pitt. No doubt most of the settlements would have to
be abandoned; Pitt was the only one built to withstand cannon
fire. A major muster of rebel militia would be required to meet
and throw back Byrd's army when it came. Much had to be
done, supplies collected, men alerted, drilled, and organized.

Sutherland felt weary, his body longing for rest after all he
had done; but his spirit spoke to him, and he knew he must go
on until his duty was done.

Once again an uneasy premonition of death came over him.
He stared at the crackling fire, not feeling its warmth.

Behind Sutherland, in the darkened lean-to, Gwen lay awake,
her head on her arm. The baby was asleep between them,
snuggled against his father, and Jeremy was leaning on his
elbow, looking at the child. Gwen stirred and smiled at her
husband, who caressed her cheek with the back of his hand.
Joy and relief and love filled her, but she saw the worry in
Jeremy's eyes.

She knew he was not so worried about their safety now, for
together they would somehow get through; nor was he concerned about his new reputation as a rebel spy among the
loyalists, for that was something only time would cure. When
Jeremy just then said what was on his mind, Gwen had expected
it.

"My father'll go on alone to the settlements, and to Pitt."
He spoke without emotion, glancing out at Sutherland's big
frame, silhouetted against the glow of the fire.

Gwen said, "You should go with him?" She wanted Jeremy
to stay at her side forever, through everything, whatever might
come.

He nodded once and kissed the sleeping baby.

Gwen said simply, "Then go, if you must."

He looked closely at her, his eyes showing admiration. She well knew he did not want to go.

Just then they heard Sutherland singing softly as he poked at the fire. It was an old Scottish song, one of those happy-sad ones that spoke of the *auld country* with feeling, but also welcomed the new life, the bold future in another land. From his own bed, Tamano joined in, for they had been together on many a trail, and had learned each other's songs, just as they had learned and traded music with French and Americans and a score of Indian tribes over the years.

So nearly everyone was awake. Jeremy squeezed Gwen's hand, got up, and went to sit by Sutherland, and as the song ended, they had tea together. Gwen lay listening to their hushed voices. Tamano joined them for a while. There was some shaking of heads, apparently a disagreement, but before long Jeremy returned and lay down. Tamano, too, went back to bed, and Sutherland stayed up to stand first watch.

Gwen waited for Jeremy to speak, and it was a relief when he said Sutherland insisted on going off alone. Jeremy would accompany her and the others back to the Falls. The argument had not lasted long, because everyone knew Sutherland was right: the women and children needed to be protected, and the eastern settlements had to be warned quickly.

Jeremy was restless that night, and for all her weariness, Gwen did not sleep well. In the middle of the night, she awoke to see him sitting up, though it was not yet his watch, and Tamano was by the fire. There was much to think about, and a farewell was coming upon them once again. In these times, no one ever knew what it really meant when good-byes were said.

PART TWO

1779—1780

chapter **9**

FORT PITT

There was no more enjoyable way for James Morely to spend the afternoon before Christmas than by playing a fast, rough game of shinty on the ice. In a quiet cove not far from Fort Pitt, he and a dozen other men and boys went at the small wooden ball with curved sticks, skating back and forth, each team trying to score in the other's goal.

In the warm months, shinty was played on fields, much like the Indian sport of lacrosse; but in the winter, when the rivers and lakes froze over and people had time on their hands, the game became immensely popular, played by men of every race. Few were better at it than James Morely. It was a grueling, heady combat, and although James was not the biggest or fastest, he was clever and brave, and knew how to use what muscle he had to good advantage. He could skate wonderfully well, and his shot was quick and very powerful.

No one could handle the ball more skillfully, and it was tough to get it away from him when he was attacking the goal. He played all that day, the winning team—usually his—holding the ice against all challengers. It was cold, but clear and sunny, and many folk from Fort Pitt and the nearby settlement had come down to the river for a stroll and to spend an hour watching the competition.

Since it was the day before a holiday, James and a few of the more prosperous regular players had arranged for a bonfire, with a drink and a slice of roast pig for whoever came. Four fat pigs were slowly turning over the fire, and there were kegs of ale and a bowl of hot buttered rum that never seemed to go empty. Many a toast was drunk to the health of the well-to-do shinty players that day.

As he took a break for another glass of rum, James regarded the diverse people from the fort and settlement who gathered along the bank to share his food and drink. By the looks of them, it was obvious Fort Pitt was not a wealthy community, but it was stable and deeply rooted here in the hills at the Forks of the Ohio—the confluence of the Allegheny River, which flowed in from the north, and the Monongahela River, up from the south. These streams became the mighty Ohio, a thousand miles long, rolling westward to the Mississippi. Pitt had been a military post, first French, then British, since the 1750s, and as ever was a strategic key to the defense of the northwest. Its people were British-Americans for the most part, with a few French *habitant* and trader families left over from before the conquest.

A large portion of the crowd were soldiers, some of the few hundred regular Continental troops stationed at Pitt. From Virginia and Pennsylvania, these men would rather be back on their farms but had to serve half a year in the dismal, clockwork garrisoning of this fort far from home. Had they been home, at least they would have eaten regularly, but at Pitt they were always hungry, for military supplies were low, and what was to be had was extremely expensive. With the terrible depreciation of Congress's paper money, the garrison commander could scarcely procure food, let alone clothing, blankets, and shoes, or provide decent housing for his war-weary men. This afternoon they ate and drank as much as they could politely consume, and James was glad he could make their lives a bit easier for at least one day.

Also in the festive crowd of spectators were the newcomers, homeless migrants from the East, who were still arriving daily, though it was the onset of winter. Intending to move down the

Ohio after the spring flood, these people were also often short of food and supplies. They came down to the shinty game from where they lived, crowded along the riverbank in lean-tos, shanties, tents, even under overturned flatboats. Some were formerly well-to-do but had been made poor by the war in the East, and often they were none too sympathetic with the cause of the rebels. Few were experienced frontiersmen, and scarcely any of them knew how to fight Indians. But it was the same with the regulars, except for some Virginians, who had been brought up under the shadow of the tomahawk.

At the apex of Fort Pitt society were a handful of fairly rich and middling traders and land speculators who socialized with the threadbare, though well-connected, army officers of Pennsylvania and Virginia. These, too, came for the fun of the shinty, and to taste the roast and the buttered rum. Not there, as was to be expected, was the man whose station was far above everyone else, and who was looked up to by all—Bradford Cullen, whose likes for wealth and influence had never before been seen at the fort.

Unlike these plain people of Fort Pitt—many of whom were loudly striking up the carol "God Rest Ye Merry, Gentlemen" as James finished his rum and hefted his shinty stick—Bradford Cullen did not have to be out here on the frontier. Yet it was inevitable that he should be, James knew, for Fort Pitt was the threshold of the vast, rich northwest, and from here everything would begin. Future campaigns against Detroit; government surveys for land disposition; sales of captured Indian country; plans for the dividing of the northwest among influential and wealthy rebels—all would be arranged here when the time came. No one would be in a better position to advise Congress about the northwest than Bradford Cullen, no one more able to profit from the northwest's future. Naturally, James Morely would take his own share of that future.

Skating toward the cleared ice along with several other sweaty, laughing men and boys, James listened to the lusty singing on land, and it made him feel good. He was uplifted by the raw power waxing strong at Pitt, and knew he was in the right place. After the Indians and British were defeated, this country would be thrown wide open to white settlement. Even if the British legally held on to the northwest, American settlers would ignore international law and take what they could, defying Congress, Parliament, and the Indians.

But all was in the future; for the moment, Fort Pitt was the only real protection for many miles around, a solitary, desperate place in time of Indian war. Yet it was stout and would be defended to the end. As for the outer town, beyond the earth-and-palisade citadel—Pittsburgh, as some were calling it—it was mainly shanties and cabins, the chief enterprise of many of its householders being the seedy taverns and inns that abounded.

Still, dockyards and sawmills were already thriving, with orders for boats and for housing lumber rising steadily, and some industrious souls had even begun digging coal in the nearby hills and selling it to owners of iron stoves. There was little in the way of culture, of course, but despite the town's isolation, something exciting was in the air, something in the attitude of these newcomers to Pitt. It was as if they knew bigger things were at hand for this country. They sensed they were pioneers, not only as settlers, but as the forgers of new communities, eventually of new states. They knew the future held prosperity for those who were able to capitalize on it. And like them, James was glad to be here. He had committed himself completely to building his new company with every resource at his disposal, and every ounce of his strength. He was happy, also, to have found shinty players for diversion.

Late that afternoon, with a red sun low over the western hills, James had skated enough. Perhaps he had even overdone it, for in the more than four years since leaving Detroit, he had taken several serious wounds, and these pained him from time to time. Nor was he in very good physical condition. Long days behind his desk in the merchant house he had opened in the settlement had not improved him, and he was acquiring a small but distinguished paunch.

As he skated off the playing ice, he heard his name called from shore and saw the attorney Noah Maxwell, bundled to the nose.

Shivering, looking unhealthy and thin-blooded, Maxwell cried, "Dinner tonight! Remember? At Mr. Cullen's?"

Yes, James thought, he and Noah Maxwell had been invited as the sole guests of Cullen and his matronly daughter, Linda. Though it was a tedious way to spend a Christmas Eve, James could not refuse after all Cullen had done to help him prosper. While other war merchants—including Owen Sutherland—were obliged to wait for payment from Congress or the states, Cullen had made immediate arrangements to have Virginia pay for James's portion of the cargo to George Rogers Clark. Cullen must have had enormous influence with the House of Burgesses in Williamsburg, who had paid in highly valuable tobacco, which had immediately been converted to Spanish silver dollars, now safeguarded by Cullen's agents back in Virginia.

James had drawn on this tidy sum, the profits being enough to start his own small company. From an office in a house he rented at the fort, he was doing a lively business arranging to supply the migrating settlers swarming through the community. Until that tide of people crested this coming summer, he would not get very rich, but he was happy.

Noah Maxwell was already working as an attorney for Cullen and Company, having given up his position with the eastern land speculators. Sharp and not very scrupulous, the dashing Maxwell was doing fine with Cullen, and was even making an attempt to woo Linda—but at this last he was less than successful. James knew Linda held a flame for himself.

As James skated toward his friends, he saw a sleigh standing nearby—the one that had carried Noah here—and in it was none other than Linda Cullen. She was chubby and squat, dressed in garishly purple riding clothes of the finest quality, but the loudest taste, and in her hat was a silk rose that stuck too far out on its stem. As Linda waved admiringly at James, the rose wobbled, looking somewhat like the antenna of an insect.

James waved back, observing how Linda was becoming ever more homely, her thick features and wide cheekbones making her singularly unattractive. That might not have been so bad if only her heart had been kind and innocent, but she was spoiled, a selfish whiner of the first rank. If not for the fact that Bradford Cullen doted on her and bought her friends and favors, Linda would have learned the bitter facts of life long ago. She would probably have become a kindly and reserved lady. Instead, she was boorish and overly talkative, pushy and childish, and usually got what she wanted if she pestered her father enough.

She was yoo-hooing at James, waving for him to come over,

when the game started up again, and someone called his name
for one last score. James gratefully took the opportunity, delaying the encounter with Linda, and darted out to stop a dangerous attack on his goal. He scarcely heard Linda's squeals
of excitement and the bone-chilled Noah's impatient cries. The
game became suddenly furious, and James found himself attacking the opponent's goal, thirty yards behind which was
Linda's sleigh. He thought only of the scoring, and with all
his might fired a tremendous shot that flashed toward the goal.
The ball clipped the crossbar and sailed right at Linda. Gaping
in amazement, she did not have the presence of mind to move
from her seat.

James gasped. Everyone stopped to watch. He whispered
"Duck!" Linda did not budge. The wooden ball struck the silk
rose, snipped it off, and tore through the sleigh top, leaving
her unscathed.

Squealing, Linda clapped her hands with excitement and
stood up in her seat, her adoring eyes fixed on James, who
was awestruck. Then Linda thought better of it, let out a long
moan, threw her stubby fingers to her forehead, and began,
slowly, to swoon.

James dashed toward her, skates and all. She took her time
before falling forward, heavily, into his waiting arms. Her
perfume almost made him queasy.

After a moment, her eyes fluttered open. An adoring smile
tugged at her mouth, and she flopped one arm over James's
neck. Next, she appeared to be asleep, or at least to have fainted
dead away.

Standing nearby, Noah Maxwell tipped his hat back, grinned,
and helped James right Linda in the carriage seat. Then he
climbed aboard and yanked James up. Someone tossed James
his shoes, and off went the sleigh. Maxwell winked at James
in admiration. He was a sport, acknowledging that James had
won Linda—and all the wealth she represented. If James wanted
her. It was true, James certainly coveted Cullen's wealth, but
not if Linda had to come with it.

Later than evening, after Linda had recovered, they met in the
magnificent Cullen residence. Wearing a flowered pink brocade
that reminded James of decayed swamp lilies, Linda babbled
on about how distressed she had been, how James had saved

her from a terrible fall, and what a powerful shot he had taken at the "enemy's" goal. She was as noisy as her gown, which had a plunging neckline that would have made Marie Antoinette blush, and her heels clattered like hammers on the floor as she came to take James's arm, ignoring Noah Maxwell.

"La!" she said, fluttering a green silk fan before her face—even though it was December—her eyelids moving almost as rapidly as the fan. "But I am so pleased you've come for Yuletide dinner, my dear Mr. Morely!" She sashayed, so that James was jogged a bit from side to side as they went down a candle-lit hallway toward the dining room where Bradford Cullen would soon appear.

Glancing back at Maxwell, James said that he, too, was glad to be here again: "I've been too much kept away by business since my return from downriver."

Linda pulled him to a halt, saying with a coy wink that she well knew James had been trying to get his new company, Morely Trading, off the ground, without the help of her father.

"You are so very bold, Mr. Morely," she fluttered. "La! Don't you think so, Mr. Maxwell?"

Maxwell grinned and bowed slightly to her, saying with a sideways glance at James, "Some would say rash, Mistress Cullen—but, yes, our friend is bold in his ambitious designs for success."

James was casual, taking Maxwell's cynical remarks with a smile. Indeed, it was something to challenge Cullen and Company directly. Despite his rising stature in the Fort Pitt commercial community, James was feeling the vast bulk of Bradford Cullen looming over every aspect of economic ventures, from land sales to shipping, construction to money-lending.

Still, it had helped James enormously that Cullen had promptly found a way to turn into cash George Rogers Clark's promissory notes for the goods James had brought to the Falls of the Ohio. James could not deny the attraction of all that an alliance with Bradford Cullen could give him, and there were times when he thought he should take the offer and help manage Cullen and Company. Yet he was making a mark on his own, and doing quite well at it.

And now he had been invited to Cullen's lavish home, along with Noah Maxwell. There must be something important behind it, something more than just a social visit. Cullen seldom invited anyone to his house.

As Linda chattered idly on his arm, propelling him forward again, James took in the carved balustrades, the Chippendale furniture, ornate and beautiful, and the thick Persian carpets on highly polished floors. For all his purported Puritan upbringing, Bradford Cullen had spared nothing in the opulent decoration of this mansion on the edge of a wilderness. James could not think of a single house in all the northwest that could compare with Cullen's residence here in the center of the citadel. It had been two houses once, and Cullen had remade them into a stout fortress from without, a palace within.

James hardly heard Linda cooing and *la*-ing as he walked into the lamplit dining room. He was too absorbed by the incredible richness of everything. Linda was talking effusively about the new English furniture she had ordered that had just arrived directly from New York. How it had come James could not imagine, for New York was in British hands. Linda declared that she was sure James would adore her choice of style. Indeed, he could see that for all her clumsiness, garish dress, and awkward manners, Linda did have excellent taste in the furnishing of a mansion, in the trappings of limitless wealth.

The long table in the dining room fairly glittered with silver and candles and gleaming crystal. On one wall was a full-length painting of a severe, thin woman, whom James recognized as the deceased Helen Cullen, Bradford's wife, and one of the two people in the world who could tell the old man what to do. Linda was the other. James suspected that it was Linda who had invited him tonight, and perhaps Maxwell was there as an up-and-coming young employee who interested Cullen. Whatever the reason for his own presence, James Morely was now glad to be here. It had been far too long since he had taken the time to experience firsthand the fruits of Bradford Cullen's immensely successful labors in a mercantile empire that spanned the globe. Chippendale chairs at rebel Fort Pitt, fresh from British New York, indeed!

James smiled to himself, and he saw Maxwell wink, as if the lawyer could sense James's admiration of this place. As Linda was seated in a flurry of fan and frilly clothing, James moved from behind her chair, pausing a moment when he heard ponderously slow shuffling and the clump of a heavy cane coming down the hall through which they had just walked. The door opened, and in floated the French manservant, Auguste, tall and thin, with a nose like a downturned teakettle spout. Auguste had been silent, as ever, walking in the hallway. The steady shuffling came closer until into the light of the room moved Bradford Cullen himself, squat and fleshy, with a mighty curled wig, old-fashioned, and spilling over his sloping shoulders. He looked like a toad with glittering, small eyes that saw everything.

James and Maxwell bowed, and Cullen paused to observe them, measuring them until he appeared satisfied with what he saw, and then he bowed graciously, for all his bulk, to his daughter. He kissed her pudgy hand and wished her a happy Christmas. As he straightened as much as he was able to, Cullen raised the silver head of his cane to acknowledge the two young men.

Cullen looked every bit the refined gentleman of wealth. When the man smiled, he appeared almost kindly, grand-fatherly, with the charm of a born politician or businessman. James had no illusions about Cullen's ruthlessness, but at moments such as these, he admired Cullen's ability, by a simple glance, to make those around him feel important. After all, Bradford Cullen was one of the leading men in America, even in all the British empire.

Cullen wheezed, his belly jouncing as he chuckled and said in a hoarse voice, "Mr. Morely, it does do these old eyes good to see you at my table once again!" He shook hands, and though he was fat, his hand was strong and cool. "It's been too long since you've visited me and my darling daughter—" He smiled at Linda. "Too long especially for Linda, I'll warrant!"

She again pretended coyness, and her eyes fluttered behind her fan. James smiled politely and noticed Maxwell grinning. The lawyer was enjoying Cullen's none too subtle remarks about Linda's romantic feelings for James Morely, who was uneasy to hear them.

Then Cullen said, almost seriously, "And too long for myself as well, sir! How ever will I keep track of what my competitors are doing if I cannot have them at my table and pick their brains while they are distracted by good meat and drink?" He stamped the cane. "Little enough good meat and drink there is in this country these days!"

It was all formal and correct, though amicable enough, and James found himself easily flattered by Cullen. James did not mind the idle talk and the free-flowing compliments, and during the course of a sumptuous meal, he found himself again aware that Cullen had considerable respect for his abilities as a merchant.

It was difficult for James to believe the terrible accusations about Bradford Cullen, especially those from Owen Sutherland, who even suspected Cullen of having arranged the murder of James's own father years ago. Cullen had only words of admiration and respect for Garth Morely, having known him in the frontier trade ever since the French wars. As for Cullen's having allegedly hired gangs of killers to prey on the Frontier Company over the years, James had once believed that, but could believe it no longer, now that he knew the man better.

Cullen was no angel, but no one in frontier commerce was— not even Garth Morely, a hard and shrewd man. James believed it when Cullen said Garth had been more influential in establishing the Frontier Company than had Owen Sutherland, though it was Sutherland who got all the credit. Certainly Cullen ought to know, having competed with the Frontier Company since its inception. The old man was a mercantile wizard, and nothing escaped him.

Cullen seemed to know everything that happened out here, and he brought that point home to James once more as, over after-dinner brandies, he said, "Mr. Morely, in the months since your return from the Kentucky country, you've put yourself in a position to double your profits!"

James smiled, saying it was so. Cullen apparently had taken close inventory of James's interests in lumber, gunpowder, and flatboat building. James's prices and the quality of his firm's work had attracted considerable business.

In between Linda's occasional empty-headed spouting, Cullen remarked that another ten thousand emigrants would be passing down the Ohio River in the coming year, and he said the way things were going, all of them would know about James's firm before they even arrived here from Virginia or Pennsylvania. He wondered aloud why that was.

Noah Maxwell interjected, "Settlers know about Morely's firm while they're still as far away as New Jersey, New York, and Connecticut. Remarkable!"

James blushed a bit. He had established a network of agents on commission throughout the populous, war-ravaged middle colonies, arranging presigned contracts for boats and supplies to be ready at Pitt for prospective emigrants. Contracts were made even before the traveling parties had departed their home towns. Most emigrants traveled in groups and were well organized, with leaders and the rudiments of self-government before they reached the frontier. James had organized a system of credit whereby the travelers were first informed about what they would need, and then were persuaded to sign contracts for Morely Trading goods and wares because his prices were so low. James employed only the most reputable agents, men known and trusted by the prospective travelers, and that had done the trick more than anything else.

At first, James did not intend to reveal the workings of his credit and contracts, but it soon became clear that Cullen's informants had already discovered it. Cullen was again generous in his praise, saying that Noah Maxwell was the one who had managed to uncover all the details of this clever new system.

Cullen said, "And Mr. Maxwell is now a respected member of my firm—a minor partner, I'm pleased to say."

As Maxwell beamed, James nodded and said Cullen and Company was fortunate to have him. Though he did not voice it, James wondered whether Maxwell was still maneuvering for Linda's hand and the Cullen inheritance. His thoughts were abruptly altered, however, when Linda said in a childlike way that obviously startled even her father:

"We would so love to have you with us, too, Mr. Morely. La! We would, indeed, wouldn't we, Papa? Oh, with all our hearts, Mr. Morely!"

Cullen chuckled as Maxwell smiled and said, "Then we wouldn't have to spy on you to keep track of your blessed inventiveness! And with us, you wouldn't find it necessary to be so blessed inventive just to keep yourself afloat!"

Linda's fan fluttered rapidly. Maxwell glanced at Cullen, who was stolidly gazing at James. James said he was flattered by the offer, then looked at Cullen and added, "If offer it was, sir."

After a moment of silence, in which Auguste elegantly poured coffee for all of them, Cullen breathed out slowly as he eyed Maxwell and Linda.

"Perhaps," he said to his daughter, "Mr. Maxwell would enjoy taking coffee with you in the parlor. Mr. Morely and I will join you momentarily."

Linda was obedient, as was Maxwell, who James thought would make a good attorney for Cullen and Company. Maxwell was brilliant, especially when it came to looking out for his own interests and making a profit wherever he could. Maxwell knew much about land speculation in the northwest, and Cullen could not have a better ally to help him compete with strong eastern syndicates of speculators.

James and Cullen were left alone. The doors were closed, and the dining room was silent, except for the crackling fire and Cullen's rasping breath. The atmosphere seemed to darken, to become more intense.

James remarked that Linda and Maxwell looked to be a fine couple, but Cullen guffawed, and with a wheeze said the attorney was not the man for her.

He eyed James closely and said, "What about it, my lad? Will you join Cullen and Company as a partner? A *major* partner?"

James could not help but feel a thrill at the prospect of sudden wealth and power, but he fought down that feeling, for he had plans for his own company, plans that would one day prove him every bit as successful as Cullen, and honest enough for Owen Sutherland.

Smiling politely despite his pounding heart, James considered a moment before he said, "I pray I might be worthy of such an offer, Mr. Cullen, but as you know, I have good prospects for my own firm, and so I must regretfully decline to accept." He paused, then said, "Of course, I would be happy to collaborate on joint ventures."

Cullen laughed, his wet, red mouth glistening in the light of the lamps. "Ah, yes, you are an ambitious and precocious young man! Well, I won't do much business *with* you, for I want *you*, not your business! Yet I daresay it won't be easy for me to compete with so youthful a genius at the trade, not as old and decrepit as I'm becoming!"

James was embarrassed and tried to mutter away Cullen's

self-deprecation, saying he was sure Cullen knew more than he himself would ever know. Cullen almost rudely interrupted, waving a finger and saying that was not true.

"The world is fast changing! Times are becoming far more complex than I ever knew them to be! Why, there are banking houses springing up everywhere, and they are the real force of the future, not the bold and clever trader and merchant who takes his chances and wins a contest of wills here and there! No, it's the financiers, the bankers who will rule one day, not merchants! Times are not what we once knew. International finance will supplant international trade, and nations will rise and fall on the whim of a few bankers, whether those bankers be in Paris or London or Philadelphia!"

He seemed thrilled by the prospect of the world's commerce, kings, governments, and economies being ruled by a handful of men behind the scenes. James had to admit it was an interesting, unexpected thought. It made sense when Cullen said capital was the power of the future, not goods, not wares, not even armies.

Cullen leaned over the table and whispered, "I have built an empire scarcely matched on this continent, but I built it in another time, in the old way, controlling a market, a commodity, and . . . with some clever imagination!" His expression became gloomy, his small eyes distant. "But my empire cannot last in the face of what is coming. Already, millions of French *livres* are beginning to flood the independent states, changing the complexion of our economy. Only the man who can comprehend, manipulate, and master the money game, international finance, the banking game, the game of huge loans and interest and denial of loans and interest—only he will endure the mighty quakes that will shake our way of life to its very foundations! Shake Cullen and Company, shake America, England, France! Only men like Noah Maxwell and yourself can build upon what I have created, can perpetuate the name, renew the vigor of Cullen and Company, and see to it that my blood heirs will be masters of their destinies, masters of America's destiny, masters of the age to come!"

Cullen was sweating from the emotional outpouring of this inflamed speech. As an aside, James wondered whether the man really expected to have blood heirs born before he died. Linda was past marriageable age, with no prospects in sight save for Maxwell; but Cullen had just said he would not accept the lawyer as his successor.

Cullen's beady eyes were fixed on James, who remained calm, well aware that if anyone knew what was coming upon the world and America in the next few years, it was Cullen. James knew Cullen had firm ties to wealthy loyalists in British-held Canada as well as to powerful rebel statesmen. No matter who won the rebellion, no matter whether the northwest was free or still a British colony, Cullen would make the most of the situation. For all James's ambitions, he knew Cullen and Company would remain well on top for many years to come.

Then, out of the blue, Cullen said, "I would give all I owned to the man who gave me a blood heir!"

James was startled, especially when Cullen's eyes were so penetrating. Neither man moved.

After a moment, James looked at the table top and said, "Maxwell could—"

"Not Maxwell!"

James stared back, their gazes locked—not challenging, but rather searching, questioning what the other was thinking.

James cleared his throat and said, "The man who marries Linda will be most fortunate—"

"Everything!" Cullen slammed the table, so that it shook and the silverware rattled, the candles flickering.

James smoothly recovered. "Forgive my presumptuousness, sir—if presumptuous I am being—but I do not love your daughter."

They stared at each other again, Cullen finally softening, a smile creeping over his face. He leaned back, letting his hand slide slowly over the tablecloth as he began to chuckle.

"Love . . . yes, yes, that's what I expected." He laughed, shaking his head slowly. "Well, my lad, you are indeed a man of the times, yes you are! Not so long ago your worthy father—rest his soul—and I would have arranged the match, and you both would have been obedient and appreciative! But now you would marry for . . ." He chuckled lightly. "For love!"

James smiled, for Cullen exuded good feeling and friendliness. James said, "Times have changed, sir."

Cullen cocked his head and, looking at James, whispered, "The girl loves you, do you know that?"

James flushed, and scratched his forehead, saying, "No, I did not."

"With all her innocent heart, she does, indeed!"

Innocent? Hardly.

Cullen pressed. "And I have ever striven to please her, for she means more to me than all the wealth and all the power!" He was actually becoming sentimental, and for the first time, James saw the depth of this other aspect of Bradford Cullen— the tyrannical merchant prince as a doting, indulgent, and almost desperate father. He wanted not only a blood heir, but a man to make his daughter's life complete, happy.

Cullen's shaky voice was pitiable as he said, "I have given her everything, everything . . . but this! She would be so overjoyed for the rest of her days, and . . . and at the same time, she would give me an heir!" He nodded, his expression almost pathetic as he looked at James and repeated, "An heir!"

James had no reply. After a moment, he sat up straighter and said only, "I understand, sir."

Slowly, Cullen collected himself before saying, "I would be proud to have you as a partner in my company, but prouder still to have you as Linda's husband."

James found himself unexpectedly agitated, moved powerfully by the thought of wealth beyond all imagining. Yet he had his own plans, and in the back of his mind was the thought of Susannah Sutherland. She was still too young to marry, but when her time came, she would be a woman any man would be fortunate to have as his wife. Linda Cullen was not for James Morely, but could he say that to her father?

He tried: "As I said before, sir, I do not love—"

Cullen hissed, "You need not love her, man! Don't you see that? Just marry her, get her with a son, and treat her kindly, is all I ask!" He leaned forward, his hand almost touching James's. "Just never betray her openly, whether you love her or not, and swear that your son will be my successor!"

"Mr. Cullen!" James stood up quickly, and Cullen leaned back, eyes half closing. It was hard for James to go on, and he was breathing fast, thinking of the incredible prospects, his emotions whirling. "Please, sir, let us go no further with this! I'm happy as I am, with my little company, and as a bachelor!"

Cullen became cold and relaxed once again. "As you wish."

With effort, he stood up, and a genial smile crossed his face. He clapped James on the shoulder and said they should join the others. "Should you wish to renew the subject, Mr. Morely, I am at your service." Then he gripped James's arm and said in a whisper, "Everything!"

As they went out to join Maxwell and Linda, James believed he would never want to renew this conversation unless he were in desperate straits. To possess Bradford Cullen's estate would be wonderful, and James could manage it so that it would be a blessing both for himself and for the greater good of America. But to marry Linda to have it was too much to ask.

In any case, he would not join Cullen and Company as long as his own prospects looked so bright.

chapter **10**

TIDINGS OF WAR

"Do you bite your thumb at us, sir?"

"I do bite my thumb, sir."

"Do you bite your thumb at us, sir?"

Upon a puncheon platform, backed by the wide Ohio that was frozen and white in the January sunshine, Benjamin Sutherland leaned over to speak to a short Virginia boy. Both were dressed in flowing robes and feathered caps, just as Susannah Sutherland imagined two Capulets would have paraded about Verona in the setting of *Romeo and Juliet*.

Benjamin liked this scene best of all, though it was only the lighthearted opening of Shakespeare's tragedy. He was cast as a troublemaking kinsman of Juliet Capulet, and also on stage with him and the Virginia Capulet were two youths as Montagues.

The last question had come from a Montague, and Benjamin winked at his Capulet companion, asking, "Is the law on our side if I say aye?"

"No," was the answer from the Capulet, who stared brazenly at the two young Montagues, who were just as eager to pick a fight. As it happened, the Montagues were Pennsylvanians.

Benjamin smiled smugly at the Montagues. "No, sir, I do not bite my thumb at you, sir..." He bit the tip of his thumb, his other hand resting lightly on his father's heavy claymore, which portrayed the deadly rapier that would have suited a Verona dandy of the age. "...but I bite my thumb, sir!"

He bit it again, close to the surly face of the Montague, and the throng of blanket-wrapped frontier folk crowding about the stage stamped their feet and clapped their hands in approval of the Capulet's insolence. They called for blood.

The Montague felt for a wooden sword at his belt, inadvertently getting his hand tangled in his unaccustomed robes. He hesitated, looking down at the fouled weapon as he demanded, "Do you quarrel, sir?"

The audience shouted, "Aye! Quarrel! Bite your thumb! Bite his nose! Gouge his eyes! Go on, lads."

The rest of the dialogue was drowned out by the enthusiastic mob. Sitting on a bench set up in a wagon, with colorful banners streaming overhead, Ella Sutherland watched Susannah become fidgety and pace back and forth at the side of the stage. After all the work getting these lines right with the cloddish boys, Susannah wanted them to make their words heard, and she waved her mittened hands for the audience to be quiet. She was bundled warmly, save for her head and the flowing curls that had fallen from where she had pinned them up.

Susannah was as nervous as any young play producer must be at her first attempt, especially because *Romeo and Juliet* meant so much to her. She had taken heart when the entire community had enthusiastically approved the idea of creating a performing company. It was made up mostly of young folk, with a few older ones pressed into service for roles that simply had to have them, according to Susannah's thinking. This was the very first performance.

"You lie!" rose above the crowd, from the Montague boy trying to tug his sword clear of sheath and flowing robe. Susannah gasped as the robe was torn. After all her sewing! The crowd roared in approval.

Benjamin Capulet yelled, "Draw, if you be men!"

Out came the swords, including Benjamin's claymore in defense of the Capulets, and the fight began, mock at first, but when Benjamin took an accidental whack on the nose, he shoved a Montague, who tumbled backward, legs tangled in his over-long robe. The other Montague used the wooden sword on Benjamin's shins, but Benjamin dared not even defend himself with the dangerous claymore, and he swung his free hand at the fellow. The fallen Montague sprang to his feet and went at Benjamin while the crowd cheered.

On cue from a frantic Susannah, an energetic Benvolio arrived, shouting far more often than the script called for, "Part, you fools!" Then, "Leave off, drat you, lunkheads!"

Benvolio was tall, lanky Mel Webster, friend to the Suth-erlands, an eccentric inventor and teacher of the Indians, who had adopted him, calling him Singing Bow, for the magic of his fiddle. Mel-Benvolio could have used some magic just then, if only to get the play to move along past the opening brawl. His cap was knocked off as he tried to keep Benjamin from punching the boy with the wooden sword, and his blond hair caught the bright sunlight as he darted between the combatants. Mel must have been a tempting target for Benjamin's insolent protector, the mute blue jay named Punch. The bird appeared from nowhere, struck Mel a resounding peck on his head, and turned him around in a spin, flailing and cursing while the audience loved every minute of it.

All but Susannah, of course. She saw her work being ruined in a stupid moment of temper. It was just like these quarrelsome Virginia and Pennsylvania backwoodsmen to look for a fight, but for Benjamin it was unforgivable. Furious, Susannah threw herself into the fray, knocking aside one Capulet, or perhaps it was a Montague, and grabbing Benjamin—who was a head taller than she—by the ear. She yanked him away while the crowd stamped their feet and applauded, and the ever-alert Mel-Benvolio recovered from his stinging head to clear his eyes, which were tearing, and to call upon Tybalt, waiting in the wings. Tybalt hurried up the steps, followed by a few others, backers of Montague and Capulet, who joined in the now prop-erly staged brawl.

Lady Capulet—a young Pennsylvania farm girl—and her husband—another Pennsylvanian, who had pasted on some facial hair plucked from the tail of a white deer—also strode onto the stage. They were joined by Virginians as the Mon-tagues, and the Shakespearean insults flew, followed promptly by the arrival of the Prince of Verona, whose entrance was tardy, and so he was dragged onto the stage by Susannah. The prince was big, good-looking Tom Morely, wearing a false gray beard, and he could not help giggling as soon as he began, "Rebellious subjects—"

Tom was the older brother of James Morely and was a fun-loving fellow, dark and boyish, happily married to Sally Cooper Morely, who had been raised by the Sutherlands as a foster child. Sally was near the stage, in the pit, gesticulating for Tom not to laugh. That made things worse, as he fought down his mirth and managed to bluster, "Profaners of this steighbor-stained neel!" Which should have been "neighbor-stained steel," and that did it for Tom, although most in the audience had no idea why he was in hysterics, not realizing his mistake and not caring, for it was all such good fun.

Susannah was leaning in from the wings, calling out the correct lines, but that made Tom all the more giddy. Ella Sutherland was trying not to laugh herself, seeing how upset Susannah was.

For months, Susannah had been preparing this play, and the whole settlement and the fort garrison had been eager for it. Soldiers had built the wooden puncheon platform, and many women had sewn the pennants, streamers, and costumes, using old clothes and whatever spare material was at hand. The players, adults and children, had rehearsed night after night for weeks, with Susannah patiently coaching them. But now it was nearly ruined.

Susannah was just about in tears, while everyone else was delirious with laughter, for any kind of entertainment was a much-needed relief from the hardships of winter here at the Falls. Around the audience several bonfires burned, and a bower of pine boughs had been erected nearby for a feast that would follow the play.

Now, if only Susannah could either get control of the play, or start to enjoy the hilarity like all the rest. Of course she was to play Juliet, while a boy from North Carolina was a halfhearted Romeo. He was handsome and tall and a beautiful speaker, as Susannah had deemed essential, but he was awkwardly shy before an audience. That problem would come later, if Susannah could get them through Tom Morely's giggling.

She did, loudly crying out the prompting words, "Once

more, on pain of death, all men depart!"

The accommodating Tom repeated those words, too late realizing they were the cue for him, in particular, to depart. He backed off the stage, surprised, still laughing, leaving the others to carry on with the tragic tale of ill-starred young love.

It was quite a success after all, and Ella thought Susannah a captivating Juliet. The people of the settlement had not had so much fun in years, certainly not since the Indian wars broke out back in 1776. The feast that followed was joyous, with everyone contributing some special, hoarded goods to the table. Mel brought out his fiddle, as did Sally Morely, and with a jew's-harp, pennywhistle, and a couple of enthusiastic singers, the dancing got under way upon the hard-packed snow in the center of the settlement.

In the midst of the dancers was Colonel George Rogers Clark himself, robust and hearty, red hair falling over his buck-skin shirt. He was not yet thirty, but no man in America bore such responsibility for defending so much territory.

Ella, in her own flatboat, which was now pulled up on shore, watched the younger children and kept the babies happy. More than once she cast her gaze across the frozen Ohio, wondering where her other loved ones were.

Late that afternoon, when the dancing had ended, a courier to Clark arrived, tramping across the ice, and brought Ella a letter from Vincennes. To her joy, it was from Jeremy, who said they had reached there safely, thanks to the fear Clark's army had instilled in the Indians of the Wabash and the Illinois. There had been little danger after the encounter with Amaghwah, said Jeremy, adding that he and Tamano knew so many of the Indians in that region that they were aided at every turn and sent safely on their way to Vincennes, reaching there by Christmas.

The letter told of Owen's mission, and Ella tried not to let that upset her, for she had every faith in her husband's return, and it was too hard to think of what he might be enduring right then. The next troubling news was word that the baby, Richard, had been sickly, the constant exposure being too much for him. There had not been enough time to rest and let him recover fully during the escape south.

"Depending on flood waters, you can look for us in April

or May," Jeremy wrote, "and we will then plan whether to stay at the Falls or make our way upriver. But I fear Richard will not endure the journey, and we may be compelled to stay in one place until he becomes stronger."

Jeremy did not write of the imminent British attack that spring, for if such information fell into the wrong hands, it might cause panic and immediate flight eastward. It was up to Clark to explain other matters further, Jeremy wrote, adding, "It would be well for you to be prepared to move as soon as we arrive, for there may be little time to travel in safety, as you soon will learn."

That very afternoon, Clark himself called the settlement together, and as he stood on the puncheon platform, he told them they should prepare for the worst. The people were quiet as they heard the news. The celebration was over.

"Whatever the adversity, friends, we'll not run without a fight!" He seemed taller, stronger, as he stood above the silent people, and it was apparent to Ella why he was the great leader he was. His voice was steady and carried across the settlement. He was decisive, clear, without a trace of doubt or anxiety.

"We have learned that the threat comes not alone against our eastern frontier, but against the Illinois as well, and even against the Spanish settlement of St. Louis, according to our agents."

He paused, and it might have been that he was looking into the heart of every man and woman there, to discover whether they would stand or flee. Ella knew that plenty of small land speculators and otherwise uncommitted newcomers were here simply to stake a claim and sell again at a profit. These always fled when trouble broke out, leaving permanent settlers in the lurch. It might have been to these men that Clark was speaking next.

"The land office at Harrodsburg will be closed immediately, and no sales will be permitted, by my order according to the authority vested in me by the sovereign Commonwealth of Virginia."

Grumbles and questions rose in the crowd, but he spoke loudly to still them.

"Furthermore, patrols will be stationed at the mountain passes, to prevent the enemy from cutting off communication with the seaboard country . . ." He paused significantly, before adding, ". . . and to forbid the flight of any able-bodied men from the frontier."

At first there was silence. Then followed a shout of approval from those who had put down roots, who had fought alongside Clark. They cheered him wildly, and it was a thrilling moment for Ella. Everyone knew failure meant death or captivity, and the loss of all they owned, all they had built up over the past bloody years of danger and sacrifice. Clark, if anyone could, would meet this great threat, and his people would be there with him.

Late that evening, as Susannah and Ella lay in bed—Benjamin, with Heera, was out on patrol—Ella sensed that Susannah was troubled. She rose, left her small sleeping alcove, and went to look in on Susannah, who was lying close by. The flatboat was hushed and darkened; the only sound was the soft snoring of Tom Morely from the alcove where he and Sally and their son, Timothy, slept.

Ella opened Susannah's curtain, and by the light of a moon shining on the snow outside the window, she saw her daughter was awake. It was still remarkable to Ella how she and Susannah were able to communicate without speaking. An instinctive understanding bound them, an understanding beyond words.

Ella sat down on the edge of the bed and touched her daughter's hand. Susannah took hold, and they stayed in silence for a while. Ella knew the girl had been shaken by the sudden heightening of danger, but also sensed that the danger was not what was keeping her awake just then. She waited for Susannah to speak, which she did after a while.

"Must all love . . . true love . . . must it always have such profound sorrow with it?"

Ella saw the glint of tears in her daughter's eyes. Susannah turned away, as if to hide them, and sniffed softly.

Ella understood what she meant. "Romeo and Juliet are merely characters in a play, dear one. You are not Juliet, any more than that boy was Romeo today."

Susannah looked back at her, taking a shaky breath and sighing as she said, "Oh, I know that, Mother, but . . . it just seems that the love such as Romeo and Juliet shared was too good for this wicked world. And that . . . that their love could not have ended any other way than it did. In sorrow. Or maybe some would call that a beautiful death, but I'd much rather they had lived happily."

She looked at her mother, intensity in her moist eyes as she said, "Romeo was rash and proud and even foolhardy, perhaps, but he was so fine, so good in his heart, though the Montagues hated him. . . ."

She stopped, as if what she had to say was too foolish, but Ella pressed, "You want to say he was like James Morely, don't you?" Ella tried to smile, but Susannah's heartache was simply too heavy for that. Susannah sighed that it was so. Ella replied, "But none of us hate James, or wish him ill, Susannah."

"Sometimes I think Pa does not like him, hard as he tries, and that's so unfair, Mother! He doesn't understand James, and maybe never will."

Ella gripped Susannah's hand, though still trying to be light, and saying, "He'll never think James a Romeo, or you a Juliet!"

Susannah withdrew her hand and let it drop to the covers listlessly.

"No, Pa is so unromantic, so unfeeling about such things. . . ."

Susannah said that all her father understood was war and commerce and smelly Indians. Ella closed her eyes, thought about Owen's passion, how he had swept her away in the midst of an Indian war, and how their love had grown from an unsuspecting first glance to what it was today—lasting, unshakable, and beautiful beyond words.

She said gently, "Be kind when you speak of your father, dear, for you are not old enough or woman enough to know what you are saying."

Susannah obviously felt that, and it gave her voice a twinge of annoyance. "I understand enough—maybe more than all of you think! Especially my father!"

"That may be, Susannah, but only time will tell—time and your good character . . . and the good character of your Romeo."

Again, Ella had meant to be light, but Susannah did not take it that way at all.

"If Pa was all that you say he is, then why isn't he here now, with us? Why has he always been away during this war, instead of home with us, where he should be? If he loved us so much, it wouldn't be so easy for him to go off—"

"Enough!" Ella stood up. "It's not for you to judge him, Susannah! But just remember one thing: he's ours with every bit of himself he can give, but he belongs to others, too—to America itself! And I love him all the more for that. I love him all the more for what he gives our people, because I know there's no place on earth he'd rather be than with us right now. When you're woman enough to understand, you'll know that, too!"

Susannah made no reply; she seemed hardly moved by Ella's speech. Ella gathered herself, but tears were welling up. It hurt to have Susannah be so hard on Owen at a time like this! Ella understood, however, and so would he. If only he would return to them soon. She needed him now. How she ached for him, as did Susannah, though the child did not know it herself.

On a ridge overlooking the vast white expanse of frozen Lake Erie, a lone figure hurried along a trail, breaking his way through drifted snow, moving and moving without pause to rest.

The legs lifted and fell, one stumbling after the other, in a supreme effort to cover ground. A stinging wind whipped off the frozen lake, icy and mixed with snow, concealing the man's tracks almost as soon as they were made. The sky was cloudy, telling of a storm close behind that wind, and Owen Sutherland prayed the bad weather would hit soon, for he could not run much farther.

He clambered along the face of a rock outcrop that hung over the edge of the lake. He kept to the cover of the cliff, pushing on hard, his breath coming in burning gasps, and his body like lead, aching all over. He found a place to slow and look back at the shore trail over which he had come. There was no sign of them yet, and if they did not close with him soon, the wind would wipe away his tracks, making it difficult to follow. Unless those Shawnee could smell his spoor.

Breathing hard, he peered along the edge of ice, where a massive rise of high ground concealed the rest of the trail from view. Surely they were there, somewhere, coming on, and they must know he was still in front of them. For two long weeks they had been after him, forcing him to dodge, to hide, to backtrack and lie low for days at a time. But always they found his trail and hunted him like wolves.

Yes! He saw the first one, running along the snow-covered ice, staggering more than running, carrying a rifle as though it weighed a hundred pounds. No wonder the warrior was exhausted, for he and his companions had been in sight of Sutherland on and off for three days, close enough to fire once or twice, and for him to fire back when he had to. Now he could cut down this first man, but the others might not be far behind and would hear the shot. There was still the slight chance that he might throw them off by following this icy rock path, which left no tracks. But that chance was slight indeed.

He looked once more at the Shawnee. The man was giving out, and he fell momentarily, remaining on hands and knees, head down. He was tough and fast and determined, fighting to his feet again. If he kept up his grueling pace, he might just catch Sutherland. It would be the last thing he ever did, though. Yet Sutherland hoped he would not have to shoot the man and thus give himself away. He had another plan, one that was desperate and a gamble, but if the Shawnee had trouble finding his trail, it just might work.

He pushed on against a gusting wind. He stayed to the rock, slipping painfully now and again on ice, until his body was skinned and bruised, his clothing wet and stiff. He made his way along the frozen track, avoiding leaving prints in pockets of snow. He hoped against hope that he was right in believing his destination was just beyond these outcropping rocks.

Soon, he came around the outcrop, into a cove, and the wind lessened, giving him a chance to catch his breath. Shading his eyes against the gray glare, he stared for some sign of what he wanted to find, his chest heaving, every breath raw and cold.

There it was! Smoke rising from the trees at the edge of the lake told him this was the place he was seeking. He had to try it, for he could not outrun his pursuers much longer. He struggled on, making right for a tiny Indian village.

chapter 11

MEN OF THE NORTHWEST

One afternoon in early February, James and Maxwell went skating on the Allegheny River, below the ramparts of the fort. As usual, Maxwell was saying how James had lost his mind to decline an offer of partnership in Cullen and Company, and as usual, James said he did not want to talk about it. James had mentioned nothing of how Cullen had tried to get him to marry Linda, because Maxwell was still working at his own chances to win her hand.

Maxwell said, "I know you think old Cullen is an ogre and scarce to be trusted, but it doesn't matter, for he won't last another two winters, and he'll never make a trip back east again!"

James was enjoying his skating, and he leaped and pirouetted, hardly hearing what his friend was saying. Maxwell, a clumsy skater at best, doggedly followed, this being the only way he could get a chance to talk privately with James for any length of time, because James was such a hard worker, almost driven in his obsession to make Morely Trading Company a success.

"Hear me out, please!" He skated toward James, who flew through a figure eight and began to circle him so that the lawyer's arms flapped as he tried to turn and keep his balance. "He's already given over his legal affairs into my hands, and I practically handle all his bookkeeping as well! Will you stop circling! He's richer than even he knows, and men such as you and I could redouble the fortune in no time! Hey, I'm getting dizzy!"

Maxwell's feet almost skidded out from under him as James changed direction and he tried to keep up. James laughed and took a moment to show him how to stay up on his runners and push off, from one foot to the other.

Maxwell gamely struggled with it, but his thoughts were elsewhere. "Look, man," he blustered as he caught himself on James's shoulder, "I'll be Linda's husband soon, and with you as my major partner, we'll make Cullen and Company greater than ever before—"

"You'll have to stop Morely Trading Company first!" He skated away, enjoying Maxwell's near helplessness.

"Dash it all, man! You're going against the grain! Against the current! Crosswind! Don't you see? Even with the old man still alive, we can manipulate the books, the legal matters, all in our favor, so that we will become Morely and Maxwell and Company, and Cullen and Company will be the name only! Even the old ogre can't do a thing about it once we gain control!" He bent over, hands on knees, legs trembling from the effort to balance himself.

James slowed, skating sideways, feet askew, thinking of the gravity of what was being said. Maxwell was actually offering to alter Cullen and Company documents in order to take power even before Cullen died. James wanted no part of it and shook his head.

"You'll certainly make a good accomplice for Cullen, Noah!"

Maxwell was annoyed and followed James, but as his quarry again changed direction, he found himself unable to stop while he grumbled, "And what precisely is that supposed to mean?" He managed to turn awkwardly, but James was no longer there. Instead, he was rushing across the ice toward a distant figure who was approaching slowly, coming out of the snow-covered forest on the other side of the river.

Maxwell attempted to follow, but James left him far behind,

skating swiftly toward the tall, buckskin-clad man on the ice.
It was Owen Sutherland.

James saw that Sutherland was weak, gaunt, and exhausted.
He caught him under the arm and held him up as the Scotsman
said with a faint laugh that this was a pleasant coincidence.
Sutherland looked wan, even though his skin was burned from
snow and sun. He swayed slightly as he moved onto James's
shoulder, and James took the rifle, asking why Sutherland had
come here like this.

"And what about the others?" he quickly added, his fear
rising. "Are they all right? Have you been attacked?"

Sutherland slowly shook his head. "What day is it?" James
told him. "The month?" He seemed relieved, saying, "There
is yet time." Briefly, he explained how he had come down from
Detroit with the warning for the settlements and Fort Pitt.

"I've got to see the garrison commander, laddie." Sutherland's voice was dry, hoarse, his eyes hollow. "Got to warn
him, got to get him to organize the militia."

James could see that Sutherland had been many weeks in
the woods and had suffered much; an old trade blanket hung
over his shoulders, and his clothes were worn and tattered, his
beard thick. It looked as if he had not eaten for much of that
time, and indeed it was no wonder, for no rebel scout could
have come through that country and lived—no one but Owen
Sutherland. James was ever being reminded of Sutherland's
stature, a man above the rest in so many ways.

Maxwell arrived to lend a hand, and soon Sutherland was
carried by sleigh to James's house in the settlement. Sutherland
was exhausted, but his will was indomitable, and he would not
rest or eat until he had seen the garrison commander and told
him everything. James stayed behind to ready a bed, clothing,
and food.

Sutherland walked alone through the town, his mind nearly
empty because of exhaustion. He should have felt cold, for the
wind whipped in off the rivers, but he was too numbed by
weariness to consider wrapping his frayed blanket closer about
his shoulders. Normally he would have been too proud to be
seen in such miserable condition on the streets of any town,
but he was simply too spent to care.

He had his crucial message to deliver, a defense to help

organize, and after all he had endured in the past two months, he took no interest in what was happening around him as he plodded through the town.

Sutherland was familiar with Pitt and made his way as quickly as his tortured legs would carry him. There were many others in the street, all of them heading for the central market, it seemed. Men were spilling out of taverns, mugs of ale in their fists, laughing and jostling as if a fair were at hand. In the distance he heard the slow rap of military drums, the familiar beat telling him a soldier was about to be punished for some serious crime. The American army used generally the same military system as the British, and Sutherland was sure the drumbeat he heard meant there would be a public flogging.

He put that gory ceremony out of his mind. He had to find the commander of Pitt, Colonel Daniel Brodhead, who was in charge of more than four hundred regulars from two regiments, one Pennsylvanian, the other Virginian. Sutherland knew Brodhead was a tough, stubborn man, one who had refused to send regular troops to support Clark last year. That was no wonder, though, for Brodhead's garrison was starving and sickly, and half of the soldiers were in hospital or on sick call. Brodhead was in such difficulty that he was forced to buy food from nearby Christian Delaware Indians.

Sutherland had heard all about the weakness of Pitt from the village of neutral Wyandot Indians who had protected him during five weeks of winter, when trails were snowbound and roving parties of Shawnees were on the hunt for him. Over the years, he had made many friends among the Indians, and this time none served him better than old Ido-lana, headman of this Wyandot village on the southern shore of Lake Erie. Years ago Sutherland had saved Ido-lana's life and had hunted game for his people, who were without black powder and dying of hunger during a terrible winter. Now, throughout January, Ido-lana had hidden Sutherland while the Shawnees came searching for him, departed, and came again. Later the Wyandots had disguised him, given him valuable clothing from their own small store of possessions, and accompanied him on a difficult trek until he was close to Fort Pitt. The debt of those Wyandots to Sutherland was now paid.

Many other Indians also knew of the miserable conditions the rebel regulars were suffering. It was said Fort Pitt would have to be abandoned if Congress did not soon provide funds and essential supplies to keep them alive. Thinking about that as he trudged along, Sutherland was disgusted with the inept rebel government. Indeed, he saw many gaunt faces—bleak, cynical expressions on the soldiers he passed.

Pittsburgh was a heap of wretched hovels, but Fort Pitt itself was in good repair, the cannon serviceable, its hungry-looking sentries sharp as they challenged Sutherland on his approach to the earth and palisade citadel. He was told Colonel Brodhead was in the town, supervising the whipping of a deserter—the third one this week, a sentry said with a sidelong glance at his companion.

Sutherland turned around and went to the market. There the troops were paraded in a hollow square, about two hundred of them. On opposite sides of the square were Pennsylvanians in faded dark blue tunics and dingy white smallclothes. They looked poor but proud, and were clean and disciplined. The Virginia soldiers in the other two sides were clad in worn buckskin hunting shirts—the rank and file without the fringes reserved for officers—and wide-brimmed hats with feathers. While the Pennsylvanians carried short muskets with fixed bayonets, the Virginians were armed with long rifles. With the sound of the slow march rapping in the background, Sutherland paused to locate Brodhead.

He thought these men looked military enough, for all that they were haggard and threadbare. Some had no stockings, others had stockings that were torn, and every uniform was patched several times over. Then Sutherland spotted Brodhead, a strapping, barrel-chested man with a large, square jaw, standing with his officers in the center of one side of the square. On Brodhead's right were blue-coated Pennsylvania officers, and on his left, with the fringes on their hunting shirts, the Virginia officers.

Just as Sutherland asked a sergeant nearby to tell Brodhead about his arrival, the downcast deserter was brought into the hollow square. In the center stood a tripod of long poles, to which the unfortunate man was lashed, hands and feet spread wide apart. He was naked from the waist up and appeared to be almost elderly, as were many of the conscripts these days. Men sixteen to sixty were drafted for frontier defense, and this man was near the high end of the scale. His gray hair fell glistening to his shoulders, he was wrinkled and skinny, but his eyes were defiant.

Behind the paraded soldiers were townsfolk, the curious, the fascinated, the morbid. This was army life, American or British, rebel or loyal or professional. Sutherland wanted no part of it. He wanted to be off, to take Brodhead aside and tell him the worst about the march of Captain Byrd's army that spring. He was relieved to see Brodhead stride rapidly toward him before the sergeant-at-arms commenced the whipping.

The lash began to crack as Brodhead hurried Sutherland away toward his headquarters in the fort. Before they had gone from the market square, however, they encountered a number of women and children, gathered in a tight group, blocking the street. Apparently they were relations of the man being punished, and were Irish, for they began to sing the melancholy "Shule Aroon," all of them staring hatefully at the distressed colonel. Brodhead wanted to find a route around the women, but for a moment could not see just which way to go. One of his aides pushed forward, politely asking the women to move, then becoming annoyed when they kept singing, standing their ground.

The song carried the refrain "Johnny has gone for a soldier," and told of the heartbroken woman left behind, lamenting "And through the streets I'll beg for bread . . ."

Visibly shaken, Brodhead called off his indignant aide and set out on another course through a back alley toward the citadel. Behind him, the song rose, plaintive and haunting, punctuated by the sharp whack of the cat-o'-nine-tails.

At moments like these, Sutherland wondered what would come of this revolution, this "Glorious Cause," as its most ardent supporters named it. Was there any way to win it without the lash, without having soldiers' wives starve? He did not know, and was far too tired to think about it.

At the spare, almost crude quarters of the colonel, Sutherland told what he had learned.

The commander sat at his desk, head in his hands, saying, "There's nothing I can do to stop it! I have too few troops, too great an area to patrol, no supplies, no money with which to procure supplies. . . ."

Sutherland knew he was right; but the officer agreed to try.

• • •

While Brodhead set into motion all the military defense mechanism at his command—including expresses riding to Williamsburg and Philadelphia with pleas for aid—Sutherland went to the house of Bradford Cullen. It was a handsome place, freshly painted red and yellow, with a white picket fence and a green door sporting a big brass knocker. Sutherland had been through this once before, coming to Cullen for aid in the defense of the rebellion. That had been back in Montreal, when cannon were desperately needed to help in the siege of Quebec, a siege that ultimately failed with disastrous results and heavy losses for the rebels. Cullen, in authority back then, had come up with all sorts of reasons for refusing Sutherland the needed cannon. The siege had failed for lack of cannon.

Sutherland had suspected Cullen then of playing both sides, of feigning rebel sympathies while carrying out espionage and collaborating with the loyalists. If the loyalists and the Crown somehow defeated the rebellion, Cullen would declare himself a secret liaison all the while and profit from the defeat of Congress's forces. If the rebels won, Cullen could claim he had been a key supplier of goods and munitions to the rebels, and a financier of the cause of Congress. Yet in this rebel service he never went too far, lest he anger his secret loyalist allies, or help tip the scales too much in favor of the rebels. Until peace negotiations were completed, Cullen would wait before committing himself fully to either side.

Sutherland could prove none of this, but he believed it with all his heart. Cullen was a blackguard of the first rank, but he might be willing to help in the defense of Pitt, at the very least. After all, he lived here, and he was too old to escape what was about to descend on the community. Indians on the rampage were not to be controlled, and the sacking of Fort Pitt could easily cost Cullen his life.

Cullen's manservant, the tall and gangly Auguste, turned up his nose when he saw this disheveled, ragged figure at the door. When he realized it was Owen Sutherland, however, he nervously went to inform his master. Auguste well knew the wrath of Owen Sutherland. The last time he had tried to prevent Sutherland from entering Cullen's house, back at Montreal, the residence had nearly been destroyed as a result.

Conscious of his miserable appearance, Sutherland left the Indian blanket at the door, straightened up with force of will, and looked imposing enough in spite of his worn buckskins and leggins. He would have liked to have his claymore at his side, at least. Then, with a wry smile to himself, he wondered whether he even had the strength to lift it. Perhaps the claymore was best with young Benjamin these days.

Soon Sutherland was shown in to Cullen's dark office, where the fat merchant was seated behind a large mahogany table. In the lamplight, Cullen's eyes gleamed, framed by the huge wig. He did not offer Sutherland a seat, nor did the Scotsman take one. Sutherland loathed being here, before this man, but for his cause he would do what he must.

Cullen rasped and chuckled, saying, "I thought you'd never come to me again, Sutherland. Do you need work? I can use hunters. Meat will bring a small fortune here at—"

"The Indians will hit the settlements in the spring, and Brodhead needs supplies, and the settlers downriver with Clark are in the same situation." Sutherland saw a look of guarded nervousness about Cullen. "Will you sell us the goods?"

"Hah! Sell to your Congress? They won't even pay their own miserable soldiers!" Cullen was clearly uneasy, but he was bluff and arrogant as he scorned the undependable delegates to Congress in Philadelphia.

Sutherland wasted no words. "I will sign the note, and I will collect payment from Congress."

Cullen was quiet a moment, his breath rasping in and out before he said with a sneer, "Congress already owes you plenty for what you sold Clark in your misguided generosity!"

Sutherland made no reply, but he was angry, especially because Cullen always seemed to know the details of any transaction of importance, wherever he was.

Cullen leaned forward, one hand in the pool of light illuminating the desk. "Once I offered you to ally with me, Sutherland, and you refused." A slow, burning stare settled between them. "I can still use you, man! Forget all your idealistic allegiance to Congress. Whether they win or lose, they don't want this country. After the war, this country'll be here for the taking. It'll be a whole new land, and I'm the one to rule it!"

Cullen opened and closed his fist before his face. "Join me,

Sutherland!" He spoke almost in a whisper. "Your Frontier Company exists in name only, but ally with me, and together we'll breathe new life into it!"

Sutherland had heard all this before. Cullen's company was strong, but the old man could not have a better partner to control the northwest than Owen Sutherland. Although Cullen was enormously wealthy, he was widely despised and feared, and the Indians hated his traders and agents. On the other hand, Sutherland was loved like a brother, despite the fortunes and temporary enmity of war. Cullen's mind, Cullen's money, Cullen's network of shippers and suppliers could quickly master the rich, uncharted wilderness, if only Owen Sutherland would be his right hand. If Cullen and Company had to battle the Frontier Company every step of the way, Cullen would never live to see his empire stretch unchallenged across the western wilderness.

"Admit it, Sutherland! Admit you cannot beat me now!"

Sutherland felt a new strength within, as if the very presence of this despicable schemer gave him a surge of power. By comparison with the toadish Cullen, Sutherland was a magnificent figure of a man, even in his present weakness, and after all he had suffered.

Sutherland said, "You know what the army needs—will you supply it?"

Cullen's face became red, and he slammed the table with the palm of his hand. "I cannot! I have none of what you want and will not have it for months! See that young upstart Morely about your needs. Then be off, hero, saving wretches who'll neither thank nor repay you!" He turned away, his jaw moving from side to side. "You'll never learn, never! If you had any idea what could be done, us together! But you're imprisoned by your . . . your honor! Trapped in discredited, defeatist ways!" He spun. "Get out, Sutherland!"

But there was no one there. The door stood open. Cullen cursed foully. Even now, he could not sink his clutches into Owen Sutherland. Even now! And it appeared he never would.

James Morely's apartment behind his large trading house was simple, solid, and clean. It was spartan in taste, although the furnishings were all of the finest quality. A fire crackled away in an iron stove in one corner, and a bright winter sun pouring through the windows lighted the main room, with its cheerful curtains and rugs. James had an extra bedroom, which was prepared for Sutherland.

It was not long before Sutherland returned. He sat wearily at the table, eating soup that James's maid had prepared, and a pitcher of ale was at hand, along with bread, butter, olives, and bowls of preserves. Sutherland gradually explained what had happened at Detroit, how Gwen was rescued, and how the British were preparing a powerful thrust to wipe out the settlements.

Sitting across from Sutherland, James heard this last with surprise and dismay. He was no ardent rebel, but he was shaken by the news. Of course the killing that would result shocked him, but also he would lose much business if the settlements were destroyed. The impending disruption of his richest market might spell disaster to plans for expansion and rapid development of his company.

Sutherland explained that he had gone directly to Bradford Cullen to ask for gunpowder and supplies for the regulars and the militia of the settlements, and that Cullen would give nothing on credit.

In reply, James said, "Cullen has very little powder and supplies at hand, for I've bought up most of what's available, and his new shipments won't arrive from the East until late spring." James explained that Cullen had unloaded most of his hard merchandise in various obscure dealings, apparently to finance great tracts of land he had bought up lately. Cullen had concentrated his attention on these speculative efforts, allowing James to purchase most of the supplies that had come overland to Pitt this autumn. Cullen had not cared about this small disadvantage, for he meant to strike back hard that summer, filling Pitt with cheaper goods that would compete with Morely Trading.

Sutherland said he now knew all that. "Cullen told me you're the man who can outfit the militia. We'll need food, guns, flints, black powder, lead, shoes, blankets, cartage, a few dozen yoke of oxen and their harness, enough cattle to feed us for a two-month campaign. . . ."

"Owen?" James had a very important question to ask but

was afraid he would not like the answer. "Who will pay for all this? Those settlements have no money. The garrison commander here has little hard money. Will Virginia or Pennsylvania authorize the expenditures? Congress surely won't or can't. It'll cost twenty thousand pounds sterling to equip the army you ask."

Sutherland said simply, "No one has authorized payment yet, but if this army is not mustered, the entire frontier will be devastated."

James stood up and walked toward the stove, thinking hard. Then he turned. "Who will sign for this merchandise? Who will guarantee to pay me?"

Sutherland sat back and looked at the table a moment before saying, "If need be, I will sign."

James felt a wrench of remorse within, but he could not help but say softly, "And what collateral do you have, Owen?"

Sutherland looked up sharply, his expression intense, face lined and taut. "My honor."

James relented, though he was thinking that Sutherland's honor was all he had left. Unlike Cullen, who had such close connections with the Continental Congress, Sutherland would not be paid for many months to come—if ever—for the credit he had given George Rogers Clark. James had some bad news to break, and he advanced to the table and looked intently at Sutherland as he gave it.

"Do you know there are many in Congress and even in Williamsburg who object to Clark's rash campaign?" Sutherland did not reply but looked away, as if he was not very surprised to hear this. "Matters and men have changed in Congress, *and* in Virginia, and there's a whole new set of leaders, with other ideas—ideas that do not include the northwest territory for the states. Ideas that do not include Clark's plans to take Detroit, even to hold Kentucky!" James came around the table and leaned forward, saying, "These men are powerful, and they want peace with Britain as soon as possible, and they are perfectly willing to give up the northwest to do it."

He declared that Fort Pitt and the Ohio Valley would be the boundary line of the new United American States if those men had their way. They desired trading rights with the British empire after the war, and in return would gladly surrender the northwest to get those lucrative rights. They did not want to spend further for frontier campaigns.

"Owen, George Clark's drafts on Virginia are not at all certain to be honored. There are those who demand that he be recalled from the frontier, and who accuse him of being an adventurer out for himself and no one else! He is personally in impossible debt, and many of the rebel merchants who supplied him are clamoring to be paid."

"I and the Frontier Company are not." Sutherland suddenly looked old, and yet there was a majesty about him, an aloof magnificence that James greatly admired. James wished that he himself might have such a bearing one day.

But, he wondered, was Sutherland aware of the seriousness of what was happening, that Clark's bills might never be paid, and that all the Frontier Company had given him would be lost? James did not think so.

"Owen, if Virginia and the Congress do not pay Clark's bills, the Frontier Company will be ruined—"

"No!" Sutherland stared so fiercely that James had to move away. "Hurt, perhaps, laddie, but not ruined. Not while there's life in me; not while the others stick together. And if you were still one of us, you'd understand, and you'd agree!"

James walked away slowly, head down. He sighed. "Times are changing, Owen, and the men you once counted on for financing your enterprises, and for credit, are gone. The old order is almost done, and the new one is yet unknown." He swung around, anger rising. "But George Rogers Clark is a man of the old order—a young, brave rebel, yes, but now that the war is nearly won, the men in the East who are leading the Revolution don't need him or—"

James caught himself before he said, "you!"

He might as well have said it, however, and Sutherland laid his mug on the table, thinking. As James paced to the stove and leaned on the mantelpiece, Sutherland turned in his seat and stretched out his weary legs.

"You, laddie, are part of the new order."

James looked around and waited.

"You are the hope of this new country, and so I've come to you, as George Clark might one day come to you, and I'm asking that you honor my name, my word, and equip and feed the army that I will raise—an army of men with the same ideals as the old order, no matter who sits in the Virginia House of Burgesses, or in the Continental Congress."

James clenched his fists, turning away as Sutherland slowly went on.

"We know nothing of old and new orders, for our troubles are the same, our needs are the same, and we mean to survive, whatever it takes. We mean to go on, no matter who rules.

"There are five thousand settlers out there, in a hundred little communities, all waiting for the British and Indians to strike, and they will not run without fighting for their homes. They mean to stay."

He paused, before adding, "I know you well enough, James, to understand that you're aware of what I am saying. You're a man of the northwest. You understand."

James looked right at him, and again was moved by the undeniable greatness of this man, a man who had walked through a frozen hell to get here, to save people he did not even know. Whether James helped or not, Owen Sutherland would find a way to meet the enemy head on, and would stand against them with every ounce of strength, until his last breath. No, it was not necessary for James to question Owen Sutherland about collateral or guarantees. A lifetime of respect and experience lay between them, a lifetime in the northwest, where old and new orders had seldom affected anyone fundamentally, for life had gone on as ever, no matter who was master, or who held the forts and trading posts.

James took a long breath. He was indeed proud to be a man of the northwest.

He asked Sutherland, "What do you need?" Sutherland rapidly ran through the list, including even tools for building fortifications against artillery. It would stretch James to the very limit of his resources.

James said, "I will give you all I can; but I expect payment from your rebel government within six months, otherwise—" He was about to say he would be ruined, but that was not to be admitted in the company of Owen Sutherland, a man who did not know the meaning of defeat or ruin.

Sutherland stood up, his legs shaky, and with a smile offered James his hand. James asked about Susannah, and Sutherland said he had not seen her since leaving the Falls of the Ohio. James grinned and, from a writing desk, fished out a letter from Susannah that had come not long ago. He offered it to Sutherland, and as he watched the man sit beside the fire to eagerly read the words of his daughter, James felt good inside. In promising to aid the settlements, he had done the right thing, even though it was risky beyond all good sense.

chapter 12

PRELUDE

The weather turned mild early that year, and the rivers gave up their ice as warm breezes gently brought the land back to life. One afternoon, Noah Maxwell invited James to join him and the Cullens in a sailing outing.

James knew Cullen seldom left his house, but one special pleasure the old man had in life was to sail for a few hours on the rivers. Cullen's new boat was large and finely equipped, built like the durable keelboats that plied eastern rivers, and manned by a crew of six Massachusetts sailors, all wearing smart dark-blue uniforms. The master of the boat stood on a pulpit aft of the deckhouse, from where he managed a wide-bladed steering oar. He was Bill Bartholomew, a muscular, red-bearded tough, reputed at Pitt as a mean brawler, but also an excellent pilot, who knew the waters hereabouts the way a scout knew the woods. Under Bartholomew's hand, the boat sailed gracefully for all its weight and bulk.

If Cullen had meant to impress James with the keelboat, he easily succeeded. From the moment James stepped aboard at the Pittsburgh wharf, he was reminded of Cleopatra's fabled barge; and although Cullen's version was not gilded, it was painted bright yellow and white and fairly glittered in the spring sunshine. With the crewmen at the oars in the bow, the keelboat was propelled far out into the Allegheny for a trip upriver. Soon the square sail was unfurled and caught the breeze, and the keelboat set off leisurely upstream, watched enviously by knots of poor folk standing on the shore.

There was no boat like this one west of the barrier mountains, and no man here except for Cullen could have afforded her. Mounted forward was a small swivel gun, and another was at the stern. On her bow was painted the name *Linda,* and she certainly had the looks of Cullen's daughter—broad of beam, adorned with only the very finest, and in need of a large crew to care for her. In the white deckhouse was "spare" Cullen furniture, polished cherrywood cabinets, and a wonderful kitchen with water pipes, an open hearth, and a new coal stove, all of it managed by a steward who doubled as chef.

After a long winter penned up at Pitt, James found this journey up the Allegheny a delight, even though much of it was spent in company with the giddy Linda while Maxwell and Cullen engaged in lengthy, hushed conversation in the deckhouse.

The Allegheny was busy with canoes going to and coming from the small settlements upstream, and several boatloads of peaceful Delaware Indians came down with trade goods for the fort. As he and Linda idled in the bow, a bottle of wine at hand, James marked the contrast between his party and the impoverished settlers, woodsmen, and Indians who passed by. They all seemed awestruck, doffing their hats and gazing in silence at the magnificent *Linda,* with her full sail, gleaming paint, and her burly master on his pulpit. The sailors sang songs of Massachusetts at Linda's request, and she glowed with happiness, the sweet wine lending its part to her patina.

James could not help but see that Linda was at heart a good person, if a bit spoiled. Although she was oblivious of what others thought of her, and was often the butt of cruel jokes, she meant well, for the most part. Certainly it was clear how she adored James. He could not pour a glass of wine without having her snatch away the bottle to help, all the while her eyes searching his, so that she often spilled or overfilled the glasses, giggling childishly whenever she did so. She was dressed overwarmly in a pink riding habit and matching wide-brimmed hat, and wore skirts so full that it was nearly impossible for her to sit comfortably.

This was one of the few times James had ever seen some depth to Linda Cullen, as she enthusiastically pointed out waterfalls and other landmarks, delighted at pretty birds, and grew almost rapturous over the beauty of this country. Indeed, she was truly childlike, and more naïve than James had realized. He could see there was more to her than the image of an empty-headed, dowdy daughter of a rich man.

"La! But it seems I've never really seen this wonderful country before," she declared, clutching her hands before her and gazing at the sunny eastern bank. "Perhaps . . . perhaps it's because of your wonderful company, Mr. Morely, but the world seems ever so much more lovely to me!"

He smiled, reaching for the wine bottle, which she grabbed first. As she poured, he said, "You do me too much honor, Mistress Cullen." He looked a little closer at her just then, while she gave her attention to pouring, not spilling any this time. She really meant what she was saying, and probably few other men had ever talked at length to her, or listened to what she thought about the world and life. For the past two hours he had shared her deepest notions about the world as she saw it, and they actually had been interesting. Linda apparently knew nothing of her father's business, good or bad, and instead gave her attention simply to living well, managing his large household, and dreaming about marrying before she was absolutely too old.

"See there!" She suddenly pointed to the water, where a baby duck was flailing about, apparently lost and hungry. "Oh, my! Quick! Quick! Let's rescue the tiny little thing! La! Oh, my heavens!"

With a cry to the boat's tillerman, and frantic orders to the entire startled crew, Linda soon had them all blundering about in an attempt to "save" the bird. Husky men were leaning overboard, cooing and clucking at the bewildered duckling while Linda tossed pieces of the finest jam tarts into the water. Even Cullen and Maxwell came from the deckhouse to see what all the commotion was about.

At last, James hung over the side of the boat, a crewman

or two holding him from falling, and scooped up the bird, which seemed less forlorn after a gizzard full of tart. Cullen muttered that he thought there had been an Indian attack, and then grinned affectionately to see Linda embrace the frightened, confused, but magnificently feasted duckling. As Linda tenderly stuffed the creature with more tart, James caught Cullen's eye, seeing the man nod once and smile in a rush of good feeling. James wondered whether Owen Sutherland had ever seen this side of the old man he so reviled.

Soon, Maxwell took James's place with Linda and the duckling, and Cullen sat in the deckhouse with James, talking idly at first about the prospects for the coming British and Indian invasion. Cullen believed firmly that the enemy would not attempt to strike at Fort Pitt, but there was little hope, he said, for the defense of the settlements.

James did not agree or disagree. After all, he had already committed himself to that defense, with only Owen Sutherland's promise guaranteeing him that he would not lose everything if the settlers were defeated and driven out—or even if they were not. James sat listening attentively to Cullen's assessment of the latest military developments, but he grew bothered when the merchant began criticizing him. In short, Cullen said James should never have trusted his small fortune to the discretion of a man like Owen Sutherland.

Smoking one of Maxwell's cigars, Cullen declared with a wave of the hand, "Idealism and making war don't mix, Mr. Morely, as your mentor, Mr. Sutherland, is proving so clearly."

James was about to say Sutherland was not his mentor, but that did not matter so much, so he held his tongue.

Cullen said, "I respect Sutherland's high ideals, but ideals only start wars, never win them. Like poor, idealistic George Rogers Clark plunging about down on the Ohio, Sutherland's days as a leading man in the northwest are numbered. No one can lead anymore without the authority of some powerful establishment behind him—either a strong government that relies upon him, or a strong company. Sutherland and Clark have neither."

James said, "They have the support of the settlers, sir, and Sutherland and Clark are the sort of men who can do much with very little."

Cullen eyed James a moment, puffed on the cigar, then said,

"Ordinary people have no vision, no depth of honor. As soon as Clark or Sutherland no longer suit them, no longer are needed to protect their outstretched necks, they'll flutter away from them both, and flock right to the true source of power and influence in this country."

James did not deny that. "But at the moment the settlers need Clark and Sutherland and will do whatever they say. With the settlers in arms, organized, and supplied, Sutherland and Clark can win a great victory, and military victories do much to enhance reputations, and serve well to attract those flocks of ordinary people you mention, sir." Cullen did not immediately reply, and James went on: "I believe that, for the moment, I have chosen the right course of action, and have committed my funds and efforts judiciously."

Cullen stared out the open window, thinking.

James said, "I mean to be on the winning side in this bloody war-within-a-war out here, but I'll always reassess my investments, perhaps to think again and to change."

Cullen tossed his cigar through the window as he spoke casually: "It's truly a pity, though, that you've tied up all your worldly assets in this little adventure, for Mr. Maxwell and I are engaged in an enterprise that one day will be profitable beyond your most ambitious dreams!"

He paused theatrically, then leaned over to a large wooden chest that had been sitting nearby, unremarked by James. He opened the lid, and James nearly sprang to his feet. In the chest were Continental dollars, more than James had ever seen in his life. Even though they were greatly depreciated, there was a tremendous sum in that chest, and James marveled for some time without speaking.

Cullen's chuckling brought his attention away from the money, and the old man said, "This is my ambitious enterprise, Mr. Morely! No great boatloads of peltry, no massive shipments of grain, or whiskey, or food, or gunpowder . . . just one modest chest filled with paper currency."

James was polite enough not to ask how much was in the chest, but he said he did not understand the reason for its being here.

Cullen idly waved at it, saying, "Today, all that money's not worth what it cost to build this boat. But in another three or four years, when Congress is in full power and begins to redeem these notes at a good face value, I'll turn them in and come away with a profit one thousand times what it cost me to acquire them!" He laughed again, his fat belly rising and falling as he considered his clever manipulation of the current financial situation.

It was all clear to James, and it explained why Cullen had little merchandise to sell to Sutherland: after trading for land, Cullen had sold the rest of his goods last year in return for these continentals—currency that was considered almost worthless because of the rapid depreciation it had suffered since being printed by Congress during the past years of warfare. Cullen obviously had an insider's knowledge of Congress's plans for redemption of its paper money, and James guessed that before too long, continentals would be worth far more than the pittance Cullen had paid to acquire them from the desperate, impoverished folk out here at Pitt.

Thousands of people coming westward with the tide of migration carried Continental dollars, paid to them for service in the army, or for supplies bought from them by the rebel government. The dollars' value had plummeted soon after the first batch was printed, with nothing to back them up save the dubious promises of an impoverished rebel government. It was illegal, punishable by imprisonment, to refuse to take a continental in payment, but most people in rebel-held America tried not to accept them anyway, willing to risk the penalty. "Not worth a continental," the expression went—but Cullen apparently knew better.

He was not exactly cheating the people who sold them to him for far less than their face value, but it was certainly a cunning way to take advantage of them and the situation. James remarked with admiration on this.

At that, the merchant leaned forward, eyes half closed, and whispered, "Forgo your foolish bargain with Owen Sutherland, and let me manage the sale of your goods in return for a thousand times their value in continentals, Mr. Morely. I'll make you a very rich man."

For a moment, James felt the thrill of that lucrative proposition. Once again Cullen had stirred up something hungry, almost lustful, within him, and he thought about the offer longer than he knew was honorable—for it was not an honorable proposition. Not that buying up continentals cheaply troubled his conscience—but James would not go back on his word to Owen Sutherland.

He collected himself and said this to Cullen, who showed no disappointment. Instead, Cullen nodded and, after a moment, spoke with much intensity. He said he was glad James had passed the test. James was startled and asked what test was that.

Cullen chuckled to himself, saying, "You are a man of your word, Mr. Morely. You have proved that to me, and now I am sure of you, more than ever."

James did not know what Cullen was getting at, but just then Linda entered the cabin, distracting her father's attention by displaying the duckling and crooning over it. The mood changed, and in came Maxwell, who searched James's expression, as if for some hint that Cullen's latest offer had been taken. James said nothing, and nothing else was spoken of continentals or promises that cheerful day on the river.

By April at Fort Pitt, the first convoy of supplies and equipment was ready to be brought to a staging area downriver. Soon, the militias being raised in the settlements would send men there to be issued supplies. It would take time to gather the troops into an army, but at least Sutherland and James Morely had worked fast to collect most of what was needed.

Scouts had told of the main British force rumored to be gathering on the Auglaize River, southwest of Lake Erie, with thirteen hundred Indians joining a hundred British regulars, as many loyalist rangers in green uniforms, and a detachment of artillery. The British had six guns in all—four small swivels mounted on horses for rapid movement, and two brass field cannon. They were not expected to strike until mid-July, for Indian parleys were notoriously long-winded, and Indians refused to march far without stopping periodically to fast and pray, consult their manitous and medicine men, and feast and dance, all of these requiring specified numbers of days.

As it was, Captain Byrd would need many weeks to traverse hundreds of miles of river and forest north of the Ohio, with the cannon and great loads of baggage and equipment to haul behind him. Further, his Indians would often be scattered, out hunting or attacking small settlements that were off the line of march. It would be extremely difficult for Byrd to maintain any sort of coordinated advance, and the Indians would seldom be at hand in full numbers at any one time.

Sutherland knew that for every week the enemy was delayed, the settlers would be that much more prepared to fight back. None of the stockaded communities save for Pitt could withstand cannon fire, however, and he had been trying hard to persuade militia leaders to abandon most of the settlements for the duration of the campaign. No one, except men from the very smallest hamlets, would listen to this advice, for to leave their homes would mean losing everything. Sutherland knew this well, for during the past weeks he had divided his time between visiting far-flung settlements and rushing back to Fort Pitt, where he worked with James to collect and organize the supplies.

To make matters worse—and much to James's annoyance—Colonel Brodhead, the Pitt garrison commander, had requisitioned a large share of the stockpiled goods. Sutherland agreed to this, however, because the men at Pitt had to hold out. If Pitt fell, the frontier was lost.

Trees were showing the green of new leaf when James and Sutherland took the convoy downriver. Their destination was Fort McIntosh, the northernmost rebel fortress, near the mouth of the Beaver River. Fifty regulars went along as escorts, and there were as many hired laborers to manhandle the goods. There were also forty militia volunteers from the nearer Kentucky settlements, men who had come up promptly to take their own share of the supplies back to their settlements.

Sutherland and James stood at the square prow of a flatboat, behind a protecting side wall of thick planks that rose to their chests and would serve as a defense if the convoy came under attack. As Sutherland leaned against the wall, gazing at the dark forest off to the right, his instincts told nothing of any enemy lurking over there. For now, he believed, they were not in danger.

The wind was fair and gusting in his face, the river white-capped, foam seeming to flow upstream, fresh and lively. He felt strong again, renewed, though he had rested but little in the past few weeks. It was as if spring had invigorated him, just as it had the beautiful upper Ohio Valley. This was a good country, for all that it was perilous and blood-soaked, and would

be for a time to come. He looked at James, who was holding
a rifle tightly in both hands, staring hard at the woods, anxious
about an ambush. James had everything to lose if these goods
were destroyed or captured.

Sutherland spoke gently: "Don't be worrying here, laddie.
There's not a redskin between this part of the river and ten
miles inland, according to our scouts." James glanced around,
licked his lips, then went back to squinting into the afternoon
sun.

Sutherland chuckled softly. "We're a strong force, I'm
thinking—too strong for even one of Girty's big war parties
to try to surprise us."

Indeed, as Sutherland looked back at the eight other flatboats
wallowing in the turbulent stream, he saw many a rifleman
standing watch on board, most of them nervous like James.

Sutherland said, "Even our hired laborers look like soldiers,
the way we've dressed them up in old uniforms."

Tensely, James replied, "The laborers won't be much use
as troops if we do get hit; half of them don't know the business
end of a musket from the butt." The boat rose and dropped
suddenly, and James looked a bit seasick. "I'll be glad when
we reach the fort."

The boat pitched again, nearly throwing them off their feet.
Up above on the deckhouse, a burly riverman from Pitt cursed
and fought with the tiller to keep the boat from turning stern
about. Sutherland and James had all they could do to avoid
being thrown to the deck as the craft lifted and fell in the
eddying current, cold spray soaking them. The boat heeled,
the steersman swore and screeched at the wind, but then he
gave in to the river.

The boat was turning steadily now, and the steersman let it
come around so that the stern was headed downstream first—
stern or bow, both were snub-nosed. Grunting and complaining,
he set about carrying the long steering oar to another oarlock
in what had been the bow. He set it in place and, in compromise
with the raging Ohio, began to steer once again from there.

Recovering, and seeing James once more at his post, Sutherland said, "I don't fear attack now, but when the regulars
relieve the garrison at Fort McIntosh, and those lads go back
to Pitt, we'll be short-handed."

James added, "And most of the Kentucky men'll take their

supplies and go home as soon as we land." He shook his head. "I wish we had this affair over with and the goods all distributed, Owen. I don't like it, sitting down there at little McIntosh, with British and redskins snapping all around us."

Sutherland did not like it either, but this was the only way to get the supplies and ammunition distributed to the settlements in time. It would have taken too long for the settlers to come all the way upriver to Pitt to be outfitted. Byrd would strike hard and fast when he got this far, and small groups of militiamen laden with precious supplies and powder would be easy targets.

James seemed to relax, taking Sutherland's advice that this stretch of river offered no good opportunity for ambush. He swigged some water from a ladle in a bucket, took a deep breath, and said he was glad everything had gone well so far.

"We were wise to get away from Pitt under cover of darkness, and no one who shouldn't know has much idea what we're carrying or where we're going. I'm glad that not even the regulars have been told we're planning to make a supply base at Fort McIntosh."

Sutherland said, "I hope you can trust him." He nodded toward the bow, indicating Noah Maxwell, who was tricked out like a sport as usual, and bantering with an unmarried settler girl who was doing her laundry in a tub.

James smiled as he saw Maxwell, so debonair and charming, making the buxom girl blush, and entertaining her simple mind with his worldly witticisms.

"Noah said he was coming along to help me," James said with a laugh. "But I think she was as much a reason as any. She's from a farm not far from McIntosh, and her family's all coming back with the convoy now that it's spring again." James said the family had fled the region last summer when the raids had started, but they believed they would be safe now with so many soldiers posted at the fort.

"They may be safe," he said, "but ever since Noah met that wench, he's been after her!"

Sutherland replied that those kind of people were the most difficult to protect from raids, for they would not remain at the forts, but insisted even in times of trouble on working their fields and taking grave chances.

"We'll patrol one farm, find it safe, and pass on to the next, but before we've been gone an hour, the first place is hit, everyone killed or taken, and all we see is the smoke."

In the past weeks, Sutherland had often roved about as a scout, taking the best men with him; but the task of watching all the trails for enemy parties was simply too much for so few to undertake. And until his recent travels around Pitt, he had not truly realized how many new settlers had reached the Ohio Valley. They posed a serious defense problem: not only were too few of them able to fight—most were farmers or former townsfolk from back in the states—but they were too stubborn for the most part to abandon their hard-won new homes.

He said, "If Simon Girty's leading the advance parties of Byrd's army, he'll know a dozen secret trails in this region, for he was raised not far from here, and fought hereabouts in three wars."

James looked at him a moment, then said, "You're worried about our families, aren't you?"

Sutherland nodded, gazing at the river. He greatly feared for Ella and the others, who were still at the Falls, the most far-flung outpost of all.

"I, too," James said. "I've heard that it's expected the British will strike there first . . . but, Owen, I don't believe it."

"No?" Sutherland pursed his lips. He wanted to agree with James but could not, for the settlement at the Falls was a logical first target for Byrd and his raiders.

James shook his head and took a deep breath. "As soon as Byrd attacks, word will run like wildfire through the frontier settlements, and we'll know exactly where he is. And he won't easily take the Falls, with all its fighting men and Clark in command. If Byrd's delayed there, everyone else will be able to come in and arm and get ready. . . ."

Sutherland pondered that, just as he had already pondered it over and over. He hoped Byrd's army would be discovered before it had a chance to surprise any of the settlements, but there were so many scouts flung out in front of the enemy army that it was impossible for even the best rebel rangers to get through the screen and locate the main body.

There was one hope for Sutherland, however, and he said slowly, "I've written to Ella to bring the women and children up to Pitt as soon as possible; they'll be safe there."

James agreed, becoming enthusiastic. "They'll be able to

come up to Fort McIntosh first, with the remaining militia from Kentucky as a strong escort!"

"I hope so," Sutherland said softly. "I hope they can come away soon." He was quiet a little longer, and could not help but say—for he needed to voice it to someone—"I fear for Benjamin."

"Ben? Yes..." James understood. Benjamin had been a close friend of his, an avid shinty player, one who had learned from James himself, and played even better than he did. "You don't think the lad will come away?"

Sutherland did not reply. He well knew Benjamin would stay and fight, no matter how dangerous it was. He would have done the same.

Ella and the others ought to have started for Fort Pitt by late April, but they had been delayed at the Falls by several false alarms that had taken the militia into the forest to protect out-lying farms. People were edgy, rumor and fear mingling into tales of Indian parties that had vanished by the time the men arrived. Or were the Indians out there in force, but for some reason avoiding a fight, keeping away from the militiamen? No one was really sure, not even Clark.

Ella had been overjoyed to receive Owen's letter and had prepared immediately to get under way, but they could not go until the militia was ready, for travel on the river was dangerous without a strong escort. The delays seemed endless, but on the good side, Ella had been reunited with Jeremy and had met her daughter-in-law, Gwen. Nothing, however, had been quite like taking Richard, her grandson, into her arms for the first time. He was her only grandchild, and although her foster daughter, Sally Morely, had a three-year-old son and expected another baby before too long, Richard was Ella's own flesh and blood.

He looked so beautiful, though sickly. His cheerful spirit shone right through the weakness that had overtaken him on the journey, and that made Ella love and cuddle him all the more. Gwen was an indulgent daughter-in-law, liking Ella immensely from the very start. Gwen, too, had been weakened by the harsh journey from Detroit, and she was glad for Ella's help in caring for Richard.

Susannah Sutherland normally would have doted on her

nephew, but she was distracted by a long letter from James Morely, a letter that she read and reread until it was grayed and worn. She kept it under her pillow or inside her blouse, and every word took on a different meaning each time she read it. Sometimes happy, sometimes puzzling, every turn of phrase, each hint, and each thought that might be behind the words was given meaning by Susannah, until at last she did not know just what James was thinking at all.

Actually, the letter had been mostly news of his business and daily life at Fort Pitt. It had contained a few mild expressions of his good feeling for her, some vague remarks that he would like to see her again, but no passion, no restrained romantic emotion that would have told a Juliet more than any written words could have done. Susannah could tell James was very busy, and she was happy he had cooperated with her father in the supplying of the settlements, but she wished he had said something more, dropped some small suggestion that would have let her know he really cared for her.

Still, it was a letter for her alone, and that could be judged as a statement of his feeling for her. So she hoped; but she could not be sure of anything with so many miles between them. Soon, however, she and her family would be setting off to Fort Pitt, and in a few weeks she would be with James once again. She could scarcely contain her excitement, and more than ever she hoped that her father would at last be changed in his opinion of James.

Life had never been more exciting and stimulating for Benjamin Sutherland. His long months as a prisoner of the Shawnee had made him look at things with a clearer eye, made him appreciate small things, like his mother's cooking, a good book, or his half brother's company.

Benjamin and Jeremy had always been close, and the younger brother could not have had a better teacher. Jeremy and Gwen did much to broaden Benjamin's education during the weeks of uncertainty and preparation for departure at the Falls. The young couple were generous with their knowledge, and Benjamin was so hungry for what they could teach him in the way of Latin, Greek, archaeology, and natural philosophy that he had a profound urge to give the world something back in return.

So it was that Benjamin decided to draw Little Jake under

his wing. Jake was slow to forgive himself for having betrayed Gwen, although no one held it against him, and everyone took interest in his well-being. He lived with the Bentlys, but was often on the trail with Benjamin. From the start Benjamin tried to cheer the fellow up, and found the very best way was to teach him woodlore.

Just as Benjamin devoured booklearning, Little Jake blossomed as a woodsman. He also took great interest in Punch, and Benjamin found it easy to make him laugh with the bird's trained antics. But for a while, the bird was slow to show he trusted Jake, and seldom went to him.

One hot afternoon, Benjamin and Jake were sitting talking near the blockhouse where Colonel Clark had his headquarters, when Punch fluttered down, dropping something shiny into Jake's hands. The boy was startled and gave a cry of delight.

"He's brought me a present!" He took Punch onto his finger and held up a silver ring, like the ones used to put official seals on wax, and he laughed, saying, "Punch means to be my friend, Ben! And—"

With a yelp, Benjamin snatched the ring away, and the frightened Punch flapped into the air. Benjamin shook his fist and pointed at the bird.

"I told you to stop your thieving, you scamp!" He was pale and glanced around, glad it was dinnertime and the place deserted. More than once Punch had flown into windows and stolen something precious, and no matter how apologetic Benjamin would be when he brought it back, he was roundly scolded as an irresponsible trainer of naughty birds. "Every time something gets lost in this settlement, Punch gets blamed, and me through him. Oh, Lordy!"

He examined the heavy ring, which was beautifully worked, with an emerald set in a coat of arms inscribed with Latin words. Benjamin took a moment to examine them, at first pleased with himself that he could understand the words—that is, he was pleased until he understood everything. "Heavens to Betsy! This is the ring of the colonel himself!"

Jake gasped, and both boys were afraid of what would happen if the severe Colonel Clark found his seal had been stolen by Punch. By now, the bird was haughtily, innocently preening on a branch high overhead.

"There's only one way..." Benjamin muttered, feeling his

hands tremble as he thought of what had to be done.

Jake guessed what he meant and, snatching the ring away, cried, "I'll do it!"

"What? Hey! Give me that—"

"No!" Jake declared. "I'll show you I kin sneak about like some Injun, just like you taught me, Ben."

Before Benjamin could protest, the boy darted away to peer around the back of the colonel's blockhouse, which stood solid and silent in the afternoon heat. Still, few people were in sight. Whether Colonel Clark himself was inside Benjamin did not know, but if he was, then Jake had better be a very good Indian to get in and out unnoticed. Benjamin worried that there was no way Jake could get away with this.

As Jake vanished behind the blockhouse, slipping into the midst of six or seven unlimbered carts, Benjamin could not help feeling proud of the lad's courage and pluck, but as he thought of what might go wrong, imagined the consequences of Jake's appearing like a thief himself, he began to sweat. Getting up from the bench where he sat, he glanced up and down the quiet main street of the fort. What should he do?

The front door of the blockhouse was wide open to let in fresh air, and the blackness inside seemed forbidding. Yet it was Benjamin's pet that had started this, and it was up to him to face the consequences before things got further out of hand. He started toward the blockhouse, his father's claymore dragging at his side, so that he had to balance it, keeping the tip of the scabbard off the ground. He felt very much a boy just then. The closer he came to the gloomy blockhouse, the more apprehensive he was. Overhead flitted the blue jay, who, to Benjamin's dismay, flew right into the open door. Benjamin dared not cry out, but glanced again from side to side, saw no one, then hurried across the yard to the door. He did not know whether to call first for Colonel Clark, for Jake, or for Punch, or for all three at once. He said nothing, approaching the door silently, trying not to appear too suspicious to whoever might be watching.

His mouth was dry, heart pounding, hands and brow running with sweat. He drew a deep breath. There was nothing else for it but to rap on the door and accept his punishment from the colonel.

Then, at the last moment, he realized he did not have the

ring. What would he say? He had to find Jake first and get the ring back. His knuckles were just inches from the open door, but he backed off and began to make his way around the blockhouse. He hoped the boy was still back there, staring at a window, thinking of how to get inside. But just as Benjamin came around a corner, he caught sight of Jake's feet as a window swallowed them.

"No! Well, that does it!" he whispered, kicking the ground, and nearly tripping on the claymore as he turned back to the front door. "Nothing for it now but to go inside and pray all he'll do is fetch me a clap on the side of the head."

He trudged around to the door and again raised his hand to knock, imagining the inevitable shout of anger that would tell Colonel Clark had discovered Jake slinking about. Suddenly, Punch flapped back through the door, causing Benjamin to duck, only to be rammed full force in the gut by Little Jake, who came barreling out. Both of them tumbled heavily to the ground.

Benjamin rolled and grunted in pain, the wind knocked out of him. Jake hopped about, shaking his right hand, which had smacked against the hilt of the claymore. Benjamin tried to sit up, wheezing for breath as Punch lighted on his shoulder. Jake blew furiously on his hand, all the while whispering something that sounded to Benjamin like, "I done it! Ouch! I done it!"

Benjamin desperately wanted the ring from the boy, but was too breathless to squeeze out the words. Jake just kept on hopping and mumbling and blowing on his fingers, ignoring Benjamin's gestures for the ring.

Then Clark himself suddenly was in the doorway. Thickset, wearing a blue officer's tunic over a linsey shirt and leggins of buckskin, he seemed to have just awakened from a nap, for his red hair was tousled, and his tunic and shirt were half open.

"Was I dreaming, or did one of you come into my room just now?" The voice was gruff, the words sharp, like the whack of a paddle on a boy's behind. He closely eyed them both. Jake tried to stop shaking his injured hand, and Benjamin wheezed for air as he tried to speak.

Clark demanded, "Well, what is it, then? You got some business here? Or did this lad just give you a licking, Sutherland?"

Unable to speak, Benjamin's face was red, and Jake stood

up a little straighter, trying to ignore his throbbing knuckles. Before either of them could reply, Punch landed on Clark's shoulder, and the officer chuckled as the bird pecked at his gold epaulets.

"Hello there, trouble," Clark said, smiling at the jay and lifting his hand to stroke its feathers. "You, at least, are keeping out of mischief, though I have my doubts about your master here."

Just then, Benjamin was stunned to see the ring was on Clark's forefinger, the same finger being used to stroke Punch. Apparently Clark himself was surprised to see the ring, and slipped it from his finger.

"Strange," he said to no one in particular, "I thought I took this off before I lay down. . . ." He replaced it on his ring finger, thought briefly, then again gave his attention to Punch before sending him on his way and bidding the boys to keep out of trouble. He turned and went back into the blockhouse.

Jake was beaming. He sauntered off, the amazed Benjamin coming behind—still crouched over for lack of wind, and trying to speak: "Did—did you?" Benjamin gasped. "Do you mean you went . . . went right in and . . ."

Jake whistled merrily, and Punch landed on his finger. The boy shrugged and said, "Best not mention it, Ben." He shrugged again and grinned at Punch, whose beak touched his nose lightly. "After all, 'tweren't nothing for a honest-to-goodness scout. Right, Punch?"

The day finally came when the women and children were ready to go northeastward to Pitt, and to Ella's joy and relief, the men of her party were assigned to the escort that would guard them on the journey. Benjamin would be with her after all, as would Tom Morely, Mel Webster, and Jeb Grey, Tom and James's stepfather. As a favor to the Sutherlands, George Rogers Clark had arranged this before he had hurriedly set off westward. He was traveling in disguise, in utmost secrecy, intending to counter what he believed was a dangerous British and Indian move against the Illinois and Mississippi valleys. When Clark appeared in a region, the Indians there thought deeply before making trouble. He was feared by most of them, but he could not intimidate anyone if he were known to be off somewhere else.

For now, with Clark gone, there was no single leader of comparable merit in the lower Ohio Valley to organize and inspire the militia. Clark had delegated authority to his officers, however, and the settlements were ready, their plans being for people to evacuate to Harrodsburg, Ruddle's Station, Martin's Station, or the Falls of the Ohio as soon as the first contact was made with Byrd's army. Clark was worried about the enemy's cannon, but not even he could persuade the families to flee to Pitt, leaving their homesteads while he led an army of their menfolk in the field. Byrd had the initiative, and for now Clark had to protect the vulnerable, strategic Illinois outposts.

One aspect of recent events seriously troubled Ella, and that was the amazingly lackadaisical response of many settlers to the news that Byrd had field cannon with him.

It was Jeremy Bently who voiced her feelings one morning as he spoke to a group of men gathered near Ella's dwelling. He said, "No one can underestimate the power of Byrd's army, gentlemen! None of your forts can withstand the guns, save for Pitt, and that means you must evacuate to the strongest defensible positions instead of huddling in your own tiny palisades, like Ruddle's Station, for example!"

The militia did not want to hear this, at least not the men from Virginia and North Carolina, who were most numerous hereabouts. They knew from long experience that Indians could never take a palisade that was bravely defended, and they simply refused to believe that the British and Indians could manhandle cannon of any size through the dense forest all the way from Detroit. Men from the East, however, had a different opinion of just what British soldiers could do—and they had seen cannon in action and knew their destructive effect on timber palisades. But they were in the minority here.

As Ella watched from her doorway, most of the militia laughed at Jeremy's warnings, and one by one they turned away, leaving him alone on the bank near the boat. Some of them muttered under their breath as they departed, and there were even a few insults and wry comments that he was "too British," too "afeared of 'em Redcoats," and had been in the British army too long. Jeremy turned to Ella, and she saw how worried he was. Neither spoke, for they both knew only too well what might happen if Byrd arrived with a large force of Indians, and the cannon to clear the way for them.

If Byrd's force slipped through the Kentucky borderlands before the valley's militia could gather in strength to oppose him in the field, he would have the individual settlements at his mercy. Ella only hoped that if the worst should happen, Captain Byrd would be able to restrain his Indians after gates were battered down and the people were left defenseless.

chapter **13**

ATTACK

The weather was warming up by the time Sutherland's supply dump was established in sheds and cabins just outside Fort McIntosh. The fort was too small to hold the great quantity of barrels, bales, crates, and bags of everything from gunpowder to axes.

With the good weather came the news not only that Indian raids were beginning again, but also that desertions at both Pitt and McIntosh were becoming more frequent. As far as many soldiers were concerned, the war in the East was more pressing than the stalemate in the northwest. British and loyalist troops were besieging Charleston, and crack loyalist cavalry under Colonel Banastre Tarleton was wreaking havoc in backcountry settlements, where rebel militias were few in number and poorly organized.

Most rebels in America had considered the war as good as won, with only terms of a truce to be drawn up; but this British offensive in the South, threatening the homeland of many of the Virginia troops, agitated and infuriated the men at Pitt and

McIntosh. How could they care about the frontier, when their own wives and children were being driven from their homes?

The regulars were rotting here, unpaid for a year, badly clothed, seldom decently fed. Sutherland did not blame them for their outspoken hatred of Congress and resentment for leaders who apparently cared little for their welfare.

With all these complications setting in—combined with the British threat to the Mississippi Valley and the Illinois country—Sutherland found himself trying to be everywhere at once. He led scouting parties into the woods, engineered defensive works for new outposts to watch for the British advance, and helped James Morely organize the supply base at Fort McIntosh.

More difficulties arose as a large number of defenseless refugees arrived, making their way overland or upriver toward the strong post at Pitt. These people were running out of food, having to live for the most part on the scant remainders of their winter stores. Their men were off on duty, roving the Indian paths, or else had been called up for the militia companies at the blockhouses. This left women and children and the elderly in growing, muddy encampments that had to be supplied and protected.

James gave freely of what he could for the sake of these people, and Sutherland was glad to see that. Although James did not trust Congress or the states to pay for what he sold the army and the militia regiments, he was openhanded about giving to the distressed. Unlike Sutherland, James had never thought very highly of the Revolution or of its leaders' motives, and still had not changed his opinion. He was supporting this effort to supply the frontier militia and army in part out of loyalty to Sutherland, and in part because he had made up his mind that his business interests lay in the settlers' holding their ground against British-led Indians. If the British won this campaign, and the Crown held on to the northwest lands, then the development of the Ohio Valley would be stunted for years to come. There would be continual warfare that would prevent population growth. If the rebels won, however, and these settlers held their ground, attracting thousands more, Morely Trading would thrive.

• • •

On a warm June day, Sutherland and James were at dinner in a cabin just outside Fort McIntosh, when there came a shout of alarm, followed by the sound of a horseman galloping in. They rushed outside, into bright sunshine, and saw it was the lawyer, Noah Maxwell, his coat flapping as he jounced up and down on his horse.

Maxwell rode recklessly through a crowd of workmen and shouted to Sutherland that a farm over the hill was under attack, the family doomed unless aid came immediately.

"Big war party!" he gasped, sliding from the horse into the arms of James. "Must be forty or more! I was there visiting this morning when they came out of the woods, killed the master of the house in his field, and bottled up the rest in the cabin!"

Maxwell had romanced a few of the local girls, and no doubt had been trysting at the farm when the Indians attacked. The place was more than a mile away through the woods, on a trail that was good for setting an ambush. While Maxwell babbled on in fear, shouting for men to go save the family, others cried that the regulars from Fort McIntosh should go out there. But Sutherland knew they could do little but be taken by surprise if they dashed off like brave fools.

Sutherland thought quickly. This called for the best men he could round up, and he immediately set a plan into motion. After sending two experienced scouts down the trail for information, he quickly organized the few capable men from among the laborers, ordering them to take up a defensive position a quarter-mile along the trail, to hold the ford of a stream there. Then he rushed to the fort and was given command of half the able-bodied men, about thirty in all, to begin the counterattack. It was not much, but with some of the laborers, it might be enough.

Soon Sutherland's force was closing in on the farmhouse, from where firing could be heard in the distance. They slipped through dense forest, moving in open rank, spread across a hundred yards of woods, a reserve of fifteen men following behind. The day was windless; mosquitoes and flies buzzed about their heads. The sound of gunfire grew louder.

Deploying his men swiftly, Sutherland soon had the farm flanked on two sides. He took a position on the right, on higher ground overlooking the open fields, and as he observed the distant farmyard, he saw the Indians clustered in small groups near the barn and along fencerows. The cabin's defenders were firing back rapidly; at least a couple of men must have been inside, and they knew how to shoot. The Indians were moving in cautiously, a few of them hiding behind an overturned hay wagon, where they were preparing to make a rush on the house from the right side. Once under the windows and loopholes, they could shoot inside or grab hold of rifle muzzles. It would not be long before they attacked. Sutherland had to make his move.

By prearranged hand signals, he brought his men closer, to the very edge of the field, where they collected in a creek bed and lay waiting for his command. The Indians apparently had no idea they were almost trapped.

Sutherland readied his attack force, about two dozen picked men. When he reached the farmyard, the troops in the woods to his left would hit the retreating Indians from the side. It would be bloody but simple.

He ordered his men to take aim. The exposed backs of the Indians were easy targets. "Fire!" A brutal volley rippled along the creek bed, and the Indians went down in groups, the survivors leaping up, startled.

Sutherland gave a shrill Highland battle cry, and his men surged forward, yelling and screaming as fiercely as any Indian. He swung his tomahawk over his head, bellowing in battle-madness, the men at his heels as he dashed across a cornfield just plowed, the earth still black and moist. He leaped over the bloody, scalped body of the farmer, who lay behind his plow. The mule, still in its traces, had also been killed, just for the sport of it. Sutherland charged onward, and the Indians scampered from the farmyard, now about sixty yards away. If not cut off, they would melt into the woods and have to be run down, one by one.

But suddenly the Indians turned as a group and opened fire in a sharp volley that sent slugs flicking past Sutherland's head. A man beside him groaned and stumbled, and another cried out, the sound of death in his throat before he even hit the ground. There were still some Indians aiming to fire, and the whites slowed their rush, for three had been hit in the unexpected volley. Who would have expected the Indians to stand their ground like soldiers, when they always fled to fight in the trees, where they had a better chance?

Indians fired again, when Sutherland was just forty yards from them, and another white man was hit. More Indians had reloaded and were ready to fire.

"Take cover!" Sutherland shouted, and his men dived to the side as these warriors opened up. He himself did not take cover, but saw to the wounded, hauling a moaning, half-conscious man behind a large pile of boulders, at the same time assessing the situation. The Indians had loaded and fired like trained regulars, so there was never a time when they all had empty guns. To charge into that would have been slaughter, even though Indians were notoriously poor shots.

Sutherland was recklessly pacing back and forth among his men, who were now exchanging sharpshooting with the enemy and had begun to cut them down.

"Make it hot for 'em, lads!" he cried to his troops, who were spread out at the edge of the cornfield, behind boulders and a rail fence. The exposed Indians now were outmatched, and with a braying screech from their leader, they withdrew slowly, firing, and carrying their dead and wounded. In a few moments they would come in range of Sutherland's flanking party, which with discipline was holding its fire.

Smoke hung gray and acrid over the pretty cornfield, sunlight slanting down on dead and dying littering the ground. The people in the cabin shoved open a shutter to wave and shout encouragement as they continued to fire at the withdrawing Indians. About to order the advance, Sutherland was surprised to see the warriors again regrouping, this time at a hedgerow just beyond the farmyard. They meant to continue fighting back. Normally they would have retreated instead of risking heavy loss, for even one death in a victorious war party had to be mourned for days before any reveling would be permitted in a village.

Determined to drive them off, Sutherland swung the tomahawk like a sword. "Let's move," he called out, and his men rose to crouching runs, to take new positions in the farmyard, behind wagons and dead cattle and a small chicken coop. They closed on the Indians, who kept firing back, and two more whites fell.

"They want us to rush them!" a man shouted angrily, waving a knife. "So let's give 'em cold steel!"

Others cursed as the dead and wounded were dragged to shelter. It was not in the nature of the white fighting man on the frontier to be restrained when his blood was up and friends were dead or dying. Sutherland was suspicious, however, and knew what could happen if brave men threw caution to the winds. These Indian raiders were behaving too methodically, as if there was some plan he could not yet detect.

"Let's get 'em, Mr. Sutherland!" a man with a wounded arm cried from behind the chicken coop. "I owe 'em a lick!"

"Afore they turn tail and get away!" another shouted.

But Sutherland stood there at the corner of the cabin and took in the scene. The Indians were too bold, too confident against so many armed whites. Bullets flew and hummed around him, and he counted the enemy holding the fencerow. One good volley from his own men, followed by a determined frontal attack, would normally be enough to dislodge them. Already the Indians had lost heavily, and at his feet was a dead, painted warrior they had not had the time to carry off.

Just then, a rebel came scampering through the whizzing lead and dropped next to the Indian. A scalping knife came out, one foot held the head down at the neck, and in a trice the hair was lifted. The white man howled like a savage, waving the bloody scalp as other whites jeered riotously. Sutherland scarcely noticed. He was peering through the smoke, searching for something that would tell him what he wanted to know. But his men's patience was finished.

"Have at 'em!" someone growled.

"Lead us on, Mr. Sutherland!"

"Red skunks! Give us the word, Mr. Sutherland!"

The Indians egged them on, hooting and hurling insults in colorful English—well-learned from trappers and traders— calling Sutherland's men white bastards and sons of bitches, and shouting at them to "Come on if you're men and not dogs!"

"Goddamn *Bostonnais!* Fight us, cowards! Fight if you be men!"

That did it. A big soldier near Sutherland howled and sprang to his feet, charging past at the Indians. But quick as any bullet would have done it, Sutherland grabbed him bodily and threw him to the ground.

"Hold on!" Sutherland ordered all of them. "There's more to this! You'll get your fight yet."

"But, Mr. Sutherland, those slimy red niggers—"

Sutherland stood there in a hail of bullets, and his men stilled their complaining. He had seen something. Now he knew why these raiders were so bold. From back in the woods, fifty yards behind these first warriors, he saw a feather flicker here, a movement there, the glint of sunlight on metal.

Another party of Indians was behind the first, lying in wait at the edge of the trees. It was an ambush, as if Sutherland's stroke had been expected by the enemy leader. Whoever was leading these Indians knew his business, and likely had expected the rescue force to come out of the fort. He had readied this reserve in the woods to counterattack at the moment the rebel troops were caught in the open, when they thought they had all the Indians on the run.

Sutherland commanded his men to hold their positions, and sent a messenger back to order his own reserve through the woods further to the left, to fall upon the Indians hiding in the forest. So far, Sutherland had seen no whites with the Indians. That was strange for a war party so large, and so well disciplined. Somewhere in those distant woods was a military commander who knew his business: Girty, or even Mark Davies. Perhaps he would soon find out.

At the right moment, Sutherland advanced his troops another ten yards, moving slowly from cover to cover, under bullets from Indians behind the fencerow. These warriors were bold, standing their ground as they enticed Sutherland to lead his men headlong into the ambush. But he would not charge yet. Not yet.

He felt the lack of his claymore. When the time came, this would be an all-out frontal charge, and he would have welcomed his officer's steel. His trade tomahawk would have to do, and he brandished it as he strode back and forth, in plain sight of the Indians. In some ways, he was an old-fashioned commander for wars in the northwest. Old-fashioned officers always stayed on their feet in a pitched battle, no matter how bitter the shooting. Sutherland had been conditioned to that tradition, even though out here all men usually fought from cover like Indians, officers included.

Bullets zinged past, cut the grass and kicked up dirt all around as every Indian took aim at him. More than once he felt the whiz of a slug as it sang close to him. He knew his brazen disregard for the enemy's marksmanship would have its effect on their morale. Indians were sensitive to honor and insult, and if an enemy showed himself utterly unafraid of them, they thought twice when that enemy went on the attack.

The moment came. Suddenly, Sutherland's reserve in the woods struck the hidden Indians. Firing became hot and heavy in the trees, the shots and screams of battle erupting behind the startled Indians still fighting in the open field. They looked back, confused, to see some of their companions being driven out of the woods where they had been hiding. This was Sutherland's moment. He yelled for the attack. His men rose in one body, tomahawks and knives in hand, their rifles left behind, and hurled themselves across the remaining yards to the fence-row.

The Indians did not stay, and streamed off to the right, few firing back, most dashing for their lives as some of the swifter whites caught up with them. Sutherland collected the rifles and led half his men against the Indians concealed in the woods and, combined with the reserve's vicious assault, drove them out, to flee into a tangle of swamp and undergrowth, death at their heels.

With the people in the farmhouse out of danger, Sutherland organized his rangers into small parties to trail the retreating enemy and to make sure they had taken enough for one day. Then he rapidly led a party back toward the supply dump. His men were excited, many of them praising him, calling him brilliant, wishing aloud that he would lead them again against the approaching enemy army. But Sutherland was uneasy. Although his fight had been a success, it still did not feel right to him. Something was wrong.

Then, when they were less than half a mile from the fort and supply base, the answer came. The earth shook with a tremendous boom. With sudden anguish, Sutherland knew the worst had happened.

"At the double!" he cried, and led them down the trail at full run. The supply camp had been hit. That was their gun-powder blowing up.

When Sutherland burst recklessly out of the forest, he found the cabins in roaring flames, the storage buildings still exploding as black powder went up, keg after keg. The enemy was already gone, not a living rebel in sight. Sutherland stopped at the edge of the camp, horror and fury boiling in him as he stared at the destruction, which sent billows of gray smoke into the blue sky. He had been brilliantly outmaneuvered, and he harshly blamed himself.

He did not excuse himself by saying the people of the farm would have been wiped out had he forsaken them, and that there had been no other choice but to go to their aid. It did not matter that the enemy had suffered heavy losses in his sortie. All Sutherland could think of was that the precious powder and supplies were gone. There was little left with which to aid the endangered lower settlements now.

Then he thought of James Morely. Was he dead? Sutherland's bitter, distraught soldiers were searching for dead and wounded amid the devastation, some of them dragging what could be saved out of burning buildings. In anguish Sutherland called for James, ran to their cabin, and found it ablaze. James was nowhere in sight. Soldiers came hurrying from the fort, and a pursuit force was hastily organized, but Sutherland advised them to move slowly, carefully, lest they meet an ambush.

The officers, disconsolate and pale, collected near the water and paused to look a moment downriver, where the enemy had fled. Some Indians had even come up in canoes and surprised the sentries that way.

It had happened in a twinkling, a horde of Indians swarming out of the woods to fall on the base camp. The cabins and storage sheds near the fort had been set ablaze, most of the guards slain as Sutherland's main body was off defeating the decoys. The soldiers in Fort McIntosh had been pinned within the palisade by heavy musket fire, while James's inexperienced men were shot to pieces. Overrun in less than two minutes.

It was all perfectly planned and timed, as if the enemy commander had understood the tactics and disposition of the defenders—had known beforehand all about the supply camp.

An officer, his face blackened from smoke and dirt, threw his tricorne on the ground and kicked it away, cursing, "They must have bloody well known most of the men left here were not soldiers, Mr. Sutherland, or they'd never have dared attack so many of them! Damned curs! But how could they have known?"

Sutherland wondered the same thing. It had been no routine hit-and-run raid, for there were too many Indians, and yet there had not been enough to take Fort McIntosh. Normally, unless they had meant to take the fort, Indians would not have come so dangerously close to it. They obviously were after only the supplies.

Sutherland said, "It smells like spies' work, gentlemen, and now it's every settlement for itself." As he said this, he thought about Ella and the others at the Falls of the Ohio. He was relieved they would be getting out before the main blow was struck.

Just then, a shout came from downstream, and two militiamen hurried up the river trail, James Morely slung between them, his legs dragging. Expecting the worst, Sutherland ran to him. But James was not wounded, although he had been beaten badly.

A soldier declared, "Injuns carried him off, sir, but didn't do for him, though I don't know why."

James was laid on the ground, and as he came to, he looked up at Sutherland, who was kneeling over him. James saw the flames and gave a bewildered start, trying weakly to rise, but Sutherland gently held him down, saying it was all over.

Sutherland wanted to know what had happened, and James flushed, as if ashamed. Sutherland had seen this look of brutal self-reproach before, when James had been a sentry and had failed to give the alarm in time to prevent a surprise attack in the Wyoming Valley. Sutherland told James, who was atremble from the shock, to steady himself.

Turning to the others, Sutherland asked that they permit him and James to speak in private. James sat up, refused a drink of water, and stared blindly at the river rushing past.

He muttered, "I should've been ready."

Sutherland said, "Do not blame yourself."

James looked sharply around, then away again. "It was Davies and Girty!"

Now Sutherland understood, and he suspected Davies had a spy or informer—someone who wanted the supplies destroyed.

James groaned, "Why did they not kill me, Owen? I don't understand. They killed so many others, before my eyes. . . ." He shuddered, as if about to break down, and seemed woozy.

Sutherland asked, "Are you feeling faint, lad?"

James hardened, mouth tight as he hissed, "Faint? Why do you say that?"

Sutherland gave no reply. A moment passed, and then he said, "What matters now is that we collect as much as we can, little as it may be, to send downriver—"

"More?" James almost squealed, gazing wide-eyed at all his valuable goods going up in flames. "You think I can find more after this? Everything I owned is there, there in those buildings! There is no more! And if there was, I wouldn't be able to pay for it!"

Sutherland saw the wild dismay in James's face, and that troubled him. He wanted James to keep hold of himself, no matter what. "There's no use for self-pity." Perhaps he said that more bluntly than he should have.

James became angrier, and gritted his teeth as he said, "Your damned inept rebel army caused this! Your fool Congress, fool states let this happen because they won't send the troops or money needed to defend this valley!"

He struggled to his feet, hands in fists as he gestured at the blazing cabins, crying out so loudly that everyone nearby heard him: "Why should private citizens have to pay for this? Why should you or I pay for this when your leaders will not even pay their soldiers who are trapped here to await their doom? Answer that, Mr. Sutherland, spokesman of the noble Revolution!"

"Steady," Sutherland said, his anger mounting. He thought to turn his back and walk away, but that would only make matters worse. "You will be paid . . . I've given my word."

James sneered, blood and spittle at the corners of his mouth: "A fine thing, your word, Owen! I respect it well, but your poxy Congress cares not a whit for a man's word, or his honor, or his success or failure! This war of yours profits a few wealthy men, satisfies their craving for power and more power, no matter who dies on either side! Your word means nothing to them, not yours or George Rogers Clark's or Dan Boone's! Your Congress scarce respects Washington himself! They can't or won't supply or pay even their troops besieging New York itself—"

James paled suddenly, his eyes rolling, and Sutherland caught him as he fell. Other men hurried over, but Sutherland waved them off. He carried James to a secluded spot in the sunshine, beside the water, and there laid him down, with his head held low to get the blood back into it. After a moment, James recovered, looking weak and miserably embarrassed.

"It's nothing. . . ." he muttered, hand to his forehead.

As gently as he could, Sutherland said, "There's no need to conceal from me what I already know about your condition."

James spat out, "My *weakness,* you mean?"

Sutherland was exasperated and took a long breath. Not far away the pursuit force was readying to depart, and the officers were waiting for Sutherland to lead them. He touched James on the shoulder, but James recoiled and looked away, the back of his hand to his trembling lips.

"James, will you help us resupply?"

Sutherland had no idea what to expect. James stared at him, as if half in disbelief, half in angry defiance at being so challenged to accomplish the impossible.

Sutherland said, "Colonel Brodhead at Pitt will authorize commandeering private goods and draft animals from the people here, and I would give my personal note to them in return, as commissary for the defense force. But they know you well here, and they trust you—it will be better if you stand for the goods, and you in turn will be paid by me."

James made a sound of exasperation and rolled his head from side to side as he leaned against a tree. "My Lord, Owen, how you live in a world of dreams and fancy."

Sutherland stood up and nodded to the officers waiting for him. Then to James, he said, "We need everything we can raise, immediately, and you know best where it can be had."

James made no reply, and Sutherland set off after the enemy raiders.

James sat there a little longer, thinking how strange it was that the attackers had not simply killed him when they broke into the cabin where he had been writing. Others had been murdered on the spot, but he and Noah Maxwell were dragged out, uninjured until James tried to fight and had been beaten.

As James had watched in horror, tied to a tree, the cabins and buildings had been torched, men killed. He still had no idea what had happened to Maxwell, but guessed that he, too, had died.

This was the most terrible day of his life; hardly anything was left, save his good name. Now Sutherland was asking him to put that in jeopardy as well. If he went to people here and asked for more, only on credit—on the dream that Congress or the states would pay in due time—he would be looked upon as a fool. His reputation would be irretrievably damaged. No one here believed, as Sutherland did, in the promises of the rebel Congress. No one in this country had any illusions about the men now in charge of the rebellion, men who cared not a damn about the northwest or its people. Ask the unhappy regulars about that.

Just then someone approached, and James was startled and relieved to see Noah Maxwell. His clothes were torn, but apparently he was unhurt. James leaped up and gripped him by the shoulders, asking what had happened.

Maxwell was pale, his eyes haunted as he glanced about at the carnage, especially at the butchered, dismembered bodies that were being carried away in blankets.

To himself, Maxwell murmured, "I had no idea it would be anything . . . anything like this." Closing his eyes, he whispered, "Lord forgive—"

James shook him. "Are you all right? Noah! Tell me!"

Maxwell shuddered violently, his breath coming in gasps, until he lowered his head, and said softly, "I'll be all right, James." He caught a breath that seemed to instill determination, and said again he would be all right. James knew this Philadelphian had never seen a massacre before.

They started off toward the fort, but then Maxwell anxiously asked to wait until all the bodies had been brought past and put from his sight. To avoid the roar of the fires, the intense heat and smoke all round, they went back to the river and sat on logs. Suddenly, as if obsessed, Maxwell scrambled toward the river and began furiously washing his hands. From where he sat, James thought the man was sobbing. That was understandable, for he must have been close to death himself. After a while, responding to James's question, Maxwell said his escape had been pure luck, that he had fallen into a bush and hidden there until it was all over. He kept washing his hands, shoulders heaving, a pathetic figure.

James glumly considered again how Owen Sutherland must more than ever think him a weakling, a man who takes fainting spells at critical moments. Well, whatever Sutherland thought, it did not matter. He threw a rock into the river and watched the splash drift away into the white foam. James Morely was one man who did not care what high-and-mighty Owen Sutherland thought of him, especially when what Sutherland thought was wrong, a result of faulty judgment. If Sutherland wanted to carry on this bloody war, let him find the goods, the supplies, if he was so sure Congress would pay, which James believed it would not.

James decided to sit out the rest of this fight, safe in Fort Pitt, where he would make new plans, change his old ones if he must. Then he glanced up and saw the dead being hauled away, and for an instant of chilling horror imagined one of those bodies Susannah Sutherland's. He felt anger and helplessness to think that she and a thousand others like her might be dead before this foul work was done.

Then he closed his eyes, shaking his head and sighing as he accused himself of being a fool, just like Sutherland. Yes, he knew he would try again, somehow, to collect what was needed to protect the settlements. In a determined voice, he told this to Maxwell, who was staring at the sand where he crouched. Maxwell turned, a frantic look in his eyes.

"But you can't!" he cried. "You mustn't!"

Surprised, James asked why not.

Maxwell glanced about almost wildly until he replied, "Because the enemy is . . . too strong here, and . . . and will come back. . . ."

"We'll be ready for them next time."

"We?" Maxwell blustered, attempting a scoff. "You talk like you're one of these starry-eyed rebels! We? You're no rebel, my friend—you're a man of the world, as am I, and as is our Mr. Cullen. Now, be reasonable, and put all this folly behind you. Give it up, for goodness sake." He was recovering from his shock. He rose, pacing as he declared, "Bless me, James, but you do yet have the innocence of the young, for all your cunning businessman's heart."

Maxwell grinned crookedly. James saw no humor, but well knew what he was saying was true. Still, there was a point of honor involved, and a challenge by which he would prove to Owen Sutherland that he was as good a man as any. It would be a feat to collect what was needed from an impoverished countryside. He said this last to Maxwell, who guffawed.

"Bless me, James, but you do want the eye of Owen Sutherland! Why? He's a man of the past, of another age, like Boone and Clark and the rest! Why do you give a damn about Sutherland?"

James got up and began to walk to the fort with Maxwell, and after a moment said, "Perhaps it's because I have some affection for his daughter."

"What? Bless me, James, but you are a delight sometimes!" Maxwell shielded his face against the scorching blaze from a cabin and said, "You fancy some frontier wench, when you could snap your fingers and gobble up rich Linda Cullen, snatch her right out of my own hands! Bless me!"

James said, "Sutherland is a great man, and once was like a father to me, after my own father was murdered by renegades.

"I can't help myself, sometimes," he went on, "but having the respect of Owen Sutherland almost means more to me than doing business with Cullen, no matter how rich I become."

Maxwell chuckled sympathetically. "So you'll wed Sutherland's Cinderella and forsake the Cullen fortune, eh? This Cinderella must be quite a beauty, a princess!"

James said she was not yet of marriageable age, and when Maxwell blurted out a laugh, crying "Bless me," James became irritable, embarrassed, especially while they were surrounded by so many gloomy people, weeping over the dead.

chapter **14**

A MINOR SKIRMISH

The next few days were hell for James Morely.

After the success and honor he had earned over the past months, the loss of all his supplies in one astonishing disaster had apparently shaken the confidence of many who once had been eager to do business with him. For that or for some unexplained reason, James found no one willing to extend him credit, and there were even a few who bluntly said he had been rash to put all his eggs in the rebel basket. These sounded almost like Bradford Cullen, as if they had heard the man say this to James.

Now there was another mood in the air at Fort Pitt: doubt over who would control the Forks of the Ohio when the war was done. Since many people here had little love for Congress or the rebellion, some would willingly turn their coats to the British side if need be. James could not deny what they were saying about the prospects for defense now, for their pessimism had the ring of truth.

Strangely, even many who had been ardent supporters of the rebellion were uncooperative with James—once more, it was as if they had been put up to it by someone. James went to prosperous farmers to buy cattle, only to find the herds had been driven far away into the woods, allegedly to prevent their being requisitioned for a pittance by the hungry regulars at the fort. When he went to gunsmiths to buy muskets and rifles, it appeared every gun had either been bought up recently by some anonymous purchaser, or the gunsmith was not working because of illness. Three gunsmiths were said to be sick with the flux all at the same time.

It was likewise with the owner of the Pitt powder mill, a man of ambiguous leanings in the rebellion, but one who normally sold to anyone—including illegally to Indians, it was suspected—for the right price. He told James that he had no powder on hand, and would not go to the trouble of starting the manufacture of more without a large cash down payment, much more than James could afford.

Most grain mills refused James the same way, and every shoemaker at Pitt seemed to be out of stock. Even his own boatyard had trouble buying lumber for a gunboat that Sutherland had suggested would help hold the river crossings.

James was ashamed at this chill reception. Few were willing to extend the least credit to Morely Trading, and he found himself virtually bankrupt, with no prospects of recovery. Certainly he could not supply Owen Sutherland. He was failing. Obviously he was not the success he had once believed himself to be.

Early one warm morning, James was about to depart for Fort McIntosh to meet Sutherland, when Maxwell hailed him on the wharf. Gloomy and feeling beaten, James was also suffering from lack of sleep and from nervous strain. He stood sullenly on the wharf, watching what few goods he had been able to collect for Sutherland being loaded into a flatboat. Maxwell approached, looking fresh and trim.

Well dressed as ever, the young lawyer obviously had recovered from the horror of the Fort McIntosh slaughter, and he greeted James heartily. "My, you look the worse for wear, my friend! Bless me!"

James needed no such comments and said so. He was about to make for the gangplank when Maxwell touched his arm and drew him aside a moment.

"Won't you reconsider Mr. Cullen's generous offer?"

James licked his lips, glanced about at nothing in particular, and felt very tempted to say yes.

Instead he said, "Out of weakness? That's not good business practice, Noah."

Exasperated, Maxwell raised his hands, then clapped them together, as if James's comment had been a complete misinterpretation of Cullen's intentions. He said what had happened was a tragedy, but certainly understandable under the circumstances.

"Mr. Cullen means only the best for you, James! He does not mean to, ah . . . take any advantage—"

James moved away to escape Maxwell's hand on his arm. "But it would be the same as coming to him out of weakness."

"Nonsense!"

"You know it." James would not crawl for any man, and if he joined Cullen, it would be only because it was the wisest step, not out of desperation. He said this, adding, "I will not admit so soon that I am beaten, Noah."

Again Maxwell was good-naturedly exasperated. "Mr. Cullen needs you, James. I need you. Listen, my friend, if we wanted anyone else, we could have him—a hundred of them! It's you, James Morely, we want with us!"

James felt that. He knew Maxwell was sincere, and it gave him a lift of spirit. Thanking his friend, he said, "I'll consider it further, then."

Maxwell was delighted. "Excellent!" He shook hands with James and clapped him on the back as they walked to the gangplank. "Mr. Cullen would be proud, you know that! And no matter what your final decision, you know he'd never make malicious remarks about you the way Owen Sutherland has."

James bristled. "What remarks?" He was startled to hear this, though ready enough to believe such an accusation against Owen Sutherland, who he believed certainly had no high regard for him.

Maxwell hemmed and muttered an apology, saying he had not meant to bring it up, had not meant to "poison" anything. James insisted he explain himself. On the boat a man was calling that the wind was fair for Fort McIntosh, and they had to go.

Maxwell shook his head, gestured toward the boat, and said James should think no more of it. "Surely they were just inadvertent comments said in the heat of anger and disappointment—nothing to worry about, and nothing for you to hold against the man." James wanted to hear more, but Maxwell refused, as if trying to give James a cheery good-bye.

The lawyer was startled when James suddenly grabbed him by his coat and drove him back, lifting him off his feet, demanding, "Tell me, Noah! Tell me what he said, or so help me—"

The men at the boat fell silent to see two wealthy men grappling. Maxwell flushed, and insisted that James let go before he would talk. This James did, though the anger did not leave him. Maxwell straightened his coat, and James angrily picked up the lawyer's hat, waiting impatiently for the reply.

Softly, so the men would not overhear, Maxwell carefully said, "Just rumors, of course . . . nothing I can prove he said—"

"Tell me!"

"Well . . . he said you were not strong. Something to the effect that, with the beating you just took—all the losses, I mean—that you didn't have the strength of character to recover, and that now no one stood between the Frontier Company and that—that 'bastard,' he said—'that bastard Cullen.'"

James flushed, fury mingling with disappointment that Sutherland might say such a thing. It was bad enough that so much had been lost, but James could not stand to lose like this. He would not stand for anything that belittled his reputation.

"How do you know he said that?"

Maxwell shrugged. "It's all over the town. Ask anyone."

"Ask anyone?" James shook his head slowly. How could he simply ask anyone such a question, a question that made him out to be an insecure failure on top of everything else? He glanced at the men in the boat, and told himself they might very well be thinking what Maxwell had just said: Owen Sutherland soon would be back at Cullen's throat, but James Morely had been only a flash in the pan.

No, James would ask no one about this but Owen Sutherland himself. He almost felt as if he had been set up for this defeat, had been dragged by Sutherland into an extremely vulnerable position that had cost him all he owned in one sudden raid. He went onto the boat without bidding Maxwell good-bye, striding to the other rail, where he stared hard at the shadowy forest across the Monongahela River.

The boat lurched, wind filling its sails, and drifted into the current. James felt or saw nothing around him. He was thinking about Owen Sutherland, wondering what the man was really about. Had he some reason to try to demean James at every opportunity?

Sutherland himself would have to answer that question, next time they met.

Benjamin Sutherland moved quietly through the woods, close enough to the Ohio River to hear it rushing beyond the tall trees behind him. He was scouting the land near an encampment where his family and friends had stopped to repair one of their whaleboats, which had been driven by wind and current against the rocks that morning.

Overhead, the blue jay, Punch, flitted noiselessly through the trees, and Benjamin glanced at him once or twice for any indication that the bird knew Indians might be near. Punch located Indians and often attacked even peaceful ones on sight. Ahead, the white husky, Heera, walked easily on the narrow trail. Close behind Benjamin came Little Jake, armed with only a small bow and a belt of arrows. Jake was learning quickly and kept alert as they explored.

The camp was a hundred yards back on a sandy, treeless peninsula at the end of this deer trail. There were ten men and twice as many women and children, traveling to Pitt in three whaleboats. They were on the southern side, the Kentucky side of the Ohio, where it was relatively safe, but Benjamin could take no chances, and moved silently through the forest in search of any sign that war parties might be at hand.

He did not wear his father's claymore because it was too unwieldy in the woods, and he was still too slight for it. A tomahawk hung at his side, and he carried a loaded and primed Pennsylvania rifle as he glided through the underbrush, not making a sound. Little Jake was doing almost as well behind him. The trees were young, the undergrowth a tangle of bracken and brambles. The ground became lower and swampier, until Benjamin worked his way to higher rocks overlooking the river. There, still in concealment, he paused a while in the fresh breeze to observe his people down below.

Heera joined him, sitting panting, ears pricked up. Jake sat nearby, his dirty face scratched by thorns, his hair caught with twigs, but he looked happy. Benjamin grinned at the boy and rubbed his head, not speaking, for they would try not to speak at all until they were back at camp. Benjamin enjoyed the steady, cool breeze after the murk of the swamp. He looked through the trees at his people and noticed that some men in the party had already pushed the damaged whaleboat back into the water to test it. Soon they could get under way again, and he was excited that in a week or so he would be rejoining his father. He could see his mother and Susannah sitting together on a sunny rock, and the others were idling about, a couple of men standing guard.

Not far away to the east was the mouth of the Licking River. Upstream in that direction were several stations, including Ruddle's, Martin's, and, farther to the southwest, Harrodsburg, the largest of them. Many settlers lived there, especially North Carolina and Virginia people, the sort who were so confident— overconfident, as Jeremy had said. They had been fighting Indians all their lives and did not greatly fear the sudden appearance of a large war party before their gates.

Everywhere scouts were out, and as soon as the enemy was discovered in force, the militia would be called into a large body, and more troops would be sent down from Fort Pitt. The frontier could raise a thousand good fighting men with rifles in a couple of weeks, and the approaching British-Indian army would be hard pressed. With the people and their livestock protected inside palisades, and the crops not yet ready, there would be little foraging for the enemy this time of year. Before long they would be hungry and would find themselves harried and hunted on their flanks, until at last they would be lucky to escape back home with their lives.

At least so everyone believed—except for Jeremy and Gwen Bently, who feared the cannon. Benjamin Sutherland was inclined to go along with the opinion of the settlers, however. Frontiersmen were fighting for their families and homes, and would not be driven out like so many pigeons—

Just then Punch flew down and struck Benjamin in the face with his wings, startling the lad, almost making him laugh . . . until he knew this was a warning. At the same moment, Heera growled low in his throat. Indians! Swinging around, Benjamin moved toward the far side of the rock on which he sat and looked down at the open swampland to his left. His heart leaped, pounding wildly as he saw at least a hundred Indians slipping through the swamp grass, making for the encampment. There was barely time to outrun them, for they were already on the move, ready to attack. He had to give warning!

There was only one thing to do. He raised his rifle and took careful aim at a warrior who was feathered and painted like a chief. The man was only thirty yards away. He would fall, the others would momentarily take cover, and Benjamin could spring into the bushes to catch up with his family. The sound of the shot would be enough to warn them, and they would be in the boats right away.

Suddenly, Benjamin felt an icy chill. Little Jake was still sitting on the rock, gazing calmly at the river, unaware of danger. He would never get away in time.

Benjamin acted swiftly, scrambled up to Jake, and yanked him close, whispering, "Indians down there! You go now! Fast! Way we came! Tell them to run! Tell them not to wait for me! Go!"

Jake was terrified and wide-eyed, but he made not a sound as Benjamin gave him a shove and sent him along the trail, only a dozen yards ahead of the first Indians. Then Benjamin turned to find a target. He could hear the enemy by now, just yards away. They were all around him.

Ella was speaking to Susannah, telling her to buck up, and that if James Morely truly loved her he would show it.

"You know your father and I will not stand in your way if—"

The sound of Benjamin's rifle sent fright coursing through her, and she leaped to her feet. Seconds later, Jake dashed out of the woods as fast as his feet could fly, wailing that they had to go.

"Ben says to run!" Jeremy caught him up, shaking him for a clear answer. "Ben says don't wait! Indians everywhere!"

The others scurried about, whaleboats being shoved into the water. Jeremy and three men grabbed rifles and headed in the direction of the gunshot. There came another shot, and suddenly the forest erupted in smoke and fire. Indians rushed out of the trees sixty yards away, firing and yelping as they came. Jeremy dropped to one knee, as did the others, and fired back. These first shots hit three Indians and drove the attackers back into cover. Ella caught up a rifle and ammunition and joined the men in a line to cover the boarding of the boats. Sally was hurrying the children into the water, and bullets zinged past, striking the boats and splashing into the river.

"Ben!" she wailed to Jeremy, whose wild expression was as desperate as hers. He loaded and rammed home the bullet, and Ella cried out, "We can't leave him!"

Jeremy yanked out the ramrod, and with Jeb Grey at his side, charged headlong toward the trees, in the direction of another rifle shot, and the distant sound of Heera snarling and barking. Ella began to follow, heedless of the consequences, but suddenly Jeremy stumbled, his left leg spurting blood, and Jeb swung to grab him up. An Indian leaped from the trees and sprinted at them, tomahawk raised. Jeb did not see him, struggling as he was with the wounded Jeremy.

Ella screamed, and Gwen was there, too, her baby in arms. The other men were all dropping back, more of them wounded. They had to get out now, or they were finished. The painted warrior was almost on Jeb, and Ella whipped up her rifle and, scarcely aiming, fired. She missed!

The warrior came on. Almost too late, Jeb spun to see him, but could not get his weapon up to fire. Then Cape was there, snarling and snapping, a brown fury as she hit the Indian and went for the throat. The Indian was knocked off balance, his blow missing, and Jeb's rifle banged, dropping the man in a heap. Other Indians came out of the woods, firing and moving forward, dodging the return fire.

Ella flew to Jeb, who had thrown Jeremy over his broad shoulders and was lumbering back toward the boats. Gwen was there, too, the wailing baby still in her arms, as frantically she sought to discover how badly Jeremy was hurt. Under the steady fire, they embarked, as Ella and the rest of the men formed another line to cover the escape.

There was no panic, no confusion. The firing line blunted the enthusiasm of the first attackers, who had made their charge before the main body was able to come up to support them. Ella was terrified for Benjamin, but she did not break down. Loading and firing like one of the men, she moved slowly backward as the rest of the party got into the boats.

She heard the name Benjamin being spoken over and over again, and as she moved back into the water, she realized it was her own voice, calling desperately for her beautiful son.

It was almost two weeks later when James Morely finally had the chance to confront Owen Sutherland, who had been on a long scout toward the Shawnee towns, a dangerous and arduous journey through country swarming with small enemy war parties. Sutherland had been lucky to get back alive, and had brought word that the enemy army had moved southward, to cross the Ohio and strike at the Kentucky settlements first.

James met the weary Sutherland in a rebuilt cabin outside Fort McIntosh, and at first listened patiently while the Scotsman related what he had told the rebel commanders. Sutherland was gaunt and exhausted, and had been bruised and cut in hand-to-hand fighting with enemy scouts. Soon after he told James all the news, he nearly collapsed onto his cot, closing his eyes, obviously about to fall fast asleep.

James knew that Sutherland needed this rest badly, but he could not hold back, and drew up a chair next to the man's cot, staring at him in the hope he would respond. But it appeared Sutherland would be asleep at any moment.

"I have to ask you something, Owen."

Eyes closed, Sutherland mumbled, "Aye, laddie?" Already he sounded far away.

"It's very important."

"Aye?" He muttered something unintelligible until James gave the bed a rough shake, and he came back to consciousness asking what was the matter. Sutherland looked at James with a glaze of weariness in his face until he apparently realized the fellow had something serious on his mind. With much effort, Sutherland leaned on one elbow. "What is it, then?"

James drew himself up and said, "It's said you have declared me incompetent, unable to resupply you because I am not . . . not good enough."

"What?" Sutherland seemed unable to comprehend; he sat up, rubbed his eyes, and was about to reply, but James spoke first.

"I have always known you held me in low esteem because

I'm not a fighting man like you, or like my father was—"

Sutherland's voice was a croak. "Don't bring your father into this."

"Don't tell me what to do!"

Sutherland looked up sharply, as if temper was almost getting the best of him. That did not worry James, for he had a temper as hot as any man's.

Sutherland restrained himself, however; he sighed, saying, "I'm not surprised that you can't resupply us now, but I don't blame you."

"Then whom do you blame?"

Sutherland sat up as if his entire body ached, and said, "Cullen, and your friend Maxwell. They've either bought up all that's available and sent it somewhere out of reach, or have placed orders with suppliers on the condition that none of them do business with you."

"Preposterous!" James refused to be dragged into the old, bitter quarrel between Sutherland and Cullen, a quarrel that Sutherland more than Cullen seemed eager to perpetuate, as far as James could see.

"Is it preposterous? Are you so knowledgeable, so experienced—" Sutherland caught himself again, and with a wave of the hand, said, "Ach, James, Cullen wants you with him, and first he'll break you to do it."

"You'd think Cullen was the devil himself, the way you talk, Owen!" James's anger was mounting. He did not like Sutherland's self-righteous attitude, especially because the man seemed to be trying so nobly not to argue.

Sutherland rose and went to get a glass of whiskey from a sideboard near the window. "He is the devil, laddie, and he's the man that killed your father—don't forget it."

"Don't change the subject! There's no proof of that—"

Sutherland swung, his eyes fierce. "No proof! No, perhaps not the proof you bright younger folk need, tied up neat and legal and wrapped in the technicalities of the law of knaves like Noah Maxwell! No, not that proof—but I'm a man who uses common sense, who can smell the stench of Cullens and Maxwells, and I don't need you to tell me who they are!" He drank and poured another. "I hold nothing against you."

James cursed under his breath, his hands in fists. He realized that he was on his feet. The precise matter of the rumor was unimportant now, for it was obvious that Sutherland's low opinion of him was coming out all at once.

James said, "How you feel about me is quite clear."

Sutherland waved off James's reply, declaring, "If you had the common sense, you'd know Cullen and Maxwell were somehow behind the attack on our supplies."

"You're mad!"

"Am I? Perhaps it's you who's mad! Either mad or on your way to becoming just like them, with Maxwell's law on your side, wrapping crimes up in legalities to mask the stink—"

"That's enough!" James turned away, then spun back on his heel to glare at Sutherland, who was calm, for all his intensity, pouring another whiskey with a steady hand while James was shaking from head to foot. "Your old hatreds won't poison me, Owen, nor will I let them stand in my way!"

Sutherland looked around sharply at that. "What do you mean?"

"None of your business." James would not tell Sutherland about Cullen's latest offer, nor would he stoop to trying to convince the stubborn Scotsman that Cullen was not the utter villain everyone in the Frontier Company believed him to be. "Think what you want, Owen, and say what you want about me."

There was a pause, and James wished Sutherland would interject that he had never spread a bad word about him. Sutherland said nothing, however, downing the whiskey and pouring yet another, before putting the bottle back on its shelf and going to sit at the small table in the middle of the room.

Through clenched teeth, James said, "You cannot blame Bradford Cullen for all the ills and evils of the northwest! I'll wager you're as much to blame as anyone for the troubles out here—you and your damned rebel Congress, those tight-fisted tyrants who make Cullen look generous!"

Sutherland slowly finished his whiskey. James saw in him a once-powerful dreamer whose cause had tarnished, had lost its luster, a man who was aging but could not admit it.

His voice steadying, as if he felt pity for Sutherland, James said, "You're an idealist, Owen, an idealist who has been betrayed by his ideals, betrayed by the powers-that-be in a rebel government that'll turn out no better than the one you're rebelling against." He shook his head. "I don't understand."

Sutherland sipped, gazing at the window as if emotionless, and at the moment James thought him more like an Indian than a white man.

James leaned forward, his hands spread in a gesture of appeal. "What is it that makes you do what you do, Owen? I don't understand why you give everything you own for the rebel cause when you could remain neutral, do a fine business, and stay untainted by the choosing of sides in this ugly conflict. Why is a man who is normally so practical now so fanatically idealistic when it comes to a revolution that is led by conniving rascals who don't give a tinker's damn about your ideals?"

Sutherland looked at James, who felt as if he were in the presence of a being of superior character, of high nobility. That impression made James feel less a man than Sutherland, and, as ever, the feeling irritated and angered him. He cast it off with a gruff sound of exasperation, and walked away to the other side of the room. James did not want to think of Sutherland as someone better than he. Then it came to him that what he was actually seeing in the character of this man was simply old-fashioned gentility—an out-of-date mannerism, a habit, nothing more. Sutherland was just human, like the rest of them, and no better than the next man.

James spun, resentment welling up, and he declared in a strident voice, "You won't admit that times have changed! Our times are passing your old ways by, Owen! You embrace your brittle pride, and you presume to tell me what to do or not to do with my life, as if Bradford Cullen might corrupt me, might defile me so that I become unworthy of Susannah's hand! Well, you won't rule me at all! And you won't unfairly defame Bradford Cullen again in my presence."

Sutherland now replied, slowly and calmly, putting down his glass on the table, "You'll have to learn for yourself about Cullen, James. But as I've said before, join with him and I'll never give you Susannah's hand."

James felt anger rise again, but he contained it.

Sutherland looked closely at him, saying, "I'm sorry, laddie, but that's how it is. My lass'll not have anything to do with a man who backs Bradford Cullen."

James was boiling, but the right words would not come. He wanted to tell Sutherland to stop being so damned self-righteous, so damned stiff-necked, and to look at the world with modern eyes.

Outside, there came the sound of running, and someone rapped quickly at the door, announcing himself as a courier from the Kentucky country. James let him in, and he handed over a letter for each of them.

James's letter was from Susannah, and he was self-conscious at first as he sat down on the chair near his cot to read it. Sutherland anxiously tore open his own.

Ella's letter was only a few lines, written in a trembling hand, and hastily. Sutherland could scarcely get past the first sentence. His breath caught, and it was as if his heart stopped.

> Oh, my dearest one, how can I tell you what so breaks my mother's heart, but our darling Benjamin is no longer with us.

"Dear Lord . . ." Sutherland murmured, "no . . ." His hands shook. His mind was numb, unwilling to believe, unable to understand that it could actually be true. His beloved Benjamin dead?

> . . . We fled to Harrodsburg after the attack, and there I awaited some word of him. I could not believe that he had not escaped, though his situation had been so desperate. Owen, he had given his life for us.
>
> I cannot go on, my dearest, save to tell you Jeremy went after him with a strong party of men and found his body, untouched by the enemy, concealed among rocks where he had crawled after being wounded. Heera died there, too.
>
> Oh, Owen, God grant that you may be with us soon. We cannot come to you until the river is safe. God keep us all.
>
> Your faithful, loving wife, Ella.

Owen Sutherland wept, and James came to him, having read similar dreadful news in his letter from Susannah. Sutherland softly asked to be left alone, and James departed, shaken and sorry.

Whose imminent death had Sutherland sensed after all? He

had thought it had been his own, but it had been his son's. It hurt so. Oh, how it hurt, as nothing else he had ever felt before. To live was agony. To live, and never again to be complete.

That very same afternoon, Sutherland set off alone for Harrodsburg, a week's travel downriver through country controlled by the enemy. He left a brief note for James, telling him to do his best supplying the defense forces, and saying that if anything happened to himself, that Ella would see to it all debts were paid. If there was some problem collecting from Congress, then James was to send a copy of this letter to Benjamin Franklin, who would do all he could to persuade the rebel officials to repay James for what he had spent in service of the cause.

When James read this, he knew Sutherland was walking the path that led to an encounter with death. The forest was crawling with the enemy, and there was little hope for saving the lower settlements until a militia army could be mustered and supplied at Pitt. That would take weeks. Sutherland had gone, alone, but he was as dangerous as he was fearless, a force to be reckoned with even by an army of fifteen hundred men.

James's scorn of Sutherland's old-fashioned attitude gave way, as it had before, to awe. If anyone could turn the tide by operating alone in the Ohio Valley, it was Sutherland. No one else could; certainly not James Morely.

Feeling insignificant, useless, James wondered now about his own path, and about Susannah. He thought of her letter, and its closing words. "Pa will have need of another son, James."

But James Morely did not believe he was the one to take Benjamin's place. He wished he was man enough—by Owen Sutherland's standards—but he believed he was not, and never would be.

chapter 15

BETRAYAL

It was morning, and Owen Sutherland stood in the midst of the enemy camp. Beside him, Shawnees were chanting around a fire, drinking diluted, Redcoat-issue rum. Nearby, grim-faced Frenchmen were looking forlorn after a hard march over hundreds of miles. There were also hollow-eyed Redcoats, trying to ignore the semidrunkenness of their excitable Indian allies. With the soldiers were a few dozen experienced loyalist rangers dressed in dark green. These last were men from New York, whose homes had been taken by rebels when they refused to join the uprising.

There also were several hundred other Indians from the northwest, mainly Ottawas, Delawares, and Senecas. They all had a grudge against the rebels, who had steadily fought and defeated their peoples over the past five years. Now they were on their way to take bloody revenge.

Beyond the rowdy encampment, across a grassy meadow where dead horses and cattle lay rotting in the spring sunlight, was the fort called Ruddle's Station. It consisted of a few cabins protected by a blockhouse and a palisade of twelve-foot tim-

bers. The walls were stout, normally good enough to keep out
Indians, and there was a spring inside for fresh water. The
people here could have held out for months, if things had been
different. The flags of Virginia and North Carolina fluttered in
defiance over the blockhouse, and twice in the past three days
the defenders had refused Byrd's demand to surrender.

Sutherland had seen both demands go out under a white flag
of truce, the officer in charge being none other than Mark
Davies. The man was lithe and strong once again, as if this
campaign had rejuvenated him. He was dressed in his scarlet
uniform, no longer wearing the buckskins and green of a partisan woods ranger. He would see the campaign through as a
regular, with a force of the British army and cannon behind
him. The time had passed for Davies to slip through the woods
with Indian raiders, attacking isolated cabins and unsuspecting
travelers on forest trails. This was now all-out war, and Ruddle's Station was to be the first major blow of the campaign.

Sutherland had been with the British, loyalists, and Indians
for three days, disguised as a Wyandot, in the clothing that the
tribe had given him for protection last winter. He wore a fur
cap with a feather, and his face was shaved, blackened with
soot, and streaked with war paint. There were few Wyandots
in the army, so he was left alone, and it was possible to observe,
unnoticed, everything of importance that occurred. When the
time came for the rebel counterattack, he would slip away with
his intelligence and lead the militia assault against whatever
weaknesses he uncovered.

Not far away, he knew, Ella and the others were huddled
in the fort called Harrodsburg. He had not yet attempted to get
inside that stockade, because the action was here, at Ruddle's,
and he wanted to witness everything Byrd intended to do.
Between here and Harrodsburg the forest was filled with roving
Indians and enemy scouts, and even a Wyandot traveling alone
toward the rebel fort would arouse suspicion. Sutherland dared
not risk being exposed and having to escape, for it was most
important that he gather all the knowledge he could about the
main army. When the time came, he would be at Harrodsburg
to defend his loved ones.

This sunny morning, Sutherland shared mess with several
Frenchmen from Detroit, all of them scouts who had much
influence with the Indians. In other circumstances it might have

amused him that they did not recognize him, for he had supplied them in times of peace, and often traded for their pelts.

As he ate, he kept from meeting their eyes. He made sure that his long, greased hair hung over his face, and he was dirty enough to avoid being looked at too closely. He had hidden his fine Pennsylvania rifle—better than any poor Wyandot could have owned—in the woods nearby. He ate off a bark plate, devouring stew with his fingers, sitting cross-legged as he listened to their conversations. There was only one man who might trouble him, and that was the scout Simon Girty, more Indian than an Indian, and shrewd enough to take notice of Sutherland and become suspicious.

Girty was no longer with the army, however, having once too often argued fiercely with Davies, whose superior attitude irked Girty to no end. Davies finally had ordered Girty out on a prolonged scout, and it was plain to everyone that Girty would not hurry back, perhaps not even until the campaign was ended. Girty despised Davies but served him nevertheless, partly because Davies, for all his haughtiness, had a high regard for the man's abilities in the woods, but mostly because Girty's whole life was scouting for the British army. And Girty remained a big man with the Indians as long as he represented the army that fed, armed, and led them.

Sutherland knew the attack on Ruddle's Station was to begin before long, for both of the wheeled cannon were drawn up and aimed at the fort. The regulars were to be called to arms in an hour, and Byrd would demand surrender one last time. If the rebels refused, the gates would be blown apart. If that still did not move them, the troops would charge in and force capitulation without further ado. It was to be simple, apparently, but Sutherland feared otherwise.

Already he had heard Indians joking to themselves about how they would drink the blood of the rebels after the guns did their work. This was a tense time for Sutherland, sitting in company with relaxed, chattering Frenchmen who were merely curious about the battle's outcome. They did not give much of a damn for English—loyal or rebel. They had been paid well to scout, and that was why they were here.

When the moment came, Sutherland stood behind the main body of Indians, not far from where Mark Davies was stationed

at the side of their older chiefs. Mounted on a gray charger,
Byrd gave the command, and the guns blasted apart the doors
of the fort with three well-aimed shots. The Indians howled in
glee. The soldiers let out a hurrah on order, and up went the
white flag over the blockhouse. Byrd rode to the captain of the
guns to salute him with a brief removal of his hat, and at
the same time drums rolled for the advance guard to occupy
the fort. Feeling downcast, Sutherland saw a handful of leaders
from the settlement appear at the shattered doors, women and
children behind them. It could have turned out no other way.

It had been so quick and easy. Byrd beamed, prancing about
on his horse, and the soldiers stepped in rank, fifes shrilling
over the beat of drums. Then to the cries of sergeants, they
swung into a column, four abreast, while "The White Cockade"
rang out in gay triumph.

Then it happened. Sutherland thought he saw Mark Davies
give a hand signal of some sort, and the Indian chiefs suddenly
sent up a bloodcurdling war cry that was lifted by their warriors.
The mass of a thousand Indians rushed forth, dashing past the
startled troops, their yelling drowning out the drums and fifes,
which quickly fell silent because the musicians were horrified
by what they saw. The Indians were bent on total massacre.

Sutherland was powerless. Byrd and another officer spurred
their horses into the path of the Indians, but like a tide, the
warriors swept around them, screaming and yelping. The terrified people of Ruddle's fell back as the Indians drove at them,
overwhelming them, killing and scalping men, women, children in a cruel bloodlust that made them wilder with every
scream of triumph.

His own blood up, Sutherland went after Davies, but the
man had swiftly mounted his horse and was riding toward
Captain Byrd. Sutherland could not get at Davies, and he stood
staring at Captain Byrd, who was frantically shouting orders
at his white troops, trying to get them between the frenzied
Indians and the helpless settlers. It was no use. A scene of
ferocious butchery exploded before Sutherland, and he rushed
forward into the fort, groping his way through smoke that
billowed from the already flaming cabins.

He was in the midst of fire and blood, murder and terror,
and could not turn without confronting another scene of horror.
He threw himself at two Indians attacking a kneeling, wounded

white man, whose head was bloodied and laid open. Sutherland swung an ax handle he found somewhere and drove the Indians back, startling and angering them, but he dared not strike them lest they and others try to kill him.

A Redcoat suddenly ran out of the smoke and snatched up the injured settler, dragging him away as Sutherland fended off another shrieking Indian who was after an easy scalp. This time, Sutherland—who looked much like any other Indian in that doomed fort—caught the man a glancing blow and sent him reeling. Other young Indians cursed him, one raising a rusty old musket and presenting it at Sutherland's chest. The Indian was astonished to have the gun whipped away and broken on the ground. Sutherland threw it into the man's face.

"Cowards!" he roared in their Ottawa tongue. "You shame your people! You blacken the name of Ottawa!" They glowered at him, then slunk off for better pickings.

Next, Sutherland dragged a wailing, delirious woman out of a raging cabin, and when she screamed for her baby, he bounded back into the flames, yanking a log cradle from the floor. With his other arm, he lifted the woman, hauling her toward the private who still stood guard over the wounded settler. The soldier was just a boy himself, but he fought like a man against Indians who charged him, threatening, demanding the victim. Neither Redcoat nor Indian dared kill one another, but there were blows and scuffles all around the burning settlement.

When Sutherland joined the private, the Indians backed off, seeing him as a tough adversary. Then another soldier arrived, bruised and tattered, with a weeping child under each arm. An Indian appeared suddenly and plucked at one, a little girl, but the soldier turned and kicked with all his might, cursing and spitting until the warrior backed off with a snarl.

Sutherland said nothing to the soldiers, but after almost twenty minutes of struggling, the three had a dozen wounded, helpless whites behind them, an island of mercy in the midst of evil. Smoke was black and choking, but they dared not move, lest they run into a large mob of Indians. More people came to them, some brought by soldiers, others miraculously making their way themselves. Eventually, there were twenty or more, until Sutherland could not count them for the need to fend off attackers.

Then, through the smoke, he saw a burly white man swinging a maul, his clothes torn, blood running from wounds. He was surrounded by Indians with knives and tomahawks. They were having fun while he was screaming defiance. Sutherland rushed toward him, called for him to surrender and come with him.

"Don't be a fool!" Sutherland shouted, as the Indians mocked the man and threatened to close in.

"Surrender?" He glared at Sutherland. "You Tory dog!" He swung the maul, and Sutherland barely avoided the sharp head that whisked past his face.

"Give up!" he yelled. "Come with me, man! You've no chance!"

"Never!" He went at Sutherland with the maul, but Sutherland ducked under it and came up with a solid grip on the handle.

"I'll save you, man! Listen!"

For just an instant, their eyes locked, and it was as if the settler wanted to believe Sutherland—wanted to believe this dirty Indian with a white man's voice; but he could not. There had been too much treachery, too much death. Perhaps his own beloved kin were already dead.

He bellowed, "Never!"

Sutherland wrenched the maul from him, thinking that now the man had to give up and be protected. But suddenly an Indian leaped in, silently bringing a tomahawk down on the back of the man's skull. Blood spattered Sutherland, who stood there, mouth open, eyes wide, the maul in his hands, the body at his feet.

Indians fell on the body like wolves, some of them even congratulating Sutherland for such great courage in disarming a true warrior. He held that maul, heard the carnage and din of slaughter like the sea against a stormy shore, and closed his eyes, helpless, utterly devastated.

But he could not be overcome. He threw down the maul and whirled about, running back to rejoin the soldiers with the other settlers. By now there were twenty soldiers, and fifty or more refugees from the destroyed station. Other Redcoats were lugging dead and dying toward this little knot in the center of it all, but by now the heat from the burning cabins and walls was too much to bear. At a cry from an officer, the people

were hurried out, but at the gate their path was blocked by a
crowd of jeering, laughing young Indians, some waving scalps,
others threatening to shoot. The Redcoats suddenly went at
them with their bayonets. In a hoarse shout of fury, the soldiers
drove the Indians from the gate, clearing the way. Though no
one was injured, the Indians were bitterly angry to be frustrated
at their bloody sport.

Sutherland stayed in the fort, which was crumbling all around
him, and at the last minute he found a little girl huddled in a
half-filled rain barrel, her hair singed, eyes kept tightly closed.
He lifted her out of the water and tried to speak gently to her,
but she would not open her eyes for fear. Her hands were
clutched against her thin breast, and her legs were drawn up
tightly. Quickly, he carried her away as a building collapsed
with a roar close behind. He clutched her against him as he
ran. At least she would live.

Bodies were everywhere. Indians ran about through the
smoke, trailing bolts of bright cloth, wearing hats or ladies'
bonnets, wrapping colorful ribbons around their brawny arms,
drinking rum, eating bread, and carousing for all they were
worth. Sutherland knew they soon would go for the rest of the
prisoners, even if it mean fighting the soldiers to do it. He ran
with the child through the crowd, cuffing a warrior here, kicking one there, and got out of that inferno, seeking the protection
of the Redcoats somewhere outside.

How he wanted that poor little girl just to open her eyes,
to see she was being cared for. She trembled like a leaf in a
wind.

"You're safe now, child!" He ran almost blindly through the
smoke and dust and mass of hurrying bodies. "You're all right,
little one—"

The next thing he knew he was tumbling, trying to keep
from landing on the child, trying to break his fall, knowing he
had been hit a tremendous blow from behind. He twisted and
crashed onto his back, keeping the child up. He was dazed,
and could do nothing when strong hands yanked her from him.

He fought for his senses, and through a bloody haze saw
someone with the girl. He would not give her up to be killed
by Indians, and screamed in protest, struggling to rise. But he
was hit solidly again, and went down, groggy. No! He would
not give up! He battled the dizziness and grabbed at the man,

wrenching him off his feet, and with sheer ferocity dragging him down, shaking him violently.

Suddenly, Sutherland realized this was a soldier who had hit him and had taken the child. Through a fog, he saw the girl sitting there in the grass, eyes still shut tight, teeth set, hands gripping against her chest.

The soldier belted him again, and Sutherland rolled off, letting the man get up. He watched the Redcoat corporal stagger to his feet and lift the child tenderly.

The corporal said with a vicious curse, "I oughta kill you, Injun! You motherless dog!" Then he stumbled away, at the limit of his strength, face streaked with blood and smoke, to find a place of safety for this innocent creature.

Sutherland sat a moment, head bowed, throbbing with pain. The crackle of flames mingled with shouts of triumph, screams of despair. Sutherland would have to fight on, to save who could be saved.

He looked up and saw Redcoats in a ragged line, clubbing back mobs of Indians trying to kill the soldiers' helpless charges. Operating in tight little squads, the Redcoats had gathered up perhaps a hundred unfortunates who were able to walk or crawl, or who could be carried to safety. Now these all were huddled with the Redcoats, like some herd at bay, attacked by wolves, in the midst of the common ground before the flaming fort.

Sutherland would never be able to get through the seething mass of redskins gathering now, and it seemed as though the blood-mad Indians intended to kill the survivors even if it meant fighting their allies to the death.

Then a hunting horn rang out, pure and clear. Over the chaos, the Indians heard and recognized it. It was a signal to retire, and they became quieter, though they longed to drink white blood, to spend their fury on a defeated enemy. For a moment, Sutherland wondered whether the Indians would heed that call, and they grumbled, beginning to shout again. Then the horn sang out once more, insistent and sharp.

The Indians looked at one another and at their chiefs, then slowly withdrew, leaving at last the exhausted—in some cases, weeping—soldiers and the battered settlers from the ruined station.

It was not the hundred angry Redcoats who had finally stopped the killing. It was Captain Davies's horn—by the direct orders of a furious, ashamed Captain Byrd, Sutherland eventually learned.

But it had been too late to save half the folk of Ruddle's Station, for they lay in the burning ruins. Those who could be protected had been hurried away, and the sight of them being herded like cattle to safety in the middle of the Redcoat encampment had wrenched at Sutherland's heart. The loss of Benjamin, and now this, were almost more than he could take. He had to get away, into the forest, to decide what to do.

He knew the next target was Martin's Station, and after that would be Harrodsburg, where Ella and the others were. Certainly Byrd wanted to prevent another slaughter, but could it be done?

Sutherland had to find Davies and kill him. That night, after retrieving his rifle from the woods, he returned to the camp and made his way to the Redcoat tents, where the weeping, suffering settlers were cramped together around the fires. Davies must be here somewhere.

He approached the street of two dozen bell-shaped tents, but was confronted by a surly, red-faced sergeant, who blocked the way to the white settlers and cursed him for a red-skinned rascal.

"Keep back, you, or I'll break you with my bare hands! Go on, get back to your own dogs!"

Sutherland recognized this man as Sergeant Bailey, the one from Byrd's overturned boat. In the dimness, with only the flickering of firelight to see by, Bailey did not know him. Sutherland looked over the forlorn people, crowding together in family groups, the wounded swathed in bloody blankets, the dying in the arms of loved ones.

"Go on!" Bailey growled and raised a big fist.

Sutherland withdrew and, once out of Bailey's sight, made his way through the edge of the trees around the soldiers' camp, until he was close by Captain Byrd's tent. From the shadows, he observed the commander and his officers sitting in chairs around a camp table. They were downcast, shaken by what had happened at the fort. Only one was erect, eyes alight as he listened to Byrd. This was Captain Mark Davies, who seemed to have been completely renewed by the day's gruesome business. Sutherland would get at him somehow.

Byrd's voice was low, trembling with dismay: "I have told the savages in no uncertain terms, gentlemen, that His Majesty's forces will not again accept such dishonorable behavior. . . ." He gave an oath and said, as if to himself, "And under a white flag of surrender!" He had trouble going on. Most of the officers did not look at Byrd as he spoke. He must have felt very alone just then, Sutherland thought, for his words lacked the ring of confidence or decisiveness.

Byrd had lost considerable weight in the hard journey from Detroit, and his face was sallow, his sunken eyes shadowed in the light of lamps that hung on poles around the canvas marquee. He said the Indians had promised to behave after Martin's Station was captured, and not to attack without direct orders.

"Their chiefs had the gall to tell me that they were happy to have drunk so much blood today."

Byrd's officers fidgeted at that, some of them shaking their heads, others bent over, looking very unsoldierly. All but Davies.

For just a moment Sutherland wondered whether a bullet now would put an end to this bloody trail. He was sure he could get away in the darkness. He began quietly to load his rifle.

Just then Davies was called away by some chiefs who begged Byrd's indulgence, and he vanished in the night. After Davies left, Sutherland heard Byrd mutter that the captain was the only man who could keep the Indians in hand.

Sutherland knew it was otherwise, and that Davies was the one setting them upon the settlers. Even more than the Indians, Davies would have his revenge, over and over again, on the rebels he despised with all his black heart. What would the gentlemanly Byrd think if he knew about that?

chapter 16

MARTIN'S STATION

If Sutherland had been able to catch Davies alone, he would have murdered him that night. He went through the camp, looking for the man among the Shawnees, but he was nowhere to be found.

Early the next morning, the army set off on the march toward the stockade called Martin's Station, five miles away. All that day the Indians capered and joked, ran off into the woods to kill cattle and horses, against Byrd's orders, or to hunt out unprotected families that had not reached the fort. Byrd's Indians were not only soiling the man's honorable reputation, but were hurting their own chances at ultimate success by their uncontrollable lust for killing. So far, they had slaughtered thousands of beef cattle, pigs, and horses, and the path of the army was littered with rotting stock that should have been captured to be herded along as provisions for the long march back. It took great quantities of supplies to feed fifteen hundred men in hostile territory, and Byrd did not have a large pack train behind him.

By the looks of Byrd as he rode past Sutherland on the way

to and from various parts of his army, he was miserable, and appeared too ashamed even to look his men in the eye. For all their fury against rebels, even the loyalist troops were shaken by what had happened at Ruddle's Station, and they were among the most ardent defenders of the prisoners whenever any Indians approached to abuse the captives.

With a thousand warriors scattered across the countryside and under the authority of Mark Davies—if anyone could really be said to have authority over them—the soldiers advanced in column along the well-beaten path between Ruddle's ashes and Martin's Station. It was not a bold, proud army, for the sullen Redcoats did not have the heart to sing. The drums beat out only the orders of the officers, and the fifes were silent. Trailing the troops were nearly two hundred downcast, battered prisoners, mostly women and children, guarded by the white loyalists. It was an army of death, not victory.

Ella Sutherland would never be the same. Yet she had to live, had to help the others go on—especially Susannah, who had been shattered by the death of her brother.

Ella worried more about Susannah than about anyone else, although she knew that Owen would take Benjamin's loss hardest of all. Since arriving at Harrodsburg, Susannah had cried every day, and had taken ill, though she declined to lie in bed.

For her own part, it would have been easy to mourn and mope and drag about Harrodsburg, and Ella would have been forgiven if she had done that. She refused, however, to be overcome by her sorrow. Her only indulgence was to mother Little Jake, who was as heartbroken as Susannah at the death of Benjamin. The child was in need of affection, and Ella needed to solace him.

Each day, she fought off grief, laboring with the others to prepare for the attack that could come any time now. News of the tragic fate of the Ruddle's Station people had already come in, but not from scouts of the settlers, for the place was too tightly ringed by the enemy for that. It had arrived in a blunt, harsh message written by Captain Mark Davies, who had told of the killing at Ruddle's and demanded immediate surrender to avoid another catastrophe.

The people of Harrodsburg now were even more defiant.

They had strong walls, and they believed in their ability to
stand off any direct attack. Though Gwen Bently had told Ella
of the power of the cannon, there was little point in worrying
too much over it. There was nothing anyone could do about
it, anyway. It was obvious that surrender might mean death for
many of them, never mind what Davies's letter had promised
about sparing all those who laid down their arms.

Harrodsburg would fight, and Ella was not afraid. She just
wished Owen could be at her side if she had to die. She had
no idea where he was just then, but if he had received her last
letter about Benjamin, she was certain he would be on his way,
no matter what the danger.

Northeastward, at Fort Pitt, James Morely saw the pitiful prep-
arations for a field force to march against Byrd in the Kentucky
country. Plenty of fighting men were available, from a hundred
communities, many of them well mounted, all with good arms
and ammunition; but they had food for only a few days.

He was standing on the walk leading up to Bradford Cullen's
front door, and with him was the dapper Noah Maxwell. They
paused there to watch a mounted troop of Pennsylvania militia,
hard-looking men in full uniform, with black leather helmets,
green plumes, and blue coats. They had everything they needed
for war as they thundered proudly through the street before the
mansion—everything but food.

Even late springtime in the backcountry was a hungry season, with folks eating the last of what they had stored, and
beef cattle still thin after the hard winter's ordeal. Here at Pitt
there were few cattle, even less corn for feed and bread, and
scarcely any salt to be had. James watched the splendid horse-
men ride by, their mounts healthy enough from the grass of
the fort's common ground—but the men were on half rations,
like all the soldiers here.

"It's a defensive army," said Maxwell, clucking his tongue
and moving toward the front door. "No one can collect enough
food for more than a few days for the number of men needed
to face down Byrd, and nobody wants to sell to the army
anyway, because they don't trust Congress to pay—"

"I've heard it all," James said testily, waving a hand to shut
Maxwell up. "The so-called patriots around here've run their
cattle and draft animals into the woods, or sold them to some

anonymous buyer, it seems—some rich fellow who for his
own reasons has herded the animals out of reach and beyond
forcible procurement."

Dust swirled up and settled on their fine clothes as they
went to the door, James thinking gloomily of the fighting he
had heard was raging down the Ohio. He was afraid for the
safety of his mother, his stepfather, his brother's family, and
his many friends, all of them shut into Harrodsburg. There was
nothing, however, he could do to help them now. That agitated
and gnawed at him, kept him awake nights, and made him feel
all the more helpless. He looked haggard and felt worse.

On top of all this, a curt reply had come from Congress that
the goods James had sold to Owen Sutherland were to be paid
for by Sutherland, and were in no way the responsibility of
Congress. That redoubled James's resentment, for he knew
Sutherland was still waiting to be paid for the goods the Frontier
Company had sold George Rogers Clark. Sutherland had no
way to pay James for what had been destroyed at Fort McIntosh,
and would not until Congress or Virginia first honored Clark's
bills. Clark had captured an enormous country more than a
year ago, but even he had not been paid for what he had spent
out of his own pocket. It was a lamentable mess—shameful,
as far as James was concerned.

Try as he would, he could not put any of it out of his mind
as he joined the Cullens in their magnificent parlor for afternoon
tea. Cullen had invited him for no apparent reason—though
James knew he was expected to sit beside Linda and thrill her
with his presence. Yet he was satisfied to be there, to share
some intelligent talk about the political and military situation,
and to hear what Cullen's latest thoughts were.

Even Linda seemed less abrasive to him as he got to know
her better, and she was quite easy to charm for an entire day,
if he once commented favorably on her dress, or on a painting,
or on the cake she had concocted for the occasion.

She left them early on this particular afternoon, for the
conversation had been a bit boring to her, though it had been
sharp and precise, analyzing the difficult rebel position. No
one could be more blunt than Cullen when it came to that. The
men spent an hour in the parlor, which was kept dark, as Cullen
favored it.

Seated on a cushioned divan, he pontificated eloquently and

with astonishing awareness of the most minute yet significant detail of the war's developments. It was a lesson for James, and he relished it.

At one point, Cullen said James should not worry about the British and Indians striking at Pitt. Sitting forward on his chair near a heavily curtained window, James set down his teacup and asked, "How, sir, can anyone be sure of the British and their unmanageable Indians? If they should come this way—"

Cullen made a noise in his throat. "They won't, they won't! We don't have much they want . . . not yet, in any case, and there's rich prizes to be won downriver." As if Cullen sensed the chill that came to James at mention of the vulnerable forts, the old man looked away and glanced at Maxwell. The lawyer stared uneasily at his teacup.

James subdued his own emotions, forcing them to submit to his urge to know what Cullen thought.

He said, "Surely Congress won't abandon the settlements. They'll *have* to send supplies before matters get much worse!"

Cullen sat back, his vast body filling the divan, his wig hanging dolefully over his sloping shoulders. "Enough of your dreams, my fellow! Enough, if you want to make something of yourself!"

Maxwell softened the mood, saying, "Surely, James, you know Congress is already scraping the bottom of a very empty barrel just to supply General Washington, and he leads the most important army the rebellion has in the field. How can Clark or Sutherland expect them to open their stingy purses for the sake of a few hundred far-flung settlers in a country Congress doesn't expect to own after the war's done?"

James protested: "What about the honor of Congress, and of Virginia, which sent Clark to capture the frontier in the first place?" Even as James asked this he felt foolish, like some child first learning about the grim realities of life.

Cullen's sneering reply was: "Virginia's being harassed by British invaders, and it's likely she'll even have to abandon her capital, Williamsburg, before long. Honor means little to politicians in times of dire distress, and no Virginia politician dares authorize George Clark to spend any more than he has—certainly not in an attempt to capture a country that might be negotiated away to Britain afterward."

In a way, Cullen seemed almost amused by James's inability

to find the needed supplies for the rebel armies, yet he refrained from making sport of it. Still, after asking Maxwell to attend to some business elsewhere, he did not waste the opportunity to point out a better path for James to follow: "Linda Cullen as Linda Morely means a whole new beginning for you." He was cool and yet sincere, and certainly was right as he said he knew perfectly well James had fallen on hard times. "You're almost penniless, unable to acquire much credit, and yet you should be encouraged that I still have such faith in you!"

To himself, James restlessly thought: more faith than Owen Sutherland ever had shown. He left Cullen's presence later that afternoon without giving any definite reply, and Cullen had seemed satisfied with that. Perhaps the old man was glad simply because James had not turned down the notion, as in the past. To be truthful, James did not really know what to think. He well knew, however, that he was sick to death of being poor. If he had money, he might have been able to do something to save his people.

That thought, too, he put ruthlessly from himself, for it hurt too much.

As for one day marrying Susannah Sutherland, she was sweet, but still too young. James was becoming more pessimistic with every day that passed—although he would rather have said "realistic." As he walked home through bustling Fort Pitt, he fought against his deepest emotions, for in his heart he knew he loved Susannah Sutherland.

Linda Cullen was really not a bad sort, and she did indeed care for him—that was obvious. On the one hand was a pretty young girl with an overbearing, proud father who might give James no peace. On the other . . . on the other was the whole world, and it would lie at James's feet.

The disastrous loss of his supplies at McIntosh had been a bitter pill, but a valuable lesson in practicality. James never should have put his faith in the whims of Congress, no matter what Owen Sutherland said. Cullen had been right, as usual.

An empire would lie at his feet. More power than any American his age could boast of. It was a dazzling proposition, especially when compared with the forlorn situation that confronted him—a frustrated little merchant struggling against impossible odds to raise a few thousand pounds sterling worth of fodder and ammunition for a lost cause. James wondered whether he was behaving like a fool after all. Perhaps by sticking to the side of Owen Sutherland he was proving Sutherland's low opinion of him. Proving that he was not the strong and independent man he believed himself to be.

So far, James had been a failure because of his idealism and some unforeseen circumstances. He despised the very thought of failing, and yet, if Bradford Cullen had confidence in him after all that had gone wrong, then perhaps it was time for James Morely to take the most decisive step of his life. Opportunity such as this would never come again.

It *was* a dazzling proposition, and Linda Cullen really was not so bad after all.

Before the coming of the Indian marauders, the land around Martin's Station had been a pretty place. The fort was a strong stockade of high timbers set in the middle of a broad common ground where the dwellers let their animals graze. Around the stockade had been a dozen neat cabins, each with a garden and rail fence, but now they all were ablaze, sending their gray smoke into the sky while the Indians danced about them, whooping, and firing rifles in a frenzy.

Sutherland watched from nearby, looking at the silent fort with its flags fluttering bravely. The rebels were waiting, and surely had heard of the destruction at Ruddle's. Sutherland believed Byrd would do his utmost not to let it happen again.

Just out of good rifle range, the two heavy guns were trained on the fort's main gates. The sullen crews were awaiting orders from Byrd, who was back in the camp, while drummers beat the call for the chiefs to come to him. All the whites were tense, unhappy, afraid of the nightmare that might happen all over again.

Sutherland drifted on the edge of the Indian mob as they patiently listened to Byrd, who stood in the center of the mass. With a finger wagging, his foot stamping for emphasis, Byrd told them they must obey orders. He commanded them to take prisoners and not harm anyone who did not carry a gun.

The Indians were silent, very glum. Sutherland grew uneasy again. Byrd's attitude was haughty and scolding, and the Indians clearly did not like that. After seating himself on the ground and motioning the twenty or so chiefs to do likewise, Byrd passed a pipe among them to solemnize his words; but when the pipe came back to him, he took out a handkerchief and wiped the stem before himself smoking. This was a discourtesy of the first order, but Sutherland could tell that the officer had no idea the Indians were extremely disturbed.

For a while, Byrd waited for a reply from the chiefs, but none of them rose to offer the usual flowery speeches of agreement. The Redcoat captain looked up uncertainly at Mark Davies, who stood casually, close at hand. Byrd wanted some assurance that the Indians would not again perpetrate a massacre.

"Captain Davies, do these people understand precisely what I expect from them?"

Davies leaned forward, a chill smile creeping over his face. "They do, sir."

"They do?" Byrd harrumphed, looked over the chiefs, who were sullen and inscrutable, then shifted his ample bottom on the ground. "Well, will they obey? Do they realize they must obey?"

Davies glanced at the Indians, then said, "The chiefs have told me that they will obey, sir."

Byrd harrumphed again, nodded, and said, "Very well, then, there it is!" He heaved to his feet, impatient to get started with the attack. Normally, a white leader would have begun a war song to inspire the Indians—they being his children, since he was the representative of the king, their white father across the sea. Byrd had no such intention, however. He was all Redcoat military formality.

"Mr. Davies! Order the beat to arms!" He strode away toward the Redcoat camp, where the soldiers had not yet finished erecting the tents. At the rattle of the drums, they threw down everything, grabbed coats, hats, guns, and ammunition, and rushed to the designated parade ground to fall in by company.

Sutherland climbed into a tree to observe all this, and saw how miserably small was the Redcoat contingent compared to the Indian force. Only a hundred troops, along with a few loyalists who would stand by them and back Captain Byrd— but there were so many Indians. The redskins gathered, armed and painted for battle. They drifted close to the edge of the no-man's-land between the soldiers' camp and the fort. They formed a great ebbing and flowing mass of humanity, adorned and feathered, most stripped naked, all armed to the teeth.

They were strangely, ominously silent. Sutherland had seen
much of Indians at war, but never before had he seen so many
who were preparing to fight standing in absolute silence. Had
the chiefs not given their word through Davies, Sutherland
thought, he would have believed there was a conspiracy among
the warriors. . . . Then the shock hit him. There was a conspiracy, indeed. The chiefs were not at the fore of their men,
as was usual, but stood, unarmed, in the rear, with Davies,
and close to Byrd's position. As Davies had said, the chiefs
would obey Byrd's orders not to attack the defenseless fort—
but the warriors had made no such promise.

Sutherland sprang down from the tree, which was at the left
wing of the Indian main body, not far from Davies and Byrd,
who was mounted. He began to run to the British commander
to warn him of what was about to happen. Just then drums
rolled—a dozen side drums, two bass drums—and a half-
dozen fifers struck up music to stir the blood. The fort remained
silent, the British cannon about to be fired. The Indians were
hushed, excitement in every savage face. Sutherland moved
quickly through the massed Indians toward Byrd. But even if
Byrd threw all his Redcoats into their path, Sutherland feared
it was already too late to stop them.

Two resounding blasts sent balls crashing against the Martin's
Station gates, and that was all that was needed. The timbers
cracked, the gates shivered, then gaped uselessly on their hinges.

The Indians were milling, for a moment uncertain what to
do. Sutherland tried to reach Byrd without causing excitement
or giving himself away, but there were just too many Indians.
Then the commander spurred his horse forward, calling for an
officer to ready the flag of truce. Sutherland could hardly get
through the Indians, who also began to move forward, hesitantly at first, then more sure of themselves. He saw Davies
not far away, a vengeful grin on his thin face, as the chiefs
stood impassively all around him. Byrd was calling for a drummer and an officer with a white flag to go and make terms.
Sutherland wanted to scream that the Indians would not keep
back, but that would have been too quick a death. He was
surrounded by bear-greased, painted bodies, and could hear
the warriors whispering in a half-dozen languages that it was
now time.

Davies made a movement with his hand, and this time

Sutherland saw it clearly. It was a signal to attack. Sutherland glanced in dread at the fort, seeing the white flag of surrender shoot up the flagpole. Immediately, he was buffeted by the movement of the entire Indian mass, and there was a guttural shriek, a war cry that was caught by a thousand voices. Byrd's horse rose on its hind legs; the drummer with the truce party stopped beating, and its officer whirled around to yell for the Indians to halt where they were. To no avail.

The chiefs did not move, as they had promised, but the warriors attacked, howling like wolves, the crescent of Indians driving forward as one man, nearly unhorsing the helpless, shouting Captain Byrd. The Redcoats and loyalists sprang forward on command, breaking formation, and running desperately to outrace the Indians to the gate of the fort. Byrd had lost control of his terrified horse, and as it plunged, he could not get out of the thronging Indians.

The fort was still silent, as if unable to grasp what was happening. Not a shot was fired at the wave of Indians, who swiftly outran the soldiers. The Indian mass headed off the small cluster of scarlet tunics, and by sheer numbers kept them back from the gates as the rest of the warriors surged through in brutal triumph, falling upon the helpless defenders.

Sutherland recoiled, pushed his way clear of the Indian attackers, and went after Davies. But the man had again gone, mounting up and riding off toward the Redcoats—either to rally them or cleverly to delay their reorganization. In a moment, Sutherland was left standing in the middle of that empty field, watching another hideous massacre.

chapter **17**

CAPTAIN BYRD

Sickened, Owen Sutherland backed off to the edge of the woods while the fighting went on for much too long before the outnumbered Redcoats at last got themselves between the murderous Indians and the settlers.

Sutherland had never before witnessed such abomination. It was even worse than the first massacre, and this time the mob of Indians at the gate was too dense for him even to try to get through to help the soldiers.

With tears in his eyes, he leaned against a large oak tree, hearing the death screams, seeing the settlement go up in flames, and watching the weeping survivors being led away by downcast Redcoats with fixed bayonets. If Redcoat honor had not been defiled by this treachery, then at least the self-righteousness of the British government had been proved a lie. Parliament, by using Indians in the war, had forfeited any right to rule this land, to determine its future.

It was more than an hour before Byrd managed to save all those who could be saved, and to get them out of the inferno

that had been a fort. There were at least a hundred of them to
add to the couple of hundred from Ruddle's, who were massed
under guard in the woods somewhere downriver. Sutherland
saw Byrd go riding by alone, white-faced, horrified, and helpless. The man seemed not to know what to do next. He had
been on the verge of one of the greatest triumphs in the history
of wilderness fighting, with the ability to drive nearly every
rebel from the frontier, but he could not control his Indians,
and that had brought the most humiliating dishonor upon him.

Then, just as Byrd rode by, his horse stumbled in a rut,
nearly pitching him forward, his hat falling off and landing
right at Sutherland's feet. Sutherland picked it up as Byrd
recovered, his horse standing up, unhurt. Byrd reached down
as Sutherland returned the hat. Was this the moment for Sutherland to reveal himself, to get Byrd alone and ram some sense
into his spit-and-polish mind?

But Davies and some other men came riding close behind,
and Sutherland backed off as they galloped by. Davies had an
expression of satisfaction on his face, and again Sutherland
had the barely controllable urge to leap out and kill this villain;
but that would not be enough to stop what was to come. Byrd's
Indians were increasing in confidence, and their ferocity would
be even worse when Harrodsburg was attacked. Even if Sutherland gave up his own life to kill Davies, the fate of Harrodsburg was sealed unless Captain Henry Byrd found the will
to regain control of his Indians. Even without cannon, a thousand confident Indians could take Harrodsburg.

Sutherland stayed by that tree, watching Byrd gather his
officers before his tent. The Indians were in another orgy of
killing, this time slaughtering cows, pigs, and horses, and the
soldiers could not stop them all. The food for an army of ten
thousand men was ruined in minutes of pillage and madness.
All the while, the downcast Byrd moped in front of his tent,
while his officers milled around him, anxious for some decisive
command.

Sutherland knew the Redcoats and loyalists were tough and
brave, and if Byrd gave the word, they would fight to the death
to protect the whites. But such a conflict within the army would
mean the end of Byrd's triumphal campaign and his chance to
make a name for himself, even though his two victories were

besmirched by the cruelty of his Indians. Byrd was plainly at a loss for what to do, and for how to govern a thousand savages.

Long after dark the next day, at the largest settlement in the region—Harrodsburg—a shadowy figure slipped over the wall, passing a sentry who was experienced and sharp-eyed, but not good enough to detect Owen Sutherland.

Wearing his own clothes now, Sutherland had crept through the Indian positions surrounding the settlement and climbed the palisade by using a small grappling hook fashioned of hickory forks and a rope stolen from the British camp. He had come not to warn the defenders of what they were to expect— they all knew by now—but to see Ella and Susannah once more, perhaps for the last time.

After reporting all he knew to the fort commander, Sutherland found Ella and the others housed in a stable, asleep in the straw. He came in darkness, seeing Ella by the faint light of a tallow lamp hanging nearby. She seemed to be sleeping, and he knelt at her side for a little while, looking at her as if to remember every beautiful feature.

And there was Susannah, tucked close to her mother, a shawl draped over her shoulders. So lovely were they both. Sutherland drew up his daughter's shawl, leaned over, and kissed her softly. He sighed, feeling love and sorrow rising at the same moment. He touched Ella's cheek, so lightly that she did not stir. Then he kissed her forehead and moved back, half expecting her to awaken, not sure he wanted her to. She moved, put her hand on Susannah, and drifted away into deep slumber again.

Perhaps it was better this way. Perhaps it was better that there be no last parting. Sutherland did not know the right thing to do, but he wanted to cause them no more heartache. He had to confront his fate that very night, had to face death before the morning came.

Let them sleep.

Then he saw something moving on the ground, like a doll that was alive. It was Gwen's baby, Richard, awake and crawling as his mother slept nearby. Jeremy Bently apparently was on duty somewhere. Sutherland smiled and picked up Richard. The baby was a warm and squirming little fellow, arms and legs wiggling. In the dimness, Sutherland could just make out the light in his grandson's eyes—the light of the future. He kissed the baby and laid him between Ella and Susannah, pulling the shawl up so that Richard would take the wool against his cheek, suck his thumb, and sleep.

Sergeant Ned Bailey tramped along the perimeter of the soldiers' camp before Harrodsburg, making sure no Indian was sneaking past his sentries to frighten or abuse the prisoners clustered around the bonfires. His men were thinly spread out, quartered in a large circle around the captives, scarcely enough troops to stand guard, let alone allow some of the men to catch a bit of sleep. Sergeant Bailey himself had not slept for three days, having spent night after night watching over the three hundred people.

He grumbled as he strode along the edge of the woods, complaining about "red devils," cursing army life, wishing he were back in India or had retired from the army last year, as he had intended to.

"God-rotting army got me into this! Poxy army, after all I've given it, shames me like this, so I'm no better than a nursemaid to poor civilians! No more'n a bedmate to murdering, heathen fiends—"

He heard a noise. A rock clattered nearby. He spun toward the sound, but saw nothing. He was alone here, not far from Byrd's tent, where a guard of three men stood watch over the sleeping officer. Bailey peered into the woods. The night seemed darker than ever, though many fires gave light, and the smoldering heap of a rebel's cabin glowed in the distance.

Again he heard movement. His hand went to the knife at his belt. "Who's there?"

"Owen Sutherland."

Sergeant Bailey caught his breath. A lesser man might have run or shouted for help. But he steadied himself, searching the blackness where he thought he had heard the voice.

"Then show yourself, Mr. Sutherland."

The voice was behind him. "Here, Sergeant."

Bailey spun again, hands flexing. He shrugged his shoulders. He still could not see Sutherland. Bailey had been outmaneuvered, and was aware he could have been killed without a sound. Then the sergeant saw Sutherland's tall figure, sil-

houetted against the camp firelight. Bailey said nothing until
Sutherland told him what he wanted.

"Take me to Captain Byrd."

Bailey became momentarily uneasy. "You armed?"

"No."

Bailey took Sutherland's word for it, as any man who knew
Sutherland well, or who knew enough about him, would do.

"Follow me, then." Bailey threaded a path through the captives lying in groups all around, and Sutherland stayed close
behind. Sutherland knew some of these people, but he was
unable to look at the empty faces, and loathed hearing their
miserable groans and weeping. He even thought he heard his
name called, but did not answer.

He and the sergeant approached Byrd's tent, and a guard
presented his musket in salute to Bailey before gasping Sutherland's name. Bailey told the dismayed man to stand easy and,
with Sutherland, moved toward the tent entrance. By now, a
dozen other soldiers had seen Sutherland, and many of the
settlers had recognized him. Word was passing through their
midst about his presence, and many of them were sitting up to
look toward the captain's tent.

As Bailey went inside to report to Byrd, Sutherland sensed
someone else approaching quickly. It was Mark Davies, followed by a number of Indians. He was stamping straight toward
Sutherland, hand on his sword. Although unarmed, Sutherland
was sure he could overpower Davies and strangle him right
there—but he had more important plans for this night, and
Mark Davies would not hinder them. Just before Davies could
reach him, Bailey came out of the tent, noticed the officer
coming, and put himself squarely in his path. Davies growled
for him to stand aside, but Bailey held his ground—an unforgivable sin for a noncom. He said Sutherland was in his custody.

"You fool!" Davies snapped. "I'll have you lashed if you
don't get out of my way!" He gave the burly sergeant a shove,
but he might have been going at a granite boulder, for Bailey
stood fast, saying nothing more.

The Indians had their tomahawks out, and Davies drew his
sword partway from its scabbard. Suddenly the sentries were
beside their sergeant, bayonets at the ready, in a startling display
of defiance and near insubordination.

Davies blustered, recoiled, then suddenly whipped his blade clear, cursing, "No common knaves will dare challenge my authority!"

Just then Byrd stuck his head out of the tent. He was wigless, his hair cropped short, eyes dark and melancholy. When he saw Davies and the soldiers in a standoff, he became fierce:

"As you were, Captain! Sergeant Bailey, usher your . . . your companion into my tent!"

He withdrew, and Bailey held the tent flap while Sutherland entered, ducking low, and finding Byrd half dressed, standing before him. Byrd threw on his officer's tunic, his hands trembling as he fastened his waistcoat buttons. It seemed he was taking this time to collect his thoughts. The tent was lit with candles, and there were two folding chairs near the officer's cot.

"So, it's . . . it's you, Mr. Sutherland," Byrd almost stammered, and seemed unable to look his visitor in the eyes. "And you have come into the lion's lair. . . . Lion?" He glanced about, finished buttoning the waistcoat, and muttered with a wry laugh, "Or you might say the den of the jackal, eh?"

Now he stared at Sutherland, lip pouting, eyes hard. He had mastered his emotions. He offered Sutherland a chair, and as they both sat down, there was a moment of silence between them. The sounds of many captives buzzing in conversation rose outside. Surely they expected something to come of the unexpected arrival of Owen Sutherland.

Byrd went on. "Have you come under a flag of truce, sir? No? Then does that mean you have surrendered yourself to me?" He looked away and chuckled with irony. "No, I suppose you would not do that; I suppose you are only too aware what happens to those who put their trust in me. . . ." Eyes dark, he looked at Sutherland and asked, "What do you want, if not to give yourself up to my . . ." His jaw was set, but his voice trembled as he said, ". . . to my well-known mercy?"

Sutherland was calm. "You must call off this campaign immediately."

Byrd did not flinch, but he stiffened visibly; after a moment, he said hoarsely, "On the brink of final success? In another month, Fort Pitt itself will come under my guns."

"That is doubtful."

Slowly, Byrd nodded, saying, "You esteem your rebels too

highly, Mr. Sutherland. They cannot resist my advance, and will undoubtedly flee back across the mountains before the month is out. You cannot deny it."

"Captain, I've not come to persuade you with strategic reasons for turning back now, though I do have reasons enough, based on simple military logic."

"Go on."

"George Rogers Clark is raising the countryside against you."

"Bah! Clark is in the Illinois, taking our feint, as we had planned."

Sutherland said, "By tomorrow, half your redskin allies will believe he's here, ready to pounce on them, and you know how they fear him." Byrd's eyes narrowed as he listened. "Surely you, sir, better than any British field officer, know the power of a terrifying rumor spreading among the Indians."

Indeed, Byrd had been defeated with St. Leger in the Mohawk Valley because of false rumors that a huge army of rebels was descending on the British and Indians laying siege to Fort Stanwix. Byrd's Indians had melted into the forest in their fear, forcing the entire British army to withdraw because of lack of numbers. This setback had resulted in St. Leger's failing to link up with General Burgoyne, who, isolated, had subsequently been defeated at Saratoga. Yes, Byrd well knew how Indians could be influenced by rumor, and no other name could move them like the name of Clark.

Byrd swallowed as Sutherland said he had already started such a rumor. "Do you recall the Wyandot Indian in the tree yesterday, the one who picked up your hat when it fell off?" Byrd was becoming troubled. "That was me, and I've been a very talkative Wyandot, a man who knew all about Colonel Clark, and had even seen him scouting around your rear." He smiled. "Ask the Indians. Many already are wondering if Clark's coming after them."

Byrd waved a hand angrily. "I'll hold enough to me to do what I came for."

"Perhaps. But you can hold them all to you, and you'll still never escape alive from this country, Captain."

"You're extremely brazen to make so bold with me, sir! Foolhardy!"

"How will you get your captives back to Detroit? Or will

you let the Indians kill them all? How will you feed them? How will you feed your men? How much deeper can you go into our country before there will be no escape?" He leaned forward, touching a map that lay on Byrd's cot, indicating Harrodsburg, Fort McIntosh, Fort Pitt, the Falls of the Ohio, and several other settlements that had not been taken.

Sutherland said, "They will fight you to the death, after what you've allowed to happen. You have three days to withdraw from here, no more. Any longer, and you can be sure Colonel Clark will indeed be on your flanks, will harry and nip at you until you try to cross the Ohio, and then he'll be there, when you don't expect it, with five hundred riflemen, and you'll never escape."

Byrd remained calm, though Sutherland could see his ominous picture had taken effect. Yet it was obvious Byrd was not a man to yield to fear. He stood up and paced a moment before turning to Sutherland.

"I did not come here to murder innocents, Mr. Sutherland. I came to drive out rebels, not even to take three hundred wretches prisoner."

Sutherland nodded once. He knew Byrd's victories at Ruddle's and Martin's had not been in the British plan, for the settlers there had been expected to flee at the first rumor of so strong a British force. Instead, they had boldly stood their ground—much to their own regret, but also to the regret of Captain Byrd. Now Byrd was responsible for all these captives, whose lives were forfeit if the Indians got hold of them. Captain Byrd was a man of honor, and he had to protect those people if he was to have any reputation left at all.

Sutherland said, "Colonel Clark ordered the settlements to fight, and they obeyed him, just as the united militia will obey him when he comes for you."

"Enough of your insolence, sir!"

Byrd began to pace again, hands behind his back.

After a while, Sutherland said, "But I did not come to persuade you with military reasons for giving up this campaign." Byrd stopped pacing. Then he sat down to listen. "You cannot manage your Indians because they are under the secret influence of Captain Mark Davies." Byrd was silent, intense. "Davies signaled them to attack—I saw it myself at Martin's, and at Ruddle's."

"Impossible!" Byrd's eyes were wide, and he sat back. "Against my direct orders? Unthinkable! Can you prove it?"

"Bring him in here now and ask him."

Blustering, Byrd was about to do so, when Sutherland requested that Davies be confronted in a certain way.

A few minutes later, a sullen, scowling Mark Davies stood before his seated commander, with Owen Sutherland sitting casually nearby, a confident look on his face. Byrd asked whether the Indians could be contained after the Harrodsburg gates were down.

Davies shrugged, standing erect, with his hat under his arm. "I can do only so much, sir; and you know how they hate the rebels, how their lands have been taken, their wives outraged, their honor blackened."

Byrd pressed: "Can we trust them to stay out of it this time if the rebels surrender, Captain Davies?"

Davies glared at Sutherland, then steadied himself and said, "Once their blood is up, sir, it's . . . well, you know. But we must have them with us, or we're not strong enough to take the fort, gates knocked down or not."

Davies was uneasy and clearly did not like being so sharply questioned while the insolent rebel Owen Sutherland sat smugly watching. He became tense, but remained correct and formal.

Byrd sighed, "I fear for what will happen."

Davies leaned forward. "Sir, we're so close to victory . . . and this is war! I . . . I regret as much as anyone what has happened, sir, but we must go on, if you'll permit me to be so bold. And I believe the Indians will be satisfied after one more victory." He grinned. "You know how savages are, sir— like children, spoiled and naughty, but if they're handled properly—"

Sutherland suddenly spoke out: "Your commander is calling off the campaign. You turn back tomorrow."

Byrd remained unmoved as Davies recovered from his initial shock. Davies glanced from Byrd to Sutherland, turning livid as his neck bulged out of his black stock. He could barely speak. "You can't! Not now! We have them! You can't do it! Damn you, Sutherland!"

"It's done." Sutherland had played him perfectly.

Byrd was troubled, his mouth turned down at the corners,

but he said nothing, letting Davies vent his wicked fury.

"We have them! Those rebel dogs in Harrodsburg are in our power!" He clenched his fist as though squeezing Harrodsburg and all in it. "You can't listen to this rebel, sir!"

Byrd interrupted: "That is not for you to decide."

"Damn you! In our power!"

"Captain! Hold your tongue!"

Davies boiled over, hand on his sword hilt. "We'll break these bloody rebels once and for all, don't you see?" His voice was almost hysterical. "Sutherland's blinded you! He's played you for a sentimental fool, because his own family is in that fort, and he knows, he knows, he knows"—Davies was almost raving now—"he knows that once we crack that gate, we'll have them, have them all, like this—" His hand squeezed, tighter and tighter, his eyes bulging, teeth clenched.

"The campaign is over," Sutherland said, with a calmness that infuriated Davies all the more, and when Sutherland smiled, the madman's face changed into the mask of a murderer.

Sutherland asked, "What will you do now, Davies?"

Davies hissed, "We'll have them all, Sutherland! I'll have my vengeance, and every last one of your kind will die! My warriors will tear them to pieces—"

"As you did at Ruddle's?"

"Yes!"

"And at Martin's?"

"Yes! Yes!"

"You ordered them to do it!"

"And I'll order them again! To wipe your vermin from the face of the earth, to purge our empire of rebels and traitorous swine—" He drew his sword.

Byrd leaped to his feet, crying, "Captain Davies! Hold, or I'll have you put under guard!"

Davies recoiled, eyes blazing. "You'll do nothing of the kind!" He barely governed his vicious temper, barely refrained from striking his superior, for which he would have been executed. Then he snatched at his silver officer's gorget, tearing it from where it hung at his throat, and threw it on the ground. "Hereby I resign! You have no more power over me!"

Sutherland was ready to go for the man if he moved at Captain Byrd, but in came Sergeant Bailey and another sentry, and they wrenched the sword away, taking positions on either side of the wild-eyed Davies. Like many a soldier, they hated him, and would have relished manhandling him into irons.

Byrd, shaking with fury, might still have arrested Davies, refusing to accept the resignation, but he, too, saw something far deeper and more dangerous in this drama.

Governing himself, he said gravely, "You well know I could have you shot for this, Captain."

Davies was quaking with anger, and there was a sudden look of uncertainty about him, as if he realized the seriousness of his predicament. Still, he would not back down. He had resigned his commission.

Byrd said, "I'll accept your resignation only on the condition that you call off the Indians, send them all home immediately, and warn them that if any of my captives are harmed, I'll come for them with soldiers and burn their villages to the ground . . . and then I'll come for you, wherever you might be, and I'll kill you myself for what you've done!"

Davies backed up and whined like some animal, hands shaking in front of him. Indeed, he looked more beast than human.

Byrd stepped forward. "Swear it! Swear it or I'll have you shot!"

Davies slowed his breathing by force of will and, glancing hatefully at Owen Sutherland, swallowed and said, "I so swear!"

"Begone!" Byrd commanded. "Before I give you into the hands of Mr. Sutherland!"

At this, Sergeant Bailey could not keep from snorting loudly, grinning right at Davies. In the next moment, Davies and the soldiers were gone, and Byrd was left alone with Sutherland, both standing in the grayish light, as dawn broke over the eastern mountains.

Byrd collapsed in his chair. "Dear God, I am so sorry. . . ."

Sutherland, too, was shaken, feeling utterly spent and miserable.

After some time, Byrd said with utmost solemnity: "You saved my life once; you are no prisoner, and may return under a flag to the rebel fort." His eyes dropped their gaze to the floor. "Tell them we will withdraw in peace if they permit us to go unmolested. Otherwise . . ." He moved away and rubbed his eyes. "This is a strange and melancholy war, Mr. Sutherland."

He looked back and caught his breath. "There is no glory

for us, no right and wrong about it, no clear path, no well-defined enemy or friend. Dear God, I would that it were over!"

Harrodsburg and Owen Sutherland's family were saved. The next morning, Captain Henry Byrd withdrew his unhappy Redcoats and loyalists from the fort's gates, regimental standards furled, drums and fifes silenced. In a brief speech to the furious, astonished Indians, he had told them their behavior had dishonored their nations and the British army, and that he would not go on fighting at their side.

It was no small thing for Byrd to be so blunt, for these Indians outnumbered his white troops by more than ten to one; his only hope was that they would not yet dare to make war on the British, who supplied them and traded with them. Still, the hatred in these warriors was deep, for they had been insulted and bitterly disappointed to be denied further glory, further scalps. Sutherland believed this was the beginning of the end for British-Indian cooperation against the settlers on the frontier.

As the British herded their captives back toward the Ohio, Sutherland stood on the ramparts above the closed gates of Harrodsburg, his arms around Ella, and Susannah at his side. The people of Harrodsburg were silent, dour, though they had been spared. In the distance they saw friends and relations being led away by Redcoats and loyalists for the long journey back to Detroit. Many would never be seen again.

Sutherland's heart was heavy, the recent events and the loss of Benjamin overwhelming whatever relief he might have felt.

As soon as the enemy was out of sight, he, Ella, and Susannah went to Benjamin's grave. It was near the river, in the little cemetery by a burned-out log church. He carried the claymore he had given his son, and leaned on it as he knelt at the grave. Ella and Susannah, their faces streaked with tears, put wildflowers in an earthen vase on the mound.

Once, Sutherland had such hopes for the boy.

Throughout all the danger, he had never really expected this, though he should have. Yet how could any father expect this, even consider it possible?

Benjamin had been the best son any man could have asked, and because there was no other way to be now, Owen Sutherland was grateful for the blessing of having had him as his son.

Susannah was sniffing, trying with all her might not to cry as she stood back from her parents, now both on their knees. Ella leaned against her man, and he took her hand.

She said softly, "We live because of him. . . . We should live for him, for all that was good about him . . . and we should be happy."

It was so. Benjamin would have wanted it no other way.

Just then, there was a flutter of wings, and the blue jay appeared, landing on the hilt of Sutherland's claymore. Punch had not been seen since Benjamin was lost. Susannah spoke softly to him, glad he at least was back. She took him on her finger, and dropped to her knees between her parents. Her father put his arm around her and held her close.

"We go on," he said.

Susannah put her trembling hand in his. "Stay with us, Pa. We need you so!"

"Aye, lass. I'll never leave you again."

A little later, Susannah wandered alone near the river, only Punch for company, while her parents lingered near the grave. Her mind turned over and over with thoughts of despair, thoughts of hope. She felt so much like a grown woman, so much so that she was sure she knew her own mind and understood feelings and emotions that once had been a mystery. She also felt very alone.

Her mother and father were as one, for all that they loved her as much as anyone could; but she was changing, moving away from them and from their life. They wanted to live in the heart of this vast wilderness, to be far away at Valenya, while she had no clear notion of where she wanted to live, or how. She wanted to be where there were good people who understood her, who knew her heart, and who accepted her as a woman, as an equal. She was growing up, and all the world should see it.

Out here were sorrow and fighting and loss, and it would be so for years to come. She sighed. How she would miss her brother! But if they had not chosen this wandering, warring life, they never would have lost him. He would be with her now, and she could tease him, joke with him, tell him things he did not realize would interest him until after the telling. . . .

She felt about to cry again, but fought away the unhappiness. Calling to Punch, she tossed him a piece of bread from the picnic basket she had brought. In her hands was her Shakespeare, though she did not recall having taken it from the basket. She looked at the worn book, idly thumbed through it, and found the dog-eared page that always seemed to fall open for her.

Romeo is parting from Juliet, saying he is certain they shall meet again, and she has a haunting vision of him, dead. Into Susannah's mind came the image of James Morely, whom she would not see any other way but alive, cheerful, and handsome. Romeo bids farewell, and Juliet, left alone, declares:

> O, Fortune, fortune! All men call thee fickle:
> If thou art fickle, what dost thou with him
> That is renowned for faith? Be fickle, Fortune;
> For then, I hope, thou wilt not keep him long,
> But send him back.

Send James back. James Morely was just a week's journey from this place, but in her heart, Susannah unexplainably felt he was far, far away from her, farther than he had ever been before, and she did not know why.

PART THREE

1780–1781

chapter **18**

SUSANNAH

The news of James Morely's marriage to Linda Cullen
came as such a shock to Susannah that she did not leave her
bed for two weeks. Owen and Ella were fraught with worry
for her, not only because she was so heartbroken, but because
her melancholy brought on sickness. The parents were not sure
what to feel about James's marriage, for they had not been
enthusiastic about the match between him and Susannah. Still,
they regretted seeing her so dejected.

By the end of the summer, however, Susannah was much
improved, although she did not renew her teaching of the children. For a long time she remained lethargic, as if nothing in
the world was of any importance, nothing worth a laugh. To
Ella, Susannah's heart, which once had been so light, seemed
filled with despair. And yet the girl was becoming even more
beautiful, as a soulful, drifting mood came over her, giving
her features a certain spirituality. It was as if she had experienced a lifetime in the briefest of moments. She was no longer
a child.

Months passed, and Susannah settled into a state of withdrawn, but alert, contemplation. She seemed to be seeking some hidden truth of life, a truth that eluded her, a truth that would explain why a young man of the highest character would forsake love in favor of worldly things. In time, she began to understand it, for her father and mother were gentle, loving, and they reasoned with her about what so often is life's greatest tragedy: the willful decision to follow the desire for earthly power, while betraying one's ideals and forsaking those things that can give real happiness.

When Susannah Sutherland understood this, accepted it, she forgave James Morely for spurning her. She allowed him to be human and imperfect. To Owen and Ella, the change for the better that came over their daughter in those long months of 1780 was a great relief. By winter, she was no longer despondent, and had returned to most of her responsibilities in the community with renewed dedication, if not vigor.

Yet she still was not up to teaching, and her parents were sorry for that. Much of her physical strength seemed to have been lost in her lonely time, and she was a frail young woman these days. It was as if, for all her understanding and acceptance of her destiny, she was still bleeding within and did not know it.

Winter passed, and the war went on all around the Falls of the Ohio—now being called Louisville, in honor of the king of France, America's new ally. Susannah's father often was called away briefly to fight, to scout, or to counsel with George Rogers Clark and the regulars at Fort Pitt. He did not leave for long, however, for he had promised to stay with them, never again to undertake a dangerous mission of many months. The Sutherlands had suffered enough.

Like every other family on the northwestern frontier that year, the Sutherlands were weary of the endless fighting, unexpected raids, petty hurts and losses, and the nagging reports of isolated killings that were more like common murders than warfare. In revenge for the British campaign that had ravaged Ruddle's and Martin's stations last summer, Clark had led a thousand mounted frontiersmen against some Shawnee towns, reducing them and their corn harvests to ashes. It had been a bitter, starvation winter for that tribe, but even with such a harsh retribution, the Indians did not cease their raids. Their hatred flared hotter, and the frontier killing raged more fiercely than ever.

The evil Mark Davies was still out there, this time as a freewheeling partisan raider with a little army of hard-case followers, men as desperate and cruel as himself, honoring nothing but their own greed and profit. Davies perpetrated many of the wickedest killings, and was known to long more than ever for revenge against Owen Sutherland. Yet whenever Sutherland heard reports of Davies's whereabouts and went after him with a fighting force, the man slipped away. Apparently Davies was biding his time, satisfied to torment Sutherland by killing and escaping, not ready yet to challenge him face to face.

It was a doleful, anguished year for the frontier, from New York to the Mississippi, and nowhere was it harsher than in the valley of the Ohio.

From her detached perspective, Susannah observed the world of forest and river, rifle and tomahawk, with silent pity. In her life she had known many Indians—perhaps some of them she knew better than the rough Virginians or leathery Pennsylvanians who so recently had taken this wild country. She saw the right and wrong of both sides, the hatred and passions, as if they were part of a Shakespearean tragedy—one that had no end, only violent climax and uneasy interlude, acts and scenes of desire, fear, misguided hope, and forgivable delusion.

Susannah forgave them all, red and white, just as she forgave James Morely for choosing a selfish path in joining Cullen and Company, and breaking with his past. She knew his heart had been betrayed by his mind, and she believed he had loved her as much as she had loved him.

And Susannah forgave her father for having alienated James once too often. Owen, too, was human and imperfect, for all that he was the bravest man she had ever known.

Susannah was forgiving but withdrawn all that difficult spring and summer of 1781. She went on bravely, asking no one for pity, or even for understanding. She only wished, now and then, that she knew just where it all was leading.

"Will we ever see Valenya again, Mother?"

Susannah asked her question without looking up from her sewing. She sat in late summer sunlight that spilled through the doorway of the cabin they had bought from settlers who had fled the frontier not long ago. She sat on a bench at a puncheon table, and her mother was spinning, as always she seemed to be these days. To Susannah, it was as if her mother entered some merciful dreamworld when she treadled that wheel, as if her thoughts took flight and all her troubles were forgotten.

Ella kept spinning, her head slightly nodding in rhythm with the foot pushing down the treadle.

"You ever can read my thoughts, daughter." Ella smiled as the sunlight revealed wrinkles that had not been there before Benjamin died. "But if you can read them, you must know that I do believe we will go back one day." She paused, kept on spinning, then said, "But who knows when?"

Susannah found it difficult to believe they would ever get back to Valenya. The course of the war in the East had changed sharply, with a British army under Cornwallis tramping back and forth across Virginia. With that army was the turncoat Benedict Arnold, a former rebel with whom her father had fought in the Canadian campaigns. Susannah recalled how hurt her father had been to hear last year that the brilliant Arnold had betrayed the cause and gone over to the loyalist side. Sutherland had not been one of those ignorant loudmouths who reviled Arnold in the most despicable terms—loudmouths not fit to clean Arnold's boots.

Sutherland knew the man well and understood why he had gone over to the loyalists. Arnold had been one of the few consistently successful rebel field commanders, but time and again he had been overlooked by a dithering Congress, when he should have been promoted. Even Washington had said so. Like George Rogers Clark and Sutherland, Arnold had remained unpaid for immense out-of-pocket expenses in the service of the rebellion. He had not even been given the credit for winning the critical battle of Saratoga.

Unlike Clark and Sutherland, however, Arnold had become so embittered, so disillusioned, that he had recklessly seized the opportunity to win fame and fortune in service of the Crown. Arnold's treason had been a blow to the cause, and it was a dishonorable end to a brilliant career as a rebel general.

But this, too, Susannah Sutherland saw in terms of a play, of a great human tragedy: so much wasted effort when peace, not war, was what was wanted for the good of America. She

forgave them all, and did not voice her disbelief in her dear
mother's cherished hope that they could rebuild their lost way
of life. She did not believe it possible, no more than they could
bring back Benjamin, or she could marry James Morely, even
though she was sure he still loved her.

That last, unexpected thought startled her, and she accidentally stuck herself with the needle. James did love her, for all
his imperfection and misguided ways. She considered that as
she absently sucked the drop of blood from her finger. It would
be fine to see him once again, to look him in the eyes—those
beautiful brown eyes—and to see for herself that he was really
still noble of heart.

She was thinking of this when Punch, the jay, hopped in
the door, followed by Owen, whose moccasins tramped down
the fresh sand that was spread daily on the dirt floor to keep
it clean. Susannah saw he was downcast, his anger contained.
He sat heavily in a rocker before the small cooking fire in the
clay-and-stick chimney. Ella slowed her spinning and, like Susannah, waited for news of the meeting Sutherland had just
had with Clark and the militia leaders of the frontier settlements.
They were to discuss Clark's daring plan for a strike that very
season against Detroit.

"They won't do it," Sutherland said with an exasperated
sigh. "I can't say I blame them, for their men are spread too
thin as it is, and every little garrison is hard-pressed to protect
its own folk in time of alarm. But . . ."

Ella stopped spinning to listen, as Owen said the entire
frontier had fallen on the defensive. Thomas Jefferson, governor of Virginia, was no longer able to support a campaign
he had called for, to send two thousand men and artillery into
the northwest to capture Detroit, thus defeating the enemy at
his very supply base.

"Jefferson is so thwarted by the British campaigns in Virginia that he's resigning as governor in favor of a military man,
and there's not a regular soldier to be spared to help us defend
ourselves." Sutherland rose and went to the doorway, where
he stood in the sunlight, staring out at the muddy grounds
around the cabin. Just then Clark and some of the officers from
the upper Ohio walked past, deep in conversation. Clark looked
haggard and dejected.

Sutherland said quietly, "Clark has the authority to flatly

order them to send him their militia, and he could have marched them north, and I believe he would have triumphed if he did it, just as he triumphed in the Illinois. . . ." His voice trailed off. "But things have changed, and the war's growing harder on the settlements. There's even danger of attack from the British to the East." He ran a hand through his hair, and Susannah thought she had never seen her father look so trapped, so harried by circumstances he could not control.

Ella said, "Too many settlers have died, Owen, and too many have gone away. The fight's gone out of the rest, and it's all they can do to hold their little blockhouses and help each other plant a crop."

He said nothing, but kept staring out the door. He was facing the river and Indian country; facing Detroit and Valenya.

Ella spoke again: "Clark could have ordered them to go, but he won't, and that's at the very heart of our new democracy! That's why we're fighting in the first place. Clark has the legal power to command them to leave their homes and fight, but he won't do it unless they believe in him, the way those men in the Illinois believed in him and did the impossible for him!"

Susannah could not help being a bit more blunt about it, and she kept on sewing as she said, almost casually, "Maybe he's afraid of more bad defeats. Doesn't he still blame himself for the loss of the Westmoreland County men?"

Ella pursed her lips, and Owen turned to come back into the cabin. He said, "Aye, lassie, that he does, that he does, and I fear it's hurt him deeply."

Susannah recalled the terrible distress that had come upon the settlements a couple of months ago, soon after Clark had arrived with nearly three hundred militia volunteers to plan the campaign that had just been called off. Clark had originally been expected to wait far upriver, to be joined by a hundred additional militiamen from Pennsylvania's Westmoreland County. Those had been brave souls, from the only frontier county that had resolutely sent their militia in a body for the campaign. Clark had been tremendously gratified by their confidence in him, and by their self-sacrifice.

But because his own men were deserting daily, he had decided to depart for the Falls of the Ohio, just a day before the Westmoreland hundred arrived. His force floated down the Ohio uneventfully, but the Pennsylvanians never caught up.

They were ambushed and wiped out, not a man escaping. Clark's plans had been undermined by the disaster—his plans, and his rough-and-ready self-confidence.

Six years of civil war and constant danger had crushed many a good man on the frontier, and now, it seemed, it was Clark's turn. Some people had already forgotten how it had been when he and his greatly outnumbered army had taken the Illinois country and the British lieutenant governor in one brilliant and courageous stroke. But now Clark had no supplies, no money, and few fighting men available to do anything except protect the homesteads against Indian raids—and even that was becoming daily more difficult. His own state of Virginia would not back him, or could not, yet he was expected, single-handedly, to lead the defense of the settlements.

Ella said, "We need another winter, and the rest from war it will give us."

Sutherland agreed. As usual in winter, the war would come to a standstill for a few months, and that was good for the struggling states, because every day that passed brought ultimate victory nearer. Every dead king's soldier, every French *livre* that came to America, and every British merchant ship captured on the high seas offered up that much more hope for American liberty. The states needed a winter, but more than that they needed one solid victory over the British, perhaps in Virginia, perhaps with the French or Spanish fleets triumphing at sea.

As her father spoke, Susannah knew she had heard this all before: "One more victory! One victory to shake Parliament, to cause the Tory government to fall and a Whig government that is against the war to come to power!"

Susannah asked, "Until then, what do we do?"

He sat back, gazing at her. Finally, he said, "What would you like to do, lass?"

That question surprised her, for she had expected him to speak grimly, to say with hard resolve that they would stand fast, hold on, fight to protect the settlements.

She could not resist saying what was in her heart.

"I would like to visit Fort Pitt." Both her parents observed her intently, obviously wondering what she was getting at. She did not know whether to be lighthearted about it, or to speak in a voice that revealed her deepest need.

Trying with all her strength to speak plainly, she said, "I would like to see James Morely one . . . last time."

Her lip quivered as she caught her breath. She smiled wanly at them, unable to keep tears from creeping into her eyes. "Yes, that's what I would very much like to do."

"My dear Susannah!" Ella breathed, herself about to cry, and she looked over at Owen, who was on the edge of his seat. "Our daughter, husband—she's coming back to us."

Tears were running down Susannah's face. "I'd just like to . . ." She shrugged once, for she did not know why this was happening now, after all this time, after all these months of her understanding everything and offering forgiveness.

Sutherland said softly, "Of course you do, lass . . . of course you do, and we should have known that long ago. Of course we'll take you to Pitt."

James Morely was not a happy man, but it could not be said he was unhappy, either. He was a man who once had desired great wealth and power, and now had both beyond his dreams. He was virtual manager of Bradford Cullen's western operations, and had already made two trips to Philadelphia to begin the process of his taking charge of the American—and eventually the worldwide—commerce of Cullen and Company. It was exciting work, with which nothing else could compare.

Marrying Linda had been a small price to pay, James had been told often by Noah Maxwell, now a principal partner and James's right hand. It had been a small price, indeed, in comparison with all the benefits that had come to James. He lived in Cullen's great mansion, had built onto it, and had established himself as the most important personage, next to Cullen, on all the northwestern frontier. Cullen still kept many business affairs in his own tight fist, and often held private meetings without James—secret appointments with shadowy figures who came in the night. But despite his occasional uneasiness, James did not press his father-in-law for an explanation, and chose not to believe Owen Sutherland's accusations that Cullen ruthlessly played both sides of the war for his profit.

There were plenty of times when James thought Cullen rude and overbearing, the kind of man who had to have his own way, who had to keep James down a bit, if only on principle. And Linda was always her father's best supporter, making it useless for James to seek her aid in any disagreement. Still, James freely ran the daily business of Cullen and Company, and was doing wonderfully well at it. Cullen's expectations that James would learn quickly had been justified.

Life had far more good points than bad. Linda was tolerable enough—pretty well useless as a wife or companion, but so busy with domestic details and frazzled by the end of the day that she was no real problem for James. How could she be a problem, when his own waking hours were so fully occupied with creating new and better commercial ventures? It was work in which he took such delight!

Building boats; outfitting pioneers, settlers, lumbermen, miners, and tradesmen of every description; land and currency speculation; organizing small and large settlement companies whose member families were deeply indebted to Cullen and Company; planning for future trade with Spanish territory once the war was over—all these things were welcome, fascinating tasks for which James had been born. Everyone said so, especially Noah Maxwell.

Merchants and suppliers often commented on how pleasing it was to do business with James—who was honest and fair—instead of with the stingy, grasping Cullen, who soaked them for all they were worth. James still made a handsome profit, and in a few years would command the entire western mercantile empire. Perhaps he would eventually move to Philadelphia or New York, but for now there were plenty of challenges and ways to profit at Fort Pitt.

Before long the fighting would end, and vast reaches of land would be opened for sale to speculators. Bradford Cullen already had persuaded important members of Congress to make sure his company would have first chance at purchasing millions of acres for ultimate resale. That, to James, would be great fun, a new undertaking. Indeed, all of it was becoming an exhilarating game of speculation, risk, and chance; but with all the Cullen resources and influence behind him, James seldom failed to profit, or to win regularly.

When unexpected word came from the Sutherlands that they meant to visit him at Fort Pitt, he was only a little disturbed by the prospect of again coming face to face with Susannah. He felt somewhat guilty about leaving her as he had, having written only one letter, back then, to explain himself. Her reply had been surprisingly reserved, as if it really did not make much difference to her what he did with his life. Since then, he had been caught up in the whirl of marriage, joining Cullen and Company, and reshaping his world, and had not allowed himself to think very much about Susannah.

Now, however, with her coming to see him, he was faced once more with deeper feelings that surprised him with their intensity when they suddenly surfaced. Yes, Susannah was far different from Linda Cullen Morely.

James wondered how she had changed after two years. He decided it would be good to see her again, if only to place things in perspective, to clear his mind, and to put whatever he once had felt for her well behind him, forever.

That should not be so difficult to do, for James was sure he had made the right choice. Cullen and Company was the fulfillment of his dream, and Susannah Sutherland had been merely an ideal. James Morely had dreams, not ideals—ambitions, not illusions. There were moments when he still wondered about people like Owen Sutherland, who lived for ideals and the illusions they bred. He could not quite understand why anyone of intelligence would choose that course of life, when by making hardheaded decisions, calculated to produce success, a man could forge ahead at almost breakneck speed.

What made Sutherland seem such a tragic hero? What had made loving Susannah such a romantic ideal? James did not understand it. But, then, there was little time for philosophizing these days. In only one lifetime, he had the world to conquer— through the force of Cullen's money and his own wits. He needed no store of heroism, no lofty ideals, and that suited him just fine.

chapter 19

HEART'S LOVE

An autumn rainstorm hung on the western horizon, dark clouds lowering over the hills across the Allegheny River, as James Morely stepped from his carriage and went down to Cullen's wharf near Fort Pitt, where his newest boat was being finished.

This was no ordinary freight craft, but one that had been built according to James's specifications. She was a beauty, forty feet long, modeled after Cullen's keelboat *Linda,* but much sleeker. Though James had designed her for light commerce and personal travel, she could also carry cannon and would serve as a means of inspecting the riverbanks for likely places to build trading posts, sawmills, or gristmills, or to settle new communities. And she would be a joy for just sailing. James considered her a luxury he could now allow himself.

Dressed elegantly in fine, dark broadcloth and silks, wearing a new bicorne hat, he stood in the wind gusting off the river and bade the workmen good day as they departed early. It was Saturday, and he allowed them to leave by midafternoon if they had met certain goals that week. The hull had been caulked and painted, but the interior of the deckhouse was lacking trim and cabinetry, and there was no rigging for sails as yet. She floated gracefully, tied up to the wharf, and it gave James a thrill to contemplate having her at his whim. It was a new freedom.

He heard his name called, the sound of distant thunder almost drowning out the cry, and he turned to see Owen and Ella Sutherland disembarking from a crowded whaleboat that had just arrived at the fort's landing. It was Owen shouting for him, and James waved, glad to see him for the first time in well over a year. His past disagreements with Owen Sutherland had pretty much healed over, and although the two of them no longer did business together, they still had too much in common for a complete break.

He approached Owen, who was well-dressed in a long coat and knee breeches instead of the more usual buckskins. As they shook hands, James saw the strain of hardship on the man's lined and weathered face; but Sutherland was as robust as ever, perhaps even stronger in a certain way—a way James could not put into words.

"It's a pleasure, Owen, after all this time!"

"And for me, James." Sutherland smiled, and James knew he genuinely meant it, for Sutherland did not say what he did not mean. "I'm glad to see you're well."

Ella came next, wearing a white bonnet and cape, and James thought her beauty timeless. They embraced, and he felt her squeeze him warmly, as one might embrace a long-lost member of the family. That gave him a good feeling, one he had not experienced in all these heady months at Pitt. He laughed as Punch fluttered down onto his shoulder, another old friend.

Ella said, "Your mother and Jeb send their regards, as do Sally and Tom." She quickly related that his family was hoping to have him come downriver to visit soon, and James was glad to hear they were over their initial anger at his having joined Cullen. They had even spurned his offers of financial help, which had not surprised him. He listened with pleasure as Ella said that his nephew, Timothy Owen, looked a little like him, and that there was another child, a girl named Maria.

There followed a rush of questions, as James asked about Jeremy and Gwen, who had remained at the Falls, where their presence was becoming essential to the well-being of settlers for many miles around. Unfortunately, their baby was still weak, unable to travel. Ella told James that Tamano and his family would stay in the Illinois, where an Indian who was a virtual outcast from his people could do well in the trade with the French and Spanish. Those folk cared little for a man's background and more for his talents. The others had all remained in Kentucky, still hopeful of a rebel push against Detroit one day, a move that would recover their lost homes. James knew that push seemed more difficult with every passing season, but did not say that to Ella.

In his excitement with Ella's news, James did not notice that Susannah was being helped up from the boat by her father. When he looked around to see her, he stopped talking and gazed in wonder. She was incredibly beautiful. She was more beautiful than he remembered her, more beautiful than anyone he had ever seen. Her hair was pinned up under a white, wide-brimmed hat, and she wore a dark cloak that made her fair face seem to shine with loveliness.

Awkwardly, James greeted her, accepting her hand self-consciously, and bowing to kiss it, feeling at the last moment as if he could not meet those large, blue eyes that held him so steadily in their placid gaze. Could Susannah really have changed so much? Could she have grown, been formed by some magic of nature into the breathtaking woman who stood before him?

His next words were almost whispered: "How . . . old are you now, Susannah?"

She did not immediately reply, and then he caught himself, straightened up, and a little laugh escaped him as he apologized, saying, "Forgive my forwardness . . . for you're now a young woman, and I ought not to—"

Again he was at a loss for words. Susannah's eyes were so deep, so searching, so impossible to look away from. She was smiling, and he felt his whole being filled with warmth, as if her enchantment had set him on fire in the purest, most magnificent way imaginable. No, it was not possible for a man merely to imagine this at all. How could anyone imagine this? How could anyone dream about this feeling, without first having experienced it? Hardly noticing Punch perching on his hat, James was feeling something that he had never known before.

And yet this was really the same Susannah!

She withdrew her hand and was perfectly formal as she said, "Wealth suits you, James."

"What?"

"I can see you are in the position in which you were meant to be, and it suits you. I hope you are doing some good with it."

He did not know how to reply, but lamely gestured at the new boat. Becoming enthusiastic, though a bit forced, he showed the Sutherlands toward it. Punch sprang onto Ella's hand as she admired the boat. Sutherland mentioned that it would make a good gunboat, for which he got an elbow from his wife, who said he had promised not to talk of war for a while.

James was aware that Owen and Ella Sutherland were a bit uneasy, obviously about Susannah, who stood there as if without emotion. James looked back at her parents, who appeared somehow more vulnerable than he had seen them before. He suddenly realized that he, too, had changed much, having wielded great power, moved hundreds of men and thousands of pounds sterling with the wave of a hand. He was becoming used to his new prosperity—abundance—but now, in the presence of the Sutherlands, he felt almost like an unshaven boy again.

That was an annoying, uncomfortable feeling; but then Sutherland altered the mood by saying he and Ella would like to have James as their guest for dinner that evening. First, however, they would arrange for lodging in the town, if James would be good enough to escort Susannah for a couple of hours.

James saw Susannah give a start at that and look at her father, who was genial and calm, already offering his arm to Ella. For just an instant an expression of anxiety passed over Susannah's face, but then she recovered, like some courageous soldier preparing to do her duty.

Ella, too, was anxious, but she forced it away and glanced up at the sky, which was darkening, licked by flashes of lightning.

"Stormy weather," she cried with a laugh, like a young girl, tossing the voiceless Punch into the air. "Come on, husband, I've only one traveling dress, and I don't want it all muddy."

She dragged Sutherland away, the bird flying above them. James took note as Sutherland glanced back at his daughter, who was gazing— With a start, James realized she was staring right at him.

Susannah saw James's restlessness and was sure it was caused by a strong feeling—a feeling he still bore in his heart for her. To think that gave her a thrill, and yet it also hurt to know he had forsaken and repressed feelings that even now he could not mask completely. For a moment she felt herself tremble, but she contained it, ignored it, and let him see nothing of her heartache.

After all, was she not over it by now? This powerful emotion in her was just an echo of a past delusion, a remnant of something that must no longer be, and had best lie forgotten. She felt sorry for James as he gazed at her like that, as if he were somehow in her power. If she gave him a little push he might crumble to dust.

"James," she said with a demure nod that startled him back to the moment, "may I see your new boat?"

He was all clumsy and accommodating, and as he led her across the gangplank, Susannah moved gracefully in her long dress. She could have lifted her skirts and bounded in one leap over the unpainted railing, but she enjoyed playing the role of a lady, and compelling him to try to be a gentleman. James was not very experienced at it, and Susannah took mild pleasure in making him a bit uncomfortable. She knew her manners, and she waited graciously until he realized he was supposed to help her down to the deck. Then, with merely a look of benevolence, she set him back on his heels as she slid ahead of him into the doorway of the deckhouse.

In spite of his fine clothes and wealth, James was still the unpolished fellow from a frontier trading post, while Susannah, thanks to her mother, had the ways of a lady, and she continued to prod him ever so slightly, ever so pointedly, so that he was unsure whether to treat her as a childhood friend or as a lady of high breeding. She was both, but now more lady than friend.

She did not, however, fawn, with "Sir, you are too kind," or with coy exclamations and helpless little gasps. She made James follow her lead as he awkwardly showed her through the handsome deckhouse, often causing him to beg her pardon for being in her way, or to excuse himself for not opening doors promptly. Eventually, it might be said, she had him in the palm of her hand. He doffed his hat at her polite request, offered her a stool when he saw her discreetly looking about for a place to sit, enthusiastically commented on her traveling clothes when she asked directly for his opinion. And when he could not help himself and again dared to inquire her age, he was forgiven for being a bit too forward. He never received an answer.

For Susannah, it was actually fun to toy with him, and as she did so, it told her more about the change in herself. She was indeed a woman, and obviously James could not help but take notice. He was even sweating a little.

They were alone in the boat, with rain pattering down outside. His carriage with its horse stood waiting to take them to town, but it was peaceful in the deckhouse, the lightning flashing far away, only the distant rumble of thunder to be heard over the sound of rain on the boat.

After a while, Susannah had no idea how long they had been there, but both had asked all the questions, explored all the little byways of conversation still open to friends whose lives had grown apart. There came a quiet period, and for the first time Susannah began to feel uncomfortable under James's steady gaze. She was on the stool, her back to the windows that faced the river. He stood near the open doorway, which had not yet been fitted with a door. The light fell on her, and she could not see his face well, though she felt him staring, and was not sure she liked it.

Glad to think of another subject, she said, "Do you still read Shakespeare?" He said there was not much time for it, and his voice seemed far away, as if something else was on his mind. She went on: "I used to read *Romeo and Juliet* all the time, but it's become too dreary to me . . . or perhaps I should say too sad, too real."

"Sad? Once you thought it beautiful beyond description, lofty, and magnificent." He moved away from the door and came to lean against a sawhorse closer to her. "You've indeed changed."

"Indeed." She almost began to explain her feelings, to say she was not criticizing some shortcoming of *Romeo and Juliet*, but that the play was too poignant, touched her too deeply. She did not say that, however. She would not bare her soul to James now. Besides, if he did not understand, he was an oaf. Still, it was good to be with him again, and she felt much better to see him, to talk with him, and to come to accept him as a new person, just as she was a new person.

She said, "And you have changed."

He folded his arms, brass buttons glittering in the soft light, and as he smiled, he said, "For the better, I hope."

"Are you happy?"

"I have what I want."

"Do you want *all* that you have?"

He laughed, as if to throw off the irony in her pointed question.

She asked, a bit annoyed, "Do I amuse you?"

He caught himself again, and in a gentle voice said, "Exquisite beauty is not amusing, Susannah."

How that surprised her! It had the power to make her blood surge, though she did not want that at all. But it did, and she had to look away. He became master of the moment.

He said, "Do I embarrass you?"

"Married men who have what they want in life do not embarrass virtuous women with flattery." That came out more sharply than she had expected. She hardened, her eyes flashing, but his eyes also intensified, though there was a hint of humor in them. She was not sure whether it was the good humor of an old friend or the patronizing behavior of a man who teases a child. Either way, Susannah was vexed by it.

James said, "Truth is never flattery."

She looked at him, then out the door, where another carriage had stopped beside his own. She paid no attention to the carriage, especially when she realized suddenly that James was reciting the words of Romeo when first he sees Juliet dancing at a ball:

> "O, she doth teach the torches to burn bright!
> It seems she hangs upon the cheek of night
> As a rich jewel in an Ethiop's ear. . . ."

It thrilled her, for all that she did not want it to, and she longed to close her eyes and listen to his fine and gentle voice, the voice of Romeo. Her heart beat so that she almost could hear it.

"The measure done, I'll watch her place of stand,
And, touching hers, make blessed my rude hand.
Did my heart love till now?—"

"Stop!" She would not hear this, not now! She recovered,
but James had not, and he closed his own eyes as he went on
with words that pierced her, excited and hurt her all at once.

"For I ne'er saw true beauty till this night."

"Please stop, James!"
But he did not, or would not, or could not. Eyes still closed:

"If I profane with my unworthiest hand
This holy shrine, the gentle sin is this—"

"James . . ." She was shaking with emotion, unsure if she
was angry or simply overwhelmed by passion.

Perhaps, if just then he had opened those eyes of his, reached
out and taken her hand, she would have melted; but all he did
was continue to recite, his eyes remaining shut as if he were
in some dream.

"Stop!"

"My lips, two blushing pilgrims, ready stand—"

"Stand no more!" She gave the legs of the sawhorse a mighty
kick, and James fell back, head over heels, thumping down
into a pile of sawdust. As he sat up, shocked, squashed hat
askew, Susannah's anger became delight, and she giggled, hand
to her mouth. Recovering, he laughed, too, and as she laugh-
ingly begged his forgiveness, he struggled to his feet. Through
her giggling she helped him get up, and for just a moment they
were in each other's arms. Startled, Susannah would not let
that happen, and so began to draw away, still laughing, until
there came a noise at the open door.

"What is the meaning of this, James?" That voice, nasal
and loud, came from a broad shadow blotting out the light.
"Why, it's the Sutherland girl!" Linda Cullen, like some enormous bird in cape and feathered hat, was outlined against the
rainy background. Her voice became a wail, penetrating and

harsh. "What are you doing to her? Oh, my heavens! Not at a time like this!"

James moved toward her, the blood draining from his face. "Dearest . . . it's not at all what you think—"

"Oh, no . . . not at a time like this! Not now! Oh, Papa! Not her again! Oh, Papa!"

"Linda! Stop!"

But she was stumbling away to her carriage, her cape flying in the wind and rain, and James started after her. At the doorway, he gave a helpless, confused look back at Susannah, and that was enough of a delay to allow Linda to urge her driver to start up and hurry her home. Watching the carriage spin away, James let his arms drop to his sides. His head went down, and he drew a long, sad breath.

"Forgive me," they said to each other, simultaneously, and for an instant they almost laughed; but it was not really a laughing matter. Susannah knew Linda would go to her father immediately, and James was in for trouble.

"Your poor wife is with child, Mr. Morely! Do you realize that?" Bradford Cullen looked like a devil, an ogre, as he leaned over his polished mahogany desk, his wrinkled fat face just inches from James, who sat, impassive, before him. "With child! When she told me just now, I should have been overjoyed, as indeed I am, but now you have betrayed her, as I warned you solemnly never, never to do!"

"I betrayed no one, sir. It was simply a lark—"

"A lark! An interlude with that Sutherland wench, that worthless little baggage—"

"Sir!"

"What? What do you want me to say? That she's a sweet and beautiful and innocent—"

"She is innocent, and there's no cause for any of this suspicion—"

"No cause?" Cullen wheezed and stumped around his desk, his face a flaming red. It required all his strength to move as he leaned on his silver-headed cane. "No cause, when my daughter comes raving in here, suffering already from carrying the burden of a babe two months along, and she cries out that you are dallying with another woman, and for all to see?"

"A friend, that's all."

"A friend? A Sutherland! A former sweetheart, and you cannot deny it! We all know it, and so does my poor Linda! Stay away from that wench! I warn you!"

And so it went, a half hour of lambasting and accusation by the infuriated Cullen. Nothing James could say was enough to change the man's mind. James was humiliated, angry, helpless. Cullen still feared the Sutherlands, that was obvious. For him it would be the ultimate shame if rumors of James's "infidelity" with Susannah began to spread. Although James truly regretted that Linda was so upset, he was fiercely resentful of Cullen's crude accusations. More so because he had learned from Linda that he was to be a father only after Cullen had been told in the woman's outburst of rage and jealousy.

That news itself was a mixture of excitement and strange hollowness that James could not explain. He was all the more shaken because the accusation that he was being unfaithful, engaging in an affair with Susannah Sutherland, had solid justification within his own heart. He knew that he still loved her, and now more than ever.

"Have we done the right thing, Susannah?" Owen Sutherland asked his daughter that evening, as he and Ella strolled with her idly past the fort, where the river lapped at the shore close to the earth-and-stone ramparts. The setting sun had come out, and the wind was fresh, the countryside tinted orange and pink, everything beautiful.

Sutherland had heard what had happened when Susannah and James were on the boat, and James had sent word asking to be excused from dinner, hinting at some difficulties at home. That troubled Sutherland, but mainly he wanted to know how Susannah had endured seeing her former sweetheart again, and so did Ella.

They flanked the girl as they walked, father at the water side, mother with a hand in her daughter's elbow. They looked the part of a well-to-do merchant family, although Sutherland's financial prospects were still uncertain. Any day now they expected a messenger from yet-solvent company partners in Albany, who would send funds with which to pay James and to reestablish the Frontier Company at Pitt in some small way. For now, however, Sutherland's concerns were for his daughter, and he was glad to see that her spirits had lifted in spite of the embarrassment with Linda Cullen.

Susannah thought a moment before answering. "Yes, Pa, I needed to see him again, and to know . . . to know I was not simply a misguided child to have held such strong feelings for a . . . a character of my imagination."

Sutherland did not know what she meant, but it was Ella who asked her to explain herself. Susannah smiled and squeezed her mother's hand as she said, "James Morely is a fine man, such a good and sensitive man, wonderful in a way . . ."

Sutherland's eyebrow rose. "Lass . . ."

"But he's also a man who has gone his own road in life, and I accept that fully. He's also a married man, though not happily, and for having made that choice . . . for that I can only forgive him."

Sutherland breathed out in relief. "Good for you, lassie." He put his arm about her and drew her close as they walked on.

Ella said, "And you don't blame us, that we might have helped cause him to make that choice?"

Susannah shook her head. "I blame no one for anything." Her eyes shone dreamily. "It's over, though I don't deny my own feelings still are powerful when I see him—"

Sutherland cut in: "Now, lass!"

"But that will pass, I assure you both."

Sutherland exhaled again. It was not easy being the father of a daughter. He hoped that soon some fine young man he could approve of would arrive from somewhere and lift her completely out of the James Morely morass. He could tell Susannah was not yet purged, but she was doing very well, and was growing stronger. He exchanged glances with Ella and guessed she felt about the same.

"Listen!" Ella declared abruptly. "Shall we go on to Philadelphia for the winter?"

Susannah was excited, but Sutherland said that this was much to ask of him. He was expected back at the Falls, to help Clark with the defenses that winter, preparing for the spring raids. In a moment of quick thinking, he said, "Why don't you both go, and stop in on Dr. Franklin's people? They'll help you arrange your stay, and I'll come by Christmas!"

It was a good plan, a good change for all of them, and they would not be apart for too long. The women could accompany a detachment of soldiers whose time was up in a few days and who were riding all the way back to eastern Pennsylvania. Later, Owen could join them until springtime. They all agreed the idea was splendid. Ella and Owen believed that if Philadelphia could not shake James Morely from Susannah's impressionable mind, nothing would.

chapter **20**

CULLEN'S MEN

Three full days passed before Linda would even speak to James. In that time he dared not go to Susannah, lest Cullen's spies see him do so. Eventually, he partly soothed his wife's jealous indignation, and they began to talk of the baby on the way. That did the trick, and Linda became calm at last; but like her father, she insisted that James never again even see Susannah Sutherland.

Of course, such a demand infuriated James, and the trouble started all over again. He declared he would see whom he liked and when he liked, and no one would tell him otherwise, and that included Linda's father. Off she went again, crying through the house, to her father's arms. When Cullen called for James— using an embarrassed Noah Maxwell as the messenger—James flatly refused to go and left the house.

He went directly to the Sutherlands, who had rented a cottage at the edge of town. Owen Sutherland had received his expected funds and had undertaken trade negotiations with several honorable smaller merchants who were disinclined to deal with Cullen. Sutherland even paid back a portion of the debt owed James for the Fort McIntosh disaster. It was apparent to James that Sutherland had every intention of restoring his business, despite his accumulated setbacks and despite the fact that neither Congress nor Virginia had yet reimbursed him for the small fortune he had expended to aid George Rogers Clark nearly two years ago.

James was told that the Sutherlands were about finished with their business at Pitt and would separate, the women departing for Philadelphia and Owen for the Falls in a few days. Late that afternoon, James was once more allowed to sit alone with Susannah. It was obvious that the young woman's parents wanted them to resolve their relationship once and for all, that they meant to have Susannah's mind clear and at rest.

In the common room of that humble cottage, with a bright fire crackling in the hearth, James sat across from Susannah while she nervously embroidered. He wondered just what she thought of him, and knew this was probably the last time he would be able to speak frankly with her about his own feelings and what had happened between them in the past. Before long she would be out of his life, perhaps forever. He was uneasy, for in his heart was a feeling for Susannah that he dare not voice. He had hurt her too much already, and would not risk distressing her again. He suspected that she still was vulnerable to him, and he did not know what to do.

It was Susannah who initiated the conversation, saying plainly, "Does your wife think we are lovers, James?"

There was not the slightest emotion in her voice, but her words stirred him, the very thought of their being lovers disturbing and exciting him. Yet he suspected she would not stand for it if he attempted to romance her—and if Owen ever thought he had such designs, there would be hell to pay. It was clear the Sutherlands trusted their daughter, allowing her to be alone like this with James while they went for a walk. James guessed that Susannah herself meant to break their relationship cleanly.

He cleared his throat. "Perhaps Linda does think so . . . but whatever she thinks, she and her father are extremely agitated about . . . everything, and have tried to forbid me to come here."

"Indeed? Then why have you come if your master, Mr. Cullen, has forbidden you?"

James resented that and said so, almost angrily, adding that Susannah was being intentionally cruel, ". . . trying to get even with me for how I so clumsily treated you in the past!"

Susannah looked up, her eyes cool and steady as they held his gaze. "That's true." She put down her embroidery. "I had thought it would do me good to hurt you in return, but, alas, I see it does not."

She smiled, completely unexpectedly, and again James was irresistibly moved by her beauty.

But then she said, "I wish you to go back to Linda, and to all that you want, and never to visit me again, James."

He sat stock still, regretting she had said that. "Indeed, you do yet hurt me, Susannah."

"I want to hurt you no more, nor you to hurt me, and that's why you must leave me alone forever, for I cannot do anything else but hurt you if I cannot have—" She caught herself and looked away, her guard dropping, her proud attitude failing her.

James stood up, close by. "If you cannot have me?"

She would not look up. "Please go now."

He released a sigh and held out his hand for hers, asking, "Forgive my poor manners, lady, but . . . but if one last time, I might . . ."

Hesitantly, she raised her hand to his, and he bent to kiss it, their eyes meeting and holding. He saw all her sadness, and felt his own sadness, wondering whether she understood how he, too, hurt.

"Farewell, Susannah, and do not think harshly of me."

She shook her head, not crying, but unable to speak.

He smiled bravely, and so did she. Fighting down his surging passions, James asked calmly if he might write to her from time to time, ". . . as old friends."

"It would be fine," she said. "And may the Lord bless your family, James."

What a power she had to move him! He could not help himself. He did love her!

She bade him farewell, and he knew there was no other way but to go, if he was to keep his sanity.

With a heavy heart, James went out the front door of the cottage, into another drizzling autumn rain. He paused to recover, breathing in the cool air. He had neglected much important business in the past few days of quarreling and unhappiness; but he felt better, as he hoped Susannah would feel better. He was resolved to go right to Bradford Cullen and tell him to back off and stop trying to run his life.

Just then, as he crossed the street, he saw a carriage in which sat Noah Maxwell, Cullen's best spy. Maxwell was alone. He called James over and said they must talk. Upon James's asking, Maxwell said Cullen already knew he had been with Susannah. James said nothing more for some time.

Soon they were out on the road to the stone quarry, a winding track that met with other roads that cut across fields, so they could ride around and around for some time without having to go out of sight of the fort.

"I'm here to give you a warning, James," said Maxwell. "Nothing in Cullen's life is dearer to him than his daughter, but now you have injured her. He will not easily forgive you for that."

Annoyed, James said he was not surprised, but that he was his own man, and anyway he had done nothing wrong—save for what he felt in his heart. He let that last confession slip.

Maxwell clucked his tongue. "You do indeed love that Sutherland girl, then."

"What does it matter? I'll not be unfaithful to Linda; I stand by my word, Noah."

"Bless me," Maxwell said with a sigh. "Bless me, my friend, but I hope you'll never be so rash as to reveal your feelings about Susannah Sutherland to the old man's face."

James gave a little laugh. "I trust you to keep my secret, Noah."

Maxwell seemed uneasy, a bit pained, and he replied, "I, too, depend on Cullen for my livelihood, James, and I ask you never again to compromise me by telling me any intimacy that places you in a bad light with Cullen."

"Will you tell him what I've just said, then?"

Maxwell looked sideways at James, then gave the horse a rap with the reins. "No need to; he knows it well already, and now I have orders to take you to him. Sorry, James, to be so conspiratorial, but we'll talk again, and you'll forgive me, I believe."

They swung off the main road and headed for the quarry, a secluded, water-filled hole ringed by thick trees. It had been dug thirty years ago to build part of Fort Pitt, and now was unused. James wondered aloud why Maxwell was driving along this quiet track toward it.

Maxwell said, "Because Cullen has instructed me to. James, unless you and I can change matters with the company, neither of us will ever be our own man."

"What? Change matters? What do you mean?"

Maxwell seldom said anything like this that did not have some significance to it. He surely was getting at something serious, but before James could press for an answer, they drove around a dense thicket and he saw another carriage, this one Cullen's, parked near the edge of the quarry.

Maxwell drew the horse to a stop, and James sprang down from the carriage, angrily stamping toward Cullen, who was seated in regal comfort. The driver was tough Bill Bartholomew, Cullen's bodyguard.

"What is the meaning of this, Mr. Cullen? Must you play such games with me? I feel like I've been kidnapped!"

Cullen raised a fat hand, an ugly smile coming over his face. "Not kidnapped, my man, but let us say . . . you have been compromised." With a flick of his silver cane, Cullen indicated something behind James, who turned. To his dismay, he recognized the notorious British officer Mark Davies, and a scraggly man in buckskins he was sure must be Simon Girty—both men with rebel prices on their heads. Just knowing their whereabouts and not reporting it would be a crime by rebel standards.

Davies was wearing partisan green, and James recalled the rumors that he was now roving the forests as a murderous volunteer raider, a man without true allegiance to anyone but himself and his band of Indian and white killers. Supposedly he was still fighting in the loyalist cause, but the army had little control over him. Simon Girty, on the other hand, was no renegade, but a loyalist scout for the British army.

James was furious, and knew immediately that Cullen was engaging in some secret dealings with these men, while at the same time pretending to be a leading rebel. Sutherland had accused Cullen of that, but James had not believed it. Mark Davies was grinning, as if well aware of the embarrassment his presence caused James. Girty was sullen; it appeared he did not want to be there at all.

As Davies politely greeted him, James ignored him and

swung on Cullen. "What's the meaning of this? These men are enemies of this community!" Cullen's piggish eyes glittered merrily, and suddenly James felt utterly defenseless. He was unarmed, and the thought came to him that Cullen meant to murder him for having upset his daughter. That would be madness! But then, Cullen would soon have the blood heir he wanted. Perhaps he no longer needed James. . . . These thoughts whirled through James's mind, and he whipped back to confront Davies and Girty, picking up a stick with which to fight if he had to.

Davies laughed, and so did Cullen from the comfort of his carriage. Maxwell was silent, looking downcast, as though James could expect no help from him.

James readied to fight, but Cullen called out in his hoarse, wheezing voice, "You are in no danger, son-in-law. Put down that stick." James turned to face him again, one eye on the partisans. "Now, sir, you are at last a trusted initiate in Cullen and Company, and you see plainly the full diversity of our dealings. These two gentlemen are here on business with me . . . they require guns, ammunition, liquor—the usual needs of warfare. In turn we have our own bargain, our own private arrangement."

James said with a snarl, "You're a British sympathizer after all!"

Cullen laughed, and was joined by Davies, who strolled toward James. Davies had a sword at his side and obviously was unconcerned about the stick James still held.

Cullen said languidly, "Now you know how I could be so sure that Pitt was not in real danger. . . ." He nodded to Davies, who came a few steps closer to James; the man looked menacing, though a mild smirk was on his face. "My two acquaintances here told me the true aim of Byrd's campaign was merely to punish and drive out the settlers, not to trouble us at Pitt."

Davies said, "Mr. Cullen and I have been acquaintances for some years, and throughout this rebellion, we've . . . let's say we've cooperated very well together." He looked slyly at Cullen. "To our mutual satisfaction." He said to James: "I trust you and I will do the same, my friend."

James gripped the stick, hatred about to get the better of him. He himself had fought Indian raiders sent by Davies against the Frontier Company, and had been wounded in the fight. He wanted to lash out, to smash Davies for all the evil he had done. It appeared the villain was ready for that, for he had one hand casually on the hilt of his sword.

James was quivering, the stick coming up as if on its own. Davies tensed. Maxwell cried out for James to be steady, and rose in his seat. The horses whickered nervously. James knew he was no match for Cullen's men, but his honor required that he defy them. If not, what honor did he have?

"Don't be a fool!" Cullen called with a light cackle. "If you want to be angry with someone, be angry with me, sir, for Mr. Davies merely obeyed my orders—"

James swung on Cullen. "And it was you who betrayed the supply camp!" Cullen smiled, as if flattered. "You told this devil how to attack us, and what we had there!" Suddenly James realized that Noah Maxwell must have been in on the conspiracy, too, and he gaped at his friend, who looked embarrassed, his face flushed. "Noah! You were the one who gave the alarm about the farm being hit!"

Mark Davies clucked his tongue. "Tut, tut, Mr. Morely, but you are a self-righteous fellow! But you yourself really haven't chosen a side in this war, have you?"

"Shut your mouth!" James roared and slashed with the stick, but Davies's sword was out, hacking the stick in two. The point of the blade circled just inches from James's face. "You're a bastard, Davies! A murdering—"

Davies became enraged, his face contorted, and he lost control. Ignoring Cullen's shouts of warning, he lunged at the unarmed James.

Suddenly Simon Girty was there, knocking the sword aside, grappling Davies to the ground, and cursing at him to "mind yer god-rotting manners, you hotheaded English varmint!" He grasped the man's sword arm as Davies tore and scratched at him with the other hand. "Varmint! Drop the steel, you fool!"

That made Davies all the more wild, and with tremendous effort he broke free of Girty and, still on the ground, slashed at him with the sword. The scout scrambled backward, but he had taken a nasty cut across his chest—not deep, but painful.

Both men were panting, and Girty was almost as enraged as Davies, who sprang up. Girty took the tomahawk from his belt, hissing that Davies had best govern his temper.

"Or you'll see what a backwoods white man can do to an English—"

"Enough!" Cullen was livid, standing in his carriage, but it was not he who stopped the fight. It was huge Bill Bartholomew, who leaped from the driver's box. Towering over the other two, he held a brace of cocked pistols in his fists. Cullen wheezed, "No one's going to kill anyone here! You men remember your orders to work together, or I'll report this to your higher-ups, and you'll both be broken before I'm done! Enough!"

James saw how these partisan fighters despised each other and were forced by circumstances to work in a tormented alliance. Catching his breath, he nodded to Girty in thanks for helping him. The scout spit out a wad of tobacco mingled with blood.

Davies backed off, sheathing his sword and knocking the dust from his hat. He eyed James with contempt, but he was recovering his senses again.

James turned his attention to Cullen, who was smiling once more. James was pale, trembling with anger. "So you come out on top, no matter whether rebel or loyalist wins!"

Cullen chuckled, long and slow. "That, my man, is why I wanted you for my successor. You understand me. You are clever and forthright." Then abruptly he hardened, his voice cutting as he said, "You have your task within our company, and you will indeed be my successor, with all the wealth and influence you could require. I will handle these more delicate matters. You'll not have to soil your righteous hands in any way—just profit from it! But now you know it all, and if you wish to avoid being enmeshed in what your rebel friends would consider the mortal sin of supporting the Crown, then keep away from the Sutherland wench, once and for all!

"I can arrange that you be further compromised if I have to, and no one will link any of it to me." He banged his cane on the floor of the carriage. "Go back home! Raise my heir, and make my own child the happiest woman on earth! I warn you now!" He looked vicious. "Do not further provoke my anger!"

It was as if a terrible thunderstorm had broken, as if the very earth trembled with Cullen's wrath. But then, just as suddenly as it had risen, the gale abated, and Cullen was all sweetness and good humor once more.

"Do you understand me, young man? Let us not endure such unpleasantries again."

James might have replied, had he not been so fuming with rage, and had Cullen's attitude not suddenly changed to mild benevolence. The man was a sorcerer, a master of the moment. James shook with hatred, but kept himself outwardly steady. Cullen chuckled again and held out a hand in James's direction.

"Enjoy your promising new life, my man. Make the most of what I and Providence have laid at your feet. Go home to Linda now, and be content. Go home and thrive, for the sake of your unborn child. Do this, James, and forgive an old man his irascible whims."

Whim? This was cunning at its most evil.

James got back into Maxwell's carriage and rode toward Fort Pitt without saying a word. At first, Maxwell seemed ashamed and sorry. As for James, he loathed his life, and knew he was again faced with a crucial choice: leave Cullen and Linda for good, abandon all his hopes, forgo the treasure that already was his, or . . . or what? An awful ache rose up inside him, and he burned with anger and remorse all at once. He wondered what sort of man he really was after all.

Before they reached the fort, Maxwell said in a doleful voice, "I understand, James. This all came as a shock to me when first I learned of Cullen's double-dealing." There was a pause.

Maxwell leaned forward and sighed. "Truly, James, I had no idea of what terrible things would happen at Fort McIntosh . . . about those poor lads who . . . That savage Davies, worse than the Indians! I had no idea what would happen!"

He almost whimpered that Cullen had ordered him to spy on the supply dump, to report everything about it, and to make contact with Davies in the woods on the day of the attack. James thought there was even a tear in the lawyer's eye as he went on:

"They promised you'd be safe, James, and they told me they would just take the men prisoners and burn everything." He looked almost bewildered, and shook his head. "I only pray that you'll believe me in this, James. I meant no harm to anyone." He swallowed, his voice shaking. "You know how

Cullen can be, how he can force a man to do his bidding. . . ." His teeth clenched. "He's a despicable dog! I hate him! How I hate him!"

James said nothing, but let his body sway with the rhythm of the carriage.

Maxwell said, "Cullen's pulled so many men down to his level. But it's still possible for you and me to rise above it . . . to, let us say, make the most of our advantageous situation."

"How? What situation?" James wanted to know how to get even with Cullen, but did not want to lose everything—yes, he had already made up his mind not to break rashly with Cullen. He would see this crisis through, and would ultimately triumph simply by outliving the old scoundrel. He would inherit it all one day, and would have the last laugh.

Maxwell thought a moment before replying, and said, "I have complete charge of all the company's legal documents and contracts, James, including Cullen's will. . . ."

Noah Maxwell knew every in and out of Cullen's business affairs, and had probed more deeply into secret documents and official papers than Cullen ever had intended him to.

As the carriage neared the center of town, Maxwell said, "The old man will die soon, that's plain; and now that he'll be assured an heir in a few months, I think he'll likely allow himself to shrivel up and die with a smile on his ugly face, thinking his unholy blood will continue to run in the veins of some future world leader."

James told him impatiently to get on with his point, and they drew up in front of the Cullen mansion while Maxwell explained further. He said, "Cullen has threatened to write you out of the company altogether if you displease him once too often."

James was not surprised to hear this.

Maxwell said, "Now, I know you well enough, Mr. Morely, to guess that you're already in for another collision with Cullen, and in a month or two you may suffer a demise that will cause Linda and the child legally to be taken from you."

James sat glumly listening, aware Maxwell was right. Cullen had the capacity to do just that. Even an occasional casual letter to Susannah, for example, could touch off a storm that would cost James everything. He refused even to consider this prospect. He had become too used to the good life, and had too many grandiose plans of his own to let that happen. He meant to be greater than Cullen, and would not be stopped now.

Maxwell went on to say he had secretly prepared all the proper documentation, with all the needed registered seals and forged notaries, to smooth the way for deposing Cullen from his position at the head of the firm. There were a few others in the brewing plot, men who hated Cullen, who would profit one way or another, and who would do their part, swearing to be witnesses to anything that was needed. They already approved of James as the leader of Cullen and Company.

James was astonished. "But he'll fight you! He has influence beyond either of us—"

"Name one man who loves him! Name one man who will do his bidding, besides Mark Davies, perhaps! Name one man who won't gleefully stand by and laugh if we outsmart Bradford Cullen and legally depose him!"

James shook his head. "He has the wealth to hire the lawyers, buy fighting men . . . Noah, it'll be a mess."

"You're a man of courage!" Maxwell chuckled. "Besides, two can play the same game: we can force him to keep quiet by threatening to expose his treasonous activities with Davies and Girty and all the other loyalists! I'm the man that can do it, too—perhaps the only one who can! And before he can even protest, we'll have the machinery in place to have him arrested in a twinkling, if need be. There's many a rebel officer who'll gladly throw him in the clink for a few weeks while awaiting judgment from higher authorities. The wait in an unheated cell alone will kill Cullen. He won't dare risk it." He laughed aloud. "Think of the victory you'll savor! Cullen'll be miserably defeated, as he deserves. He'll do whatever we demand, and you and I will take his place!"

"As equal partners?"

"In everything. Except Linda. She's yours, my lad!"

As James went into the house, his thoughts were running wild. It all was possible! Old Cullen could be beaten, could be put out to pasture permanently, and James and Maxwell would lift Cullen and Company to new heights, cleansed of the corruption and ruthless duplicity that Bradford Cullen had employed as his most important tools. It could be done!

Just then, a maid cried out from somewhere down the hall, and an excruciating, groaning wail from Linda caused James to spring away, shouting that he was coming. When he reached Linda's chambers, he found her curled up on the floor, the distraught servant crying and begging James to fetch a doctor.

"The baby!" howled Linda in pain and anguish. "The baby! The baby! I'm losing my baby!"

Linda miscarried, and she was inconsolable, but not nearly so devastated as was Bradford Cullen. James did not see him at all for days, and the man did not even have the strength of will to attend the small, private funeral. Only a few tersely worded messages came to James through Maxwell, who made it plain that Cullen was so distressed that he might soon die from it.

By the time the worst was over, however, and unhappy, desperately sick Linda was able to sleep a bit at night, it became apparent that Cullen would not yet die of grief. Still, Maxwell suggested to James that the old man was on his last legs.

"When he heard about the miscarriage, he collapsed, clutching his chest, and if the doctor hadn't come and given him a double dose of foxglove decoction, his black heart would have seized up for good." Maxwell said this as he chewed on a cigar and shared some brandy with James in the privacy of the company office at one end of the mansion. "Hadn't been for that damned manservant, Auguste, fluttering about and dashing off for the doctor, the old bastard would've been done for there and then."

He snorted and downed his drink. "Bless me if I'd have gone for help! Him gone'll make our plan that much easier."

James thought Maxwell truly heartless, so full of hate he was for the overbearing Bradford Cullen. Should James ever be in the same situation, he did not know whether he could let Cullen die without trying to fetch a doctor. He did not say so to Maxwell, however. James would be satisfied if the bereaved Cullen did die soon, though he worried about the failing Linda, and it was a real pity that the baby had been lost.

A pity, James thought absently, but wondered why he felt no particularly deep sorrow.

chapter 21

NATURAL CAUSES

The travelers bound for Philadelphia assembled on a mild October morning, with the air unusually heavy and damp for this time of year. The men were in good spirits, a few of them making sport with Punch, who darted from shoulder to shoulder in search of crumbs of biscuit the men offered. The soldiers were impatient to be on their way home at last, after twelve long months at Fort Pitt's garrison. They also were pleased at the prospect of having two charming women in their party, which would afford them all a chance at displaying gallantry, while the women could do their part by baking for them over the campfire from time to time.

It would be an adventure for Susannah in particular, for she had not been in Philadelphia in years. The greatest city in America, once the second-largest city in the British empire, Philadelphia was virtually the center of the entire New World and was still rich and prosperous despite the war. Susannah was indeed excited at the thought of visiting there, but she felt sorry and worried for James Morely and his gloomily changing life.

She knew all about the miscarriage and of Linda's worsening condition, and Owen had hinted that Bradford Cullen was likely to be extraordinarily hard on James these days. Try as she would, Susannah could not put James's troubles from her thoughts as she prepared to mount her waiting horse, which was held by a groom from the hotel where they had stayed the past two days. The women were dressed in warm beige riding coats, which, like most of what they were taking, had recently been purchased at Pitt. Of all the packhorses, theirs was the most lightly laden.

Ella was already mounted, holding hands with Owen in a last farewell. Susannah kept watching the far end of the street for some sign of James coming to see her off, but he was not there. No doubt he was too busy with pressing family matters or business affairs.

Standing nearby, the captain of the thirty soldiers called on his men to mount up, and touched his hat to Sutherland, saying it was time to depart. Then he walked to the mule train and ordered the skinners to ready themselves. There was a flurry of shouting, last good-byes, and someone started a song of the trail, which the soldiers caught up as they turned their mounts into file and moved toward the edge of the town, where they would regroup and form a long column.

Sutherland came to his daughter and held her close, saying it would be a safe trip, for there was no chance of enemy raiders east of the Forks of the Ohio. Anyway, it would not be long before the travelers reached the far side of the barrier mountains, where the land was thickly settled and well guarded.

"Give my regards to Dr. Franklin's people, lass," he said fondly, obviously glad to be giving Susannah an opportunity to recover from her hardships, and to remind her that there was more to the world than a lonely wilderness settlement. "Promise me you'll think only of the future for the next few months!" He smiled, and they embraced, Susannah feeling a rush of affection for her wonderful father.

Still, she was distracted as she spoke words of parting, and kept looking over her father's shoulder for some sign of James.

Then he was there! Running full speed, holding on to his hat, coattails flying, he waved at them from down the street. The soldiers were drawing up, the mule skinners starting up their packtrain, and there was a general bustle among the people of Pitt, who were waving to friends. Barreling through the mules, rushing into the midst of the crowd came James, calling to Susannah. She could not help herself and pulled away from her father, at the same time speaking James's name.

But she felt her arm held fast, and looked back into her father's admonishing eyes. He would not let her run into James's arms.

"Easy there, lass," he said before carefully letting her go.

She knew he was right. Recovering, she tried to smile, then found herself standing before James, who was able to restrain himself, to catch his breath, and remove his hat. Remembering his manners, James first went to Ella and bowed politely, wishing her a good journey. Ella smiled uneasily, then exchanged glances with her husband as James returned to Susannah.

Before he could speak, Susannah blurted out, "How is Mrs. Morely?"

He stammered a bit, flushing as he said she was not much better, and had taken a turn for the worse last night.

"I haven't seen her this morning yet, for I've been busy; but her father's been at her side for some time. . . ." Then he changed the subject, saying, "Godspeed, Susannah, and may Philadelphia be good for you . . ." He smiled warmly. "As I know you'll be good for Philadelphia."

She laughed lightly, nervously, and stood staring at him, thinking she might never see him again. Had her parents and all the others not been at hand, she surely would have thrown herself into his arms and hugged him close. As it was, tears were coming, and she felt awful, being unable to stem them. Ella called out that it was time, and Susannah let James kiss her hand. She did not allow the kiss to linger, and drew away, trying to maintain her composure. After all, she had thought her feelings for James had been resolved! But then why was she feeling all this surging emotion?

She mounted, helped by her father, who promised to join her in Philadelphia before too long, and as she prepared to turn her horse away, she took one last look at James, who seemed utterly downcast, unable to conceal his feelings for her.

Just then there came another shout from down the street, and a two-horse carriage thundered toward them. It was Cullen's, and Bill Bartholomew was standing up in the box, obviously being urged by his passenger to drive faster.

The carriage bore through the crowd, forcing people to leap aside, and Bartholomew lurched it to a stop just a few feet from James.

From inside the cab, Cullen's voice rang out, "You unfaithful dog! Get in! Get in and come to see your wife's lifeless . . ." His voice broke, and he sobbed, "My daughter is dead because of you! Get in! Get in now!"

James was wide-eyed, shocked, and Susannah watched him spring at once into the carriage with Cullen. Her horse whickered and became jumpy as the carriage lurched past, turned, and whirled back down the street. For an instant, Susannah thought she saw a face look out, as if James was searching for one final glimpse of her. But then she realized it was the face of Bradford Cullen, and he was staring, full of hate, right at her.

"Poor James," she whispered. "Oh, poor, poor James."

Then her father was there, squeezing her hand, and urging her to catch up with the troops. Shakily, Susannah bade him farewell and hurried her horse away, finding it painful to look back.

The following day—one of the most miserable of James Morely's life—he met in his private office with Maxwell to plan what had to be done next. As he walked the floor, James thought of how Linda's death had further revealed Cullen as a cruel despot, vicious and destructive. No one dared go near him, save the mild-mannered Auguste, who had no choice but to wait on him.

James himself was weak and for hours had been feeling faint and nauseated. Sitting nearby, Maxwell was white with tension and fear, and it was apparent he was worried about whether James was able to go through with his plan.

"It's now or never, James!" Maxwell suddenly whispered, trying to be calm while James paced back and forth. "We have to act now, or the old man'll cut you out of the company . . . maybe worse, if he gets Mark Davies to do his dirty work."

James fought down a wave of feebleness that made him stop and steady himself on the mantelpiece. He hated himself for this weakness at so critical a moment. He would be ashamed if he fainted in the presence of Maxwell, so he battled with all his will against succumbing to a fit. He was pale, sweating, finding it hard to breathe.

Maxwell said, "Don't worry about Bill Bartholomew, for he's in my pay already. And Auguste will be no problem, for Bill will scare the hell out of him if he tries to back up Cullen." He slammed his fist into his palm. "It's all ready. The documents are drawn up! Everyone knows Cullen's going mad with grief. He's unfit to command! Why, even Linda's death is playing into our hands—"

He caught himself suddenly, for James gave him a dark look of anger, saying, "I'm sorry for her death, Noah! I don't want to benefit from what I—" He swayed and put a hand to his forehead. Concerned, Maxwell came to him, but James said he was all right.

Maxwell asked forgiveness, saying he meant no insult to Linda. "And yet we must strike while the iron is hot, while Cullen is nearly raving, out of his mind! We'll prove him incompetent, a madman, and we'll threaten him with confinement if he attempts to oppose us in taking over the company!"

James nodded, breathing deeply. "Then let's be about it. When is he willing to see us?"

"He expects me in two hours. Come along—if you're up to it."

That last infuriated James, for he hated any suggestion that he was not strong enough. "I'm up to it! Never doubt that, Noah! Never!"

A knock came at the outside door, and Maxwell let in Owen Sutherland. James had no desire to see anyone just then, but he would talk to Sutherland. At James's request, Maxwell departed, and Sutherland came into the room, both men sitting down as Sutherland offered his condolences.

Sutherland saw that James was suffering from his fainting spells, and he felt sympathy for the man. Sutherland had come to say good-bye and to offer to help James if help was ever needed.

"You've made yourself bad trouble with Cullen, my friend, and he could be dangerous."

James nodded, his eyes foggy as he tried to compose himself. After a moment, he focused on Sutherland and asked an unexpected question: "Owen, do you really believe it was Cullen who had my father murdered?"

Sutherland could see a change coming over James. He was not sure if it was for the better. A fierce and profound bitterness was taking root. The young man was finally coming to realize Cullen's true character, but what that would mean for James, Sutherland was not sure. As he looked into James's hard, cold eyes, Sutherland felt a shock of recognition—for there was a striking similarity there to Cullen's own eyes. That gave Sutherland pause. Slowly, he replied that he was sure Cullen had put the killers on Garth Morely's trail in order to deal the Frontier Company a crucial setback.

For a moment, James said nothing, but his expression became harsher, even ruthless, it seemed.

Sutherland said, "Your father was a wise and prudent man, James, and would have counseled you not to do anything rash."

James glanced up at that, a sly look coming over him as he said with a faint smile, "Nothing rash, Owen—just calculated, cunning, like Cullen himself. What he deserves!" He looked away, mouth turned down at the corners.

Sutherland drew a deep breath and stood up; James also rose, and they shook hands. Sutherland said he was leaving right away, going downriver a few miles to visit friends. Afterward, he would be in Kentucky for a month or so.

He added, "If you need help, send for me—but think twice about whether I would approve or not before you send your summons."

James nodded, but his thoughts seemed elsewhere as he went with Sutherland to the door and said good-bye. Then the two men went their separate ways.

Susannah Sutherland was riding with the others on a pretty trail through the hills southeast of Fort Pitt. She was thinking of James, wondering whether their paths would ever cross again. She considered the death of Linda Cullen to be tragic, and would not let herself think that it might clear the way for some future reconciliation with James. She must not think that, for James had caused her too much heartache already.

The horse she rode was gentle, and after almost two days

on the trail, Susannah was not much the worse for wear. The men were moving slowly, for the women's sake, and they had not made much progress as yet. The wind was becoming chill, telling of rain, and both Susannah and her mother, who rode in front of her, were warmly bundled with capes and shawls. It was peaceful here, the sky gray with heavy clouds, the forest leafless. For the first time in ages, Susannah felt almost reconciled with the world. Punch flitted down over her head and landed on her shoulder. Susannah laughed and told the jay he would love Philadelphia's rooftops.

Then she heard the sound of a horse galloping up from behind, and the men of the rear guard called out a challenge. Susannah turned as a lone rider came into view, a man she had never seen before. He waved a letter, then handed it to one of the soldiers who had stopped, and the soldier in turn brought it to Ella. The captain of the troops rode back to see what was happening.

Ella tore open the letter, saying it bore James's seal. "No!" she gasped. "Owen's been wounded! He's near Braddock's Field, and badly hurt!"

Frightened, Susannah spurred her horse forward to join her frantic mother, who passed her the letter and began to make arrangements with the captain. The letter was signed by James, and asked for the two women to come back immediately with this messenger, who would guide them to Braddock's Field. There they would find the injured Owen.

They had their packhorse cut from the train, and they parted hastily with the troops. Philadelphia must wait. Susannah prayed the wound was not too severe. What would she do without her beloved father? They had to get to him fast, before it was too late to see him again!

James and Maxwell knocked on the door to Cullen's office and heard a grunt for them to enter. The old man was hunched behind his wide mahogany desk, staring at nothing, until he noticed James. He hissed and tried to stand, but clearly was too weakened to do so.

Instead, he cursed and demanded of Maxwell: "You said nothing of this swine coming with you!"

Maxwell was pale, barely able to stammer, "Sir . . . sir, we . . . ah . . ."

Cullen roared, "Get him out of my sight! Out! Get out, both of you!"

Coolly, James stepped forward, and Maxwell seemed to fade into a dim corner of the poorly lighted room. James was all alone now, as Cullen glared at him, eyes white, burning with hatred.

"You get out of here, Morely! You are in a precarious enough position! Do not dare anger me further—"

"We have come to tell you something, Mr. Cullen." James felt his body tense and stiffen, as if his blood were running cold. He had no fear of this man, only loathing. This was the man who had killed his father, and he deserved no mercy, no quarter.

James's voice was sharp, the words like the blows of a hammer: "We've made a complete change in the company."

"You?" Cullen chuckled malevolently, his fat hands stroking the desktop as he regarded James. He snapped: "You've made a change? What change, you upstart pup? You and who else?"

Maxwell did not speak up. Indeed, James was alone.

James said, "You are to remain in power in name only, and I will run Cullen and Company from now on. You have no choice in the matter."

To see Cullen's eyes dart so uncertainly from the nervous Maxwell and back to himself, James felt immense pleasure. The satisfaction at watching this beast of a man begin to deteriorate from rude confidence to apprehension gave James a sense of mastery. Cullen might begin to rage, might even threaten, but he was finished. It was James's day now. Cullen would never rule again.

Cullen's hands stroked the table more slowly, as if he were beginning to understand. He looked past James, at Maxwell. There was no need for involved conversation. Cullen was smart enough to know that if these two men meant what they said, he was indeed in peril of being deposed.

In a loud voice, he called to Maxwell: "What've you got to say, then? Speak up!"

Maxwell cleared his throat but did not come forward, as he said in a faltering voice that gathered strength, "It is true. . . . All the papers are arranged, and you can sign them, or not—"

He flinched as Cullen bellowed, almost standing up. "Sign them? Sign away my own company to a pair of whelps? Are you both so damned cocksure that you really think I—"

James brusquely interrupted: "Sign legally..." He tossed
onto the desk several documents he had been carrying. "...be-
cause if you won't, we've already forged your signature, with
appropriate notaries, to copies of these same documents. You're
declared mentally incompetent, senile, overcome with melancholy, whatever. You may as well make it all easy—"

"Easy?" Cullen slashed the papers from his desk and, with
supreme effort, heaved himself to his feet and screeched for
Auguste. But no one came. He screamed again, his face red,
eyes bulging.

"He's gone for the day, Mr. Cullen," Maxwell said carefully.
When Cullen screeched once more, Maxwell backed even farther off, leaving James to take the brunt of the old man's fury.

"You dirty, thieving bastards! You'll never succeed! You've
blundered! I'm Bradford Cullen! I'll have your heads! I'm
Bradf—" Suddenly his face changed, eyes taking on a glint of
cruel humor. He panted, "You'll end up like your fool of a
father, Morely!"

James lost his head and went for Cullen, grabbing him by
the shirt and dragging him forward over the desk, shaking him
violently so that his eyes rolled.

Then James felt faintness come over him, and he nearly
swooned. Angrily, he pushed Cullen back into his chair and
reeled away, hand to his face.

In turn, Cullen was gasping and clutching at his own chest.
He moaned fearfully. Through a mist, James tried to focus on
the man, sensing he had brought on a heart attack, but not
caring if he had.

"Help! Help me..." Cullen was croaking, his face white,
hands grasping in agony at his heart. "In the name of—" He
wheezed in excruciating pain and fell heavily to the floor.

James was leaning against the wall, himself barely able to
keep from falling. Maxwell hurried to Cullen, kneeling over
him, both men partly concealed from James by the desk. Weak,
James dropped to his knees, tried to get up, half crawled toward
Cullen, and then began to go black. Everything was spinning,
sounds coming from all around, as if he were inside an empty
barrel. He thought he heard Maxwell cursing and Cullen wailing, the sounds of flesh and bone thumping against the floor.

"Cullen?" he muttered, trying to get up, barely able to see

anything. He knew he was on his hands and knees and could make out the desk, the yellow lamplight, and the figure of Maxwell kneeling over Cullen's body. He thought a pillow from the chair was pressed against the old man's face. James could not be sure what was real and what was delusion, for his mind filled up with swirling images. He saw Susannah Sutherland . . . there was Owen, and Linda . . . and through it all he heard Cullen's muffled screaming.

When James regained consciousness, he was lying on the floor of Cullen's office. Maxwell was opening his collar and asking whether he was all right. James rolled to his side, his senses coming back, and shook his head to clear away the dizziness. It was over; his fit was passed. It had been a horrible vision, whatever it was, and he still imagined seeing Maxwell smothering Cullen with a pillow. He again shook the vision away.

Now Maxwell was all concern and nervousness, appealing for James to get up: "Something dreadful's happened, James! Get up, please, and come see to Mr. Cullen."

James rose with his friend's help and went to Cullen, who lay on his back, eyes open wide, mouth gaping. He was dead.

"Oh . . ." James gasped, regret and disgust welling up in him. Murder, he thought. "So it has come to this."

"What?" Maxwell almost jumped with fear. "What do you mean? He had a heart seizure, that's all! Perfectly normal for a man his age! Look! He died of natural causes!"

Maxwell got up and stamped around a moment, running his hand through his hair. He looked ghastly, terrified. James wondered what to think, wondered what had indeed been real, and what illusion. Cullen's screams of death still rang in his mind. Or had it been he himself who had killed Cullen by handling him so roughly, bringing on the attack? Who could tell?

Anyway, the man was dead. The papers and his will were all arranged, and there would be no need for further unpleasantness because of Bradford Cullen. It was just as well. In a cold, rational moment, he thought that they might as well have two funerals at once, Linda's and the old man's. It would be less bother that way, less wasted words on what was past. James stood up and stared down at the bloated, lifeless body at his feet.

A black and ugly wrath rose up in him to think of all the

evil this man had done. "Good riddance," he hissed.

From now on, anyone like Cullen who stood in the path of James Morely could expect the same treatment. Cullen and company would be the name, but James Morely would be the force behind it. A force to be reckoned with by every man and woman in America and, in time, all the world.

Just then, Maxwell, who was rummaging about the papers in Cullen's drawer, gave a cry of alarm and held up a note that appeared to be a copy of an original, for it bore no seal and had been written in Cullen's hand on smaller paper than that meant for letters.

James looked at him, feeling utterly hardened and unemotional. "Well? What is it?"

Maxwell was trembling and handed the copy to James, who snatched it away and began to read. It was dated yesterday.

Captain D,
    As previously discussed, immediately carry out your plan to intercept the two women. Payment to be arranged at Braddock's Field. By this express you are hereby authorized to make the women prisoners, as justifiable in the plan to take Sutherland. Should you ever be accused of kidnapping, simply show this note to your superior, and surely they will press no charges, for you will be on a military mission at my express instruction.
    Protect yourself at all times, for these rebels are dangerous, men and women both.

Your servant,
Epius

James was jolted. Epius was the name of the Greek who built the wooden horse used to deceive and capture the besieged city of Troy. No doubt it was also Cullen's code name as a loyalist agent, and this letter was a means of legitimizing an attack on Susannah Sutherland. Should she die, Davies could not be accused of murder by a British court, for the letter proved he was acting under orders in an attempt to capture the infamous rebel Owen Sutherland. James shook with terror for Susannah.

Maxwell voiced James's fears: "He wants to hurt you the way the death of Linda hurt him. I dread it may already be too late!"

"No!" James threw down the letter, grabbed Cullen's personal wax seal from the desk, and dashed to the door, crying, "Get word of this to Sutherland, if you can find him!" Then, leaving Maxwell behind to take care of Cullen's body, he ran through the house to his room, to change into traveling clothes. He intended to mount a horse and race to Braddock's Field, the site some miles from town where the French had defeated the British back in 1755.

James had no idea how much time he had, but his best hope was that Davies would keep the women alive until Owen Sutherland got there. In the back of his mind was the thought that he could deal with this on his own, without anyone's help, especially Owen Sutherland's.

Soon James was out on the trail, in a mad gallop eastward. He had to go alone, for if he should ride in as a threat, with fighting men at his back, there was no telling what the unpredictable Mark Davies would do to the women.

James was confronting Davies as the leader of the mighty Cullen and Company, and that ought to be enough to stay the man's hand.

chapter 22

BRADDOCK'S FIELD

The wind and rain picked up, the sky becoming darker as Susannah and Ella rode hard behind the sullen, untalkative messenger. The man was ordinary, dressed in shabby clothes, but he had a good rifle, a fine trade tomahawk, and carried a brace of pistols. He looked like any poor inhabitant of Pitt, save for the expensive weapons that told he was a fighting man.

As he led them through the woods, both women were anxious and desperate to get to Braddock's Field as quickly as possible. They took back trails, rocky and steep at times, but they were good shortcuts. Indeed, the messenger knew the area well, for before nightfall they were in the rocky, wooded gorge where Braddock's doomed army had been surrounded by French and Indians and cut to pieces. Here fell Ella's first husband, and although he had escaped, saved from immediate death, he had lingered on for years before eventually dying from his wounds.

As she rode, Susannah thought how dreadful an irony it was that Owen, too, now should have been wounded here. It seemed James Morely was arranging to take care of him, but Susannah knew how quickly one could die, even with the best available doctoring. Rain spattered on her face, and she threw the hood of an oilskin cape over her head, urging her distressed mother to do the same.

The horses grew tired, steaming and blowing, as they rode into the deepening gorge, where a stream rushed through, louder than the wind in the trees. There were no fields, no residences to be seen, only deep forest and craggy hillsides. It was a lonely place, and mournful, as if the memory of what had happened here haunted the shadowy woods. The wind whipped through the treetops, sighing in a copse of pines, lamenting. Susannah shivered, glanced behind her, and drew her oilskin closer. She found herself uneasy for more reasons than just worry about her father. This messenger was an unfriendly fellow, and things felt not quite right. She wondered what it was about these woods that repelled her. It was as if she were being watched. On her saddle was a small pistol, its firelock covered against the rain. She wished the weapon were loaded. In her left hand was a riding whip, the only other defense she had.

Ella, too, glanced back, after having asked the messenger where Owen was and receiving no reply. Above them, the blue jay still fluttered from tree to tree. Susannah thought Punch would find Owen, wherever he was in this hushed glade.

Then the messenger abruptly stopped his horse and cupped a hand to his mouth, calling out in a long whoop.

Ella moved her horse close to Susannah's and said, "Has he lost his way? Doesn't he know where the camp is? Do you see any sign of James?"

Susannah watched, her glance flitting along the edge of the trees that closed in on every side. She was tense, her skin crawling. She drew out the pistol, undid the powder horn hanging on her sidesaddle, and prepared to load.

"Put that toy away!"

The voice came from behind them, somewhere within the trees. Susannah felt a chill of fear. The messenger sat staring at them, calmly grinning. Susannah snatched the cover from her pistol, fumbling to prime the pan, and suddenly Ella cried out, lifting her own riding whip to strike at someone who had rushed from the shadows.

"Flee, Susannah!" she gasped, striking again and again. Her

horse reared, snorting, and was dragged back down by his
bridle. "Flee!"

There was a shout, followed by coarse laughter. Before she
could do anything, Susannah was yanked from behind, hands
pawing at her, the pistol wrenched painfully away.

She fell to the ground, shouting, kicking, and squirming,
as a stinking body dropped heavily onto her, howling with
laughter, trying to kiss her. Ella, too, was struggling with someone, and Susannah felt helpless desperation. She was trapped,
pinned down. There was nothing she could do. Beyond the
shoulders of the man holding her to the cold earth was the face
of Mark Davies, grinning like a hungry wolf in the rain, nodding as he watched the brutality. Punch silently whipped down
to peck and attack, but he was struck by an angry hand and
had to retreat. Susannah fought, but the beast who had her was
too strong, and she was completely in his power.

"Hold!" someone yelled fiercely. "Back off, or I'll put lead
in the next dog what riles me! Get up! Get up!"

Susannah felt the weight leave her, and she fought from
under the man, crying out in revulsion and twisting away,
finding Ella doing the same, and they huddled together. Beside
them, with two pistols in his fists, was Simon Girty, his leathery
face twisted in hatred as he held off nine others, including
Davies and a pair of Indians. Uncouth and dirty, most were
more like brigands than loyalist soldiers, more outlaws than
men fighting in a cause.

Davies snickered, and his men made comments about
Girty's sudden squeamishness. They just wanted a little sport
after all their months in the woods.

"We can't all hump bears like you, Simon."

There was general guffawing.

Girty menaced with the pistols, with Davies as his main
target. He cursed at them and said, "We're here to bag Sutherland, a man, not to abuse white women! Go hump each other
like you usually do, you varmints!"

Darkening, Davies moved forward, but stopped when
Girty's pistols bore on him.

He said with a casual smile, "I have my orders, Simon, and
they are . . ." He held himself back, as if unwilling to reveal
something.

Susannah could see Girty had little chance if trouble started, but Davies would get shot first. She had never met Girty before, but she knew he and her father had been on the trail together years ago. For just an instant Susannah wondered about the truth of all those stories about the bloodthirsty Simon Girty, vicious murderer of innocents. . . . Whatever the truth really was, the man was now putting his life in peril by facing down these white renegades.

He declared, "I'll watch fer these two, and you all kin do yer work with Sutherland." As the surly men considered that, Girty glanced almost apologetically at the women, then turned again as Davies approached nearer.

Davies said with a slow nod of the head, "Very well, gentleman knight, Simon Girty, you have your solemn duty. And you can hold our horses while you're at it, thus staying well out of the fight, eh?"

Girty clenched his unshaven jaw. "You calling me a coward?"

Before Davies could answer, there was a shout from a man posted down the trail. A rider was coming. Susannah's pounding heart leaped. Surely it was her father, riding into a trap! She tried to run, but one of the men blocked her way, and she shrank back to the momentary safety of Girty's pistols.

Davies drew his sword and hastily ordered his men to their positions in the trees, then turned to Girty, saying, "Gag and bind them, and be quick about it!"

With the help of another man, Girty gagged and trussed Ella and Susannah, hands in front, before they could even think about shouting a warning. Their feet were not tied, but they were thrown to the ground and told to stay there. In the distance, Susannah heard the hoofbeats. Mark Davies took a moment to make sure the prisoners were all secured.

He said with a laugh, "Our friend Mr. Cullen is a clever forger, among his other talents, and one day James Morely will be surprised to learn that it was his name and seal that drew you and soon will draw the great Sutherland to doom."

Girty looked around at that, a hand going to one of his pistols, now in his belt. Davies snickered, saying softly to Susannah:

"Yes, dear one, no matter what your friend Simon says, your fate is sealed, for Mr. Cullen has told me to kill you."

Girty moved, but he was not quick enough, and Mark Davies slashed with his sword, catching the scout a glancing blow with the flat of the weapon. Girty tumbled back, stunned, a gash on his forehead. He wavered, unable to resist as Davies advanced and snatched away the pistols, sticking one in his own belt, then giving the scout a violent kick in the face. Girty grunted and rolled away.

The hoofbeats were louder now.

Davies kicked again, then ordered Girty to his feet, using the other pistol to threaten. Slowly the scout rose, groggy and bleeding.

Davies cursed him: "Be off! Be off before I kill you, too!" The pistol was cocked, a finger on the trigger, madness in Davies's eyes. Girty backed warily, glancing at the helpless women and moving away from that black muzzle. "I'd shoot you now if it wouldn't give away my ambush!" Davies waved the pistol. "Get! And don't come back!"

Girty was gone, vanishing into the thicket, and Susannah heard the branches clatter as he hurried away. Now she and Ella were alone, and her father was riding to his death.

Davies laughed softly, moving close to them and kneeling to listen with them to the approaching horseman. The next sound would be the report of a half dozen rifles. Owen had not a chance.

"Cullen will pay me well, ladies," he whispered. "I only wish Sutherland could be alive to watch what happens to you."

The hoofbeats were almost in the clearing. Susannah could take it no longer, and simultaneous with her mother, she somehow lurched to her feet, trying to break way. Davies grabbed for them both, throwing down his pistol to do so, and wrenched them under control. But he had not expected Ella to knee him in the groin, nor Susannah to butt him in the face with her forehead. He staggered with a painful grunt, and the women ran ahead, still unable to shout, whining behind their gags. The horse was close.

But there were others in the way, and two burly woodsmen leaped out to wrestle them down. The hoofbeats were almost upon them. Davies came stumbling up, raging, and raised a fist to thrash Ella.

Suddenly, someone shouted, "It ain't him!"

Davies froze as a man cried, "Hold yer fire!"

The horse cantered to a stop, and Susannah could see it through the bushes. She thrilled to see James leap down from the saddle and rush toward them, calling to Davies to leave them alone.

"Cullen sent me! I've come to . . . to take these women away!" He was breathless, and stopped running abruptly when Davies's men appeared and blocked his path, their rifles pointed.

"I'm unarmed!" James gasped, his eyes searching Susannah and Ella, to see whether they were hurt. "I've come for the women. . . . Are you all right? Oh, dear Lord!"

Davies scowled and confronted him: "You've come for them at Cullen's orders?"

"That's right! That's right! There's been a mistake, and Mr. Cullen wants them brought out immediately!" He handed over a letter with Cullen's seal, saying it would explain everything. As Davies took it, James moved toward the women, clumsily trying to unbind them. He did not get far.

Davies read quickly, obviously suspicious and unhappy at being denied a chance to do some further evil. He roughly pulled James back from the women, saying, "What about Sutherland?"

Susannah held her breath to hear what James would say next. He seemed surprised. Susannah longed to tear off the gag and tell him her father was coming, unsuspecting of the ambush.

James stammered, "Sutherland . . . ah, well . . ."

Davies stepped toward him, folding the letter again as he regarded James closely. "Yes, what does Mr. Cullen direct that we do about Owen Sutherland? You know all about him, of course."

James glanced from the women to Davies and cleared his throat. He was sweating, his eyes darting. Susannah guessed now that he did not know everything.

Davies spoke in a low voice. "You mean Cullen gave no new instructions for dealing with Sutherland?" He smiled coldly. "When Sutherland's been invited as your guest, just like those two wenches? You mean to say Cullen told you all about them, but not about the man himself?"

James hardened. "Whatever he told me, it's none of your business, Davies! I've come for the women, and there's the

letter! Stand back, release these two, and I'll be on my
way—"

Davies laughed and turned to his men. "Well, gentlemen,
it appears our benefactor, Bradford Cullen, has lost his wits."
He swung on James, his face still showing amusement. "He
has lured the rebel Sutherland here by arranging for the kid-
napping of two women, has revealed to those women that he's
a loyalist agent, and now proposes to release them, presuming
they'll keep his little secret, though their man pays for it with
his life!" He chortled and walked around James and the women.
"A good joke on someone, eh? But not on me, Morely!"

He moved close to James, who stood his ground bravely.
"Something doesn't smell right about this, Morely, and until I
get the truth . . ." He stepped back. "You may very well be an
important man in Cullen and Company, and I, for one, have
no desire to make you an enemy, sir."

He doffed his hat with a flourish, and his men liked that,
laughing all around. "So permit me to make you my guest until
the light of our party arrives and is appropriately entertained."
His men smirked. "Allow me to offer you our most comfortable
accommodations at our fireside." He became sinister again.
"These two women don't leave my sight until I've communi-
cated directly with Cullen. Now, be good enough to stay with
them at the campfire."

James was in no position to resist, but he asked, "How do
you know Sutherland will come?"

Davies said another forged letter in James's name had told
Sutherland his women were hurt and were waiting here for his
immediate arrival. The letter would have reached him by messenger that very afternoon.

"He was just a few hours from here, so he'll waste no time,
I'll warrant!" Davies grinned. "Now, sit down, and cause me
no more distraction, if you please."

The two women had their feet bound, and along with James,
they sat near a guttering campfire, the drizzle misting and
keeping the smoke low and in their faces. Cold and afraid,
Susannah was miserably downcast. She knew that James, too,
was in grave trouble now, though she understood little about
the circumstances. The same man who had brought her and
Ella here sat behind them as guard, rifle across his long legs,

hat drawn down over his face. He seemed to doze, although somehow he was aware of sudden movements or normal talking.

After a while, the haggard James leaned over to the women, who were sitting a little distance from him, and whispered that Cullen was dead. Their eyes widened in amazement, but only momentarily. That news was of no help to them now.

James looked truly overcome by all that had happened, and he said with a shaking voice, "I'm sorry . . . I'm sorry that I've made a mess of this." He glanced at the guard, whose face was hidden by the broad brim of his hat; then he whispered to Susannah and Ella, "I can't do anything for Owen now, but at least I can try to save you both."

The women looked at each other, fear and anger in their expressions. James must have seen that they would not give up easily, for he thought a moment, then licked his lips, as if he had resolved something. He glanced around and leaned again toward them.

He whispered, "Be ready." He showed them an open pocketknife, then concealed it again as the guard awoke with a start and eyed them suspiciously. There was no telling whether Davies was watching from cover, where his men were spread out, waiting for Sutherland to ride in.

Susannah was not sure what James was doing, as he picked up a stone. James watched the half-dozing guard until the man's head dropped, then threw the stone into the bushes. The guard whipped around and fell on his stomach, rifle at the ready. At that moment, James tossed the knife to Susannah, and it landed beside her. She edged forward, so that the knife was underneath her, and then she had it in her bound hands and sat still as the guard turned back, grumbling.

James laughed lightly: "Hearing things, friend?"

The man glared and spat into the fire, resting the rifle on his knees and tugging down his hat once more.

James said, "I'd be worried, too, if I was waiting to tangle with Owen Sutherland."

The man eyed him with guarded nervousness. "Ain't gonna be no trouble, not with Cap'n Davies in command. Now hold yer tongue and let me be while I think on it some."

The man soon returned to his half-alert drowsiness. Any quick movement got his attention, but he did not notice Su-

sannah slice her wrist cord and slide closer to Ella to do the
same. Time passed slowly, the drizzle letting up a bit. Soon
both women's hands were free, but they were still gagged, and
their feet were yet tied. Susannah had not dared to lean forward
to cut the ropes around her ankles, lest she give herself away.
Now she felt amazingly unafraid. She was prepared for anything, and would not flinch at endangering herself if it meant
saving her father's life.

Looking around, she considered their alternatives. The
campsite was some distance from the trail, where its smoke
could be seen and would attract her father when he rode in.
She and her mother could rip off their gags and shout a warning
before the guard could stop them, but unless they got their
ankles unbound... Susannah glanced at James, wondering if
he had some plan in mind. Ella, too, was looking at James.

As the minutes dragged by, Susannah began to ache, her
whole body stiff and sore, but she felt no weariness. She hoped
her father would come soon, before it was discovered she and
her mother were partly untied, yet she dreaded the moment
when he would come under those hidden guns. Her anxiety
was a force that made her quick and ready to spring when the
chance came. Ella looked to be in the same condition, and both
of them knew they would have to do something soon—but not
too soon, for any attempt at warning might fail if they acted
prematurely. If only they could untie their feet! But that would
be impossible without alerting the guard.

Nearby, Punch hopped about the ground, and for a moment
Susannah wished she could have wings like this bird and fly
to warn her father. Again she glanced at the morose James;
although he was untied, he could not take on the entire band
of renegades alone, even if he subdued the guard.

It was near dark when the distant sound of hoofbeats startled
Susannah. There was much movement in the bushes, as Davies's cold, wet fighting men took their places for the final act.
Susannah looked to James and saw his desperate intensity. She
realized now that he, too, would gamble everything to warn
Owen. Her heart leaped in fright for him. Yet that was their
only chance. Susannah could almost read his mind. He was
ready. The women would have to help. The guard was alert,
however, alternately watching James and looking in the direction of the horseman.

Then, with a snarl, James sprang at the man, and they grappled fiercely. Susannah slashed at her leg bindings and went for those on her mother. James grunted, and she turned to see him knocked hard to the ground by the guard's rifle butt. Suddenly Davies was coming. In the confusion, the guard had paid no attention to the women, and now he stood with his back to them, rifle pointed at the unconscious James.

The guard declared, "Tried to jump me, the bastard!"

Davies hissed, "Hold your fire, man! Wait till the rest open up, then finish him!" He took a quick look at the women, who were sitting as if still bound—and in the failing light he did not notice they were free. He turned quickly away, for the horse was not far from the clearing.

The firing would begin at any moment, and both James and Sutherland would die. It was now or never. Ella and Susannah leaped up at the same instant and sprang onto the guard's back. With horror, Susannah heard the rifle go off, and she screamed James's name. The guard went to his knees, cursing and punching, but he had never been attacked by women like this before. Susannah grabbed a rock and pounded him violently, knocking him down as Ella wrested away the rifle and swung its butt at him. It was all he could do to scramble away for his life, reeling into the bushes, bloody and stunned.

The two frantic women looked up, expecting to find Mark Davies coming at them, but he was nowhere in sight. Susannah fell to James's side, seeing to her relief that he was not shot. The only sound other than the stream and the wind were those pounding hoofbeats, coming closer. With a sinking heart, Susannah feared the alarm had failed to warn her father, for he was still coming on.

As quickly as they could, they dragged the unconscious James into cover, hoping the deepening darkness would conceal them. The only weapons they had between them were the pocketknife and the discharged rifle, but they had to do something to warn Owen. At the last moment, Susannah told her mother to stay with James, and she started for the clearing, about to scream her father's name as the horse pounded in. But she stopped in her tracks, seeing the animal was riderless, its saddle empty. Owen must already be in the woods, hunting Davies and the renegades! The alarm had worked!

Susannah turned to run back to her mother, but someone

grabbed her and dragged her down. She struggled, but was held fast.

"Hssst! It's me, Girty!"

Simon Girty released her. At his feet lay the guard, tomahawked to death. Girty whispered he would help them "foil that bastard Davies."

Controlling her rising fear, Susannah nodded, then led him through the bushes to Ella and James. The woods were deathly quiet now, and growing too dark to see well for more than a few yards.

Girty quickly loaded and primed the dead guard's rifle, saying as he worked, "Your pa and me go back a long way, and now that I've done a turn for him, I'll expect one in return when the time comes." He finished his work and looked up, like a hunted animal at bay. Susannah realized then that when the war was done, Girty would be a hated man on the frontier and would need favors from men like Sutherland and James.

He said, "I heard news that even Davies don't want to believe yet, and you'll see why I want a friend or two on your side." He peered through the bushes, listening, trying to tell whether they were being sought. After satisfying himself that they were yet alone, he whispered, "Cornwallis buggered it all up! He's been tooken with his whole army at a place called Yorktown, and the war's good as lost for the likes of me!" He was breathing hard, obviously angry, nervous, and bitter. "I gave you another chance in this here trouble, mind, and if things turn about, I'll expect—"

He motioned for them to be silent. Crouching, he moved forward, rifle at the ready. Susannah could see no one, but she knew Girty was a true wilderness scout, and he could smell an enemy close at hand.

None of them moved. The rain had stopped now, and the woods were dripping, making every sound seem like a man moving in the bushes. After a moment of breathless waiting, Susannah saw several shadowy figures stealing through the clearing, keeping low, moving toward the embers of the campfire. It seemed they were searching for the women.

Girty trained his rifle on the shadows but did not fire. There were too many out there, and he had to bide his time. It became quieter again, and Susannah was chilled, sensing they were somehow surrounded. But where was her father?

Suddenly, from not far away, there came a piercing scream of agony, and a man wailed, the death rattle in his throat. Immediately there followed Sutherland's triumphant battle cry, and Ella and Susannah huddled together, repelled and thrilled at the same time. Owen was out there, and he was stalking the enemy, one by one.

Silence followed, except for Girty's rasping breathing. He asked whether they had a drink about them. "Got a awful dry," he whispered, still not moving from his position of readiness, watching.

There was another shout, the sound of a struggle, and a howl of terror. Sutherland's bloodcurdling Highland yell followed, ringing out through the quiet forest.

Susannah shivered in horror, but Girty chuckled softly. "Go get 'em, Owen laddie! They ain't worth nothing to nobody nohow." He glanced back at the women, his black eyes flashing in the dimness. "No loss to nobody."

Immediately there was another scream, a weak cry for help, and Sutherland's own yell was closer now.

Susannah wanted to shout that she and her mother were at hand, but Girty had said he thought several of the renegades were nearby hiding, waiting for Sutherland to appear. Girty could not help but quietly snicker to himself, gleefully enjoying the terror of the darkness that fell around them.

Then Susannah heard voices whispering nearby, just a few feet away. Some of the renegades were drifting past, and they seemed to be moving quickly.

Girty whispered, "Going for their horses. They've had enough, I'll guess."

True it was. In the following moment, two riders went pounding away through the clearing, and one of them in his fear fired at a shadow. Another man screamed, and fell near the rider who had shot at him. There was confusion, the riders stopped to look, and one of them yelled that it was their own comrade they had shot. Cursing, they set off again, panic-stricken, galloping down the trail until their hoofbeats were faint.

Girty whispered, "Davies must be keeping count. Only him and one of his dogs left, I'm thinking—"

"Hssst!"

Someone was directly behind them, and a startled Girty had

no chance to swing the rifle. With astonishment, Susannah made out the figure of her father.

"Got the drop on me!" Girty said softly. "Don't shoot."

Susannah whispered, "He's helping us, Pa!"

Sutherland came through the bushes, silent as a cat, and touched his wife's hand. Susannah was swept with relief.

Girty muttered, "Only two of 'em left, eh?"

Sutherland said, "How many started?"

"Nine, and me."

"Two rode out?"

"Right. And two dead."

"Five left."

"What? You done for three."

Sutherland said, "Where's Davies?"

Girty was not sure. "He'll run, I'm thinking."

Suddenly, Susannah realized Girty's rifle was leveled at her father, who saw it at the same time. Girty grinned, his teeth shining in the dark.

"No offense, Sutherland," he said with a smile. "But I aim to be on my way." He bent to take the gear of the dead guard. "This ain't my fight no more . . . but jest remember, when the time comes, that you owe me, Sutherland."

Sutherland let him go, and Girty vanished almost soundlessly. Sutherland turned to search the woods for some sign of Davies.

Susannah whispered, "How can there be more left, Pa?"

He replied by suddenly screeching in terrible agony, and shaking the bushes all around. Then he howled the Highland war cry, and as it rang through the woods, he looked at his daughter, and she understood. But the enemy did not.

Others suddenly took fright, and they scrambled through the trees, their silhouettes visible as they made for their hidden horses. Sutherland moved after them, hissing at the same time, "Davies is there!"

Susannah followed him, watching.

With a shout to their horses, the riders broke out, and Sutherland charged them. The first one brought up a rifle and fired, the flash of gunfire revealing that none of them was Davies. Sutherland was not hit, and held his fire as they galloped away.

A fourth rider broke from the trees and went right for

Sutherland, who could not get out of the way fast enough. Sutherland's rifle banged, and the man fell, the horse thundering past.

There was no time for Sutherland to reload before the last man rode out. This was Davies, and he had a pistol in hand. Sutherland went for him with a tomahawk, and Davies fired so close that he could not miss. Sutherland was knocked off his feet by the impact of the bullet, and Davies whipped his horse around, rearing the animal so that it stamped down at the wounded man.

"Die!" Davies screeched. "Die, Sutherland, like the dog you are!"

Susannah screamed and ran forward as her wounded father rolled away from the sharp hooves. Davies drew his sword, trying to steady the plunging horse so he could dismount and finish Sutherland off. Susannah was unarmed as she ran to her father, finding him groaning, shot in the right shoulder. He was stunned from his fall, and helpless. Ella, too, came running from their concealment as Susannah dragged her father's heavy claymore free of its scabbard. It was almost too much for her to lift, even with two hands, and Davies laughed in derision as he leaped down and came at her. He moved slowly, savoring his supreme triumph. Susannah caught her breath, anger welling up to take the place of fear, and she advanced toward him, claymore held forth.

He laughed again. "Oh, you miserable rebels!" He tossed his hat aside and took measure of the woman before him. It would require only one good stroke. "What hope can you have?" He shook his head. "What hope—"

A shot rang out. Davies staggered, dropped to his knees, and gazed at Susannah in wild-eyed dismay. He tried to speak but could not. The sword fell from his hand, and his eyes rolled. "Oh, you rebels..." He tumbled forward, dead.

From the bushes came the unmistakable cackle of Simon Girty, and the cry "Remember me, Sutherland, when the time comes!" The cackle, high-pitched and surely a bit mad, drew away as Girty vanished into the northwest wilderness. He was a man whose war was lost, but who would ever continue to fight.

EPILOGUE

Mark Davies was dead, and with him, for now, went the renegade threat that had endangered the frontier. There would be other war parties, other raids and counterraids, but this symbol of all that was evil in British wilderness policy was gone forever.

News of the Yorktown surrender spread quickly through the northwest, and with the fighting stopped in the East, it seemed just a matter of time before peace terms would be made. On the frontier, however, the war kept raging—though it was now almost exclusively between Indians and rebel whites. White loyalists fighting alongside the tribes became few and far between, yet the Indians seemed to grow even bolder, more savage, as if they knew they stood alone now. They were in the death throes of their way of life. The Revolution was coming to an end, but frontier wars were sure to go on for generations, as long as whites wanted what Indians possessed—the wilderness.

• • •

Owen Sutherland recovered from his wound and returned with his wife and daughter to their cabin at the Falls of the Ohio. By springtime he would be on the trail again, defending the settlements, seeking a way to recover his home at Detroit. Soberly, James Morely returned to Fort Pitt, there to assume complete control of the mighty Cullen and Company. What this would mean to the Sutherlands and the Frontier Company no one knew.

James swore he would reform the great trading firm, but Owen Sutherland knew it was too big, too corrupt, and too powerful for James ever to achieve that without tremendous difficulty and self-sacrifice. Especially self-sacrifice, for James Morely had already become accustomed to having an empire at his command.

Sutherland would wait before passing judgment on James, who would have to overcome more temptations than most men could ever imagine.

Although it was clear James and Susannah were still in love, Sutherland would not give his consent to their union until James proved himself beyond doubt a man of noble character and unswerving honesty. And that, Owen Sutherland believed, was yet to be seen.